THE PLEA

Steve Cavanagh

First published in Great Britain in 2016 by Orion Books,
an imprint of The Orion Publishing Group Ltd
Carmelite House, 50 Victoria Embankment
London EC4Y 0DZ

An Hachette UK Company

1 3 5 7 9 10 8 6 4 2

A CIP catalogue record for this book is
available from the British Library.

ISBN (Hardback) 978 1 4072 5042 7
ISBN (Trade Paperback) 978 1 4091 5234 7
ISBN (Ebook) 978 1 4091 5236 1

Typeset by Born Group

Printed in Great Britain by CPI Group (UK) Ltd, Croydon CR0 4YY

www.orionbooks.co.uk

For Tracy

Tuesday, 17 March

7:58 p.m.

I thought everyone was dead.

I was wrong.

The offices of Harland and Sinton, attorneys-at-law, took up the thirty-seventh floor of the Lightner Building. This was a twenty-four-hour corporate law firm, one of the biggest in New York. Normally the lights stay on around the clock, but the intruders cut the power two minutes ago, maybe more. My back ached and I could taste blood in my mouth, which mixed with the smell of burnt acid rising from the spent cartridges rattling around on the carpet. A fat moon illuminated ghostly trails of smoke that seemed to rise from the floor and evaporate just as I caught sight of them. My left ear felt as though it were filled with water, but I knew I'd merely been deafened from the gunfire. In my right hand I held an empty government-issued Glock 19; the last of the rounds lay buried in the dead man at my feet. His legs fell across the stomach of the corpse next to him and, in a curious moment of realization, I noticed that the bodies on the floor of the conference room all seemed to reach out to one another. I didn't look at each one; I couldn't bring my eyes to look at their dead faces.

My breath came in short bursts that had to fight their way through the clamp of adrenaline threatening to crush my chest. The chill wind from the broken window behind me began to dry the sweat on the back of my neck.

The digital clock on the wall hit 20:00 as I saw my killer.

I couldn't see a face or even a body; it was a shadow taking shelter in a dark corner of the conference room. Green, white, and gold flashes, from the fireworks bursting over Times Square, sent

I

patterns of light into the room at odd angles, which momentarily illuminated a small pistol held by a seemingly disembodied gloved hand. That hand held a Ruger LCP. Even though I couldn't see a face, the gun told me a lot. The Ruger held six nine-millimeter rounds. It was small enough to fit into the palm of your hand and weighed less than a good steak. While it's an effective piece, it lacks the stopping power of a full-sized handgun. The only reason anyone would use such a weapon is to disguise the fact that they were carrying at all. This little gun was a popular backup piece for most law-enforcement agencies; it was small enough to be hidden in a compact purse; it could easily be concealed in the pocket of a made-to-measure suit without ruining the line of the jacket.

Three possibilities sprung to mind.

Three possible shooters.

No way to persuade any of them to drop the gun.

Considering the last two days I'd had in court, those three all had a good reason to kill me. I had an idea about which one it might be, but right then it didn't seem to matter somehow.

Fourteen years ago I gave up being a con man. No longer Eddie Flynn the hustler, I became Eddie Flynn the lawyer. And the skills I'd learned on the street leaped into the courtroom mighty easily. Instead of hustling pit bosses, bookies, insurance companies, and drug dealers, I now plied my trade against judges and juries. But I'd never hustled a client. Until two days ago.

The Ruger's barrel angled toward my chest.

This last con would cost me my life.

I closed my eyes, feeling strangely calm. This wasn't how it was supposed to go down. Somehow this last breath of air didn't feel right. It felt as if I'd been cheated. Even so, I filled my lungs with the smoke and the metallic tang that lingered long after a shooting.

I didn't hear the shot, didn't see the muzzle flash or the recoil. I only felt the bullet ripping into my flesh. That fatal shot had become inevitable from the very moment I'd made the deal. How did I end up here? I thought.

What was the deal that led to me taking a bullet?

Like most things, it had small beginnings. It all started forty-eight hours ago with a toothpick and a dime.

CHAPTER ONE

Sunday, 15 March

48 hours until the shot

My key slid into the lock.

I froze.

Something wasn't right.

The mahogany front door to the four-story sandstone building that housed five offices, including my one-man law practice, looked like any other at this end of West Forty-Sixth Street. The area was a mix of bars, noodle houses, high-class restaurants, accountants' practices, and private medical consulting rooms, with each set of offices becoming classier the closer you got to Broadway. The paneled front door to my building had been painted blue about a month ago. The reverse side of the door boasted a hand-cut, steel-back plate – a little surprise for anyone who thought they could kick through one of the panels and open the door from the inside.

It was that kind of neighborhood.

When it comes to locks, I don't have much experience. I don't carry picks; never had a use for them, even in my former life as a con man. Unlike a lot of grifters, I didn't target the ordinary inhabitants of New York. I had my sights set on the kind of individual that deserves to get his pocket picked. My favorite marks were insurance companies. The bigger the better. The way I saw it, they were the biggest con operation in the world. Only fair that they get their pocket felt once in a while. And to con an insurance company I didn't need to break in; I just had to make sure I got invited. My game wasn't all about the talk. I had the physical moves to back it up. I'd spent years studying sleight of hand. My dad had been quite the artist, a canon who worked the bars and

3

subways. I learned from him, and over time I'd developed a deft touch: a profound sense of weight, feel, and movement. My father called it 'smart hands.' It was this finely honed sense that told me something was wrong.

I removed the key from the lock. Slid it back in. Then out. Repeat.

The action was quieter and smoother than I'd remembered. Less clunky, less resistance, less pressure required. My key almost slid in by itself, as if it were moving through cream. I checked the teeth; they were as hard and sharp as freshly cut keys could get. The face of the lock, a standard double-cylinder deadlock, bore scrapes around the keyhole, but then I remembered that the guy who ran the travel agency in the downstairs office liked bourbon in his morning coffee. I'd heard him fumbling with his keys a few times, and on the one morning that I'd passed him in the lobby, his breath had almost knocked me over. A year ago I wouldn't have noticed. I would've been just as drunk as the travel agent.

Scrapes on the lock face aside, there was no denying the drastic change in the key action. If the landlord had changed the lock mechanism, my key wouldn't have worked. No discernible odor from the lock or the key, which was dry to the touch. If a spray can of WD-40 had been poured in, I would've noticed the smell. There was really only one explanation: Somebody had forced the lock since I'd left the office earlier that morning. Sundays in the office were a necessary evil since I'd taken to sleeping in the place. I could no longer afford to keep up the rent on my apartment and an office. A foldout bed in the back room was all I needed.

The landlord couldn't afford an alarm system. Neither could I, but I still wanted some measure of security. The door opened inward. I cracked it half an inch and saw the dime resting in the hollowed-out section on the right-hand side of the doorframe, the lock side, the door itself covering half the coin, stopping it from falling onto the step. In the evening, when I went out to get food, I slipped a dime into the gap between the frame and the door, slotting it into the dime-shaped hole I'd cut into the frame with a penknife. If somebody broke in and didn't want me to know, he would hear the dime fall, recognize it as craft, and be careful to replace it. The hope lay in the intruder focusing on the noise and sparkle of the falling dime and failing to notice the toothpick jammed precisely ten inches above the first hinge on the opposite side of the door.

Whoever my intruder was that night, he'd been careful to replace the dime, but had missed the toothpick, which lay on the step.

Of the building's five offices, three were occupied: a travel agency that was in the throes of liquidation, a financial adviser whom I'd yet to see anywhere near the place, and a shady-looking hypnotist who liked to do home visits. They were mostly nine-to-five operations, or in the case of the travel agent and the hypnotist, eleven-to-three operations. No way they'd come in on a Sunday, and no way they'd bother to replace the dime. If it had been my neighbors, they'd pocket the coin and forget about it.

I dropped my newspaper and bent down to pick it up. While I was resting on my haunches, I decided to retie my shoelaces. No one on my left. Nothing on my right.

Shuffling around to get at my other shoe, I scanned the opposite side of the street. Again, nothing. A few cars way down the street on my left, but they were old imports and the windshields were misted up; no way were they surveillance cars. Across the street to my right, a couple walked arm in arm into the Hourglass Tavern, theater junkies grabbing a bite before the show. Since I'd moved here I'd been in the tavern twice, ate the lobster ravioli both times and managed to avoid the mystery beer and shot special, which changed with the turning of the large hourglass on the wall behind the bar. Abstinence was still a one-day-at-a-time deal for me.

Closing the front door, I retrieved my paper from the steps, hugged my collar around my neck against the lingering winter chill, and started walking. As a con artist I'd made plenty of enemies, and I'd even managed to make a few more in my law career. These days I figured it paid to be cautious. I did a three-block loop using every counter-surveillance technique I knew: turning down random alleyways, bursting into a light jog before I turned a corner, then slowing way down once I was on the other side, picking up my rearview in car windows and Plexiglas bus-stop advertising, stopping short and making quick turns and then retracing my steps. I began to feel a little foolish. There was no tail. I figured either the hypnotist got lucky and brought a client back to his office, or maybe the financial adviser was finally showing up to either empty his overflowing mailbox or to shred his files.

As I caught sight of my building once again, I didn't feel quite so foolish. My office was on the third floor. The first two floors were in darkness.

A light shined from my window and it wasn't my desk lamp. The beam of light appeared small, muted, and it tilted and moved.

A flashlight.

My skin prickled and my breath left me in one long, misty exhalation. It crossed my mind that a normal person would call the cops. That wasn't how I was brought up. When you make your living as a hustler, the cops don't feature in your thought process. I handled all such business myself, and I needed to see who was in my office. I carried a tire iron in the Mustang's trunk, but there was no point in going back to the parking lot to fetch it, as I didn't feel like carrying that on the open street. I don't own a gun; I don't like them, but there were some home defense products that I didn't mind using.

I opened the front door quietly, caught the dime before it hit the tiles, and took off my shoes in the lobby to keep the noise down before moving to the column of mailboxes on the wall.

In the box labeled Eddie Flynn, Attorney I had all the backup I would ever need.

CHAPTER TWO

Taking a small key from my chain, I gingerly placed the rest of the keys on top of the mailboxes before opening the new padlock I'd installed. Underneath a pile of thick brown envelopes and junk mail I found a pair of brass knuckles. In my teens I'd boxed for my parish. A lot of poor Catholic kids in New York did the same. It was supposed to instill discipline and sportsmanship – but in my case, my dad had insisted upon it for an entirely different reason. The way he figured it, if I could punch out a guy twice my size, he wouldn't worry so much about my rookie mistakes when it came time to strike out on my own as a con artist. All I had to do was train hard in the gym, work smart with the grift, and make damn sure my mom didn't find out about any of it.

The lobby was in darkness, quiet and still except for the odd moan from the heating pipes. The stairs were old and creaked like crazy. Weighing my options, I decided the stairs would carry less noise than the ancient elevator. I kept my steps light and close to the tiled wall. That allowed me to watch the upper levels as I ascended and helped avoid the worst of the groans from the old boards, which barked if you put weight near the center of the stair. The brass knuckles felt cold in my hands. Their icy touch was somehow reassuring. As I neared the top of the third flight of steps, I could hear voices. Muffled, hushed tones.

The door that led to my office was wide open. One man stood in the doorframe with his back to the hallway. Beyond him I could see at least one man with a flashlight craned into the top drawer of my file cabinet. The man with his back to me wore an earpiece. I could see the translucent wire snaking down from his ear to the folds of his black leather jacket. He wore jeans and thick-soled boots. Law enforcement, but certainly not cops. Earpieces are not standard issue for the NYPD, and most didn't want to cough up the hundred dollars for the privilege of appearing either tactical or cool. The federal law enforcement budget did stretch to an earpiece for each man, but feds would've posted a man in the lobby and they wouldn't care about replacing the dime in the doorframe. If they weren't feds or PD, then who were they? I thought. The fact that they had coms made me nervous. Coms made them organized. This wasn't a couple of crackheads looking to make a quick buck.

I crawled up the last few stairs, making sure to keep my belly on the ground. I could hear whispered conversation but couldn't make it out. The man with the flashlight in the file cabinet wasn't speaking. There were others in the office who I couldn't see; they were the ones having the discussion. As I got closer, the voices became clearer.

'Anything so far?' said a voice.

The searcher closed the file cabinet drawer and opened the one below it.

'Nothing relevant to the target,' said the man as he selected a file, opened it, and began reading with this flashlight.

Target.

That word, like a shock wave, sent boiling adrenaline through my veins. My neck muscles tightened, and my breath quickened.

They hadn't seen me.

I had two good options: slide out of there, get my car, drive like crazy all night, and then call the cops from the next state. Option number two was to leave, forget the car, jump into the first cab I saw, and head to Judge Harry Ford's apartment on the Upper East Side and drop a dime to the cops from the safety of Harry's couch.

Both choices were sound; both were smart; both carried minimal risk.

But that wasn't me.

I got up without a sound, rolled my neck, tucked my right fist under my chin, and charged the door.

CHAPTER THREE

The man who stood at the door began to turn as I broke into a run. At first he was startled by the sudden, heavy footfalls. When he saw me, his mouth opened, sucking in a huge gulp of air, and his eyes opened wide as his survival instincts hit him before his training. First came shock, and then came the reaction. Even before he could call out, I could see the mental conditioning struggling to take over the panic as his right hand began to fumble toward the gun strapped to his side.

He was too late.

I didn't want to kill the guy. Someone once told me it was unprofessional to kill a man without knowing exactly who they were. Ordinarily, if I'd hit him in the face or the head, there was a fifty-fifty chance that the blow would prove fatal, either from the force of the brass knuckles cracking his head and causing massive hemorrhaging or from the poor guy breaking his own skull when his unconscious body hit the deck. My momentum easily added an extra thirty or forty pounds of impact pressure to the punch. At that kind of speed, the odds of fatal damage increased, and if I made it a head shot, I would likely put this guy's lights out permanently.

All I needed to do was disable the man.

He was right-handed.

At the last second I lowered my right fist and adjusted my aim.

The punch hit him bone-deep, right biceps, and the fingers of his hand instantly opened and then relaxed; it was just like cutting down a power line – pulverizing a big muscle like that would mean the man's arm would be dead and lifeless for hours. My momentum took me past the guy just as the first scream left his throat.

His partner dropped the files he'd been reading and swung the flashlight at me. This man was left-handed, and I met his swing. The two and a half pounds of Cleveland brass wrapped around my left fist met the flashlight and cut it in two. The bulb exploded, and the light died in a shower of sparks. At the point of explosion, the man's face became momentarily illuminated, and I saw his mouth open, eyes flash wide as shock tore across his face. Only it wasn't shock. I must have caught part of his hand with the brass knuckles. In the half-light from the streetlamps, I watched the man fall to his knees, cupping his broken fingers.

'Eddie, stop!' said a voice from the dark.

The lamp on my desk went on.

'Ferrar, Weinstein, stand down,' said the man sitting behind my desk. I'd first met him around six months ago. This was the guy I'd saved when we'd both had a run-in with the Russian Mafia – Special Agent Bill Kennedy of the Federal Bureau of Investigation. He was addressing the men I'd assaulted, both of whom were on their knees. The one with a buzz cut gritted his teeth against the pain of his ruined fingers. The other, larger man in the leather jacket rolled around on the floor, holding his arm with his gun still safely holstered.

Kennedy was the last person I'd expected to find in my office. He leaned back in my chair and placed his legs across the desk before crossing his feet. He looked at his men, then looked at me like I'd broken something belonging to him. The navy blue pants of his suit rode up a little, enough for me so see his black silk socks and the backup piece strapped to his left ankle – a Ruger LCP.

CHAPTER FOUR

'What the hell is this?' I said.

'Take it easy. You just assaulted two federal agents. Jesus, Eddie, those are my guys.'

The agent who'd held the flashlight got up slowly, his index finger pointing in an unnatural direction. Baring his teeth, he snapped the digit back into place. I hadn't broken anything. Just dislocated his finger. His pal looked a lot worse. He was pale and sweaty. Both agents made their way to the couch on the opposite side of the room from the file cabinets.

'They'll be okay,' I said. 'They might have to wipe their asses with their other hands for a week or so, but they'll live. Can't say the same for you unless you tell me what you're doing breaking into my office. Oh, and by the way, it's not assault if you're defending your person or property from a trespasser. Thought they might've taught you that in Quantico. You got a warrant?'

I slipped off the brass and let each piece fall onto a stack of documents on my desk. Kennedy shifted his feet to the floor, picked up a set, and slipped them on one hand, feeling the lethal weight against his knuckles.

He drew the brass from his fingers, let it fall onto the pile of pages on my desk, and said, 'Brass knuckles, Eddie?'

'Paperweights,' I said. 'Where's your warrant?'

Before he answered, he began to scratch at the back of his hand. That told me all I needed to know; Kennedy worried a lot and took out his anxiety on his body. The skin around both of his thumbnails appeared swollen and red, where he'd worked at his cuticles with his teeth and nails. He hadn't shaved, and he looked as though he could use a shower, a haircut, and a good night's sleep. His normally brilliant white shirt had faded to the same color as the bags under his eyes, and the skin on his forty-year-old face had thinned. From the inch of room around his collar, I guessed he'd lost a lot of weight.

When I'd first met Kennedy, I'd been representing the head of the Russian mob, Olek Volchek. The trial went south, big-time. Volchek had taken my ten-year-old daughter, Amy, hostage and threatened to kill her. In the five months that had passed since that trial, I'd tried to forget those desperate hours. But I couldn't. I remembered it all – my agony at the thought of someone hurting her, taking her young life, and that it would be all my fault. The mere thought of it made my hands sweat.

Kennedy had almost died, but I'd managed to get him to a medic before it was too late. His wounds had healed well, and he'd even helped smooth things out for me when the dust settled on the Volchek case. A lot of what I did over the course of those two days was highly illegal. Kennedy had made it all go away. But in reality, he didn't know the half of what I'd done, and I hoped he never would.

After he'd recovered from the shooting, he'd invited me and my family to a New Year's party at his place. My wife, Christine, had said she didn't want to go; things had been bad between us for a while. I'd been thrown out of our house, deservedly, about eighteen months ago, because I'd spent more time in bars, night courts, and drunk tanks than I had at home. I'd gotten clean and things had calmed between Christine and me, until the Volchek case.

Christine thought I'd put Amy in danger – that our daughter had been taken because of me. She was right. But in the past few weeks her anger had begun to fade. I'd been able to see Amy more often, and last Wednesday when I dropped her off, Christine had invited me inside. We'd split a bottle of wine and even laughed a little. Of course, I messed up when I tried to kiss her on the doorstep before I left. She'd turned away and placed a hand on my chest; it was too soon. I'd thought, on the drive back to my office, that someday it would be okay. Someday I might get my girls back. I thought about them every hour of every day.

I had gone to Kennedy's party alone, drank Dr Peppers, ate pork and salt beef, and left early. Defense attorneys don't usually mix well with the law-enforcement crowd, con men even less so. But I actually kind of liked Kennedy. For all his worrying and pigheadedness, he was a straight-up, conscientious agent with a good track record, and he'd put all of that on the line for me. I saw that stone-faced morality in his gaze as he sat on the other side of my desk, in my chair, chewing over my question. In the end I decided to answer it myself.

'You don't have a warrant, do you?'

'All I can say for now is that this little party is for your benefit.'

Scanning the office, I saw four hefty-looking metal suitcases stacked in the corner and, beside them, what looked like sound equipment.

'Did I interrupt band practice?' I said.

'We were doing you a favor, sweeping your office for any listening devices.'

'Listening devices? In the future, don't do me any favors without asking me first. Out of interest, did you find any?'

'No. You're clean,' he said, standing and stretching his back. 'You always carry paperweights around?'

'Office supplies come in handy from time to time. Why didn't you call and tell me you were coming?'

'There wasn't time. Sorry.'

'What do you mean there wasn't time? I heard your buddy over there mention the word "target," so I want to know what you're really doing here.'

Before Kennedy could answer, I heard footsteps. The door to my back office opened, and a small man who looked like he was in his fifties, with a gray beard and black-rimmed glasses, stepped into the room. He wore a long black overcoat that stopped at his ankles. Blue shirt, dark pants, graying curly hair swept back over a thin, tanned face.

'Protection,' said the small man, answering the question I'd directed at Kennedy.

He stood with his arms buried in his pockets, confident and in charge. He walked casually past Kennedy and sat his butt down on my desk before smiling at me.

'Mr Flynn, my name is Lester Dell. I'm not FBI. I'm with another agency. The Bureau are here because they're part of a joint task force that I'm heading up. We have a job for you,' he said, nodding.

'Great. So what are you? DEA? ATF? The cable guy?'

'Oh, I work for the agency that doesn't officially carry out operations on US soil. That's why the FBI and the Treasury Department are handling all the manpower. As far as the State Department is concerned, I'm here as a consultant,' he said, and as he smiled, the brown skin above his beard developed deep lines that tapered toward his eyes. Lines that didn't quite seem a natural fit for his face, as if smiling were an unusual thing to do. His accent seemed a little off, because his pronunciation was so precise and clean.

I didn't need to ask where he worked – the smile said it all. He told me anyway. 'Unofficially, Mr Flynn, this is my operation. And I can tell you've already guessed who I work for. You're correct – I work for the CIA.'

I nodded. Clocked Kennedy. He was watching me closely – judging my reactions carefully.

'We're tight for time, so you'll forgive me if I'm brief and to the point. We're here to take precautions. To make sure no one but us will hear this conversation. I have a proposition for you. In fact, I have a case for you,' he said.

'I don't do government work. That goes double for the kind of governments that break into my office.'

'Oh? I thought you might welcome some paid employment. I see you've got a sofa bed in back, clothes, TV, a toothbrush in the bathroom, and a stack of paperbacks. But I don't need to make any assumptions from this: I know all about you. Every little thing. You're broke. You're living in your office. In fact, you have twelve hundred dollars in your checking account, your office account is thirty grand in the red, and the work is slow.'

I hit Kennedy with a look. He folded his arms and nodded at Dell, telling me I should listen.

'Mr Flynn, here's my situation. I've spent five years investigating a group of very bad individuals. To be plain about it, I've come up empty-handed. I got nothing. Until yesterday, when all my prayers were answered. It turns out that a friend of those bad individuals got arrested for doing a *very* bad thing. He will be tried and convicted; it's an open-and-shut case. I'm hoping this man might be persuaded to make a deal with me, one where he gets to walk out of jail while he's still young and I get to arrest his friends in exchange. Problem is, this man's lawyers don't quite see it that way. I want you to take over his case. I want you to represent this guy, and I want you to persuade him to cut a deal. It's in his best interests, and yours.'

Checking his watch, he said, 'You have forty-eight hours, precisely, to get yourself hired by your new client, force him to plead guilty, and we'll make him a deal. If you do this, the federal government will do two things for you.'

From his coat he produced a hip flask, cranked it open, and poured a measure into the empty coffee cup sitting on my desk. He didn't ask if I wanted any, just poured and handed me the mug. He sipped lightly from the flask, then continued.

'First, we will pay you one hundred thousand dollars. Cash. Tax free. Not bad for a morning's work. Second, and more important for you, do this for me and I won't send your wife to a federal prison for the rest of her life.'

CHAPTER FIVE

Perched on my office desk, Dell took another sip from his hip flask. I ignored whatever liquor he'd poured into my coffee mug. He smiled again, unnaturally, and I let his words wash over me.

Do this and we won't send your wife to prison for the rest of her life.

I saw Kennedy tense up. He knew the fate of the last group of hard cases who'd threatened my family, and Kennedy seemed just as surprised as I was.

'Dell, tell him we're the good guys here,' said Kennedy.

'I'm talking here, Bill,' said Dell, never taking his fake smile from me.

If Kennedy or Dell were expecting a show, I didn't give it to them. Instead I leaned back in the chair normally reserved for my clients and folded my hands.

'Dell, this is all very interesting, but my wife is as straight as they come. She doesn't even jaywalk. If you think you have something on her? Fine, go ahead and use it and I'll see you in court. In fact, she won't need me. Christine is a far better lawyer than I am. That's why she works at Harland and Sinton, and I . . . well, I work here. So, thanks for the offer. The money sounds great, but when it comes with a threat I lose interest. I don't scare easy, Dell. Don't forget to replace my dime on the way out,' I said.

The fake smile changed into a real one. At that moment he looked different. Charming. Despite what he said and how he came across, there was an unexpected warmth to the man. He exchanged a look with Kennedy, then bent low and retrieved a green file from a case beside him.

'You think your wife is safe because she's an attorney at Harland and Sinton?' said Dell. 'The irony is that your wife is in this situation *because* she's an attorney at Harland and Sinton.'

'What?'

'I brought something for you to see. Actually, you can keep it. I've got a copy. So does the federal prosecutor. With the documents in here, we can file thirty-eight RICO charges against your wife and seek a combined total of one hundred and fifteen years' incarceration. Take a look for yourself.'

The file contained three pages. Neither of them made much sense to me. The first was what looked like a share purchase agreement for a company I'd never heard of. Christine's signature appeared as a witness to the agreement and sat beside that of the client, the share purchaser.

'I don't understand this,' I said.

'Let me make it real simple. Your wife signed this document on her first day of employment at Harland and Sinton, Attorneys-at-Law. Every attorney at Harland and Sinton gets the same treatment their first day. You know what it's like on your first day in a new office; you spend half the time trying to remember everyone's name, where you're supposed to sit, where your files are, and trying to memorize all the damn new computer passwords you've just been handed. Around four thirty on your first day in Harland and Sinton, one of the senior partners will call you to his office. He's just completed a share transfer agreement for a client. Due diligence has been done already, but he's been called to an emergency meeting and the client has just arrived. The senior partner wants you to witness the document for him. All you have to do is watch the client sign the damn piece of paper and put your name beside it. That's all. Happens all the time. In fact, all two hundred and twenty-three lawyers in there had the very same experience on their first day. But be under no illusions, Mr Flynn. In signing this document, your wife unwittingly became part of one of the largest financial frauds in American history.'

'Harland and Sinton? Fraud? Pal, you're badly mistaken. They're one of the oldest and most respected firms in the city. No way are they up to anything illegal. Why would they? They've got more money than they know what to do with.'

'Oh, they've got money, all right. Dirty money.'

'You've got proof?'

'Some, like the documents you just read. We don't have it all. Not yet. That's where you come in. See, Harland and Associates has had its financial ups and downs over the years, but that all changed in 1995 when Gerry Sinton came on board. The newly formed Harland and Sinton scaled down its client list to less than fifty and focused the practice on securities, tax, bonds, wealth management, and estates. Their profits went through the roof. Prior to Sinton coming on board, the firm was clean – and it's still got the best reputation. It's the perfect setup for their little operation.'

'What operation?'

Dell paused, looked at the untouched alcohol in front of me, turned to Kennedy, and said, 'Get us some coffee, Bill, please.'

Kennedy went in back and tried to bang some life into my old coffee machine.

'Harland and Sinton is a front. They practice a little law, but really they're running the largest money-laundering scheme ever conducted on US soil. The firm acts for companies that don't really exist, except on paper. They get their legitimate clients to buy shares in the companies, and those clients make a guaranteed return of around twenty percent on their investment. What those clients are doing, without knowing it, is handing over clean money, and the dirty money flows back through the dummy company accounts, cleaning it through the books, to pay the investors. The dirty money comes from drug cartels, terrorists, you name it. And your wife countersigned a document deeply implicating her in this fraud.'

'No way.'

I looked at the documents again. If what Dell said was correct, Christine was in the worst kind of trouble. The fact that she knew nothing about it didn't matter a damn. It's a strict liability offense – if you touched the deal in any way and you didn't perform due diligence – you went down. The fact that you handled the transaction is enough for conviction regardless of your intentions.

'How do you know all of this?'

'Because I spoke to a guy who nursed some of the transactions through the banks. He told me the whole setup. He was going to blow the operation wide open.'

'Then why do you need me?'

'Honest answer? Because the witness is dead. Your wife's boss, Gerry Sinton, had him murdered.'

CHAPTER SIX

Kennedy stopped in his tracks. Hot coffee in his hands. The room became still. My eyes closed and I rubbed my forehead. It felt like a torrent of lead building up in my temples.

What the hell had Christine gotten herself into?

She was the only woman I'd ever truly loved. Our wedding had been a small affair. My parents were both dead, and with the exception of Judge Harry Ford and my partner, Jack Halloran, all of my friends were either hustlers, hookers, or mob guys, but still, they were my friends. The church on Freeman Avenue had an unusual congregation that day. Her side of the church was full of upper-class New Yorkers, Manhattan's elite: newspaper owners, famous chefs, real-estate millionaires, lawyers, models, and socialites – whatever they are. My side had a judge, my mentor Harry Ford; a crooked lawyer in the shape of my then partner Jack Halloran; a six-foot-tall ex-hooker named Boo; four made guys along with their incredible wives and their boss, Jimmy 'the Hat' Fellini; a couple of old hustling buddies; and my former landlady, Mrs Wachowski, whom I didn't particularly like, but she took the bad look off the rest of them. Everyone behaved. Only Mrs Wachowski let me down by falling into the toilet after too many screwdrivers. Christine's mom had to pull her out.

I didn't care. I only had eyes for Christine. We were happy.

It didn't stay that way.

Somewhere between my crazy hours in the courtroom, the Berkley case, and hitting the bottle, Christine had stopped loving me. I could tell by her eyes, she was tired of it. Tired of me. Even though I'd lost my way, I'd never lost my love for my wife. Last Wednesday night, I'd reminded her of Mrs Wachowski's fall in the toilet and she'd snorted a mouthful of wine out of her nose. And even though she'd turned away from me on the porch, I knew there was a small chance we could be together again someday. The hand she'd placed on my chest was gentle; there was a tenderness to it that gave me some hope.

Blowing the vapor off the mugs of coffee, Kennedy stepped forward and handed me a cup. He stood beside Dell and waited for me to take a sip. It was too hot. I put the mug on my desk and lifted a pen, letting it flow around my fingers, helping me think.

'Who was the informant?' I asked.

Stifling a grimace, Dell got off my desk, moved around, and sank into my chair with a sigh as Kennedy handed him the other cup.

'Thank you, Bill,' said Dell, adding another dash to the hot mug from his hip flask.

'Since nine eleven the CIA have been targeting the heart of global terrorism – financing. For the past fifteen years I worked Grand Cayman, which is the Panama Canal for dirty money. We had a guy on our watch list – Farooq. He took orders directly from Gerry Sinton. We found out that Farooq, apart from being a corrupt banker and money launderer, traded in online images of children. He got caught in April last year through an intercontinental police task force. Farooq was traced via a pedophile network, and when the local cops caught him, they found illegal images on his computer. In Grand Cayman that meant serious time, but more than likely he would be killed as soon as he set foot in jail. The firm relied on middlemen like Farooq to move the money, and if he turned snitch he could take them all down.

'So I decided to go talk to him in the George Town police station. Turn him into an asset. He'd been cut loose by the firm a few weeks earlier because Sinton had some whole new method of moving and cleaning the money; plus he was scared for his skin. He promised us the largest money-laundering operation in the world and even gave us some evidence. Some of the documents were just like the share agreement you've already seen, and some were old bank account statements to give us a taste of what he could offer if we gave him a new identity and a life someplace else. He was giving us Harland and Sinton.'

The coffee tasted bitter – old machine and no filters. I tried to focus on the man in front of me and watch for any tells. He looked relaxed, he made and broke eye contact naturally, his gestures were unrestrained, and he didn't emphasize words or hide his mouth with his fingers.

'We were ready to deal, so we left the local police headquarters in convoy. Farooq never made it to the embassy. I don't know who carried out the attack, but whoever it was operated with military tactics – took out the lead vehicle with an RPG, blocked the road behind. My lead analyst died in one of the cars. All I can remember is her screaming as she burned. I couldn't get to her. Farooq was taken alive; the firm needed to know what he'd told the police.'

His eyes met the desk and stayed there as he said, 'He told them everything. He wouldn't have been able to hold out. We found his body – draped over the wall of the embassy. He'd been burned – head to foot – with acid. There were no fatal wounds, no signs of major trauma. We figured that he died of a heart attack or a seizure brought on by the pain of the acid burns. Imagine that – being in so much pain that your body simply dies.

'When Farooq died, so did the case. All the paper evidence led back to the lawyers who witnessed the agreements, with nothing to link the partners. Gerry Sinton took out the rest of the middlemen, and the firm started cleaning the money some other way. We got zip.

'We have one chance to get Harland and Sinton and it just fell into our lap yesterday. We think we've found a new asset. *Your* new client.'

'You haven't told me who this guy is. Why would he make a deal?'

'He'll make a deal. He's just a kid. A scared kid. Yeah, he's powerful, in his own way. But he can't handle the prospect of a life sentence. He has information about the firm – key information. That's all you need to know, for now. Get him on our side. I'll make the deal.'

'What'd the kid do?'

'Fifteen hours ago he shot and killed his girlfriend. We've got the gun, we've got witnesses that put him at the crime scene, and we've got forensics. The whole package. What you have to do is get him to fire his current lawyers, get hired as his defense counsel, and force him to make a deal with me.'

'I'll be disbarred. I have a massive conflict of interest. I can't persuade a client to take a deal that benefits my wife.'

He acted like he didn't hear me. 'We want him to take a plea before the preliminary hearing. He has to be arraigned within twenty-four hours of arrest. He was arrested for murder this morning. He was interviewed, charged, and he'll be on his way to central booking tonight. He has to be arraigned before midday tomorrow; that's your clock – fifteen hours to bump the firm and steal their client. If you manage to get hired, the judge will likely set a preliminary hearing for the next day. I want him to plead guilty before the prelim, while the pressure is on and the DA is willing to deal; that's the time when this man will be most vulnerable. Plus, it's no good if we just get the evidence from this guy to nail the partners. We want the firm's money. Take Bernie Madoff – biggest financial fraud bust in history, but it goes down as a failure for law enforcement because they didn't recover the cash. We want the partners and the money. To get both we have to move fast, before the money disappears. You do this, we make sure Christine walks away.'

I shook my head.

'I'll level with you, Eddie. This is how the CIA operates. We obtain an asset, control it, and exploit it. Your new client is that asset. We need to have him under control so we can use him. You'll be well compensated. We know you can handle the pressure after that thing in Chambers Street. We can always push your buttons if we have to, Eddie Fly.'

The mob referred to me as Eddie Fly, my old pal Jimmy the Hat, in particular. When we were kids, after we were done sparring, we'd play stickball. I couldn't match Jimmy's swing – he was a three-sewer hitter – but I had fast hands that never missed a catch. Jimmy gave me the name Eddie Fly. After I went into the confidence game, the name stuck.

I thought of Christine and Amy. Professional oaths and all, I couldn't let anything jeopardize my family. And from what Dell had told me, the client sounded guilty. Helping a guilty man fess up and make a deal to save my wife didn't sound so bad after all.

'I have to tell Christine; she has a right to know.'

Dell shook his head. 'You say nothing to her. The less she knows the better. What if she panics and lets it slip to one of the partners? She'd be dead and the whole operation would fail. Tell her nothing. You're going to buy her a ticket out of this. That's good enough.'

I saw the logic. I had no idea how Christine would react or if she would even believe me. I looked at Dell.

'Who is the client?'

'He's your mark. You catch him as a client and get him to plead to the murder in exchange for a deal with us. He gets a reduced sentence, the firm goes down, we get the money, and you get Christine.'

Dell glanced at Kennedy.

'I need to stretch my legs,' said Dell. He got up from the desk, and I noticed a slight limp. He walked it out, rubbed his thigh.

'I didn't get out of the hit on Farooq without scars, Mr Flynn. I want that firm. They took my witness, my analyst. I *will* take them.'

He moved in back, and I heard him close the bathroom door. Kennedy leaned forward so Dell wouldn't overhear us.

'The analyst who died in the Farooq hit – her name was Sophie. Dell's protégé. And his lover. I hear they were a solid item. The real thing. He's taking this personally. Cut him a break,' said Kennedy.

'He's threatening my wife.'

'He's doing his job. He doesn't want to hurt your family. He's giving you a get-out-of-jail card for Christine. You know it doesn't matter if Christine intended to launder money or if it was just an innocent mistake. Fact is she signed the document and she didn't perform due diligence first; doesn't matter if the partners lied to her. She has no defense. Dell is giving her a way out of this.'

'You still haven't told me who the client is and how he can bring down the firm.'

'He's the key, Eddie. Or, rather – he's got the key. We think it's probably best at the moment if you don't know too much about what this man has on the firm. But he's the only one who can lead us to the money. It's going to be a high-pressure couple of days. I know you're good – that's why we're here – but we can't take the risk of you letting something slip, even by accident. If the client thinks you're playing him against the firm, he might clam up. Tell him you can get him a sweet deal. He just needs to talk to a couple of your contacts. We can take it from there.'

I heard Dell coming around the corner.

'Okay, how do we do it?'

I saw Kennedy visibly relax. The two agents I'd injured, too. Dell pursed his lips and nodded; a light seemed to ignite in his eyes.

'We can help you stall his lawyer tomorrow, before he comes to court. Buy you some time. After that, you're on your own.'

'And his current lawyers are . . .?'

'You bet. Harland and Sinton.'

PART ONE

THE SETUP

CHAPTER SEVEN

Monday, 16 March

36 hours until the shot

My dad once told me that in the con game there are two basic modes of operation: short cons and long cons. The short cons usually happen on the street or in a bar, they take between five minutes and five seconds to complete, and they're low risk/low payoff. Long cons take time. It's not unusual for a long con to take six months or even a year to execute. They involve detailed planning, scouting, preparation, lots of financing, and the high risk is balanced by the potential for a big payday.

There is a third type of con: the bullet con. This is a long con that's condensed into a short time frame, between a week and a couple days. Speed is the key to it, and it's by far the riskiest method of operation. There's little time to rehearse, to plan, to prepare. Inevitably, you're flying by the seat of your pants most of the way. No one chooses to execute a bullet con unless something incredible falls in their lap, something that's too good to pass up, something irresistible: A rich mark who likes to gamble flies into town, but he's staying for only a week, or a priceless painting is unexpectedly removed from its normally secure resting place for an emergency cleanup. That type of deal. Fast, complex, dangerous.

I heard old-timers call it a bullet con because it's launched so quickly – like pulling the trigger. In reality, the name derives from the fact that if the con fails, the hustler can expect to eat a bullet.

On the morning before Saint Patrick's Day, at eight fifteen, I began the first bullet con of my career. Like most good cons, it started small. At first a series of simple moves and gestures: hustlers' tools to hook their mark, to make him worry, to make him sweat,

27

before the hustler wades in with a golden ticket that is the answer to all of the mark's problems.

That morning, as I walked into the basement holding area of the Manhattan District Court, I concealed a folded twenty-dollar bill in my right hand. The note was carefully creased in order to fit snugly into my palm. My footsteps echoed on the polished linoleum floor as I walked past the bars that separated me from the detainees awaiting their court appearance. I picked up my mark in my peripheral vision. He sat far away from the other prisoners, in the corner, head down and hands over his face. I looked directly at the detention officer with the shotgun cradled in his arms. He held the key to the pen that contained my mark and thirty other guys who were waiting for their arraignments.

Most of the men who'd found themselves in the pen that morning were there either because of drugs, alcohol, mental health problems, poverty, or gangs, and some of them no doubt owed their present incarceration to a combination of all of those things. The mark was different. Way different. He was the smallest guy in there by quite some way. He looked reasonably healthy, but just a little too thin. The orange jumpsuit hung off his bones. Somebody had already taken his shoes; I could see his white sweat socks. The guards always take away lace-up shoes just in case one of the prisoners tries to either hang themselves or somebody else with the laces. In place of their Nikes or Converse, they're given black rubber gym shoes. The mark wore no shoes, so it was obvious that somebody in the pen had taken the shoes he was wearing when he was arrested; nobody in there would want to steal prisoner gym shoes. His unkempt curly caramel hair and wire-rim glasses made him look just a little ridiculous, just a little too far this side of geek to be cool, although I doubted if anyone had ever told him that.

If you're a billionaire, people get real polite all of a sudden.

Neil, the detention officer known as the pit handler, heard me approaching and shifted the shotgun in his arms. To a defense attorney, the holding cage was an advertising opportunity. Guys watched who made bail, who didn't, who got their trial date quickly and whether they got off. And guys sitting in that pen have a lot of time on their hands to talk. Neil had been a pit handler for twenty years. My old partner handled Neil's divorce at a discount in exchange for Neil spreading the word to the regulars in the cage.

Goddamn it, how did that asshole make bail?

Eddie Flynn, that's how.

The noise from the pen was a deafening cacophony of swearing, screaming, and drunken singing. With the usual commotion, no one would notice my conversation with Neil. I'd told him as much a few hours beforehand, and we'd worked out a little routine for my arrival that morning, something that would catch the mark's attention.

I stopped in front of Neil and winked at him. He racked a shell into the twelve-gauge. That sound, that unmistakable crack and slide is enough to stop anyone in their tracks. Even with my back to the cage, I could feel the stare from every prisoner. My right hand slid out to shake the officer's hand. I shifted my stance to the left so the mark could see the move. My fingers opened wide enough for the billionaire to see the money change hands. Neil telegraphed the lift so everybody got a good view of him tucking the bill into his breast pocket. He opened the cage for me, a strictly forbidden practice, and I stepped into the shark tank. The only thing left to do was put my bait in the water.

Popo, pronounced po-po, a junkie client of mine, greeted me with a sullen tilt of his head. Originally, from LA, Popo was a professional snitch, and he'd moved out here when Fresno got too hot for him. He looked pretty good for a guy in his situation. His jeans were ripped up one side and his wifebeater bore a multitude of food stains. He smelled of old shit and cigarettes. A thick glaze of sweat covered his emaciated torso. The sweats marked the early onset of heroin withdrawal. Popo wore cheap, slip-on sneakers so that he could keep his own footwear when he was arrested, which was a regular occurrence. His real name was Dale Barnes. That was the name he always gave to the cops – but he snitched so often that he earned the street name Popo, which stood for 'police.' The origin of the word is unclear, but it seems to have started out in California; those beat cops that patrolled side by side on bicycles with 'PO' as in 'Police Officer' stenciled on the back of their T-shirts. From the back they read PO PO. For a snitch, a name like that wasn't good for business.

Popo spoke through cracked and bleeding lips. 'Where you been, lawyer man?'

He sounded a little pissed off with me, just as we'd arranged.

'Buying you breakfast,' I said, and I handed him a sack I'd concealed beneath a case file. I sat down on the bench on Popo's left. Popo was the closest prisoner to the mark, who sat a few feet to Popo's right, on the end of the bench. After I'd spoken to Neil earlier that morning, he'd put me on the phone with Popo and I'd told my client to get cozy with the geeky-looking white guy. With trembling fingers, he opened the sack and began devouring a burger. I let him eat. He offered the other burger to the man on his right. He declined. I thought then that they made an odd pairing. They were both twenty-two years old, both born in the same city, both lived in the same city, and were both cooling their asses on the same jail bench, and yet they could've just as easily come from different planets. One from Planet Rich, one from Planet Poor.

The mark was David Child. He owned the fastest-growing social media network in history – Reeler. In the three years since its launch, it had made David Child a billionaire and made Facebook look like Myspace. Hardly a month went by without some story about Reeler, or David, making the headlines. With his head folded into his chest, his hair slick with sweat, I almost didn't recognize him. Up close he didn't strike me as the kind to get involved in anything underhanded. He looked straight. But then again, a lot of straight guys are capable of murder. The kid was a genius, but I couldn't figure out his connection to Harland and Sinton. He was a client of the firm, but what else connected them? Kennedy said this kid was the only one who could lead them to the money. I couldn't figure it out, not yet. I looked at David and Popo sitting on the same bench. Crime was a great leveler.

'So how long dis time, Eddie?' said Popo.

I sucked air through my teeth. Not something that any client wants to hear.

'Well, we don't have a three-strike rule here, but considering you're on something close to your forty-third strike, I'd say, half hour, forty-five minutes tops. By that time I'll have persuaded the prosecutor to drop the charges and you'll walk.'

As I'd told a persistent offender and junkie that I'd have him out within an hour, I heard a snort of laughter. David's head turned, and he stared at me. I deliberately avoided any eye contact and kept my gaze nonchalantly on my client.

'I told ya, Eddie's the man,' said Popo, turning and sending a friendly jab into David's shoulder. 'Better not be longer, Eddie. I got places to be,' said Popo.

'I'll do my best. I'm not a miracle worker. I should have you out before ten thirty, but I'm not promising anything.'

He smiled. The truth of the matter was that Popo got arrested every other Sunday night. That was our arrangement. He got caught a couple months ago for a robbery and was looking at some serious time. His only option was to cooperate with the police, and with my help he made a deal. If you're a paid informant you have two payment options: sixty-three dollars sixty per week, or the state will pay for a legal representative of your choosing at a maximum of one hundred and fifty dollars an hour. This new pilot scheme, which paid for a private lawyer as opposed to the normal charitable or partially state-funded alternatives, was designed to ease the burden on the public defender and the other, overworked legal-aid schemes and avoid conflicts of interest for the public defender's office. It was not uncommon for the public defender to simultaneously represent both the snitch and the guy he'd ratted out. While it was a good idea, in practice most guys just took the sixty-three dollars and sixty cents.

Not Popo.

As long as Popo got arrested for possession of narcotics every other Sunday, I could bill six hours for getting him out again the next day. Somehow the fact that he was a paid police informant kept slipping his drug-addled mind, and I would have to attend and sort everything out at court on Monday at one hundred and fifty an hour. You can't be an inside man in a drug ring without carrying a little product – so getting the charges dropped would be a cinch. Even so, I normally took my time getting Popo released. With Popo's help, I billed the Justice Department around fifteen hundred a month, kicked back fifty to the desk sergeant at central booking and five hundred to Popo, who in turn paid protection money to the local dealer so he wouldn't get killed for being a snitch. Guy with a name like Popo needed all the help he could get to stay alive on the street. The dealer gave Popo the names of his employees who were slow on the corners so they got picked up and the dealer could bring in fresh, cheaper talent. After all, anyone who couldn't sell two thousand dollars' worth of dope a day on a street corner in New York really shouldn't be in the business anyway. I'd thought of it as a sweet deal for everybody. Everyone got paid, the crime statistics looked better, and the public defender's office got themselves some free time. Nobody got hurt, and the city picked up the check.

A nice little racket.

'Sit tight. I've spoken to the prosecutor. She's a friend of mine. She'll call your case first so you can get out of here fast,' I said, and gave Popo a slap on his wet back.

I got up and offered some final advice to my client.

'Be ready in about ten minutes. Say nothing and leave all the talking to me. Got it?'

He nodded. Satisfied, I turned to leave. I'd expected that I might get to the cage door before David called after me. He called out before I'd taken my third stride.

'Excuse me, Counselor, do you have a second?' said David.

I stopped but didn't turn around.

'The public defender will be in court later. I don't do legal aid or pro bono, pal,' I said.

'No . . . no . . . ah . . . you don't understand. I've already got a lawyer . . . It's just I . . .'

I half turned and cut him off. 'Then you don't need me.'

'No, wait, please stop. I just need to ask you something, please,' he said, and laced his fingers together before holding them under his chin. He silently mouthed *please*, over and over. Although he desperately wanted to speak to me, he didn't want to get up; his fear of getting up from the bench, and thereby attracting attention from his cell buddies, outweighed his desperation.

'Take it easy. It's okay. Say, don't I know you?'

He seemed to shrink and hugged his body. Last thing he wanted was to be recognized.

'I don't think we've met,' he said.

'What can I do for you?' I moved over to him.

'My lawyer, he told me last night that he would be here this morning. He hasn't shown up, and I'm worried. I've . . . I'm not used to . . .'

'You've never been arrested before. I get it. Who's your lawyer?'

'Gerry Sinton.'

'From Harland and Sinton?'

'Yeah. You sound surprised.'

'Well, a little. My wife's an attorney at Harland and Sinton. I thought they were strictly corporate.'

'Gerry and I go way back. I trust him. Have you seen him this morning?' he said, his voice breaking high and low from a raw throat. Neil had told me that David had been crying most of the night, until Popo managed to calm him down. A wise move; the men in the cage can smell weakness a mile away.

'No, I don't believe I've seen Gerry this morning, but I'm sure he'll be here soon.'

I noticed his hands were small and soft. They shook with the same fear threatening to overcome him completely. His jaw worked like a jackhammer, his eyes red and wide. He reached out as I turned to leave and took hold of my wrist.

'Hey there! Hands off,' said Neil, the guard.

The mark let go and grimaced.

'Wait, please. Could you maybe find out if Gerry's arrived? I can't call him, and he should be here by now. I'll pay you for your time. Maybe you could call your wife? See if she's seen him?'

Popo didn't have a bank account, didn't have any money or possessions other than the clothes he wore. Kennedy told me that David's net worth stood at 1.9 billion dollars, he owned a yacht, a fleet of cars, three properties, and a basketball team. Right then there wasn't much to separate David from Popo. Each of them needed their fix. Popo needed heroin, the mark needed his lawyer, and their aching leveled both men in a way that only death or disease could match.

'Christine works for Ben Harland. I don't know how much she sees of Gerry Sinton, but I'll call her anyway.'

As I pretended to call Christine on my cell, I checked my watch. Before I'd come to court, I'd tried calling her half a dozen times when I'd managed to slip away from Dell and the feds. She didn't pick up. Truth is, I didn't know what I would've told her if she had answered. I thought I'd tell her to stay home, but I didn't think she'd listen unless I told her everything. Then I decided that Dell was probably right – the more she knew, the more she was in danger.

'I wouldn't worry. He's probably caught in traffic. I'm sure he'll be here. When he arrives, he'll give his name to the court clerk and register as your counsel of record, pick up the case papers, and make contact with the prosecutor. Look, I'll ask Neil to call the clerk and check it out for you.'

'Thank you,' said the mark, shutting his eyes in the hope that when he opened them, I would've located his savior.

I closed my phone, said, 'Her cell is off. Probably in a meeting.'

I called Neil over to the bars and asked him to call Denise, the clerk, to check if Gerry Sinton had arrived in court. While Neil made the call, I gave David a reassuring smile. Neil probably called his bookie. He certainly didn't call Denise. No need. At that moment in time I had a pretty good idea of Gerry Sinton's precise location, and if everything went according to plan, Gerry Sinton didn't have a hope in hell of making it to court anytime soon.

CHAPTER EIGHT

About an hour before I'd walked into the cells, Gerry Sinton would've been sitting in traffic on the Avenue of the Americas behind the wheel of a 1968 Rolls-Royce Silver Shadow. Dell told me that Sinton had a car collection that would make Jay Leno weep, and Sinton liked to drive. At one time he had employed a driver, like most other top attorneys, but laid him off when he bought the Roller six months ago.

As he drove, the car in front of him, an old Ford pickup, would begin to veer in and out of Gerry's lane. Gerry would've seen the couple in that car arguing and he might've sounded his horn once or twice at the pickup and attempted to overtake them. The pickup driver, Arthur Podolske, wouldn't have allowed that to happen. Arthur weighed around three hundred and seventy-five pounds. He was in his fifties, asthmatic, and ranked as one of the best precision drivers I'd ever worked with. That guy could stop a boat in a heartbeat. Arthur would change lanes to block Gerry's overtaking maneuver and, at just the right moment, Arthur would hit the brakes hard at the very second that the light turned red. Gerry wouldn't stand a chance of stopping. His classic would assuredly hit the back of the old pickup.

Gerry probably got out of his car shouting obscenities at Arthur. That wouldn't last long. As soon as the driver's door of the pickup opened and Arthur spilled his considerable ass onto the street, he would begin to feign a heart attack. Arthur's wife, Eileen, makes Arthur look like a gymnast. I imagined Eileen had burst into hysterics, like she usually does, and flapped her huge arms at Gerry, and within seconds panic would overtake the whole situation. The big risk was that Gerry would use his cell to call his office and dispatch another lawyer to the courthouse to look after his client. I'd planned for that. Luckily, a passing NYPD patrol saw the whole accident, and while one patrolman radioed for a paramedic, the other would pull Gerry out of the Roller, plant him face-first into the hood, cuff him, and then bundle him into the back of the patrol car to be dealt with after the paramedics arrived. All before Gerry could dial for help.

Not an easy setup by any means, but I had help from the kind of people who can arrange for a patrol car to follow a lawyer and detain him before he could get a chance to make a call on his cell phone, who can do just about anything they think necessary.

There was zero chance of Gerry making it to court that morning.

'Your client here speaks very highly of you,' said David, holding out a hand to Popo.

'I told him, my man Eddie is the best,' said Popo, through shuddering teeth. Withdrawal was beginning to hit him hard.

I held my gaze on David, like I was taking a real look at him for the first time. His face was dirty with tears, and his hair stuck to his forehead.

'Hey, I do know you. You're . . .'

'Not here,' he said. His eyes flitted around the cage, and he gripped his knees to stop his hands from shaking. Even so, his feet jacked and, sensing my stare, he slid his feet underneath the bench.

I hadn't anticipated David losing his footwear. Sometimes you've got to improvise. Some of the best and most convincing cons were successful because the hustler saw an opportunity to sell himself as an honest man. Getting the mark to trust you is the biggest hurdle, and when opportunities arise to cement your relationship with your target, you've got to take them. In the game we called these little plays 'convincers' or 'persuaders.' Those chances have to be grasped no matter what the odds. Losing his shoes counted as a golden opportunity for me to prove to David that I was on the level.

'Hey, what happened to your shoes?'

He hung his head and rubbed the back of his neck. His feet bounced nervously, and he wrung his hands. He looked at me before shooting a glance into the heart of the pen. I saw a huge black guy standing in the center of the floor, like he owned the place. He had a lot of space around him in a crowded cage full of dangerous men. This guy was at the top of the food chain. He wore a pair of new Nike training shoes. Red slip-ons. They were way too small for him and his heels spilled over onto the floor.

Ignoring David's pleading hands and whispers to 'please, leave it,' I headed for the center of the pen and held out my hand to the giant in front of me. He was six inches over my six feet, maybe a hundred pounds heavier than me, and all of that extra weight looked like well-compacted muscle. A tattoo of a black eagle spread its wings across his broad chest, and I saw gold shining in his gums.

The big guy just stared at me.

'I'm Eddie Flynn,' I said, leaving my hand out.

Nothing.

'Can't help but notice you're wearing my client's shoes. I don't think they fit you. I'd like 'em back.'

The big man's eyes burned, and I could see the rest of the men in the cage nudging one another, ready to watch the shit go down. A heavy stillness settled over the pen. I could smell the man's sweat. My hand remained extended, and my gaze never left his face.

Instead of taking my hand, the giant's right arm shot out and grabbed my tie. He was either about to pull me close and strangle me, or just threaten me. I didn't give him the opportunity. Instead I gripped his right hand in mine and anchored it to my chest. My left arm shot toward the ceiling and took the big man's elbow with it. I kept his wrist locked low, and his elbow struck the ten o'clock position with a loud crack from his shoulder. I watched the man's expression change from anger, to amazement, then sheer, hot agony. Arms weren't designed to fold like this.

'I push my arm two inches higher and your shoulder pops for keeps. There's a lot of cartilage in there that will grind and snap. You'll pass out, and when you wake up you'll wish you were dead. You want to take off the shoes and play nice? Or you want a disability check on the first of every month?'

He nodded. I let go. The arm would be dead for a few hours; the nerves and muscle fibers shot to shit. I could tell he was thinking about jumping me.

I smiled.

He took off the shoes.

Growing up in the meanest boxing gym in the city had its advantages, even in legal practice.

I tossed the shoes to the mark. His mouth hung open. Neil broke the stunned silence. 'You know, I really should get a new prescription for these glasses,' he said as he took off his spectacles and held them up to the light.

Neil continued. 'You're up, Eddie, and your little friend is up right after. I called Denise; no sign of Mr Sinton.'

'Thanks, Neil,' I said.

I saw David lose his breath upon hearing that Gerry Sinton hadn't made it to court, managing only short, noisy gasps that made his lips curl into his mouth as he struggled to inhale the stale air. Sweat dripped from the end of his nose and mingled with fresh tears on his face.

'Can you help me, please? I don't know what's happened to Gerry. He should *be* here, but look, it's not like I'm going to get bail anyway. Gerry told me I didn't stand a chance. It's just I . . . I can't go out there alone. Can you represent me? Just this one time? Please, I'm begging you.'

All that planning, all that preparation, everything I'd done that morning was designed to elicit that plea for help. When it came I didn't say anything, because I knew if I said yes, there was no going back. I ran over all the possibilities in my mind one more time. I'd thought of little else for the last ten hours. Nothing had changed. There was no other choice, no other way out.

The alternative was to end up in a cage just like the one I was standing in, only I wouldn't be there to visit a client – I would be there to visit my wife.

'Okay,' I said.

He breathed out slowly and smiled. I felt as if a weight had just slammed down on top of my shoulders and had begun to crush me.

I moved closer, kept my voice low.

'Let's get the formalities out of the way. You're David Child, the guy who founded Reeler?'

'Right,' he said.

'What's Reeler?' said Popo.

'It's like Twitter, or Facebook,' I said.

'What's Twitter?' said Popo.

Ignoring him, I turned my attention to David. 'If I'm going to represent you, I'll need to know all about your case. It didn't seem polite to ask at first, but I'd better know now. What're you charged with?'

He wiped his face, then rubbed his sodden hands across his shirt. When he answered me, he sounded like a man who couldn't believe what he was saying. It was as if the very act of speaking those words brought fresh realization. Like trying to walk on a bad knee, having forgotten the injury, the pain a hateful reminder of reality. Eventually, he managed to spit it out.

'Murder,' he said. 'The charge is first-degree murder. I promise you, I didn't kill her.'

CHAPTER NINE

He hid his face in his hands. I needed to know more, but right then there was no point in pushing it further.

'All right, take it easy. I have to deal with Popo first. It'll take ten minutes. I'll ask the judge to pass your case for a little while, so you and I can talk somewhere private. Hopefully that might give Gerry enough time to get down here.'

David didn't look at me as I spoke. He kept his hands over his eyes.

I left the cage and kept my eyes on him until I'd walked through the security door that led to the upper levels of the courthouse. While I was waiting for the elevator, I took my new cell phone from my jacket pocket, typed a text, hit send.

I'm in. Keep Gerry out of the picture for at least another hour.

By the time the elevator arrived, I'd received a response.

You've got forty minutes, max.

My watch read nine fifteen. Not enough time.

Thankfully the elevator was empty. I hit the button for the fifth floor. The doors closed and the elevator rose and began its painfully slow ascent. Twenty-four hours before this my life seemed to be switching back onto the rails. I'd opened up my own firm three months ago. Business began picking up in the last two weeks, and I'd started to feel a little like myself again. Back in the saddle with clients, deadlines, an overdraft, and a secondhand car – a world away from my old firm, yet it felt better; it felt honest.

A year and a half ago I'd quit the law. A case went bad, really bad. I'd gotten someone hurt, not by conning anyone, or doing anything illegal, just by doing my job. And I'd lost everything – my wife, my daughter, my life. After making a pretty decent attempt at killing myself with booze, I checked into rehab, got clean, and got perspective. That was it for me. I'd decided to give up the law: no more clients, no more courtroom tricks. I was done. Then five months ago I'd been forced to represent the head of the Russian Mafia. I came out alive and fell back into the law.

And now here I was, not only about to be involved in the most sensational murder case since O. J. Simpson, but having to con my client to save my wife from a jail sentence. Conning the client to save Christine didn't bother me too much.

My new client was the forty-fifth richest man in America.

And from what I'd been told, he was guilty as hell. For a second I thought about Dell. He'd lost someone and he was hurting – that seemed clear enough. That kind of pain can do two things; you want to save others from your pain or you want everyone to suffer the same as you. I couldn't figure out where Dell fit in that equation. Not yet. He saw David's arrest as an opportunity. I guessed a plea of guilty was enough to satisfy Dell's conscience. Then he could use David to get to the firm, to the people he wanted to suffer – Ben Harland and Gerry Sinton. And Dell wanted everything from those two men – their lives, their business, their reputation, and their money.

The money.

It all came down to money.

Estimated at eight billion dollars in illegal transactions. That's what Kennedy had told me just before I'd left this morning. I had to deliver a guilty plea for David so that Dell could make a deal for a lighter sentence in exchange for the partners, the money. Get the plea or they'll put Christine away for life. Back in my office, I'd had no qualms about that setup. Now that I'd seen the kid, I began to wonder how he'd managed to pull the trigger on his girlfriend. He didn't look like he could pull the tab on a soda can without help. An ill feeling grew in the back of my mind. I tried to ignore it.

The elevator clanked to a slow crawl and opened on the fifth floor of Central Street Courthouse.

Forty minutes to get full representation from the mark.

Then another twenty-four hours to make him take a plea.

I stepped into a grand hall filled with the usual mix of people awaiting a date with a judge. Leaning against a pillar in the corner of the hall, I got my best view of the crowd. There were a few lawyers waiting around, and the ones that I recognized were not from Harland and Sinton; none of the attorneys in the hall wore anything remotely expensive. That firm prided itself on having the best attorneys money could buy, and they all got a two thousand dollar per month clothing allowance. The female attorneys favored Alexander McQueen and the men liked Armani. Most of my suits were in the cleaners. My office was a little damp, so I had to get them cleaned often to get rid of the smell. The suit I wore that morning cost three hundred dollars and it was pretty much the best suit I owned.

I was about to kick off the pillar and head to court when I saw him.

It wasn't Gerry Sinton. It wasn't a Harland and Sinton attorney either.

He looked Hispanic, he wore a black wool overcoat over a gray sweater, dark pants, and black shoes. He sat on a bench to the right of the central stairwell, maybe thirty feet away from me. His left index finger flicked across the screen of his smartphone. Quite a few court customers were doing the same thing, huddled in corners and on benches, sipping coffee from plastic cups and checking out what was going on in their virtual lives. But the man I saw was different. Even though his finger slashed across the screen in his hand, he paid no attention to it. The smartphone has become the twenty-first-century newspaper for surveillance men.

This guy was paying close attention to who was in the hall, and his gaze passed over me casually. He took a slug from a take-out coffee and eyeballed the room. As he leaned back to take another sip, I could see a tattoo on his neck, but I was too far away to see what it was. Definitely not a fed. I checked the crowd to see if I could identify who he was watching. Nobody stood out.

A sensation, almost like someone running a needle down the back of my neck, drew my attention back to the coffee drinker.

He was staring at me.

When I was little my father took me on the Wild Asia Monorail in the Bronx Zoo. As we passed by Tiger Valley, one of the Siberian tigers stopped dead and stared up at my rail car. It was looking straight at me. It didn't growl, or bare its teeth. Just stared. Even as a ten-year-old kid, I knew from those ferocious eyes that the four-hundred-pound beast below wanted to tear me apart.

I got exactly the same feeling from this guy.

He threw his coffee into the garbage and left by the stairs. I guessed he hadn't been looking for me, but he'd sensed that I had noticed him. That's probably why he left. It was only when I started walking toward the courtroom that I realized I was breathing hard.

And my hands were shaking.

Whoever the guy was, I never wanted to see him again.

CHAPTER TEN

Five minutes later, settling myself at the defense table, I caught my first break; Judge Knox shuffled into court and took his seat, coughed, and immediately laid out his plans for the day.

'Good morning, ladies and gentlemen. Just so legal counsel are aware, I'm playing golf this afternoon, so I have to be away by one thirty at the latest. If your case is not dealt with by that time, your client will be automatically remanded in custody until the next rotation. Call the first case.'

Judge John Knox didn't give a shit about justice. He liked golf, whiskey, and attractive female clerks. His favorite pastime was threatening the lawyers that appeared in his courtroom. Glenfiddich, high blood pressure, and a sour temperament brought a rosy tint to his cheeks and nose. He was short and had a big dose of small-man syndrome. Knox would sit in court for a few hours and deal with cases quickly, then rise, and everybody else got sent to jail, bail applications unheard. He'd been the subject of judicial sanction in the past and he'd been appealed plenty of times, but he just didn't give a shit.

The courtroom seemed pretty empty. There were maybe a half dozen lawyers and they represented about as many clients. That left around twenty guys downstairs in the cells, waiting on the public defender. I'd already arranged for Popo's case to get called first, then David Child. I'd called the clerk, Denise, earlier that morning. Told her I needed to get clear as soon as possible and that I'd consider it a personal favor. She obliged. I had a good reputation with the staff.

The custody officer brought in Popo. He was wearing wrist and ankle cuffs and he shuffled into his seat on my left. Around twenty feet away, I could see the conveyor line of prisoners waiting to get

44

their cases called. David Child was at the head of that line, and he looked around the courtroom as if it were a torture chamber. His eyes were wide, and even from this distance I could hear his chains tinkling as he trembled.

Julie Lopez, the prosecutor, stood at probably the same height as Judge Knox: a couple of inches over five feet. Around thirty or more blue files sat piled up in front of her in two equally proportioned stacks. Just like her files, Julie always looked super-organized; her hair was tied back with a pen, makeup understated, dark suits businesslike and impeccably tailored. She took the first file from the left-hand collection and began her day.

'Your Honor, first case is Dale "Popo" Barnes. Mr Flynn appears for the defendant. Prosecution withdraws all charges, Your Honor.'

Knox didn't sit in this courtroom very often, so he wasn't familiar with Popo. He said nothing to the prosecutor at first. Narrowing his eyes, he flicked through the pages of the file, and as he read, a look spread over his face that failed to mask his obvious contempt for me and my client.

'Ms Lopez, did I hear you right? The prosecution withdraws all charges?'

'Yes, Your Honor,' said Julie.

'But he had enough dope on him to validate a distribution charge, never mind simple possession.'

'Yes, Your Honor.'

'So why withdraw the charges?'

To add to his problems, Judge Knox was plenty stupid. Julie looked at me and shrugged. I returned her gaze and shook my head. For a few seconds we just looked at each other and ignored the judge. We were deciding what to do. It would be bad to announce in an open public court that Popo was a longtime police informant and had immunity from prosecution for a wide variety of drug offenses. Maybe I thought the name Popo would give it away. It didn't seem to work on Knox.

Most judges would take the hint and realize this guy spilled his guts to the NYPD, but Knox wasn't biting despite an embarrassed smile from Julie.

'Is there something I'm missing here?' said Knox.

45

Around fifty IQ points, was what I wanted to say, but didn't. Instead my brain suddenly came up to speed and I saw an opportunity for my second persuader of the morning.

'Your Honor, may we speak with you in chambers about this matter? There is a sensitive issue here. Also, I would appreciate the opportunity to discuss the next case on Your Honor's list in private. It's a Mr Child,' and as I said my mark's name, I looked straight at him and then back at the judge. It was a little early for the reporters to fill up the benches, and even if there were a few crime reporters in the back row, they wouldn't expect to see David Child in court, so the name wouldn't ring a bell and they wouldn't see him unless they were right at the front of the benches. There were no reporters in that position.

Knox recognized him right away, but wisely didn't want to wake up any journalists who might be in the court. A slight nod of the head was all we needed. Knox got up, the clerk said, 'All rise,' and Julie and I followed Knox through the back door of the court, down a small corridor, past the chambers reserved for this court, and into his private office, which doubled as Knox's little kingdom. There were courthouse rules about judge's chambers, but none about personal offices, so Knox exploited the loophole. I had time to look around while he got himself comfortable in his seat and adjusted his robes. The little office was painted the same color of cream that seemed to be on every office wall these days. Pictures of Knox with famous golfers hung around the room. There was even a set of clubs against the back wall. There were no family pictures. A smell that was at once familiar and yet elusive seemed to come up off the carpeted floor. Smelled like honey, bleach, and malt whiskey.

'So, Popo first, and then both of you make my day by telling me all about Mr Child,' said Knox, unable to suppress a grin.

Julie and I remained standing in front of two comfortable-looking leather chairs that faced Knox's desk. In the judge's chambers you didn't sit until you were asked. As far as I knew, Knox had never asked anyone to sit down. He was that kind of asshole.

Julie tried to balance a blue file, the one relating to Popo, on top of the backrest of the chair in front of her so that she could open it and read her notes. I had neither a file nor any notes for

Popo. I had a few of Popo's old files with me, which I just carried for show. Usually I didn't create a paper file for Popo because then somebody might audit it and realize that I wasn't doing anywhere near the hours that I would be billing the NYPD. No file, no audit. If the IRS asked questions, I would say it was misfiled somewhere and they would give me the benefit of the doubt. If NYPD wanted to see the file, I'd tell them to go to hell; it was my client's file and attorney-client privilege protected it.

I decided to jump right in with the friendly and flattering approach while Julie read her notes.

'Judge, my client Popo is a police informant. He has to carry and use narcotics in his line of work. The DA's office knows this and they let it slide, for the greater good. My client has provided information that's led to a number of good arrests.'

Knox's neck turned the same color as his nose. He was embarrassed about almost dropping the ball on a police informant in open court. I'd handed him a lifeline, a way for him to look smart and save face.

'Mr Flynn, I simply wanted to check with the prosecutor that the information she was getting from your client was worth the withdrawal of all charges,' said Knox.

'We have a continuing arrangement with Popo and he has an immunity agreement,' said Julie.

'Well, before we talk about Child, are we okay to let Popo walk?' I said.

'Who? Oh, the junkie, sure. Tell me about our billionaire. I glanced at the file. He got a defense?'

'Sure,' I said.

'What's the prosecution's attitude to bail?' asked Knox, quickly turning his attention to Julie.

'We're opposing bail,' said Julie.

'Flat out?' asked Knox.

'Yes, Your Honor. The people feel that the court would be unable to ensure Mr Child would return for trial even with the most stringent bail conditions.'

The judge leaned forward in his chair and steepled his fingers under his chin. The tip of a pale tongue escaped through his lips, and Knox made a loud sucking noise as he flicked it back into his mouth. The movement was sudden and somehow reptilian. He pretended to consider what the prosecutor told him.

'What bail conditions would your client consent to, Mr Flynn?'

This was an attempt to short-circuit the bail hearing. If I told him the conditions that my client would agree to, he would grant bail but on additional conditions over and above what I'd told him my client would accept. After I answered that question, he would probe Julie to find out what conditions she would request if he were minded to grant bail. In this way Knox could get both defense and prosecution to accept a deal on bail so he wouldn't have to have a hearing at all. That way both the defense and the prosecution would be unhappy but neither one would challenge his decision as we would both be fearful of losing what little ground each of us had gained. Knox might have been slow on the uptake, but he'd learned a judicial trick or two.

'I'm afraid I'll need to seek instructions from my client on bail terms.'

'Good,' said Knox. 'You've got ten minutes.'

I checked my watch and estimated that I had around fourteen minutes before Gerry Sinton came roaring into court and then it would all be over before we even got started.

CHAPTER ELEVEN

I knew the story already. Had it laid out for me in detail around nine hours ago by Dell. Even so, I wanted to hear it from the client. There were always multiple versions of every story. We are our own little planets, and invariably we can only see things from our own perspective, which includes our prejudices, our vices, our talents, and our limited perceptions. No two people see the same thing. When you add that any one person will give differing accounts of the same circumstances, depending on whom they're talking to, it gives you an idea of how unclear versions of events can be. A person will tell the same story differently depending on whether they're talking to a man or a woman, a college professor or a cabdriver, a cop or a lawyer. We unconsciously tailor our speech and body language so that we can gain empathy and understanding from the listener. Trouble is, you need all of the information to make a judgment call on what really happened. And that's without considering whether or not your storyteller is even telling the truth to begin with.

There are simple techniques that are designed to get the raw data, not the spin.

I used the simplest of those techniques to get David Child talking. We were sitting in a cramped gray consultation room. A dark mahogany table separated us. The table bore the scars of paper clips, knives, and pens, which had been used to dig the names of past felons into its flesh.

I'd just sat down. I hadn't told Child anything about my talk with Judge Knox.

'So, what happened?' I said.

'What did the judge say?'

Leaning back in my chair, I said nothing. My hands rested on my thighs. It was important not to fold my arms, to keep an open body posture. So that I remained subconsciously on 'receive.'

'What'd he say?'

My head tilted to the right.

'Mr Flynn?'

A few seconds passed in silence. Child looked at the floor. It's pretty hard to maintain silence when somebody is patiently waiting for you to start talking. His head popped up and he met my gaze with a pleading stare. I raised an eyebrow.

'What happened, David?' I repeated.

He nodded a few times, then put his hands up in surrender.

I didn't ask Child why he'd been arrested, or why he'd been charged with murder, or what evidence the cops had on him. The question I asked was as open and wide as possible so that I'd get a lot more information.

'Jesus,' said Child, running his hands over his head. 'I loved Clara. I'd never met anyone like her. She was perfect. So perfect. Why the hell she ended up with an asswipe like me, I'll never know. Jesus Christ forgive me, but right now I wish I'd never met her. She'd still be alive.'

He began to cry. Tears flowed freely, and from the swelling around his eyes it was clear he'd been crying a lot in the last few hours. Even so, he bent over and his back rocked with huge intakes of breath that he forced out in guttural cries. For all his supposed financial worth and power, right then, with the snot and salt tears on his face, he looked like a miserable boy.

I said nothing.

I didn't put my arm around him. No words of comfort or reassurance. I remained relaxed and silent.

If I sympathized with him, I'd be doing him no favors. I'd spend my remaining eight minutes watching him cry and blow his nose. Quickest way to make somebody stop crying and start talking is to remain silent. People get embarrassed about letting out that flood of emotion to a stranger.

Child used the sleeve of his jumpsuit to wipe his face.

'I'm sorry. I'm sorry,' he said.

I said nothing.

Seven minutes left.

'What happened, David?'

He rolled his neck, blew out a few times to regulate his breathing, and gave me my answer.

'She's dead because of me,' he said.

As he spoke he didn't look at me. He kept his eyes low, on the table. The words came out matter-of-factly, like he just told me his address or his date of birth. It wasn't a heartfelt confession, but a simple statement.

Lawyers don't usually question whether or not a client is telling the truth. That way lies madness. You do what you have to and trust the system. So, the guilty plead guilty. The innocent fight their case and the jury decides. If a by-product of that process is the emergence of the truth, then so be it, but the truth is not the aim of the process. The verdict is the aim. Truth has no place in the trial because no one is concerned with finding it, least of all the lawyers or the judge.

However, in my former career, before I was a lawyer, the truth was always my goal. As a con man you live and die by portraying the absolute truth to your mark. Not the real truth, of course. No, a version of the truth that suited the con, but that story, that line, that whatever it was, had to look and feel and taste and become the truth for that mark.

With my experience I could normally spot a lie a mile away. I expected Child to be an excellent liar, a man I would have to study before I would be able to spot his tells. I'd underestimated him. He was a mass of nerves, shock, and guilt. That made him damn near impossible to read. So I had to rely on my gut instead.

My first impression – this guy was no killer. But I'd been wrong before.

Six minutes.

CHAPTER TWELVE

The interview room echoed with the *clank* of barred doors sliding shut in the adjacent corridor. Even with the heavy door to the booth firmly closed, it wasn't enough to keep out those sounds. Crying, singing, and praying.

Child wiped his face. He sniffed and straightened up.

'I knew something bad was going to happen before I left the apartment. I checked my e-mail on my phone; I had seventeen new messages. An odd number. I don't like odd numbers, so I knew something bad would happen and it would be my fault. I know it's crazy, but I've always had this, well. The doctor diagnosed . . .'

'We don't have much time, David. We can get to the details later. Just the basics of what happened to your girlfriend.'

'I left Clara in my apartment – she'd just moved in that day. I was on my way to work – I stopped at the traffic lights a couple of blocks from my building. We have a meeting at Reeler every Friday night at eight thirty; we'd check the figures for the week, adjust the marketing plan, and bounce ideas around. The light turned green, and I moved across the white line. I got maybe twenty feet across the intersection when this asshole rammed me. He drove through his stoplight and hit my Bugatti. I could smell the booze on him as soon as he got out of the car, and then he threatened me. The police came and they . . . they asked me what happened. I told them, and then the cop told me the driver saw a gun in the footwell of my car. I told him that was a mistake, but then the cop went to my car. I swear to you, Mr Flynn, I've never seen that gun before. I don't own a gun. He asked me for my permit. I didn't have one. I told him it wasn't mine, and he arrested me. I thought I'd get a fine or something. We were only in the precinct for a few hours.

They came and took my clothes, swabbed my face, arms, hands, and took my fingerprints. I thought it was all routine. I called Gerry Sinton and he came to the precinct. Later that night they told me Clara was dead. She'd been shot. Her body was in my apartment . . . I . . . I . . .'

Panic choked him, and I saw the tears beginning to form.

'I left her in my apartment around eight o'clock. I kissed her goodbye. She was alive when I left my place. I swear it.'

'So you were questioned. Gerry was with you. You told the cops what you told me?'

'Yes, I told them the truth. I didn't have anything to hide.'

If he was a liar, he was one of the best.

'Why'd you tell me she was dead because of you?'

'The goddamn odd number. I knew it. Somebody must have broken into my apartment looking for me, to rob me – and they . . . they found her. I didn't kill her. I don't have a gun. I didn't do it . . . I . . . no . . . not me . . . I couldn't.'

His chest began pumping, and his eyes glazed over. His hands shook violently, and his face turned a shocking white just before he threw up on the desk. Then his head dropped. I caught him before he fell out of the chair, set him down on his side, kicked the consultation room door open, and called for help.

Through guttering breaths, he struggled to force out the words.

'Gerry . . . Gerry . . . told . . . me . . . no bail . . . no bail . . . no media . . . won't get bail . . . flight risk.'

'Calm down. Shut up and breathe.'

A guard rushed in, knelt beside Child, and looked at me. David was going into shock.

The guard, a young officer with large and kindly eyes, left and quickly returned with a mask and a small portable oxygen tank. Together we got David into a sitting position, back against the wall. He took two desperate sucks on an inhaler before the guard slipped the oxygen mask over David's face. We sat with him for a few minutes, letting him get control on his own. After a while his breathing became deeper, slower.

Slipping the mask onto his chest, he said, 'Gerry told me I don't have a chance for bail.'

This was my shot. I stood, opened my file, slipped a four-page document on top of the file, and placed it on David's knees.

'What's this?'

'It's a retainer agreement. You sign this, I become your lawyer. I'll get you bail and I'll keep this out of the papers. All you have to do is sign it,' I said, handing him my pen.

'But Gerry said I can't get bail. I've got four private airplanes. I'm a flight risk. And if somebody makes a bail application, the press . . . they'll . . . be all over it,' he said, the fear threatening to close down his chest.

'Just sign it. You won't last a day in jail. I can get you out. But I need to do it legally. Sign this, and I'll look after you, David.'

The pen shook in his hand as he scrawled a hasty signature. I took the document and the pen and handed it to the guard beside him.

'As he's a little shaky, witness this for me.'

The guard looked at that paper like it was anthrax and held up a hand.

'Look, it's for my protection,' I said.

'Go ahead and sign it,' said Neil, standing in the doorway. He'd come to make sure I was okay.

I looked at the guard's name tag – Darryl White. I got Darryl to sign, initial, and date the document.

'Is the doc around?' I asked.

'He's seeing one of the regulars,' said Neil.

'Can you let him take a quick look at my boy, here? Maybe give him a blue to calm him down?'

'Sure thing. Come on, son. You're in good hands now,' said Neil.

Together, we lifted David to his feet. Darryl, who was smaller than me, could have lifted the kid one-handed. He probably weighed a hundred and ten pounds. His bones felt sharp at the elbow, and there was almost no musculature there at all, as though he was held together with sinew and paper glue.

Sitting in the medical room, head back, eyes wide as though he were willing them to suck air into his lungs, David spoke. A whisper. I didn't catch it.

'Take it easy. The doc will be here in a second,' I said.

Taking a noisy gasp of air from the oxygen machine, David pulled the mask to one side and said, 'Is it okay if I call you Eddie?'

'Sure,' I said.

'Okay. I signed your agreement. That means you're my lawyer, right?'

I nodded.

'Please, Eddie, help me. I didn't kill Clara. Help me. I'm begging you.'

And there it was, the plea. A cry for help from a terrified kid.

Vibration from my cell phone.

Another text from Dell.

Gerry Sinton just walked in to court 12.

CHAPTER THIRTEEN

A female lawyer from the PD's office was taking five to sort a quick case with the prosecutor, Julie Lopez, in court twelve. Judge Knox flicked through the case files on his desk while the lawyers in front of him quickly bargained away a trial.

At first I didn't see Gerry Sinton. I'd never met him in the flesh. Last night Dell had shown me a photo, but it wasn't very recent and it didn't in any way convey the sheer feeling of power that surrounded the man like a sweet cloud of five-hundred-dollar aftershave. His blue pin-striped suit was impeccably tailored to fit his tall and elegant frame. Black curls, streaked with gray, sat on top of a large and dangerous head. Wide yet stylish glasses were perched on the end of his nose. He was tanned, lined with age, but he didn't look like he was in his late fifties. Money had a way of halting the aging process. He was kneeling at the clerk's bench talking to her, checking the listings, making sure he hadn't missed his client's appearance in front of the judge. I could see the clerk telling him that the matter had already been mentioned but not determined. He leaned closer, read the name of the lawyer the clerk had entered beside David Child's name. The clerk looked around the room, spotted me, said something to Gerry, and pointed in that way that only clerks can – *there's Mr Flynn. He's the attorney of record. Go fight with him, pal. Leave me out of it.*

Gerry's big head came up, and he whipped off his glasses and looked at me like he was ready to chew glass. There was no snarl. It was just a feeling of menace that came with the man. He put his glasses back on and started walking.

Folding my arms, I shifted my weight onto one hip and watched him as he approached. The closer he got, the more his neck flushed red, and by the time he stood in front of me, a fat vein bulged out of his starched collar. He towered over me by a foot and a half and stood close, almost like a point guard blocking the basket. From his distressed leather briefcase, he produced a lengthy document, which he tucked beneath his arm. The huge black stone in his pinkie ring caught the overhead lights and blinded me for a second. I thought the ring probably cost more than my first house.

He took off his glasses again. That's when I saw it.

It's no easy thing to kill somebody. Most murders happen when the perp is drunk or high or both. Or an argument gets out of hand, or someone suffers an extreme emotional disturbance. Most people couldn't even contemplate murder. But there are people who are simply immune to the psychological blocks that stop us from killing. They have no empathy. I didn't need to know Gerry Sinton's history to see the killer. Sometimes you just know. The man in front of me could not feel anything for another living soul. There was only self. Nothing else.

'You Eddie Flynn?' He spoke with a trace of South Baltimore still hiding in the deep tones.

'Right,' I said.

'Cut the bullshit. How much?'

'*Excuse* me?'

He took my elbow and guided me to the corner of the courtroom.

His voice was low and slow. 'So you got a tip from a buddy that a celebrity is in holding. You go down there, try to steal yourself a big fish. I get that. But this is *my* fish. You can't have him. I don't have time for this. How much do you want to walk away? Ten? Fifteen? How about twenty grand?'

'No, thanks.'

His expression didn't change. A cold hate, hidden behind a dead face. I imagined that he'd worn the same expression when he'd ordered the hit on Farooq, the informer.

'You illegally solicited my client. I can have you suspended and disbarred. Right now. Or you can take twenty thousand and walk away.'

I stood firm.

He calmed, the anger slipping away the more he looked me over. He probably saw a small-time lawyer hustling his way through the criminal lists, trying to make the rent.

'Take the money. Walk away. This is too big for you.'

'I think it's you who's in over your head, pal. This isn't a boardroom. This is a criminal court. You're in my house now. If I were you, I'd click those ruby slippers together and think of the Upper East Side,' I said.

No visible reaction. Only the slight tremor in his voice gave a hint of annoyance.

'I've got a solid retainer for this case, Flynn. You know how the big boys operate. He's my client.'

'I've got the most recent retainer. Signed by David Child this morning.'

He leaned closer, not used to arguing with two-bit lawyers like me.

'My offer of twenty thousand stands for the next sixty seconds.'

I shrugged.

'You should take the money. Bad things will happen if you don't.'

I felt my hands tighten into fists, and my voice rose. 'Back off. You don't scare me.'

'You have no idea who you're dealing with . . .'

The sound of the judge's voice snapped Sinton to attention.

'Hey, this is a court of law. If you two have a problem, take it outside. I'm reading here,' said Knox.

'Your Honor,' said Sinton, 'there has been malpractice on the part of Mr Flynn in relation to his illegal approach to my client. I'd like to discuss this matter in chambers.'

'And who are you, sir? I've never seen you in this court before,' said Judge Knox.

'My name's Gerry Sinton, Your Honor. I represent Mr Child. Mr Flynn, here, has tried to—'

'Gerry Sinton? Of Harland and Sinton?'

'Yes, Your Honor. I wish to—' But Judge Knox cut the feet right out from under him.

'I knew Mr Harland Senior – when I was in practice, that is. He would be very proud if he could see the firm now,' said Knox, smiling for once. 'Tell you what, I'm just finishing a sentencing here. Won't take long. You and Mr Flynn go on back, and I'll be in chambers in five minutes. The clerk will show you.'

Before following the clerk, Sinton turned and gave me a satisfied look. He was convinced that the old friend of the firm, Judge Knox, would see things his way. I couldn't let that happen. If I got hauled off the case, it was over for Christine.

Making my way down the aisle toward the exit that led to Knox's chambers, I took big breaths in, held them, and let them out slowly. Unless I came up with something good in the next five minutes, the watertight Harland and Sinton retainer would put me out of the game permanently.

CHAPTER FOURTEEN

The clerk led Gerry Sinton along the same anonymous corridor to Knox's chambers. She let us in and then left. With a frustrated and tired sigh, Gerry sat in one of Judge Knox's fine chairs that faced his desk. It was just us in the room. He didn't speak a word, just sat there and ignored me. He'd never appeared in front of Knox, didn't know that sitting in that chair without permission was likely to give Knox an aneurysm.

I saw my first play and decided to keep my mouth shut.

After five minutes I heard Judge Knox mumbling as he made his way along the corridor. I filled a cup of water from the dispenser and hung at the back of the room. As the door opened, Gerry stood, then sat down in tandem with Knox. I saw the look. The judicial eyebrows rising and Knox's teeth taking a bite at his lower lip.

'Gentlemen, I don't like lawyers arguing among themselves in my courtroom. It's not seemly. If you want to argue, you do that when I call your case. Now, what seems to be the problem? Mr Flynn appears on my docket as counsel of record for Child. What's the issue, Mr Sinton?'

A bulky agreement appeared from Gerry's briefcase, and he placed it reverently beneath the judge's gaze. Sinton sat a little taller in his chair and buttoned his jacket. His tone changed as he spoke to the judge; it was lighter, warmer.

'Your Honor, this is a retainer signed by Mr Child in 2013. It empowers my firm and only my firm to act for him in all legal matters. If Mr Child wishes to change counsel, he must first give us thirty days' notice. If he chooses not to provide such notice, this agreement gives us a lien on any files and documents created in that relationship. Basically, this clause gives the exclusive right to act for

Mr Child. Before signing this agreement, this clause was specifically read to the client and he was provided with separate legal advice on its implications. Any retainer signed by Mr Child today is invalid. Mr Flynn has breached a preexisting attorney-client relationship; he has illegally solicited my client, and I intend to convene an emergency state bar committee this afternoon and have Mr Flynn suspended pending disciplinary action.'

Sinton leaned back, crossed his long, thick legs, and delicately placed his hand on his lap. His delivery was polished and clean. His deep voice sounded like pebbles falling into a velvet-lined hat; it was rich, with a pure tone and, underneath, a little grit. Nothing of the cold executioner now remained. Judge Knox skimmed the relevant sections, then dropped the paper on his desk, rubbed his chin, and looked at me as I leaned against his bookcase at the back of the room. I straightened up just before he addressed me.

'What do you say to this, Mr Flynn? Have you read this document?'

'No,' I said.

Knox waited for me to say more. I said nothing.

'Would you like to read it? Mr Sinton's making some pretty serious allegations.'

I drained my water from the plastic cup, tossed it in the trash.

'Mr Sinton was not here when Mr Child's case was called. I was. I spoke to Mr Child and he practically begged me to help him. He signed a retainer with me, and one of the detention officers witnessed the signature. What would've happened if Mr Child's arraignment went ahead without Mr Sinton being present? To me, that would be inefficient representation of counsel. You have to actually *be* here to represent your client.'

The judge shot Sinton a look. He hated people being late in his court. If you arrived late, you lost. Simple as that.

'If Mr Sinton pushes this argument, I could persuade my client to lodge a complaint with the Bar Standards Committee about Mr Sinton's tardiness. My retainer is the most relevant, as it deals with criminal allegations, and it's signed and witnessed today. My guess is Mr Sinton can't handle the fact that he's been fired,' I said, placing my hands on the back of the chair next to Sinton.

'Your Honor,' said Sinton, leaning forward in his chair, shaking his head.

'Your ass, Mr Sinton,' said Judge Knox.

'Excuse me?' said Sinton, with a little more surprise and indignation than was good for him.

'I can't hear you, Mr Sinton,' said the judge.

'I *said* . . .' began Gerry, loudly.

'I wasn't talking about your volume. I was referring to your ass. These chambers and offices are an extension of my courtroom, Mr Sinton. No lawyer has ever addressed me unless they are standing on their feet. You are the first to ever address me while lounging in my chair. And who gave you permission to sit, by the way? No one sits without my permission. If you had any experience in this court, you might've known that.'

The skin pulled tight on Sinton's forehead. He knew I had let him sit down; he knew I'd let him piss off the judge. And Judge Knox knew it, too, as I could see a little smile playing around those twin slugs that passed for lips.

With a dead smile, Gerry stood, buttoned his jacket, and straightened his tie. The affable pretense disappeared – the shark was back in the room.

'Your Honor, the defendant is my client legally. I was with him in the precinct when he was interviewed. I caught this case first. If you endorse Mr Flynn's argument, you are endorsing this illegal solicitation.'

This was Gerry's big point. He'd probably hoped that he wouldn't have to use it, that the judge would do him a favor. Knox wasn't in the business of doing favors, and threatening him wouldn't work. He needed finessing. He turned toward me.

'Your Honor, Mr Sinton is making a legal argument. I think he's correct that this is a matter of legal interpretation. No matter what you decide, you're likely to be appealed. I've said enough. I'll let you consider the matter.'

Judge Knox rubbed his hands together, placed his elbows on his desk, and stared into space. While Knox had pretty good common sense and was just on the right side of severe for a criminal judge, he was piss poor on any kind of legal question. On the rare occasions when he'd had no choice but to make a decision based on the law, he'd been heavily criticized by the appellate court judges. His disdain for the criminal defendants who appeared in his court was well known, and he didn't care if he was criticized by a higher court for being too harsh – or not recognizing their rights – but having an appellate court judge tell him he got the law wrong was too much for him. Knox didn't want that. He avoided these situations. Anything not to have to make a decision.

So I gave him a way out.

'Before you decide, Your Honor, I'd just like to apologize for the scene in your courtroom earlier. It's a shame that Mr Sinton felt the need to bring this issue before you. We should have been able to resolve this between us.'

I could almost see the lightbulb go off in Knox's head.

'Mr Flynn, may I say how unhappy I am that this matter has gotten this far. Two experienced attorneys bickering over a client does not reflect well on either of you. So I'm going to give each of you another chance to resolve this yourselves. Gentlemen, I have the power to appoint the public defender as counsel. I think that might just be the way forward here. So both of you step outside for two minutes. Either you both come back in here with an agreed way forward, or Mr Child goes to the PD's office and the both of you can sue each other in some other damn court.'

'Your Hon—' began Gerry.

'Not another word, Mr Sinton. Go outside and talk this over.'

And with that, Judge Knox wiped his hands and smiled to himself.

CHAPTER FIFTEEN

The corridor echoed with our feet pacing to and fro and Gerry Sinton chipping his pinkie ring on the walls.

'Is he always like that?' he said.

'Pretty much. Look, he doesn't want to make a decision that somebody could appeal. The public defender can't object to taking a case, and we can't appeal that decision either. He doesn't want to decide either way. Why don't you leave it with me? Child's in good hands. I'm very experienced. I can offer him the best representation.'

Gerry folded his arms. 'What kind of resources do you have? I've got two hundred lawyers and a team of experts that I can work around the clock. How many support staff do you have?'

'You're looking at the support staff and the typist and the cleaner.'

'This is a mistake, Flynn.'

'I'm not so sure. I know the judges and how to play them. You might have a dozen attorneys on this, but that won't stop the DA handing you your ass because you don't know what you're doing. Although, the man power is always handy in a murder trial . . .'

'You have no idea who you're dealing with. Just take the money.'

I remembered that Sinton was the one who needed the case just as much as I did. If David Child could hurt Harland and Sinton as much as Dell hoped, then the firm needed to represent him at all costs – so they could watch him. And make sure he didn't cut a deal by handing his lawyers over to the feds in exchange for a light sentence.

'I don't want money. I want the case. This will be a huge media-hungry trial. This can make my practice. It's my case. I'm not backing down. I've got nothing to lose. Since we both can't represent him, we may as well just go tell Knox to call the public defender.'

I took three steps and put my hand on the door handle to Knox's office. Sinton reached out to stop me.

'Wait, wait. That's interesting. You said we can't both represent him. Why not? I've got the resources; you've got the experience. You take the role of special adviser, or consultant, whatever you want to call it. We'll handle the case up front.'

'No way,' I said, turning the handle.

'Wait! You could take second chair. That's—'

'Nice meeting you,' I said, opening Judge Knox's door a crack.

'Hold on,' said Sinton through gritted teeth. 'Okay, first chair. But we're a team.'

'Whatever,' I said, stepping into Knox's office.

Knox was playing Angry Birds on his cell phone. A fresh cup of coffee was growing cold in front of him.

'Your Honor, we have a compromise. The firm of Harland and Sinton will serve as my co-counsel in this case.'

The judge nodded but didn't take his eyes from his smartphone.

'Glad to hear it, gentlemen. Bail hearing in five minutes. Just wait outside for the prosecutor.'

Gerry Sinton had swallowed the bait. Christine was in this mess because of Gerry Sinton and Ben Harland. I wanted to be close to these guys. Maybe I could find something to satisfy Dell, enough to get Christine off the hook and enough so that I wouldn't have to talk David Child into a prison sentence. I had my chance now. I felt pretty sure that this was the right thing to do. I couldn't force Child into prison without at least trying something else, trying to get Christine clear another way.

Gerry Sinton put his back to the pale corridor wall and breathed slowly. He'd gotten his client back.

I'd bought Christine a chance.

And probably signed my own death warrant.

CHAPTER SIXTEEN

Julie Lopez, the prosecutor, walked up the corridor, looked at us, and knocked on Judge Knox's door. We followed her back into the room.

'We're back on the record in *People v. Child*. The defense team has grown in the last few minutes, Ms Lopez. I trust you have no objection,' said Judge Knox.

'None,' said Lopez, eyeing Gerry Sinton.

'And, just for the record, your client is consenting to this hearing in his absence, Mr Flynn?' said Judge Knox.

'Correct, Your Honor. I see no reason to drag him into open court in front of the press. We're happy to proceed here, in private.'

'Well, what are the agreed bail terms, Counsel?'

'We require the defendant to reside at—' said Lopez, but Sinton cut her off.

'Just a second, Your Honor. We haven't applied for bail. My client does not wish to apply for bail at this time. This is a media-sensitive case, and my client is—'

'Your Honor, I'm first chair. Ignore my co-counsel. Our application has already been noted by the court and we are acting on instructions from Mr Child, who wishes to apply for bail. We agree to the residence terms. Any others?' I said.

'With the exception of court appearance dates, he'll report daily to the nearest precinct before one p.m. He'll surrender his passport. No alcohol or drugs other than prescribed medication, and the defendant will submit to periodic random alcohol and drug testing,' said Lopez.

'Your Honor, the defendant—'

'Agreed,' I said, before Sinton could do any more damage.

'Bail granted in the sum of ten million dollars. Preliminary hearing tomorrow at . . .'

'Your Honor, we're ready to proceed with the preliminary hearing this afternoon,' said Lopez.

'Have papers been served?' asked the judge.

Lopez handed me a large manila envelope.

'They have now,' she said.

Rubbing his chin, Judge Knox thought about his golf game being canceled.

'What are your thoughts on prelim? If this case is going to be a media magnet, I presume you'll be waiving the preliminary hearing,' said the judge.

Most felony cases, like murder, didn't have a prelim, a hearing designed to decide if the prosecution had enough evidence to hold the defendant on the charge and put the case to the grand jury. The prosecution didn't have to prove guilt. They had to prove they had an arguable case in the form of probable cause. Usually, if there's enough for an arrest and charge, that means there's more than enough evidence for the prosecution to slide past a preliminary hearing with ease.

'What's your call?' said Judge Knox.

I already had a good guess at the contents of the prosecution file. The night before, Dell had laid out the evidence held by the cops. A prelim would be a waste of time. There was enough evidence to convict David Child twice.

'We're not waiving the prelim,' I said.

If I ignored the evidence and just listened to David talk, I believed him. He was falling apart, and I wasn't ready to let him do that, not yet. I needed to see the evidence for myself, talk to him again. I wanted to keep options in play.

The phone on Judge Knox's desk began to ring.

'Very well. Case adjourned until four p.m.,' he said, and answered the call.

Before we got to the door, the judge stopped me in my tracks.

'Wait, Mr Flynn.'

Lopez, Sinton, and I turned to the judge. He looked stricken. His face had become pale, and I saw sweat forming on his top lip. He listened to the call, his eyes moving rapidly – processing the information. Finally he shook his head.

'He's here with me. I'll tell him. We'll want a full investigation. This is outrageous. You keep me informed, Wilson,' said Knox. 'Goddamn it,' he cried, slamming down the receiver. 'Gentlemen, you'd better get down to the cells right away. Your client's been stabbed.'

CHAPTER SEVENTEEN

Hammering the 'C' button on the elevator didn't make it move any faster. Sinton stood in the corner, his hand over his mouth – head bowed, deep in thought. He hadn't said a word since Knox had given us the news.

'Come on,' I said, punching the button for the basement.

Closing my eyes, I let my forehead rest against the cold aluminum veneer that sat above the elevator control. Silently I prayed that David was still alive. In that moment I realized that I had begun to care about him. He'd looked so helpless, his world and mind collapsing around him. And for what? He was no killer. The kind of people who could pull the trigger on a loved one while sober are easy to spot. Sociopathic tendencies would be evident, like narcissism, cruelty, social detachment, and a history of violence.

Child didn't have that mean streak, or that lack of empathy, and even though his world was falling to ash around him, he wasn't angry – he was scared.

No way that kid killed his girlfriend.

I squeezed my eyes shut and tried to remember everything I knew about David. You don't get to his level of wealth without hurting somebody. And men in David's position didn't get their hands dirty. If he wanted somebody killed, he could always pay a man to do it.

I wished I could see him out of the cell – watch him outside the cold panic of a jailhouse-orange jumpsuit. Then I would know for sure. Right then, all I had was my gut telling me he was innocent.

Now somebody had stabbed him.

The elevator slowed and the doors opened with a chime. I'd heard the riot in the cells long before we'd reached the bottom floor. The detainees were going crazy. Blood in the air. The guards were screaming at the prisoners, who responded by shaking the bars, spitting and wailing back. Fingers pointed accusingly at the guards. A chant began – 'killa, killa, killa.' A guard unwound a hose from the back wall and got ready to spray the entire pen, when the medic waved at me from the offices. Running past the cells, with Sinton trotting behind me, I made it to a small corridor that led off into the first-aid room.

As I slowed, I slipped, and my feet danced at the floor, trying to find a grip until I managed to steady myself with a hand on the wall. The overhead lights were reflected perfectly on the soaking-wet floor. Here and there, on the doors, on the walls, I could still see the remnants of fresh blood. Checking over my shoulder, I saw that the trail of freshly mopped floor stretched all the way back to the cells. The first-aid room had been busy, and blood-soaked bandages and gauze poked out of the full wastebasket. Even the medic still bore bloodstains on the shoulder of his shirt. The medical couch in the corner was also stained red with blood, and even though it had been wiped, it had not yet been properly cleaned.

'What happened?' said Gerry.

'Who's this guy?' said the medic.

'It's okay. He's with me. How's our guy? Is he going to make it?' I said.

'He was alive when the paramedics took him. His vitals didn't look good, lost a lot of blood.'

'Jesus, what happened?' I said.

'I don't know. The alarm went up, and I saw a couple of guards dragging him out of the cage. Kid was covered in blood. His arms were cut bad, and he had a big stab wound in his midsection. Bitch wouldn't stop pumping. Whoever stuck it to him ripped the blade upward trying to gut him, then slashed his face pretty bad.'

'Where are the paramedics taking him?' said Sinton.

'Downtown ER,' said the medic.

'Don't go anywhere for a second,' I said, but Sinton was already running toward the door. He wanted David on his own – so that he could get me fired. I was sorely tempted to take off after Sinton. But I needed to know what had happened first. And I had time. Chances were that David would be taken straight to surgery. Sinton would have a long wait to see his client. I prayed that this wasn't my fault and that the big guy who'd taken David's shoes earlier hadn't decided to get even.

The noise had abated, and only a handful of detainees were arguing with the guards. I checked the break room. They hadn't yet mopped up, and I could see a trail of bloody footprints leading to a table. Neil, the guard who'd helped me get close to David that morning, sat with his hands over his head, his face inches over a cup of steaming coffee. Bloodstains on his cuffs. A cop sat beside him, his notebook open on the table, pen in hand.

'Neil, you okay?' I said.

His head came up quick, and he tried to force a smile but failed and coughed before wiping his mouth and leaning back in the chair. 'You shouldn't be wandering around without an escort.'

'I don't need an escort. I know these cells just as well as you do. The medic told me you pulled the kid out. I need to know what happened,' I said.

'This guy a lawyer?' said the cop, pointing at me with his pen.

'It's okay. This is Eddie Flynn. He's the guy's lawyer. Sit down, Eddie,' said Neil. 'Look, there's not much to tell. After the panic attack subsided, the medic passed Child fit to return to holding. He was in there maybe two, three minutes, when I heard a little shouting, nothing out of the ordinary. Then I saw the Mexican, the guy with the tats who wouldn't wear his shirt, he comes over to Child, says something to him. He's about to go for him when your client stepped in front of Child and got the full force of the attack. It took me ten, maybe twelve seconds to get in there and take the guy down. By then it was too late. The Mexican must have had a shiv up his ass. It's the only way it could've gotten past a search. We isolated Popo, cleared a space, and then got to work on him. We couldn't get him stable, so we moved him to the first-aid room. Damn fine thing he did in there, saving Child.'

'I don't understand . . .'

'Popo! Don't you know anything? The Mexican was trying to start shit with Child. Next thing you know, the Mexican's got a shiv in his hand and he goes for Child. At the last second, Popo jumps in, and he takes the hit. Brave kid. Maybe stupid, but brave.'

'Jesus, Popo. He never would've done it if I hadn't told him to watch out for David.'

'He'll make it. Popo is tough. And we got to him pretty quick.'

More weight fell on top of me. Dizzy. Sick. Ashamed that I'd put Popo at risk.

'Where is Child?' I said.

'He's having another panic attack. We put him in the secure holding cell one floor up. Got an officer on the door, but he can't stay there all day. I need that guard.'

I wanted to put my hands up and thank the Lord that Christine's ticket to freedom was still breathing, but I couldn't. Popo the drug addict, the snitch, the thief, the unlikeliest hero in the whole city, just stepped in and saved the life of a billionaire. My eyelids felt heavy, and I ran my fingers from the corners of each eye over the skin and then massaged my temples. Popo must've done it for me. He'd seen the hit coming and stepped in, out of misplaced loyalty to me perhaps, and he'd stopped a murder. Or maybe I was doing Popo a disservice. Sure, he was a junkie and a criminal, but there was something else in Popo. Maybe he did it purely because it was the right thing to do.

'If you hear anything about Popo, let me know right away.'

I turned and made for the exit. Because of the incident, the guards were short-staffed and edgy. There would be no more visits. Priority was restoring calm in the cages and fishing guys up the line to court and bail office or back down to holding. Everything would slow down. That bought me some time. I wondered how long it would take Gerry Sinton to realize the mistake – that Popo was in the ER and not Child. I gave it a half hour, max.

'Thanks, Neil. You probably saved Popo today.'

'There's not a lot in that kid that drugs haven't eaten away already. He's wasn't in good shape when he came in, but he's a fighter.'

A thought popped into my head and wouldn't wait.

'The Mexican, how long was he in the cage before he made his move?'

'Ah, I think he was in there a half hour, maybe longer. He went in just after you took David out to the interview room.'

I nodded and left Neil to give his statement to the cop. I called the elevator, and while I waited I watched the guard behind the security desk wiping down a whiteboard. The printed legend above the board read, DAYS WITHOUT MAJOR INCIDENT. The guard wiped off '87,' popped the cap off a fat Magic Marker, and drew a big zero on the board.

It was time to check in with Dell.

Time to tell him I'd secured the client.

And that our deal was off.

CHAPTER EIGHTEEN

I didn't notice any watchers as I made my way to the exit and crossed the street from the courthouse. A black SUV waited outside a twenty-four-hour dry cleaner called Jack's. I tossed a couple of bucks across a news vendor's hand and picked up a copy of the *New York Times* and the *Wall Street Journal*. I checked the street again. No tail.

The rear passenger door opened.

'How's it going?' said Dell as I got in beside him, dumped my case files on the leather seat, with my newspapers on top, and closed the door.

'There's been an attempt on David's life. A Mexican tried to stab him in the cage, and my client intervened; Popo might not make it. Child's okay, though. It might help us in the long run, and believe me, we're going to need all the help we can get. Gerry Sinton managed to get himself appointed as co-counsel.'

Dell made a circular motion with his left hand, and the SUV pulled into traffic. He kept his focus on the cars and pedestrians behind us, checking that we weren't being followed. The driver had a buzz cut, and I could see the fingers of his left hand taped together. He made a point of turning around and scowling at me when we hit a stoplight.

'You've already met Agent Weinstein,' said Dell.

'How's the finger?' I said.

The slim man smiled at me, flipped me the bird with his right hand and then swung around. His boss continued to check our tail for another half a block, then leveled his gaze at me.

'Co-counsel? How could you let that happen?' said Dell. I detected a little heat in his voice.

'Your men were supposed to hold him at the accident scene. He got here early.'

'The firm's security team were shadowing Sinton. Harland and Sinton employ a six-man squad of ex-marines. They look after the lawyers and the documents, but we really think they're enforcers and guard dogs for the money. Guy named Gill heads up the team. He's a former Marine and ex-NYPD – smart and ruthless. The firm's security intervened. My guess is one of them called Gill. He probably pulled in a few favors, because the cops holding Sinton got a radio call and Gerry got released immediately after that call. The officer on scene told me he got orders from his lieutenant to let him go. If he'd held Sinton for much longer, somebody would've guessed the cops had a motive. Where's Sinton now?'

'We both thought Child had been stabbed. He's on his way to the ER. I figure we have a half hour before he realizes Child is still at the courthouse.'

'You sure the Mexican targeted Child?'

'That's what I heard. Looks like the firm tried to take him out.'

From a manila folder on his lap, Dell retrieved a black-and-white photograph. He was careful not to open the folder too wide in case I saw the contents, but I saw enough to know that the file contained a thick bundle of papers on Harland and Sinton. The photo was a close-up on a guy about my age, maybe a little closer to forty, with a muscular build and light, sandy hair. His jaw looked like it could crack a baseball bat. This wasn't the same guy in the black coat and gray sweater who'd stared at me in the hall outside court twelve.

'This is Gill. Watch out for him. He's dangerous. The firm will kill to protect their operation, and Gill is the trigger man. I'd say he set up the attempted stabbing in the holding pen. We need you to get Sinton out of the picture. You can't put the pressure on Child with Sinton standing on your throat. How are you going to get rid of him?'

'For the moment, he stays. I'll need him. Truth is, Dell, I'm not convinced Child is guilty. There has to be another way. I just haven't figured it out yet.'

'Oh, he's innocent, is he? How do you figure?'

'I just know. Kid doesn't have it in him. I can tell.'

'Why don't you try explaining that to your wife after she gets eighty-five years for money laundering and racketeering? Don't be fooled by that *kid*. He's made himself a billionaire and he did it ruthlessly, so remember that.'

'Hold on. You just want the intel, right? Accounts, banks, contracts, evidence tying it all to Ben Harland and Gerry Sinton. I know exactly what you need for a successful prosecution, but you won't get any of that from Child. This guy doesn't need the skim from a dirty money wash. He's not involved. He's not the type. He doesn't know anything, Dell. He's a mark, that's it. He's just as much a victim as the other rich idiots pouring money into Harland and Sinton. I can get you the evidence you need, but I have to do it my way.'

'This guy has really suckered you, Eddie. I thought you knew what you were doing; I thought we had a deal. The evidence, the money, and the testimony in exchange for your wife's freedom. Not much to ask.'

'That was before I met Child. He's so young, and he's falling apart. I love my wife, but I won't sacrifice a life for her. Not if there's another way. I'll make sure you get what you need and you'll leave Christine alone. But I need to know how Child is linked to the firm and what he's got on them. You need to tell me.'

I handed him back the photograph, which he carefully replaced in the folder before tossing it onto the seat between us. He sighed and leaned forward. Running his hands over his face, he muttered something, then spoke clearly.

'We had a deal. We had a plan. I don't like people who break their word, Eddie. And I don't like low-life ex-con artists telling me what to do. I don't like it one little bit,' he said.

Dell's head came back to rest on the seat upright. Sliding his fingers beneath his glasses, he rubbed at his eyes. His movement was slow, deliberate, like he was fighting off the sleep that had been denied him since Child was arrested twenty-four hours before. I saw a twitch from his left eye and smelled the sweat on his forehead. The lines around his eyes were deep now.

'We stick to our original plan. The evidence against Child is more than enough to convict him of murdering his girlfriend. You know why? Because he murdered her, Eddie. You tell him you have a way out. Tell him you can save his life. Tell him you can cut him a deal. We need him to come clean about the firm. Five years is a walk in the park. It's a sweet deal for murder one. If he refuses, he goes down for life.'

'No. Either I walk away, or you tell me what David has on the firm.'

'It's too risky. We have to do this my way. Child has a problem. You're going to offer the solution. There's no other way he would part with this information.'

'I can get it,' I said.

Dell studied me, weighing his options, deciding if I could deliver. I checked the rear view. The closest car to the SUV was a good thirty feet away, and I guessed we were doing around twenty miles an hour. I knew what Dell's answer would be, and I already knew my next move.

'No,' said Dell.

'Then it's over,' I said, as I reached in between the front seats and pulled the parking brake. The whole vehicle pitched forward as the tires locked up. The driver's head disappeared into his chest as his seat belt held firm.

My right shoulder was already jammed against the front passenger seat, braced for the momentum. Dell's face went into the driver's seat, the files slid to the floor, and the car behind us fired his horn and managed to stop before he hit the rear of our car.

I gathered up my files and newspapers, opened the door, and said, 'I'm out. You're on your own.'

The driver, Weinstein, was already mouthing off – calling me crazy.

A hand on my shoulder. I anticipated it would be a forceful grab, pulling me back into the vehicle. It wasn't. The grip was one of resignation, and a final plea for help.

'All right,' said Dell.

Closing the door, I stared straight ahead, files sitting on my lap, waiting for the info, not looking Dell in the eye. The horns from the traffic behind us ceased as the SUV took off at a slow pace.

'Don't try that again,' said Weinstein.

With a sigh, Dell laid it out.

'What David Child has is not illegal. In fact, it's perfectly legal. The biggest risk to a laundry is personnel in the chain. Well, David Child gave the firm the solution that allowed them to cut down that risk. Instead of the money passing through lots of hands, it now passes though accounts at the click of a button.'

'What are you talking about?'

'He designed a digital security system for the firm. This practice has serious money floating around its client accounts, it needs an airtight security system to protect it from hackers. So David designed an algorithm. One that's based on the same principles as Reeler: a combination of random and targeted sequences. Basically, David installed an IT security system at Harland and Sinton – which is totally legit, but used in a different way, it becomes the safest and the best method of laundering money ever designed.'

'But it wasn't designed to wash the money?'

'You got it. Let's say the system David installed detects a hacker threat. If it's serious enough, then the program throws all of the money from the firm's business and client accounts into the ether. Millions and millions of dollars that normally sit in hundreds of the firm's client accounts start to move. The algo splits the money into smaller sums, no bigger than ten thousand dollars, and sends them on a random digital journey through hundreds of accounts – to protect them from the hacker. Once it's gone it cannot be traced, but seventy-two hours later the money returns to a single, high-security account. Of course, by the time the money has gotten there, it's totally clean. The firm can *test* the system as often as they like – to make sure it's operational. Because the money breaks down into sums lower than ten grand, the Bank Secrecy Act won't kick in and the sums are allowed to move without due diligence or anti-money-laundering checks. That's what money laundering is all about; it's like buying a passport for each dollar. There are three basic stages to washing money – introduction, layering, and integration. The phony share transaction introduces the money into the system; when Harland and Sinton trigger the algo, the movement of the money from legit account to legit account adds layers of provenance, and seventy-two hours later all of the money, dirty and legit, settles into one account.'

I had to admire the system; it was beautiful. The firm can treat millions at the touch of a button – in pretending to test their security system, they trigger David's algorithm and the money randomly spins through a wash cycle. Perfect.

'Because the security system is legit, you can't get a warrant, and with the money spinning, you can't trace it. I'm guessing the algo leads to the partners?'

Shaking his head, Dell suppressed a laugh.

'Yes, we believe this is how the partners get paid – they skim some of the money when it lands in the high-security account. The final account that collects all of the money is always in Ben Harland's name. We know that much. But we don't know the account number or which bank. The firm has thousands of dormant accounts in a handful of banks. The money lands in a different one each time the algo reaches the end of its cycle. It would take an army of techs to find even a small percentage of it, and we would have to know the precise time that it hit the account. We don't even know what bank it's headed for. When the algo runs its course, it sends an e-mail to the partners giving them the new account information. By that time, the money is clean and the partners take their percentage off the top before they pay the investors. We guess the laundry flows once every few months – and our best guess is the partners take around five million for themselves each time. But the key here is recovery. Think about it – every single one of the big financial fraud busts in the last few years have one thing in common – the money was never recovered. With the algorithm we can get the money and the partners.'

I thought it through, everything Dell had told me.

'You told me yesterday Farooq said the firm was getting rid of their middlemen, so the whole operation is digital now?'

'Pretty much. It's safer. We guessed if they didn't need middlemen they'd probably gone digital. At the same time the firm was cutting loose their money mules, Child became a client and designed their security system, so we started looking into it. It didn't take our techs long to figure out how it works, but it's too damn complex to track. That's why we need Child. Our whole team of techs in Langley can monitor around one hundred accounts. There are thousands. But we learned that the money disappears from those accounts and then comes back seventy-two hours later. Our surveillance isn't exactly legal – we need somebody we can put on the stand. We need Child. Our techs believe Gerry triggered the algo yesterday and the money is spinning through the air right now.'

'That's why you wanted Child to make a quick deal. You need access to the system to trace the dirty money to the partners, but you also need to be waiting at the bank to grab the money after its last wash.'

'You got it. The fact that Sinton triggered the algo after Child's arrest makes me nervous. I figure he's cleaning it, and when it lands, Sinton and Harland lift the clean money and disappear. But they don't want to do that. If they can take out David before he spills his guts about the algo, they won't have to run. We got lucky – we need to capitalize on this. If we can trace the path of the money through the laundry, we can take it all and put the partners in jail. I want Harland and Sinton – they murdered one of my people, Eddie. I heard her calling my name while she burned in that car. I need this.'

'Your analyst, Sophie. Kennedy told me about her. Said that you two were a thing. I'm sorry for your loss.'

I meant it. Didn't stop Dell from searching my face for any hint of insincerity. Satisfied, he said, 'Thank you. She was too young. It should've been me in that convoy. I know I push hard, but I'm not a bad guy. I just want the firm.'

'So what exactly do you need from David Child?'

'He wrote the algo. He must have a way of tracing how it moves the money and where it will end up. He must have a way of monitoring the money while the algo moves it. I want the route the money takes from the first dollar deposited with the firm until the payoff to the partners. He tells us where the money will land and how the cash filters to Harland and Sinton. That gives us the evidence to indict Gerry Sinton and Ben Harland and it ensures we can secure all of the firm's cash.'

I let this sink in, searching through Dell's account, looking for any inconsistencies. I found only one.

'Say I believe you. It sounds more like the truth. But if you found out that Child can manipulate the algo and you'll cut him a deal in exchange, then what the hell do you need me for? Why not go see him for yourself and make the deal? Why involve me?'

'Soon as we got the drop on David's IT system, we planned to do exactly that. Until our friends at the Bureau gave us David's psyche evaluation. The kid has a history of deep-seated authority issues – he was a hacker for many years, and he hates and distrusts the government. He's borderline paranoid, and he suffers from some kind of adjustment disorder. If we approached him directly, he wouldn't trust us. But that doesn't matter; we couldn't legitimately get to him without his lawyer finding out. Plus there's the little matter of his dead girlfriend. We can't cut him a deal without him having a lawyer. We needed Child to have an ally, somebody to trust, and we had to separate him from the firm. Made sense to bring in a new lawyer for him, one who would be sympathetic and motivated to convince Child to plead guilty and make a deal. You've been on our radar since your wife took the job at the firm. We know everything about those lawyers, every possible angle of exploitation. And when the opportunity arose, we thought we'd use it. You were perfect for the job.'

This was standard CIA fare, using people, manipulating lives to further their own needs. I'd played this game myself.

'I'm not that perfect. I won't beat Child into a false confession.'

'I know you can get a good read on someone, but you can never be sure, Eddie. David Child is highly intelligent – and all the evidence says that he's a killer. You willing to let a murderer walk? I saw the photographs. I know what he did to that girl. As much as I want the firm, I can't let a guy like that just walk away.'

A cold, dull pain lit up my right hand. An old injury. Bad memories came flooding back.

'Dell, if I thought he was guilty, I'd help you nail him. I have to trust my instincts on this. I'll get you your evidence another way. When I get it, you let Christine slide on an immunity agreement,' I said.

He rubbed his chin and said, 'How will you get it?'

'Leave that to me.'

We pulled over, a half mile from the courthouse.

'You can walk from here. Take care. I told you these men are dangerous. Now you know just how dangerous. Do yourself a favor and take the easy route – get me my plea and I'll make sure Christine is safe. But don't make the mistake of thinking I won't have Christine indicted if you cross me. Sometime tomorrow night the firm's money lands in a secured account – all of it. I need the information before that so we can be waiting. If we don't have the trace on the algo by then, it's too late. Sinton can lift the cash and disappear if he feels the need,' said Dell.

I tucked my case files under my arm, opened the door, and climbed out of the SUV onto the pavement. Dell flicked open his cell phone and turned his attention to the screen. I closed the door and the SUV sped off.

My wife or my client? Twenty-nine hours until the money lands. Twenty-nine hours to get Christine clear – *if* I gave up Child.

It had seemed an easy decision the night before. But I couldn't shake that feeling that I was on the wrong side of this, that David needed someone to defend him, not help him into prison.

Not that long ago I'd represented a man whom I knew to be guilty. I played it out and got him off. And regretted it every day since. I'd lost too much down that road.

I could no more send an innocent man to prison than I could let a guilty one go free. The system that allowed a defendant to buy a hotshot lawyer to get him off was the same system that pitted seasoned prosecutors with unlimited resources against public defenders who couldn't buy their clients a bus ticket to get them to court.

The system was wrong. It allowed the players to rule. I was a player, and whatever else I did, whatever I scammed on the side to keep my practice going, I wouldn't let the system fail for the wrong reasons.

Somehow I had to get both Christine and David clear, and right then, no matter what way I played it out in my mind, I knew if I tried to save them both I would probably end up losing at least one of them. I had to get David to trust me. I had to make a deal.

A half smile turned up the corner of my mouth as I wondered if the copy of the *New York Times* that I'd substituted for the contents of the manila folder would fool Dell if he glanced at the cover. I needed only a few minutes with the stolen documents.

A half a block away, I saw a FedEx office.

CHAPTER NINETEEN

33 hours until the shot

The FedEx office boasted six of the latest high-tech photocopiers. I threaded the pages from the file into three of them, distributing the pages evenly, no more than fifty to a machine. I hit start on each machine and waited while the copiers purred and whirred their way to making me copies of Dell's file.

I collated the copies from each machine, paid at the desk, and left.

I called Dell direct, my emergency number.

The SUV appeared within a minute.

This time I opened the passenger door and held out the papers. 'Sorry, this must have gotten mixed up with my files.'

The twitch.

Without a word, Dell grabbed the original documents, closed the door, and sped away into New York traffic, heading toward the Chrysler Building.

I had my copies slipped between the discovery pages of the old Popo files I'd carried with me that day. At that moment I couldn't read the file. I was due back at court to assist with Child's bail processing and release as soon as things calmed down in holding. I would have to read the file later. When I had time to sit and figure things out.

In taking those papers, I'd crossed a line. Even if Dell couldn't be sure I'd taken the file deliberately, he would assume it was a move on my part. I had to tread more carefully with Dell. He held Christine's fate in his hands. And I hated that.

Somehow, I had to figure out a way to shift that balance of power in my favor, and I knew the key to that was a twenty-two-year-old boy, pissing himself with panic in a cell, unable to breathe or think, never mind help anyone else.

I waved down a cab, told the driver to bring me back to court, flicked open the prosecution file Lopez had given me in Knox's chambers, and began to read. I already knew the basic facts – the victim, David's girlfriend, had been found shot in his apartment. What I didn't know before I opened that file was how the prosecution were going to run with the case, what specific pieces of evidence they had against Child, what motive they would put up in front of the judge.

It wasn't a thick file – preliminary forensic reports, witness statements, crime scene photographs, and computer logs. After I'd finished reading, I began to doubt my assessment of David Child; the evidence looked clean, and it proved, way beyond any doubt, that David shot and killed his girlfriend, Clara Reece. I thought about the kid's eyes. His panic. It was like watching him falling down a deep hole.

I found it hard to guess what way the prosecution would spin the motive for the killing. The evidence made it clear that not only did David kill his girlfriend, but it would've been impossible for anyone else to have done it.

I asked the cab driver to pull over a block away from the courthouse. I needed a walk to clear my head.

CHAPTER TWENTY

A light rain began, and I pulled my collar up and tucked the files into the folds of my overcoat to keep them dry. The sidewalk hummed with commuters, shoppers, joggers, vendors, street performers, and people talking loudly on their cell phones. I didn't hear any of it, or really see it. Nor did I see the stone columns lining the front of the court building, nor the yellow cabs lined up outside, their drivers hanging out of their windows arguing over who was first in line for pickup. None of it came directly within my view, yet I was aware of all of it, but only on the most basic level. My head was still in the prosecution file.

There was reference in the file to the existence of two DVDs that hadn't yet been served on the defense, but there were statements from detectives who had watched them and wanted to get their commentary noted for evidentiary purposes. The first DVD, according to the cop's statement, was from a traffic camera on Central Park West that captured the RTC. A drunk driver ran a red light and plowed into David's Bugatti, head-on. When police attended the scene, they saw the firearm in the passenger footwell of the supercar. Child said the gun wasn't his. The cop, Phil Jones, said that he smelled the gun and detected an odor from it, as if it had been recently fired. There was no license for the gun, and they arrested Child, put him in lockup. Then later they matched his address to the reports of the body found in an apartment – his apartment. I could tell that the cops, in their statements, were hinting that if Child's car hadn't been hit by that drunk driver, he might have gotten away clean and had a chance to dispose of the murder weapon.

As it was, fate made sure that he got caught.

Being a relatively new billionaire, Child owned an apartment in Central Park Eleven, the most expensive apartment building in the United States. The building actually sat on Central Park West, but they'd decided to christen the place Central Park Eleven. His apartment spread over more square footage than a basketball court and enjoyed a wide, wraparound balcony with the best views of the park in Manhattan. The statement from his neighbor, a Hollywood movie director named Gershbaum, began by explaining that he owned the adjoining apartment on the twenty-fifth floor and at that height, in the tower above the main block, there were only two apartments per floor. He said he was in his apartment, watching footage from a movie he was shooting that day, when he thought he heard gunfire. At first he wasn't sure. He thought it might have been a car backfiring on the street, so he opened his balcony door and leaned over the railing to check. That's when he saw the window exploding in the apartment next to him. It scared him so bad he damn near fell over his own railing. He called building security from his panic room and waited. Security were outside his door in four minutes. Gershbaum told the guard what he'd seen and showed him the glass on the next balcony. The first security guard to enter the apartment found Clara's body in the kitchen.

I didn't need to recall the guard's description of what he saw. A photograph of the body at the scene had already burned itself into my mind. She'd had blond hair, cut into a short bob. Her hair was no longer blond; now it was a mass of bloody tissue. Simply clothed in a white tee over dark blue jeans, feet bare. Her body lay facedown in the kitchen, head turned slightly to the right. Both arms by her sides. People are rarely shot as they lie facedown on the floor. And most people who get shot don't die instantly, and their arms reach out, reflexively, to break their fall as they go down from the kinetic force of the bullet. Clara's arms had not moved to break her fall. The rational explanation for that could be that she was dead before her body hit the polished, white tiles.

The medical examiner stated that Clara had been shot multiple times – most of the shots were to the head. There were two bullet entry wounds in the center of her back, thirteen millimeters apart. The remainder of the shots were to the back of her head. From the way her body was positioned, providing it had not been moved postmortem, my take on it was she'd first been shot in the head, then dropped. Two in the spine to make sure she was down, and then the killer unloaded into the back of her head. The ME couldn't confirm the number of shots to the head, as there was little of her skull left intact. A CSI's statement confirmed that beneath Clara's face, the tiles were broken and the cement held what had become a ball of mangled rounds.

On his reading of the scene, the killer had fired twice into her back then spent the rest of the clip with shots to the back of her head.

Then reloaded.

The second clip had then been emptied into what remained of her skull.

A rage shooting. That pointed to a suspect who knew the victim well, and I guessed this is what the DA's office would run with for motive. Along with the rest of the crime scene photographs was a picture of Clara, taken from her Reeler account. She was with another woman, about her age, but not as pretty. They were sitting on barstools, showing off their new, matching tattoos. A purple daisy on their respective right wrists. Drinks sat behind them, and they were facing away from the bar. Clara looked as if she was giggling. She had been naturally beautiful, her skin clear and bright, and her eyes had an effervescent aspect.

For a moment I thought of the young girl that I'd failed so miserably years ago when I'd set her attacker free.

I felt a growing heat in my stomach. My hands felt heavy and ready to fly. That feeling came to me sometimes, when I wanted to hurt someone. For Clara, all I could do was make sure that her killer could never do that to someone else. Seeing that same tattoo in the crime scene photos, on her upturned, lifeless wrist, I couldn't help but think that some part of her soul stayed behind, to watch, to wail at the life taken, and to judge. Again, I thought about David Child; could he lie that well? Well enough to fool me – a guy who could spot a tell on a mannequin? I didn't believe that he could, but the evidence against Child just got worse and worse the more I read.

If you were a tenant in Central Park Eleven, you got a key to your apartment and an electronic fob. The fob operated the elevators in the building and turned off your security alarm, which came as standard for your accommodation. Building security had Child's comings and goings logged, to the minute, from his fob. At 19:46 he entered his apartment with Clara, seventeen minutes later Child's fob was registered using the elevator to exit the building, alone. He was the last person to leave the apartment. Four minutes after that, the security guards are at Gershbaum's apartment, and then they discover Clara's body in David Child's empty apartment. The apartment that he'd left just minutes before.

A cop viewed the building's security camera recordings and saw Child entering and leaving the apartment. He wore an oversized green hooded top, baggy gray sweatpants, and a pair of red Nikes. I checked the description of Child from the first DVD, which held security footage from the car accident. He wore the same clothes.

Preliminary forensics revealed Child's hands and clothes were covered in gunshot residue. This wasn't a case of secondary transfer, like brushing up against someone who'd just fired a pistol, or walking around in a firing range. It looked like he'd taken a bath in GSR; the concentrations found on his hands, clothes, and face were consistent with him having fired a gun multiple times.

During police questioning, Child said he'd never seen the gun before the cop showed it to him, allegedly having found it on the floor of David's Bugatti. He'd told them he didn't own a gun and he'd never fired a gun in his life.

Shell casings found in the apartment were to be tested by ballistics and reports should be ready soon. However, given the similar caliber, and preliminary findings, it looked as though the gun in Child's car was the murder weapon.

The gun was a Ruger LCP.

CHAPTER TWENTY-ONE

The back stairs of the courthouse, accessed via the fire door with the faulty alarm, led me to the secure detention floor. Department of Corrections reserved this block for the most dangerous detainees and for the most vulnerable. Behind the barred entrance, two guards manned a bank of security monitors. I knew one of them by sight, told him I was there to see Child. This section of detention was not in lockdown, and he let me through after patting me down and having a thorough thumb through my files, just to make sure that I wasn't trying to slip anything to the prisoner.

The corridor dog-legged once and at the end, beyond the stretch of cells on the right-hand wall, I saw a single guard sitting outside the secure room. For a detention officer he was small, no more than five foot two. The riot stick slung from his belt looked bigger than he was.

'Anyone ask to see my client?'

'The doc came to check on him, but he left ten minutes ago. You want to see him?' said the guard.

'Sure do.'

'You his lawyer?'

'Well, I'm not his mother. Of course I'm his lawyer. Can you open the cell? Aren't you supposed to be watching him?'

'He's an AR – at risk – so I check on him every nine minutes. Wanna read my chart?' he asked.

He'd probably ticked his inspection boxes already and there would be no point in checking. The cell door opened with a metallic groan, and inside I saw Child lying on the two inches of rubber mattress that passed for a bed. Even lying down he cradled his head, perhaps afraid that unless he kept a hand on his brow the whirlwind he found himself in would spin even faster that it was already.

'I got you bail, but with some conditions. You'll have to—' I began.

'Is he alive?' said Child.

My impression of this man went up even more. When you're sitting in an orange jumpsuit with a murder charge hanging over your head, it's real easy to forget about other people's problems.

'He was protecting me,' said David, levering himself into a sitting position.

The bed was in fact a steel plate that hung from a pair of brackets bolted onto the wall on the right. A steel toilet took center stage in the cell, and on the left was a steel bench. The floor was poured concrete that still looked wet, and I could feel the dampness coming up through my feet – I could smell it, too.

'Why'd he do it?' he asked.

'I asked Popo to keep an eye on you. But I suppose it's more than that. He wouldn't have tried to stop the attack if he didn't give a shit.'

The guard closed and locked the cell door.

'I never had any friends growing up. I got bullied a lot. When I made my first million, I suddenly got popular. Maybe . . . I don't know, you think he wanted money?'

'I don't think he fully realized who you were.'

'Yeah, but I'm like, on the cover of *Time* magazine. He must've recognized me.'

'Well, I don't think Popo has a subscription to *Time*. He can't read and I sure as hell didn't tell him who you were. Social media doesn't appear on the radar if you're homeless, broke, and looking for your next fix. If he knew you were a billionaire, you bet he would've asked for money. I suppose he probably guessed that you had dough because you're white, you're clean, and you wore those expensive sneakers, but he wouldn't put himself in front of a shiv just because you were a rich white boy.'

He massaged his forehead.

'What happens now?'

'There's been a development. Gerry Sinton showed up, played hell, and persuaded the judge to assign him as co-counsel. If you want to fire him, you're going to have to go to court. The retainer you signed with Harland and Sinton is tight and gives them a lien on any attorney-client work product. You can ignore him, but it'll get messy. Not for you, for me. He'll tie me up in injunctions and try to get me disbarred for soliciting one of his clients. My advice is to keep him around, for at least a while.'

'That's fine. I was beginning to feel bad about firing him.'

I could hear the intermittent popping of the guard's bubble gum outside the cell door, so I moved closer to David and sat down beside him.

'Before we go any further, there's something you have to know. Gerry didn't want to apply for bail. He told you as much last night, in the precinct, didn't he?'

David nodded. 'He said the press would be all over it. My company's share price would hit the floor, and because I own a few planes, I'm too much of a flight risk to get bail anyway. He said there was no point in applying for bail – too many downsides.'

For some reason, at that moment, I was suddenly aware that I hadn't shaved that morning. I could feel the rasp of a day's growth on my chin. I cleared my throat and met David's eyes as I told him the truth.

'Any first-year law student could've told you that you would get bail and that the judge has the power to do that in chambers, keeping things nice and private. Plus, it doesn't matter how many private jets you've got – give the court your passport, place a big bond on the table, and with your clean record, you will always get bail. I know Gerry has little experience, if any, of criminal procedure, but I don't think he's that stupid. I think he wanted you to stay in custody.'

'Why?'

'So that you would be killed.'

CHAPTER TWENTY-TWO

He held my gaze for half a second, and then his face ran through a slide show of emotions. At first he smiled, stopped, looked at me again to see if I was jerking around, his eyebrows creased. His eyes flickered and narrowed. He didn't want to believe what I'd told him. It was only human nature to ignore what we feared the most and to cling to every possibility of hope – even if it was false hope.

'That doesn't make any sense.'

'Sure it does. What doesn't make sense is staying inside and not applying for bail. Gerry never expected you to get alternative legal advice. If what I believe is true he probably expected you to be dead by now, lying in the morgue with the Mexican's shiv in your heart.'

'No, that's not true,' said David.

'The Mexican entered your cell when you were in medical – after you had the panic attack in the consulting room. As soon as you went back into the cage, he made his move. You're not in a gang. You're nobody in that cage, and I don't think you would've done anything to provoke that guy. He smuggled the shiv in there for one reason only – he was there to kill you, David. And Gerry Sinton sent him.'

He stood and paced the room, working it through in his mind. I shut up and let him think.

A thought brought him to a halt.

'Look, you're my lawyer now, okay? I'll fire Gerry if it makes you feel better. I think it's better if I have an expert criminal lawyer like you, but don't go making crazy accusations – it scares me.'

'You should be scared. Twelve hours ago a federal task force came to me and told me they were going to put my wife in prison unless I helped them. They wanted me to get close to you and make sure you hired me to defend you in this case. Then they wanted me to lean on you to take a plea agreement: Turn state's evidence on your own lawyers, Harland and Sinton, and their money-laundering operation, and in return you'll get a light sentence for murdering your girlfriend. I was all set to do it, too. Then I met you and I discovered two things – I don't think you murdered your girlfriend and you know nothing about Harland and Sinton's money laundering. If you did know about their operation, you'd have the next best thing to a get-out-of-jail-free card. If that were the case, you wouldn't want Gerry Sinton within a half mile of you, and you certainly wouldn't want him sitting beside you when you were interviewed by the cops.'

His legs seemed to give way, and he half lowered himself, half fell onto the cold concrete floor.

'If you didn't murder your girlfriend, it sure as hell looks like somebody set you up. And it wasn't the firm. They don't want you in the pressure cooker in case you make a deal and give them up in exchange for a reduced sentence. That's why they didn't want you to have bail. They wanted you inside, where a random act of violence, totally unconnected to them, would end your life. Dead men don't testify.'

He shook his head and his breath quickened again. His hands ran over his knees, rhythmically, as he rocked back and forth, fending off the panic.

'The death of your girlfriend could be coincidental, but I don't buy it. Look, I don't have it all figured out yet. I know you're innocent. I know you're too rich and too famous to get involved in laundering cash.'

'Money laundering? This is Harland and Sinton we're talking about here. They're one of the most respected firms in New York. There's no way they . . .'

'Hang on. I didn't believe it at first either, David. But now I'm convinced it's true. If it was all a pile of bullshit and the feds got it wrong, why would some random gangbanger buy himself a life sentence by killing a one-hundred-and-ten-pound white kid he never met before? It doesn't get him any status. Yeah, guys like you might get beat up or worse in the cage, but there's no reason for any of those guys to kill you, because you're no threat. You're insignificant to them. My theory is Harland and Sinton paid somebody to make you significant. They want you dead.'

'No, this is crazy, just totally trip-out crazy. No. No way. I mean, I don't know anything about the firm doing anything illegal.'

'Exactly. I think you're on the level with that. If you didn't know shit, you wouldn't be a target for the feds or for the firm. But you are a target. I've been told your IT security system, the algorithm that hides the money if it detects a cyberattack, is being used by the firm to launder cash – millions of dollars. They're pretending that they're testing the system – but they're washing the money. The feds want your algo so they can trace the cash back to the partners. If you give it to them, we can make a deal.'

'What? My algo is not designed to launder money. It's a security system.'

'I know that. But I'm guessing the partners asked you to design their security system to a specification – so that if a threat is detected, the money starts to run. Am I right?'

He nodded.

'The feds want the money and the partners, and your algo is the key. If they can access the algo, it gives the FBI the full money trail – from the initial transactions all the way through to the clean bills. The firm triggered the algo the moment you were arrested. My guess is when the money lands in the final account, the partners will clear out. The FBI want to be there when the money lands. They want you to plead guilty, they want the algorithm, and then they'll go easy on you and let my wife walk. But I think there's another deal here.'

'I didn't kill her. I won't plead guilty.'

'I won't let you go to jail for a murder you didn't commit. We make a new deal. I'll sell them the algorithm – the price is high – they have to let you and Christine walk.'

I put out my hand, and only then did I see that I was trembling.

He stared at me, just as frightened as I was.

David shuffled backward until his head hit the wall.

'I can't,' he said.

'You have to. I'm your only shot at getting out of this in one piece.'

'No, I mean I can't help you. The feds have it all wrong. The algorithm is on a separate internal system at the firm. I can't access it.'

Lacing his fingers together, he held his hands above his head and then let them fall onto his skull. With both hands locked at the back of his neck, he swung his elbows together, then began flapping his arms. It looked like the kid was trying to blow an idea out of his head, using his arms for bellows.

'Oh God, I wish this weren't happening,' he said.

He became completely still – frozen in thought. His body came back to life as he let the idea breathe.

'Eddie, what if I could get the algorithm traced? Why should I trust you?'

It was a good question. I thought about spinning a convincing line. Dismissed it and told him the truth.

'If I were you, I'm not sure I'd trust anyone. Unfortunately you don't have a choice. The firm thinks you're a threat and they want you dead. If we can give the feds enough to take the firm down, that gives you a shot, and I got something to bargain with for you and my wife. Then I'll help you figure out who killed Clara. I don't think this was a robbery gone wrong: Nothing was taken from your apartment. You've had time to think. If you're telling me you're innocent, then you must have some idea who would want to set you up.'

'There're a lot of people that don't like me. Guys who helped me set up Reeler, guys I paid off. They were all friends once, I don't think any of them would kill somebody. But there's one person I know who might.'

'Who?'

'Bernard Langhiemer.'

'Who the hell is Bernard Langhiemer?'

'A competitor. Somebody who once told me he'd destroy me. I can tell you everything you need to know about him.'

'We'll talk about that when we get you out of here. In the meantime, I can protect you on the outside.'

'How are you going to do that?'

'I got a friend I can call. He works for an old sparring buddy of mine. This friend is a little unusual, but he'll keep you alive. People call him the Lizard. Well, to be accurate, he calls *himself* the Lizard.'

'The Lizard?'

'I told you – he's a little unusual, but I trust him with my life. And I need contact details for your family, somebody who will get down here and organize your bail money.'

'I don't have any family. Not really. You can call Holly. She can arrange the money transfer.'

'Who is Holly?'

'Holly Shepard. She's an old friend and my PA.'

'Can she bring you some clothes, too?'

'Sure.'

He knew the cell number by heart, and I wrote it down in the file. David paced the room, muttering. I thought about the evidence against him, and what Dell had told me. For a moment I wondered if David was playing me.

'Can you really trace the money?' I asked.

He stopped. Rubbed his hands together.

'I'm not sure. I can try. You think they'll let me off if I give it to them?'

The guard rapped the cell door with his stick. The viewer slid open, and I saw his dull eyes through the door.

'I got a call from the office. Your name's Flynn, right?'

'Yeah, Eddie Flynn.'

'Your wife's here to see you,' he said.

CHAPTER TWENTY-THREE

From the top of the staircase, my view of the central lobby that morning was pretty much like any other day. Security was spread out all over, with teams focused on the bag scanners at the entrance and backup dotted around, ever watchful. The floor was black, hardened, ridged rubber, for heavy-duty footfall. There were rows of pine benches bolted to the floor with steel bars. The benches ran along the walls and a couple of islands of seats sat opposite the coffee machines. There would be a steady line of defendants through the arraignment court that day, from morning until around one a.m., when they shut down for the night. That normally meant a river of family members, girlfriends, bail bondsmen, cops, lawyers, dope peddlers, reporters, pimps, probation officers, and court staff would pass through the doors.

Holly, David's PA, picked up my call.

'Holly, it's Eddie Flynn. I'm calling on behalf of my client, David Child. I need your help with—'

'Is he all right? They won't let me see him, and the firm isn't telling me anything. Is Gerry with you? Why hasn't he returned my call? Is David gonna make bail?'

She spoke faster than I could listen. But she wasn't panicked or hyper; she sounded like the kind of person who was super-organized and couldn't understand why everyone else didn't operate at the same level. It was hard to tell, but I guessed she wasn't much older than David – mid- to late-twenties, maximum.

'Let me slow you down. I'm co-counsel with Harland and Sinton. I'm a specialist criminal defense attorney. By the sounds of it, you know that David has been arrested. I can tell you he's been charged with a serious offense. I need you to come down to

97

the bail office and arrange a transfer of funds to cover his bond. Can you do that?'

'Oh my God! Is he all right? David can't cope with confined spaces. He'll freak out . . . Does he have his meds?'

'Holly, he's okay. I'm looking after him. Now, here's what you need to do . . .'

I gave the address of the courthouse, the bank information for the court funds office, the case docket number, and asked her to bring some clothes for David. She wrote it all down and said she'd be right on it. Disconnecting that call, I dialed the Lizard's cell and made arrangements for him to pick up David when he made bail. The Lizard was a former Marine and peripatetic hit man/interrogator for Jimmy the Hat, my oldest friend. The Lizard was one of his men who'd helped me deal with the Russian mob. He could handle security.

As I came down the staircase I clocked Christine. She sat on a bench close to the east wall, underneath a sign that read, No Firearms. No Photography. A leather bag sat beside her; it looked new, expensive. Her brown hair was pulled back in a ponytail. She wore a clean black suit with a skirt that stopped just above the knee. She sat cross-legged. Her left leg swung rhythmically, threatening to dislodge her polished leather high-heeled shoe. She looked anxious. The weather had been good for the past few days, and with the radiators turned up full in the lobby for the benefit of the guards on the door, the heat in the room was fierce. With long, delicate fingers, she fanned at the pale skin of her throat, exposed by an open-necked cream blouse.

Before I could reach the bottom of the staircase, she saw me, grabbed her bag, and marched in my direction. Those high heels sent deep *clacks* echoing off the walls. Her steps were purposeful, fast, and they sent the bob of hair at the back of her head swinging around with the ferocious motion of her gait.

I could see the confusion on her face, and the continued tapping with her shoe confirmed she was worried. She waited at the foot of the stairs.

The skin around her blue eyes was taut and her cheekbones were colored, as if, with the wearing of the monochrome suit and the heels, they wished to display themselves more prominently.

No matter how many times I'd woken up next to her, or turned toward her as she watched TV on the couch, or caught the scent of her in the bathroom in the morning – every time I felt that flutter in the pit of my stomach and that warm feeling that came from having found the only woman on this planet I wanted to be with. Lately, that feeling had been immediately followed by a flood of self-loathing – I'd lost the best thing that had ever happened to me and it was all my fault. I still clung to the little hope I had left that maybe the split wasn't permanent. The thought of her spending twenty-three hours a day in a prison cell if I messed this up sent a spike of adrenaline though my veins.

Before I even reached the bottom of the staircase, she started talking. She wanted answers.

'Gerry Sinton's assistant just hauled me out of a meeting because of you. I thought I was going to be fired. She told me that you're sabotaging their business and illegally soliciting one of their biggest clients. I told her there was no way you would do that. That you couldn't do that. They sent me down here to talk to you. What's going on Eddie?'

'Take it easy. Let me try to explain. You're right. I *am* representing David Child,' I said.

Her eyes narrowed. Christine was a fiercely intelligent lawyer, and she knew more about litigation than I would ever know. We'd met in law school; she was a top student and I was hanging in there by a thread. We'd shared a cab into school one morning and I'd been mesmerized by her. Unlike the other women, who were career focused and straitlaced, there was a wild streak in Christine. She had the same money and privileged upbringing that most of the other women in the class had enjoyed, but it hadn't tainted her. Instead of spending her time studying and planning job applications, she was either in the bar or volunteering at a homeless shelter. Luckily, she had the brains to excel with little or no effort. I'd never met anyone like her before.

'Why are you doing this? Don't you know this puts me in a terrible position?'

'You know I wouldn't do anything to damage your career. It's hard to explain,' I said.

'How on earth do you think you can steal one of my firm's clients? You're not a corporate lawyer. You wouldn't know one end of a law book from a Sears catalog.'

'This is going to sound crazy, but I'm doing this for you.'

She rolled her eyes and turned away from me. I saw her massage her temples, shaking her head slowly.

I came up behind her and stopped my hand in midair, just before I touched her shoulder. She sensed it.

'Don't. I know you care about my career. That's why I don't understand this. It's nothing to do with me. And I'm so pissed at Gerry Sinton's PA – she spoke to me like I was dirt. God, Eddie, I could get fired,' she said.

My hand fell to my side.

We stood there for a moment. I said nothing and let the awkward silence fill the space between us. She turned and studied my face.

'What are you doing with this client? Tell me the truth.'

'We can't talk here. Look, this isn't about you and me. There's something I have to tell you, but now isn't the right time and this isn't the place. I can come by later and we'll talk. I'm not screwing with you, I promise. I want things back the way they used to be, only better. I can do that. I'm trying to do that. Trust me, I'm doing this for you – for us.'

She searched my face for signs that I was bullshitting her. She could read me, and I sensed she knew I was telling the truth.

'Amy loves you, and I know you love her. Sometimes . . . sometimes I think there might be a chance for us . . .'

The soft look in her blue eyes evaporated when she said, 'Then you do stuff like this.'

'Christine . . .'

'No, Eddie. You've pissed off one of my bosses. I don't know what the hell you're up to, but this can't come back on me. You want to make things better? Fine. Fix *this*. Tell the client you made a mistake and send him back to Gerry Sinton.'

'It's more complicated than that. Let's take a walk,' I said, gesturing to the front door.

She slung her handbag over her shoulder and made for the door. I let her get ahead and focused my gaze on the glass-fronted entrance to the courthouse. With the overhead lights, I could see Christine reflected in the glass. I kept my eyes on the midpoint of the glass wall, concentrating on that dead center as I walked, gearing up my peripheral vision.

That was when I saw them.

CHAPTER TWENTY-FOUR

There were two of them.

The first man had been following me down the stairs. He was heavyset, early forties, checkered shirt, green padded jacket, and a light mustache to match his hair.

He had paused on the staircase to check his cell phone when I'd reached the bottom and met Christine. Even while we talked, I could feel the big guy behind me. He wore dark pants with a solid crease down the middle and work boots. That sealed it. Any guy who's got a pair of black, smart dress pants also owns a decent pair of shoes and there was no way he would come to court in his work boots.

The sandy-haired man in the green jacket kept coming, slowly, his phone in his hand with an earpiece running from the cell.

I wasn't overly concerned about this guy. I couldn't be sure, but he looked a lot like the man in the photo Dell had shown me: Gill, Harland and Sinton's head of security, although I hadn't yet gotten a chance to take a good look at his face.

The second man was a whole different story. He sat on the bench to my right. Arms folded, a newspaper spread out on the bench next to him. A long black overcoat spilled open as he lounged there, feet extended and crossed. His head back and eyes closed. He too wore an earpiece, only I couldn't see the device it connected to. I detected a strong smell of stale cigarettes that grew in intensity the closer I got to him, and then I recognized him as the guy I'd seen in the hall earlier that morning, wearing the same coat. He'd dumped the gray sweater, to alter his appearance slightly, and wore a cream button-down shirt. But the neck tattoo gave it away. He was definitely the man I'd seen earlier with the smartphone. The one who'd looked straight at me. With a closer view of him I could see a mole on his right cheek, and he was heavily tanned, making his black hair appear even darker. He had a thin, pinched mouth, almost as if he didn't have any lips, so that his mouth looked more like an open wound. It went against my instincts, but I guessed that he could only be an eye for Dell and the feds, though he really didn't look like any kind of federal agent I'd ever seen.

Christine strode ahead toward the exit, her arms swinging as she walked.

I stopped in front of the man in the black coat. Guy stank. Nicotine stains on his index finger. He must've been going through a couple of packs a day at least. Placing my files on the floor beside me, I put one knee on the ground and worked at my shoelace. I was maybe three feet from the man in the black coat. I coughed, swore. He didn't look up. I was close enough to his personal space for anyone to open their eyes, lift their head, and check what the hell I was doing. He didn't move. At this distance I could make out the tattoo on his neck. The image tattooed onto his flesh was at once familiar and yet still remained strange to me no matter how many times I saw it: a man, or a ghost of a man – his body was fluid and formed in curves that accentuated the oval head, hands clasped over his ears and mouth open. It was *The Scream*, the painting by Munch.

He didn't look at me and I was glad. I didn't want to see those black eyes again. The thought of it gave me a dry mouth.

While I opened my laces, I watched the guy in the green jacket approaching me from behind. Before he passed, he disconnected the earpiece, folded the wire, and stuffed it into his right jacket pocket. The phone went into the left pocket. From his reflection I could see him watching me. His pace increased as he got closer. He planned to walk straight past me.

I got up quickly and moved to my right, straight into his path. My right shoulder hit him just under his left arm. He stumbled, and I grabbed him, steadying him before he fell. Eyes wide, he looked at me in total surprise and embarrassment.

'Oh, jeez, sorry, pal. Damn laces. You okay?' I said.

'Don't worry about it,' he mumbled, and walked straight out the door without stopping. It was him all right, the firm's chief of security – Gill.

The man in the black coat with the tattoo, even with the noise of the collision just feet away from him, didn't raise his head.

I followed Gill out of the front doors and saw Christine propped up against one of the pillars, heel tapping on the stone, one arm across her chest, eyes on the traffic.

Gill walked past her and half ran down the stone steps.

I tucked his cell phone into my coat pocket and joined Christine.

CHAPTER TWENTY-FIVE

'I know what this is about,' said Christine, nodding.

She still wasn't looking at me. The wind picked up and blew the lapels of her jacket. She hugged herself and blinked through the cold, holding her jaw tightly closed so that her teeth wouldn't chatter. I thought she must have been so pissed off at Sinton's PA that she'd run out of the office without even grabbing her coat. Her eyes watered, and I wondered if it was from the easterly wind blowing through the man-made canyons of Manhattan, or because of the life that we'd once had, and lost. Seeing her, smelling her, listening to her voice and knowing that right then we weren't together – it was like grieving.

At that moment, I had a strong urge to lean on David, to save her. I resisted; it was a false hope and a foul thought. With the right moves, I could save them both.

There was no anger in her voice. She spoke softly. 'It's not like you, but deep down I think you're jealous, Eddie. You think now that I've got a career, I might not want you, or maybe that I don't need you. You don't have to feel that way.'

'This isn't about us. Something bad is going on in your firm. I can't discuss it here. Do me a favor. Don't go back to work. Get Amy and disappear for a couple of days.'

'Don't be ridiculous. This is Harland and Sinton you're talking about.'

This was the worst place to have this conversation. I didn't know who was around, listening. I couldn't risk telling her any more. She swung toward me, and I could see the disappointment building in her gaze. Whatever progress we'd made in the last few weeks, she thought I was throwing that away by being stupid.

'I'm asking you to trust me. I'll explain everything tonight.'

'No, you won't. This ends here and now. Send the client back to Gerry Sinton and then we'll talk,' she said.

'I can't. Trust me, this . . .' My voice fell away as her hand dipped into her bag and came out holding a ring. Her wedding ring. I wore mine every day. Never took it off. She'd stopped wearing her ring a long time ago.

'After you left the other night, I put this on. Just for a few minutes. I wanted to know how it felt.'

I said nothing, just tried to stop myself from taking her in my arms.

'It felt good, you know? Like when we were first married. I'd stopped wearing it because it reminded me of all the bad times. Now I can put it on and think that there might be something in the future – something good, for us and Amy. I put it in my bag and I've been carrying it around. I don't want to have to put it back in a drawer, Eddie. Send the client back to the firm, please. For us,' she said, pushing herself off the pillar and heading for the street.

Ignoring me as I called after her, she held out a hand to hail a cab. A taxi driver stopped and she got into the cab and left.

A digital chime sounded.

I checked my cell, but there were no messages, no texts, and no e-mails.

Scanning the crowd for faces as I moved, I turned my back to the street and carefully checked the phone I'd taken from Gill. It was a burner, Nokia, cheap, no GPS, no trace.

There was one new text message.

I clicked on 'open message.'

We're outside.

There was no name beside the message, just a cell number. It was, however, the second message in a text conversation. The first message had been sent three minutes ago.

A single statement. Three words that sent a ripple through my spine that lodged itself at the base of my neck like a block of ice. I gripped the phone so hard I almost cracked the screen.

Kill the wife.

CHAPTER TWENTY-SIX

Christine's cab had disappeared into traffic. The guy in the green jacket was nowhere to be seen. I turned and sprinted back into the courthouse, bumped my way through the security line and saw that the bench was empty. The man in the long black coat had left.

Fingers shaking, I dialed Christine's cell from the phone Dell had given me. If I'd used my own, she wouldn't answer.

The phone rang. No answer. I let it ring.

I began pacing the floor.

Two rings. I ran to a bank of pay phones in the corridor next to the inquiries office.

Oh Jesus, Christine, pick up the damn phone.

Three rings. Blood rushed to my face, and I felt my chest filling, drawing my shirt tight, but I had no breath. I sucked at the air like I was drowning and slammed a fist into the wall.

Voice mail.

I hung up, dialed again.

'Christine White,' she said. She hadn't mentioned she'd reverted to her maiden name.

'It's me. Don't hang up. You're in danger. Where are you?'

'What? Eddie?' She heard the urgency in my voice, the high pitch as I forced the words through my juddering breath.

'Where are you?'

'I'm in a cab on Centre Street. What's wrong? Is it Amy?'

I heard the first tremors of fear in her voice; she spoke fast, and she knew I was serious.

'No, it's *you*. Tell the cab driver to change lanes, as if he's turning right on Walker Street. Then ask him to check if any cars follow you into the lane. Do it now.'

'You're scaring me. If this is some kind of—'

'Do it now!'

'All right,' she said, and I heard her giving instructions to the cab driver. I couldn't quite make out what he was saying, but she repeated the instruction, forcefully.

'Did you get a death threat? I've got a right to know, and why the hell didn't you tell me this five minutes ago?'

'Christine, don't ask. Not now. I'll explain later. Have you changed lanes?'

'Yeah, we've moved to the outside. Exactly what am I supposed to be looking – wait,' she said.

The driver mumbled something and Christine replied. I couldn't make it out.

Then I heard the driver say, 'Blue sedan, three cars back.'

'Tell him to move back into his original lane, like you've changed your mind and you're going back to the office.'

She gave the instruction.

'What's going on?' she said.

'Did the sedan follow?'

The rumble of tires on the asphalt, a distant horn.

The driver again: 'There he goes, lady. We've got a tail.'

'Oh my God. What is this? What have you done?'

'I'll explain later. You're in danger. The guys in that car are going to hurt you, understand? Now, do exactly what I tell you.'

She was crying now. The driver tried to calm her.

'I'm calling the police,' she said, fear rippling through her voice.

'No, do not—'

The line went dead.

CHAPTER TWENTY-SEVEN

I called her back, but it went straight to voice mail. I called her again. Nothing.

My head spun. What the hell was I going to do? She was too far away for me to make it to her in time. I redialed.

'Eddie, I've got the police on the other line. We're going to pull over and wait for a patrol car.'

'No! Do not pull over. If the cab stops, you're dead. Do you hear me? Tell the driver to keep going. Where are you exactly?'

'On Walker. Wait . . .' I heard her talking to the driver.

'He wants me to wait for the cops.'

'Put me on speaker.'

I heard the radio and the driver in midsentence.

'Hey, if you pull over, the men in the sedan will get out, and they will kill you and my wife before the cops get to the street. You want to live? Do exactly as I say.'

'Okay, Jesus, what do I do?' said the driver.

'What's your name?'

'Ahmed.'

'Okay, Ahmed, you should be coming up on a junction with Baxter. When you get there, take a left and floor it.'

'Coming up,' he said.

'Hold on,' I said.

I don't know if Christine even heard me. She didn't say anything.

'Deep breaths, you're nearly there. You can do it. Talk to me. Tell me where you are.'

'We're passing the supermarket. Traffic's backing up. We're stopping.'

Her clothes rustled, and I guessed she was turning around, checking behind her.

'Face front, honey. I don't want them getting nervous and jumping you in traffic.'

'Wait . . .' A dull thud. 'They're right behind us. Light's still red. Oh Jesus . . .'

'Hold it together,' I said.

'They're getting out of the car!' yelled Christine.

'Get down,' I cried.

I heard the roar of the engine and Ahmed, 'Those guys have guns.'

'We're moving. We're moving, thank God,' Christine said.

'Stay down. You ready, Ahmed?'

'Oh shit, wait. Baxter is one-way; I can't turn,' he said.

'That's exactly why you're going to turn. Floor it, hit the horn the whole way. It's the only chance you've got.'

I heard the revs go through the roof. Christine let out a whimper. All I could do was listen to her wet, heavy breaths and pray. The cab was accelerating and braking, the throaty murmur of the engine followed by tire squeal and the heavy beat of the horn. Ahmed weaving through oncoming traffic.

'They haven't made the turn,' said Ahmed.

Glass breaking, metal shearing. Christine screaming. A huge *thump*. The horn stopped beating and instead blew out a long, slow note.

CHAPTER TWENTY-EIGHT

My cell phone sat still in my hand, silent. I checked to make sure that my phone was clear of calls and I stared at the home screen, willing it to ring. I called her – no answer.

I dialed, got her voice mail. Hung up. Again. Nothing. Again.

As if I was surfacing from deep water, the sound of my blood thumping in my veins was replaced with the noise from the court-house lobby. I'd tuned it out when I'd gone into panic mode. I heard the soft beeps from the bag scanner, the sound of rubber soles squeaking on the toughened-rubber tile floor, the *ping* of elevators, the electric pump firing the coffee machine across the hall, the nervous chatter of witnesses and the fake laughs from their lawyers, all drowned out by the occasional burst of incoherent, cryptic static that passed for an announcement from the PA system.

My cell stared at me, stoically mute. I stepped past the phones, checked the full length of the lobby. Still no sign of the man in the black coat or Gill. Crossing my legs, I let my left shoulder grab the wall as I checked my phone again. Nothing. I held the phone up a little, to let the casual observer think I was checking my messages, letting my peripheral vision do its work. Nobody else stood out, but that wasn't to say there wasn't anyone around with a pair of eyes on me.

I felt the ring before I heard it.

'Christine?' I said.

Running. Panting. She was barely able to speak. Pushing hard.

'I'm okay. I don't see them. Driver is okay. What do I do?'

'Are you still on Baxter?'

'Yes.'

'Run back the way you came, past the accident. Cross the street and jump into the nearest cab. Don't look behind you. Just run.'

Feet pounding. Soft flutters in her throat.

'I'm across the street. I see a cab waiting.'

'Stop running. Put your shoes on. Get in. They'll be trying to cut you off. They'll hit Baxter by heading toward Canal Street, making a left, and coming toward you from Hester. They won't be able to get down Baxter Street because of the accident. Get in the cab and tell the driver to make for the Manhattan Bridge.'

Nothing.

A car door opening. Christine getting in, giving instructions to the driver.

'I'm in. We're moving.'

My head sank against the cool wall. It felt good, easing my system down. I let Christine catch her breath. When she did, she called me out.

'You wanted the driver to crash,' she said.

'I did. I knew they wouldn't follow you. I guessed they'd want to loop around and cut you off at Hester. They can't now. Traffic is backed up on Baxter now because of your accident. Is Ahmed okay?'

'Yeah. I think so. We hit another cab. Pretty low speed. Everyone is okay, but the cars are totaled. Will they hurt him?'

'No. Too many witnesses now. This is New York. There'll be twenty people around that accident scene already.'

I checked the phone I'd taken off Gill and found that it had locked itself. It asked me for a four-digit code. Placing the phone in my pocket, I breathed in and closed my eyes. She told me there was no sign of the sedan. She'd made it.

'I have to get Amy,' she said, and broke down.

'Listen to me. Call your sister. Tell her to get Amy from school right now. Find a motel in Red Hook, close to the freeway.'

'I have to call the office, tell them I won't be back today.'

'No. You can't. Listen to me. This is gonna sound crazy . . .'

CHAPTER TWENTY-NINE

I told her everything. I told her about the share agreement with her signature on it. She half remembered witnessing the agreement for Ben Harland, who'd told her that he had a family emergency – something about his daughter – and could Christine witness the signature. She'd thought nothing of it at the time. I told her about Dell and the task force. I went into basics about the firm, their history, their financials, and then David. I didn't tell her about the evidence against him. No need. I told her I believed he was innocent. That was enough.

When I'd finished, I could hear her swallowing down the tears, the nerves vibrating through her throat. She whispered into the handset, keeping the conversation from the cab driver.

'A guy followed me today in the courthouse. His name is Gill. He's the firm's head of security. I bumped his phone, which had a text message on it, ordering him to kill you. Your bosses are scared, and they don't want me representing David Child. I suppose they figured if they murdered you, I wouldn't be able to continue with the case. Seems a hell of a way to take out the competition.'

She breathed out again, the tension sending a trembling whistle through her breath.

'They'd kill me to get you off a case?'

'This guy can hurt them. They want to be able to control David, make sure he doesn't make a deal with the cops that would shorten his sentence in exchange for bringing down the firm,' I said.

'What does he have on the firm?'

'One of the firm's money handlers, Farooq, got caught by police in the Cayman Islands. The firm had been laying off the personnel that do their laundry; they'd found a safer way to clean the cash.

The firm killed the informant before he could testify. A federal task force found out the firm is using David Child's anti-hacker security system to clean the money. They can push a button and millions disappear from their client accounts, spiraling through thousands of accounts, in hundreds of banks, before it lands, clean, in a secure account.'

'This is all my fault. He told me they'd already completed due-diligence checks,' said Christine.

'I'm not blaming you. I mean, your boss, who's a goddamn blue-chip legend, sets a document in front of you and tells you it's kosher – well, anybody would just accept that. It's not your fault. It's Ben Harland and Gerry Sinton's fault. We've just got to deal with it.'

'What have I done? I'm sorry. I'll go to the FBI. I'll testify.'

'No. Let me handle it. You stay low with Amy and let me figure this out. I think there's a way to get the information Dell wants. David says he might be able to trace the algorithm that moves the money. I don't know. If he can't, I have to rethink things.'

'If you believe he's innocent, you can't let him take a plea. Not for me. Promise me you won't do that, Eddie.'

'I promise. I need time to think.'

'My battery is getting low,' she said.

'Look, you can't go back to work. And I know that means Harland and Sinton will believe you know something, but that doesn't matter anymore; they've already called the hit.'

'And what is it you're going to do?'

My head fell forward, my eyes taking in my shoes, like I was bringing this thought up from the floor.

'I'm going to help David in whatever way I can. I'm going to try to help him get what Dell wants, then I'm going to make a deal with the feds for your immunity and his.'

'But it's murder. They can't let him walk if they think he shot and killed his girlfriend.'

I rubbed my chin and said, 'I think there might be a way around that, but you're my priority here.'

'I can't have an innocent man in jail because of me. Could you live with that?' she said.

Right then I didn't have an answer, but I knew it might come down to that choice. My father was a bookie and a grifter, but he'd never lifted money from a straight guy, never hustled anyone unless they had it coming, and never took a bet from somebody who couldn't afford to lose. When my dad taught me all the tricks of a first-class canon, he also told me never to use those skills to harm 'the little guy,' as he put it.

Because, son, we're the little guy.

I'd been a con man, using my father's skills, keeping his code, taking down scores from the worst insurance companies, from drug dealers, from the vilest lowlifes that I could find. And I'd slept like a baby. It was only when I became a lawyer that I had trouble sleeping. The line was never clear – and I'd paid for that by trying to ignore it. I'd vowed never to do that again. Even Popo and I scamming the city lawyer fund helped keep my lights on and kept the pro snitch alive. The city could afford it. We couldn't afford not to take it.

'If the firm is willing to kill me, what are they prepared to do to you?' she said.

'I can watch my own back. You know that.'

'I'll get Amy safe, and I'll call you from a motel. I've got to go before the battery dies. Be careful, Eddie,' she said, and hung up.

Vibration from the cell phone Dell had given me. A text from him:

Disclosure in the Child case is ready for collection at the DA's Office.

I was pretty sure it would only add to the evidence against David, and Dell wanted me to see it ASAP. He didn't want me fighting for David. He wanted me to believe he was guilty. Whatever was in the disclosure had to be bad news.

CHAPTER THIRTY

Child moved fast across the hall. His blond PA, Holly, was almost running to keep up with him, her shorter legs a blur next to Child's long, deliberate stride. She was dressed in jeans and a sweater and carried a cell phone in one hand and an iPad in the other, each device chiming every few seconds with a new message of some kind. On Child's right, Gerry Sinton. The big man walked with a hand on his client's shoulder. He could not disguise his contempt when he saw me. I wondered when he'd realized that it was Popo who was at the hospital and not David. Maybe when he got there.

I stepped in front of them and saw barely disguised relief on Child's face.

'I can't thank you enough,' said David, to me.

'Don't mention it,' said Sinton.

My face screwed up into a 'really, Gerry?' kind of expression. David covered his mouth and suppressed a nervous giggle. Bail joy. But as relieved as Child appeared, I could see the fear cracking through the smile.

'So what happens this afternoon?' asked David.

'We start the prelim, our first shot at testing the prosecution's case.'

'I thought we agreed to waive the preliminary hearing? This is a case that has to be won at trial. And even if by some miracle you prove at the prelim that the prosecution doesn't have enough evidence, the prosecutor can still take it to the grand jury for indictment,' said Sinton.

Essentially, in a felony case, the prosecution gets two bites of the cherry. If they don't prove to a judge that there's enough probable cause for the charge during a preliminary hearing, they can always take the same case to the grand jury: thirty members of the public who decide if there's enough evidence to indict the defendant – they only hear from the prosecutors, not the defense lawyers, and ninety-nine times out of a hundred, the prosecutor gets their indictment.

'Let me worry about the grand jury. It's one fight at a time. Right now we need to start attacking the prosecution's case. If David's innocent, like he says, he'll want to fight it the whole way,' I said.

'Eddie's right,' said David. 'The media is going to get ahold of this case at some point, and I want them to know I'm fighting it on every possible level.'

'Of course,' said Sinton. 'It's just, I have to tell you, David, the evidence against you is substantial.'

'Let's not debate this, Gerry. Get on the team,' I said.

A curt nod of the head was all I got from Sinton. David smiled again and shook my hand. When he released his grip, he palmed the business card I'd slipped him in the handshake and shoved his hand into his pants pocket. On the card I'd written instructions on how to meet the Lizard.

If Child had held up his end of the deal, he'd told Sinton that he was going to a hotel, but he would change direction, get out of a cab on Fifth Street and into a blue van – with the Lizard at the wheel. I'd meet them later at Holly's apartment.

'Prelim starts at four o'clock. I'll meet you back here at three,' I said to David, and watched him and Holly leave the courthouse and get into a cab. Gerry Sinton watched him too.

'You didn't go to the hospital, Flynn,' said Sinton.

'I only found out about the mix-up after you left. Otherwise I would've told you. Sorry. I didn't know your cell number.'

He stood back and looked me up and down.

'We're supposed to be on the same team. We both want what's best for David, don't we?'

I nodded and wondered what David had told him when they'd met just minutes before. Whatever it was, I was still co-counsel.

'I don't want you at the prelim,' said Sinton. 'I think you need to reconsider the arrangement. You have no idea who you're dealing with. The last person to cross me got burned pretty bad.'

All I could do was imagine the acid-soaked corpse of Farooq, the informant.

'Perhaps you should call your wife. Take some advice from her and walk away while you still can.' A tremor rippled over his cheek. When he spoke again, with no small amount of pleasure on his face, I knew Gerry Sinton didn't have to justify his actions to himself, and it wasn't that he simply didn't care about breaking the law and hurting people. Sinton enjoyed his work. He enjoyed threatening me, he enjoyed stealing vast sums of money, and he enjoyed taking the lives of those who stood in his way.

'I'm going back to the office. I'm sure I won't see you later, so please give a message to your wife – from me. Tell her she can't put taxi fares on her expenses.'

Like most big men, Sinton had a thick jaw. One centimeter in front of the ear, the temporomandibular joint. A flash punch to that sweet spot would shatter even the heaviest jaw like glass. I thought about this as a black Mercedes pulled up at the curb and ferried Sinton away without another word.

The only way to remove the threat to David and Christine was to get the prosecution case against David thrown out. The threat of a conviction put the heat on David, and my involvement with him put both their lives at risk. If the evidence against David got thrown out, he was no longer under pressure to give up the firm. Most dispositions, or plea agreements, happened before the prelim. That's why Gerry wanted to skip that process and remove the incentive to make a deal.

Walking back through security, I put the phone I'd taken off of Gill into an envelope and left it at the security desk. Exiting the building, I sent a text message to Lester Dell and told him to pick up the phone. Outside the courthouse the street was teeming with people. Midday in Manhattan. I lost myself in a large, fast crowd.

CHAPTER THIRTY-ONE

I grabbed a cup of coffee from a diner and took up a table in the back, close to the window. It would've been difficult to follow me on foot, considering I'd taken a number of detours. Even so, I checked the window every few moments, making sure I didn't have a set of eyes on me. A cinder-block sky hung above the buildings, contemplating rain. The coffee was hot and strong.

From the cell phone the feds had given me, I dialed Dell's number. He didn't even say hello.

'I saw Gerry Sinton put your client into a cab not twenty minutes ago. I thought we had an understanding. I thought we were clear: Get me a plea, the algorithm, and Child's testimony against the firm and we let the charges against your wife slide.'

'I told you, I'll get what you need without putting David's head on a block. Did you get the phone?'

'I got it. Where did you get it?'

'Took it off of Gill. There's a message on it ordering him to kill my wife.'

'Jesus, is she okay? Where is she?'

'She's safe. For now. The phone can put you closer to Sinton – I imagine that text came from him. That's an attempted murder charge, right there.'

'I'll get my tech on it right now. That's interesting. The firm wants you off the case by any means possible. We're close. But make no mistake – I'm not interested in nailing Sinton for attempted murder; the feds can have him on that. My job is to hurt the firm's clients – the drug lords, the arms dealers, the terrorists. To do that I need to trace the money.'

'I'll do whatever it takes, but I want Christine and David in return.'

He sighed.

'You ever truly lose somebody?' he said.

I thought of my parents. They died pretty young, before their time, certainly.

'It's like a hole, Eddie. You can't replace what's gone – but you can try to fill it with other things. New things. You can try to make it right. The firm took Sophie from me, and I need to make it right. I can do that. But think about the other victim here. Clara Reece is found lying in David's apartment with two mags of ammo in the back of her head. If I let him off a murder charge to get what I want, I'm just digging another hole. I won't go down that road. I can't. You shouldn't either. You got my text earlier – the DA has additional evidence for the prelim. Read it and tell me David Child is innocent.'

I saw through Dell's game. It was a familiar one. It's a game the justice system plays every single day in America – because sometimes it simply doesn't matter if you're really innocent of the crime; the only smart move is to plead guilty and make a deal for a lesser sentence.

'You want me to read the new evidence and tell David that irrespective of his innocence, he will definitely be convicted and his only choice is to plead guilty and make a deal to cut his sentence.'

'Bingo,' said Dell.

Happens all the time. I've done it myself. Innocent people often don't want to take the chance of losing and doing fifteen or twenty years when they could make a deal and be out in two. It's mathematics – not justice, but that's the reality.

'I'll look it over, but I'm not sure I can convince David. I'll need the GSR expert to testify at the prelim. That will help.'

'How come? Aren't expert reports just handed in at this stage? I mean, I don't see how that helps.'

He was right. At a prelim, experts weren't required to give evidence under oath unless there was a damn good reason. Their reports were simply put in front of the judge, without being tested under cross-examination.

'It's for Child. It's a convincer. One of the strongest pieces of evidence is the GSR on his skin and clothes. If the report is handed in, it has no real effect on Child. On the other hand, if the expert testifies, and I don't have shit to counter his testimony, it sinks Child even further and puts the pressure on him.'

'I see your point. I'll call the DA. This kid needs to realize making a deal is his only shot. You do, too. You should eat something. It's going to be a long day. I hear the blueberry pancakes in there are pretty good.'

Before I could reply, the call disconnected. No cars parked in the street, nobody resembling Dell on the sidewalk. Damn, he was good. I resigned myself to the idea that CIA operatives are seen only if they want to be. The waitress asked me if I wanted anything else. I ordered the blueberry pancakes.

I was relying on Dell to persuade the DA to call their GSR expert. I didn't have a chance of winning the prelim if I couldn't even get a shot at cross-examining the guy. But right then I couldn't think of a single point to put to the witness. It would come. If David was innocent, sooner or later, the ammo I needed to prove that would come to me.

While I waited for my order, I opened my copy of Dell's file and began leafing through the documents. The first batch consisted of share transfer agreements, all of them witnessed by associates at Harland and Sinton. I counted forty-plus agreements, including the one that had been witnessed by Christine.

Behind those papers was a typed list of companies. I counted thirty per page and eighteen pages. None of the companies were familiar. The list was in alphabetical order, and I flicked back to check on the name of the company in Christine's agreement. This was the information they'd gotten from Farooq. Dell's team in Langley must've been monitoring these company accounts. That's how they figured out the new laundry system.

The only other documents were photographs of Harland and Sinton's security team. I lingered on the photograph of Gill that I'd seen before.

Four more photographs behind that one. The firm's security team. Group shots of five men. Two of them wore black suits, white shirts, dark ties and had sensible corporate haircuts. The other two wore civilian clothes: button-down shirts tucked into jeans.

There were no pictures of the man in the black overcoat with the screaming man tattooed on his neck.

After a few minutes of being transferred around, I finally managed to have my call placed to a nurse at the Downtown ER. Popo was out of surgery – but still in critical condition. When the pancakes arrived I had no appetite, but I still took a bite. Lester Dell was right about one thing – the pancakes were excellent.

I sat for a while, thinking things over. In the corner of the diner were two PCs flashing the words 'INSERT COIN.' I lifted my coffee and moved to one of the computer terminals. There was a slot beside my knees, and I fed it a couple of dollars' worth of change. The screen changed and brought up the Google homepage. I typed in 'Bernard Langhiemer' and hit search.

At first the search came back with a ton of results for some other guy with a slightly different name. I hit the option to search for the exact spelling of the name and got back six thousand results – all in German. To narrow down the results, I typed 'David Child' together with 'Bernard Langhiemer' and pressed return.

One article from a tech blog came up first, showing positive results for both names. The piece was on dot-com companies, specifically why certain social media platforms took off and why some simply failed. I didn't follow this stuff myself – I wasn't on any social media – but I knew how it worked. A small section of the article looked at a social media platform called Wave and compared it to Reeler. According to the article, Wave was the brainchild of Bernard Langhiemer. It launched two weeks after Reeler, and a year later it shut down. The author figured that Reeler was more user friendly, less sophisticated than Wave, and it had gotten there first. All of which contributed to the failure of Langhiemer's project. I scrolled through another half dozen pages, but they were all in German and related to ancient family trees.

There was nothing online about any fallout between Langhiemer and David, and nothing I found indicated Langhiemer could be a threat to anyone. I thought David had probably made a bad call if he thought Langhiemer had set him up. The guy seemed vanilla enough.

I took a minute to log into my e-mail. Nothing urgent. I logged out, gathered my files, paid the check, and headed for the door.

I heard the chiming from my personal cell and hoped it would be Christine. The caller ID told me the number was unavailable.

'Hi,' I said.

'Do you mind telling me what you're doing,' said the voice on the other end of the line. Male, early thirties, maybe a trace of the Midwest in the accent.

'Who is this?' I said.

'Bernard Langhiemer.'

CHAPTER THIRTY-TWO

I looked around the diner. No one was paying any attention to me. I decided it was safer on the street, so I left and headed back downtown.

'How did you get this number?' I said.

'So, you *are* investigating me,' he said, spitting out the sentence through his teeth.

'I didn't say that.'

'Oh, you did. Don't try to fool me, Mr Flynn. I know you searched for me. What I want to know is why.'

I couldn't understand how he had traced me so fast from a single search in an Internet café. Then I remembered that I'd checked my e-mail. Maybe he'd found me through that. There was no mileage in playing this guy, so I cut through the dance and went straight to it.

'I want to meet,' I said.

In the background I could hear a female voice. Somebody shouting at Langhiemer, 'Hang up. No calls.'

I head a rasp on the mike and a muffled male voice. Langhiemer had put his hand over the phone to say something he didn't want me to hear. Maybe the voice was his girlfriend, but it was a strange choice of words. It stuck with me.

When he spoke again, his voice was clear and had lost none of the anger.

'And what would we discuss? The minimal amount of money in your firm's client account? Your overdraft? Maybe your fondness for paperback crime novels or the fact that you always have breakfast at Ted's Diner? I can go on . . .'

'You're fast, Mr Langhiemer. Real fast. If only you'd been quicker launching Wave, you might be rich by now. Too bad David Child beat you to it.'

'So this is about David, I see. I'll be in touch,' he said, and disconnected the call.

I stared at my phone in disbelief. Bernard Langhiemer just became real interesting.

Christine's older sister, Carmel, had picked up Amy from school and joined her at a bed-and-breakfast just off the 245 in Red Hook. Amy was shaken. She was quiet and would not let go of Christine. Seven months ago she'd been taken by the Russian mob, and although she'd not been physically hurt, the damage had been done. Her recovery was steady, but slow, and this was all too much for her. Christine cried on the phone. I fought down the urge to go to them, to hold them both. Whatever it took, I needed to get them the hell out of New York – someplace safe, someplace far away, where no one would look for them.

'Eddie, I'm scared,' said Christine.

'I'll fix this. I'm going to make sure you are all okay. I love you.'

She sighed, and I heard the emotion thicken her voice. 'I . . . Don't let anyone hurt you,' she said, and clicked off.

I stepped to the curb in Foley Square and headed for the DA's office at 1 Hogan Place. Security in the building was tight, and while I was there, I was in no immediate danger.

I took the elevator to the reception area of the district attorney's office. The receptionist was an old guy by the name of Herb Goldman. Herb had seen a dozen district attorneys come and go in his time. His steel-gray hair framed a liver-spotted face that was almost as old as the building.

'Come to give yourself up, Eddie?' asked Herb.

'I surrender, Herb. Guilty of being a defense attorney. Do I wait here for the blindfold and the firing squad?'

'You can sit on the stained couch over there while I find whatever dumb schmuck has agreed to talk to you. Who are you lookin' for?'

'Julie Lopez.'

Herb's eyes shot up a little as he picked up the phone and called an internal number.

'He's here,' he said.

Replacing the receiver, he told me to take a seat and I would be seen shortly.

It was coming up on one thirty p.m. Two and a half hours until the prelim started.

I barely got a chance to sit down before the district attorney himself, Michael Zader, kicked open the door and said, 'Flynn, this way,' before turning and storming back into the cavernous office.

Herb chuckled and, making sure Zader had disappeared through the door, he put his hands together, made a *wuzz* noise, and pretended to stab me with a lightsaber. The DA got a lot of shit because his surname sounded like a character from *Star Wars*. Nobody, not even Herb, would do it to his face anymore.

The outer office housed fifty of the top assistant district attorneys in the city. It was open plan, with no desk dividers, and the ADAs sat in clusters of four, facing one another. Zader encouraged his staff to discuss their cases in the office, bounce their opening and closing statements off of one another, give feedback and critique, learn from it and be better. Zader had made advocacy coaching mandatory at two hours a week and spent around five percent of his budget on the tutors. Conviction rates had begun to rise as a result. He was a real student of the courtroom and had risen through the ADA ranks like wildfire. After Zader had won his first murder trial in devastating fashion, his colleagues had stopped leaving *Star Wars* toys in his drawers.

We passed Miriam Sullivan's desk, which sat in a corner office beside Zader's, but she wasn't in. I saw the sign on her window, SENIOR ASSISTANT DISTRICT ATTORNEY. She'd run against Zader in the last election and lost, narrowly. Usually the unsuccessful candidate bows out of the prosecution game at that point, but not Miriam. I'd heard that Zader persuaded her to stay and told her that he'd nominate her when he left office in four years; he was already planning his campaign for governor.

I followed him into his office and closed the door behind me. Zader looked like an older male model. He carried less fat than most professional body builders and even though he didn't have their mass, he was plenty ripped. Sleeves rolled up, top button undone beneath a pale blue tie, and black, glossy hair – he looked like he was ready to pose for a catalog.

'Sit,' he said, as he poured himself an orange juice from the bottle he kept in a small fridge beside his desk. No bourbon in this office. He didn't offer me anything.

He sat down and flicked through a file in front of him. The office had a big-screen TV on one wall, and behind him, his shelves were stacked with books on court presentation, instructional DVDs on advocacy, and leather-bound volumes of statute. A laptop and PC in front of him, and no pictures anywhere; Zader was married to the job.

Without taking his eyes from the pages, he said, 'So, who is your connection in justice?'

I said nothing.

'You must have greased a lot of wheels, or handed over a lot of brown envelopes, to land a client like David Child. I was just wondering how you made such a high-level connection, extortion maybe?'

I sighed.

'Just curious how a low-ball lawyer like you got his hands on a big fish like Child?' Only then did he raise his head enough to look at me.

'That's privileged and you know it. I thought Julie was ADA on this case. Why am I talking to you?'

A twitch at the corner of his mouth passed for a smile. Lifting the glass, he took a long drink, draining the OJ and leaving a thick residue of orange pieces clinging to the side.

'I'd offer you a drink, but I don't have any vodka to go with the orange juice.'

Zader was all tactics. All the time. It was common knowledge around the courts that I'd dropped out of practice for a year and hit the booze hard. Nobody else had seen fit to bring it up upon my return a few months ago. It was personal, and most lawyers, even prosecutors, didn't hold any grudges against me. Shit, plenty of lawyers went through AA. No, Zader didn't have a problem with me because I used to be a drunk. He didn't like me purely because I was a competent defense attorney. As far as he was concerned, I was scum.

'I don't drink that much anymore. Anyway, it's a little early for me. I'm here to pick up the discovery in the Child case, not to trade insults. No disrespect.'

'None taken. How's your wife? I hear she's working in a real law firm. Good for her. At least somebody in the house is bringing home good money. Oh, wait, you're separated now. Sorry, I forgot.'

The wooden armrest cracked a little as I gripped it ever more tightly. I didn't need this. I was too close to the edge already without Zader taking potshots at me, trying to piss me off.

I said nothing, simply cocked my head and smiled. A sneer flickered across his features momentarily and was gone as quickly as it had appeared.

Closing the file in front of him, he leaned back in his chair. 'I got your discovery right here. I also got something else sent to my office this afternoon.'

'Flowers from your boyfriend?' I said.

He nodded as if it was game on. I didn't care if he did have a boyfriend, but Zader was the kind of homophobic tight-ass who would be gravely insulted by such a juvenile joke.

Behind him sat another desk, piled high with papers. On top of one stack sat a fat brown envelope. Grabbing it from the top of the pile, he opened it, took out the pages within, and tossed the envelope over his head.

'This is a draft plea agreement for David Child,' he said, waving the agreement in front of him.

I didn't respond.

'To be more precise, Flynn, it's a federal plea agreement. Your client admits to shooting his twenty-nine-year-old girlfriend in cold blood and he gets five years as long as he cooperates fully with federal law enforcement.'

'I haven't seen any agreement,' I said.

'I know,' said Zader. 'You're not going to either.'

Folding the pages in two, he then ripped along the fold, doubled the pages again, and ripped them again, before letting the pieces drift onto his desk as he set his hands on the mahogany.

'Destroying a federal document is an offense. You might've learned that in law school, but I suppose you were too busy doing sit-ups in the gym.'

'It doesn't become an official federal document until it's signed. We're not offering a deal here. I brought you in to tell you that personally. I don't know who you know, or who your client knows, but there's been a lot of pressure put on my office from on high to make sure this deal is signed. I've just read the case file on this murder, and I've rarely seen a more open-and-shut case. Your client is guilty as hell, and I won't be bought. Should it cost me my career, I will not allow a plea bargain in this case.'

'It's not your case. Lopez is ADA on record.'

'Things change, Eddie. Lopez is now second chair. I'm taking this case on personally. Doesn't matter how rich your client is. Doesn't matter how many federal strings he tries to pull. I'm personally going to send him to prison for life for killing that girl.'

'He tells me he's innocent, and actually, I'm starting to believe him. This case must be real shaky if you have to come on board to steady the ship.'

'They all say they're innocent. Read the file and you'll see that this guy is guilty.'

'Sounds like a bluff to me. There's always a deal. You think five years is too light, but if my guy wanted to plead in exchange for ten years, you'd bite his arm off.'

'Eddie, this case cannot be won. If your client wanted to take twenty years, I'd think about it. The way I see it, your client's conviction is written in the stars.'

'What are you talking about?'

'The gods have decreed it. Think about it. Your guy gets hit by another car when he's making his getaway? Then there's the arresting officer – talk about a stroke of luck.'

'Officer Jones?'

'Hell yeah. He's a fifteen-year veteran, although none too bright. He could never make it past the sergeant's exam. This year he decides to call it quits, gets a job in a private security firm guarding engineers for an oil company in Iraq. And on his last day in the NYPD, he arrests your client, makes the biggest bust of his career – even though he didn't know it at the time he pulled your guy in.'

'I don't believe in fate,' I said.

'I do,' said Zader. 'And this afternoon I'm gonna seal your client's fate.'

'Who are you calling first? The IO?'

A light went off behind his eyes.

'I'm going to call the GSR expert as the first witness. I could just submit his report, but I want the judge to hear this evidence because there's no getting around it. I'll sink your case with one witness.'

As he spoke, his fingers lightly brushed his jawline.

A tell.

He'd just lied to me. I felt sure whatever contact Dell had with the DA, he'd managed to persuade him to call the GSR expert, but for different reasons than Zader just gave me. Being a DA is not about results. It's about the PR you get with those results. Sure, he'd improved the figures, but anyone can massage the numbers. He was smart enough to know that he needed a high-profile murder to put his face on the national news. The Child case was his dream come true. If he kicked off the prelim with incontrovertible expert evidence that he puts before the world's media, he's golden come the state elections. Instead of handing over a report to a judge, he would put on a show for the cameras.

'I'm gonna have your client's head on a plate, and I want him to know that.'

A knock on the door. Miriam Sullivan came into Zader's office carrying a man's suit covered in clear plastic. Fresh from the dry cleaner's, just for the cameras. She was dressed in a business suit and had cut her hair short since I'd last seen her.

She laid the suit on a chair in front of the TV and left without a word.

'If you don't mind, I've got a press conference in twenty minutes,' said Zader.

I took the copy of the file from him and closed the door to his office on my way out.

I paused at the open door to Miriam's office.

'You collect dry cleaning now?' I said.

She shook her head. Took off her glasses and stroked the red grooves at the top of her nose. Miriam was a forty-year-old attractive but deadly courtroom operator who prosecuted her cases with a cold-blooded detachment that gave her the edge over most of her opponents.

'Don't, Eddie.'

'I'm not here to gloat, Miriam. You should be in that office, as DA. You're better than him. You sure as hell shouldn't let him treat you like that. It's disgusting.'

'You've never tried a case against Zader, have you?'

'Can't say that I have.'

'Watch him. He could've fired me. He didn't. He wanted me to stay on so he could humiliate me for running against him for the DA's office. He's vindictive, he's calculating, and he cheats. Come to think of it, he's a little like you.'

'I'm flattered.'

'Don't be,' she said, then leaned forward and whispered, 'I'm taking his shit because I'm recording all of it, diary entries, photos, and video. I'm building a world-class sex discrimination case.'

'You need a lawyer?'

'Why, do you know a good one?'

She held her phone in front of the dry-cleaning receipt, took a photo, and winked.

'Be careful. Zader doesn't play by the rules. He's lost only a couple of cases in his entire career, and they were years ago, when he was just learning the ropes. I'm preparing for the day when he gets tired of his little game. He's trying to make me quit. I won't. I'm waiting him out, and when he decides it's easier to fire me, I'll have enough evidence to get a great settlement, provided I don't sue for harassment. You see, I think the only way to beat Zader is to let him think he's won. Good luck, Eddie. Make sure you kick his ass this afternoon.'

'I will,' I said.

By the time I'd waved goodbye to Herb at the reception desk, I already regretted the lie to Miriam – truth was, I had no possibility of winning the case.

CHAPTER THIRTY-THREE

Dell picked up my call on the third ring. I was back in a yellow cab, headed the long way around the city, making sure I hadn't been followed before I made my way to Holly's apartment.

'The DA is taking the plea off the table. Didn't even let me read the damn agreement. Before you say anything, no, I don't think he's bluffing for more jail time for Child. Why would he? Zader is an ambitious son of a bitch, and this case will be front-page news all over the world. This is Zader's ticket up the ladder, and he wants it played out in front of the cameras.'

Silence.

'You there?'

'I'm here. Don't worry about Zader. I got that covered. You just get me my plea.'

'I can't. There's no time. The prelim starts in two hours. Once we start the hearing, the DA won't take a deal. With the press scrutiny on this thing, if the DA makes a deal, it'll look like he's soft on billionaires and hard on the poor. Zader needs to make an example of Child.'

'Are you stupid? I told you I got it covered. Call me when you've got a deal. Five years for murder as long as we get the partners and the money.'

He hung up.

Holly's apartment was in an expensive building just behind Central Park Eleven, where Child lived and where the murder occurred. I flicked through the prosecution file Zader had given to me, closing it after twenty minutes. We were three blocks from Holly's.

I'd read the forensic report from the GSR expert, Dr Henry Porter, and reread every document in the file – crime scene reports, witness statements, crime scene photographs, and computer printouts. Every single piece of evidence looked clean.

And it all proved, beyond any doubt, that David Child was a murderer.

CHAPTER THIRTY-FOUR

There was a statement from the driver of the Ford, a John Woodrow, who'd hit Child at the intersection. He'd seen the gun in the passenger footwell, backed away, and called the cops. Then there was a statement from the crime scene investigator – Rudy Noble – and his take on the murder scene. According to Rudy, the victim was shot twice in the back, paralyzing her. She fell forward onto her face. The shot that broke the window in Child's apartment and alerted his neighbor Gershbaum, was probably fired at the victim as she fell. The CSI supposed that the shot passed through her, took out the window, and the bullet made its way over the balcony into the great blue yonder, never to be recovered. Given the victim's extensive head injuries and the damage to the floor beneath her head, CSI Noble stated that the remainder of the clip had been fired into her skull, that the killer reloaded and then shot the entire second clip into the back of her head, but in reality, most of the bullets were no longer hitting bone or flesh but going straight through into the floor. Given the relationship between the suspect and the deceased and the manner of her death, Rudy Noble proffered the theory that the overkill was a classic indication of a crime committed by a crazed spouse or partner – in this case, David Child. Appended to Noble's report was a scale map of the apartment; a small, shakily drawn figure denoted the body of the victim, found in the kitchen.

Homicide Detective Andy Morgan had made several statements, most of which concerned establishing the chain of custody when he'd taken copies of the CCTV footage from Central Park Eleven and from the traffic camera at the Department of Transport. The detective's main statement concerned his discovery that Child, who lived at the address where Clara Reece's body had been found, was involved in a traffic collision minutes after the body was discovered by the building's security guards.

He went on to say that he'd ordered GSR testing on Child and his clothes and had the tests carried out by an independent GSR expert, to ensure there was no possibility of the samples taken from Child's skin and clothes becoming contaminated. The expert that Morgan had chosen proved to be an interesting angle.

Dr Henry Porter had once been employed by the state's forensic department, but now he was an independent expert. Dr Porter was pretty much unshakable on the stand – a real hard case. None of Porter's testimony had ever been successfully challenged before. He was well known in defense counsel circles as an ironclad expert witness. So when the cops caught the whiff of a high-profile shooting – one that would certainly catch headlines – they consulted the DA and brought in the supposedly independent Dr Porter to boost their case.

Porter's report confirmed the wide presence of highly concentrated gunshot residue on Child's face, hands, arms, and upper body. When somebody pulls the trigger, the little explosion that results from contact between the firing pin and the primer sends a small cloud of gas around the weapon and the bullet. This cloud contains minute particles, like shrapnel, some of which fuse together from the heat. This is gunshot residue. Some of the material can be found on the victim, or on the weapon or the shooter. Experts look for lead, barium, and antimony, or burned combinations of these, which come from the explosion, or fragments from the cartridge or sometimes even the gun itself. The sheer amount of GSR would, in Porter's opinion, be consistent with Child having discharged a firearm on multiple occasions. In the appendices to the report were the graphs showing the concentrations of material found in each sample. The samples from David's skin and clothes looked pretty much the same, but the graph depicting the results of the sample taken from the gun were slightly different; the GSR wasn't as concentrated. When you consider that the material disperses widely from the gun itself, it's easy to see why that might be the case. However, there were other differences. Lead deposits, one of the key indicators of GSR, were found on the gun, but none were found in the results from David's samples. In addition, some of the other non-GSR material found in the samples from David differed from the gun results. Again, not that big a deal. The main problem was that if David was telling the truth, then he shouldn't have had any GSR on him at all.

Porter also offered the theory that the large particles of burned rubber and nylon found in the samples from David could mean that he wore gloves. Some part of that theory jarred a little with me. Felt like the prosecution told Porter to include this in his findings so that they could argue that the lack of fingerprints on the gun recovered from David's car could be explained by the fact that he'd worn gloves.

I remembered that Detective Morgan had asked Child on no less than six occasions if he'd ever owned or fired or been around someone when they were firing a gun. Child said he'd never owned a gun, held a gun, or been around when a gun was fired. Porter's GSR report seemed to give lie to that statement.

The combination of Child's interview answers and Morgan's report pretty much nailed him. When this was coupled with the security footage of Child entering the apartment, then leaving, just before Gershbaum heard the shots and then saw the window blowing out – well, that would be all she wrote.

I thought about Porter's report. The subtle differences in the test results between the GSR on David and the GSR on the gun intrigued me. Often the key to blowing open a case lay in the small details, in the finest of inconsistencies. I just had to figure it out.

CHAPTER THIRTY-FIVE

The Lizard opened the door to Holly's apartment and stuck a Beretta in my face.

'Jesus, if you're not careful you're gonna kill somebody one of these days,' I said.

'The Lizard lives in hope,' said the Lizard.

Dropping the gun to his side, he offered me his free hand. Guy had a grip like a pneumatic press. He'd gotten a new tattoo since I'd last seen him. A bottle-green serpent's tail licked out of the neck of his plain black tee and coiled up to his jawline. He liked reptiles. And for some reason he always referred to himself in the third person. Nobody knew why, and no one had the balls to ask him. Clean-shaven, close-cut dark hair, and zero body fat over a gym-cut physique, the Lizard oozed serious. He was ex-military and had served in Afghanistan and Iraq. When he'd come home, his war had continued, only now he got well paid for it by Jimmy the Hat.

'Any problems losing the tail?' I said.

'None. Cab drove into the alley, they ducked out, turned into the next alley, and got into my van. The cab stayed put, blocking the view and their tail. We got away clean.'

He stepped out of the apartment and checked the corridor as I brushed past him. A powerful chemical smell washed over me as soon as I walked over the threshold. Holly knelt on the wooden floor, furiously scrubbing at a persistent stain. A two-gallon bottle of bleach sat on the kitchen counter above her head, and a mop bucket lay beside a battered, old brown leather chair.

She raised her head from the floor, and I saw her face flushed from her efforts with the scrubbing brush.

'He's got a thing about cleanliness,' she said, and held her palms wide. I figured her new house guest would be pretty hard to live with.

Even though the place probably cost a small fortune in rent, it wasn't exactly big. A small kitchenette on the right, TV, a couch and a leather chair on the left. Beyond the living space was a compact, square dining table surrounded by four chairs. Two doors led into the bathroom and the single bedroom, respectively.

At the dining table, Child punched the keys on his laptop. He hadn't even registered my presence. As I approached him, I noticed half a dozen shopping bags on the floor, all from the same sports store. The bags were filled with new clothes.

I was about to say hi to David when I stopped. Backed up. Picked up one of the bags and looked at him.

He wore a green hooded sweatshirt that looked as though he could fit into it twice. Gray sweatpants hung off of his skinny legs, and he wore a pair of red sneakers. The bags contained several more identical green tops, gray pants, and two more pairs of red Nikes.

I looked at Holly, who rolled her eyes in reply.

This was the exact same outfit the cop described in his statement, which summarized the security camera footage from David's building; the same clothes David had been wearing when he'd been hit by the drunk driver; the same outfit he wore as he sat at the table.

'I can make business decisions in a heartbeat, but I can spend an hour choosing my cereal brand in the morning. When it comes to everyday things, I don't like making . . . choices,' said David, still not looking up from his computer screen. 'I like these clothes. I buy a few of them, and then it's easier in the morning. I don't have to choose. All I have to do is put on the clothes in the correct order.'

I nodded, not really understanding what the right order might be.

A chime echoed from David's laptop. Then another. The chirping alert multiplied, and David began tapping on the cursor pad and running his fingers over it.

'I put an e-mail alert out on my name. Looks like I'm finished,' he said.

He got up and located the remote for the TV, switched it on, and found CNN. His picture, taken on the red carpet of an anonymous awards ceremony. The banner across the bottom of the screen read

FOUNDER AND MANAGING DIRECTOR OF REELER – DAVID CHILD – CHARGED WITH FIRST-DEGREE MURDER.

The volume indicator appeared on-screen and rose as the anchor's voice boomed from the TV.

'. . . District Attorney Michael Zader said that a David Elliott Child has been arrested and charged with murder in the first degree. The victim has been officially named as twenty-nine-year-old Clara Reece. CNN sources believe that Clara Reece was the fiancée of twenty-two-year-old David Child, the billionaire founder of popular social media platform Reeler. No further information has been released at this time, but CNN will be bringing you more on this story as soon as we get it. We hope to have our economics and business analyst report within the hour on how the stock market has been reacting to this news. As you might predict, it's not good for Reeler. In other news, New York Harbor Police have recovered the body of an unidentified male from the East River. The male is said to be in his late sixties . . .'

David killed the power and drew back his arm, ready to throw the remote at the wall.

He stopped himself, held his brow for a time and then placed the control on the couch. He returned to his seat at the table and tried to focus on the screen as his world and his business crumbled around him. Holly stood behind him, put a hand on his shoulder. He didn't flinch, didn't shrug it off, just nodded, and she let go and went back to the kitchen. I'd been warned not to get too close to David when I'd first met him. Dell told me that David had a real issue with people touching him.

He didn't have a problem with Holly. I got the impression they were closer than I'd first realized.

'In the cell, I asked you who might've set you up. You said a name – Bernard Langhiemer. Tell me about him,' I said.

'He's the devil. Langhiemer is probably the only celebrity genius in the tech world who few outside of it know anything about,' said David, looking up from the screen.

'At fourteen he hacked the Chinese Secret Service. He sent every secret agent in China a Christmas e-card. He was never prosecuted, and the Chinese covered it up. They didn't want the embarrassment of admitting that a kid in his bedroom burned their system. The CIA, the FBI, even the Secret Service tried to recruit this guy, but he said no to all of them and went to work on Wall Street. In the city, the speed at which information flows is vital. Langhiemer all but revolutionized the computer systems.'

'And how do you know him?'

He wiped a rueful smile from his lips.

'Within a month or so of Reeler's launch, Langhiemer brought out his own social media platform – Wave. Tell you the truth, it was just as good as Reeler, maybe even a little better – but we were flavor of the month and Wave died. I heard Langhiemer lost a ton of money and blamed me.

'Wave folded, and a few weeks later he tried to buy Reeler. At first he hid behind a group of backers. Then he came out in the open. I turned down all of the offers. When I stopped taking calls, Langhiemer showed up at my apartment.

'I let him up. I was curious to meet him; guy's a legend. He's in his thirties. Hipster beard, tight Armani suit, and he stood in my doorway holding Chinese takeout and a briefcase. We talked a little – who we both knew in the industry, who we liked, who we hated. He didn't like anybody. I didn't eat; neither did he. Then he got up, left the briefcase on the table, and said he'd expect an answer in twenty-four hours.'

'How much money was in the briefcase?' I asked.

'There was no money. Inside was a partnership agreement. In return for selling Reeler, he'd cut me in on his business. If I'd signed, I would own a hefty chunk of the digital world. And I'd be richer than I am now. But I wanted my own company. I don't play well with others. I got mad. Langhiemer thinks he can buy anybody. So I waited until his car pulled up outside my building and threw the agreement off the balcony. I remember him looking up at me. I couldn't see his face; he was too far away. As those pages fell around him like confetti, he sent me a message on Reeler. It said "I will destroy you."'

I pushed my chair away from the table, folded my arms.

'You think this guy set you up?'

'He's got the money, the power. He's done it before – sent illegal images of kids to the computers of high-profile bloggers who posted critical articles about Wave or were trying to orchestrate a campaign to expose the seedier side of his operations. He got away with it, too – the bloggers went to prison. Some of them were trolled so bad on Twitter and Reeler that they committed suicide. The only hits you'll find for Langhiemer on the web are what he permits to be there. I know there's a lot of people I hurt on the way up – I'm not proud of that. But they all got paid. Langhiemer is the only one who hates me enough to do it.'

I told David about my Internet search and the call that came in from Langhiemer minutes afterward.

'The article was probably a fake that he posted to keep an eye on who might be checking up on him. The article itself probably implanted a trace virus allowing him to hack the PC. When you checked your e-mail, he ID'd you and got your bank history, everything. You'd be wise to change your e-mail password and bank accounts.'

'You think he'll meet me?' I asked.

'I don't know. All I know is you should be careful. By the way, I've been working on some trace coding myself. I think I figured out a way to trace the algorithm.'

He pulled a memory stick out of his laptop, 'This program can trace every cent of the firm's money as fast as the algorithm moves it. It can even tell us which account all of the money will pool into when the cycle ends. There's just one thing – we can't use it.'

CHAPTER THIRTY-SIX

'He's been working on that thing since we got here,' said the Lizard. I turned and watched the big man checking the windows.

Holly got to her feet, wiped at the sweat on her forehead, and asked if I wanted coffee.

I did.

'Why can't we use it?' I asked.

David pursed his lips and set the memory stick on the table. He lowered his head and looked at me over the rims of his designer glasses.

'When you tricked your way into representing me, you wanted to make me plead guilty so you could get a deal for your wife, right?' said Child.

He'd been thinking more clearly since he'd gotten out. The panic had left his voice, and he seemed calm and assured. I'd been waiting for him to drop that bomb, waiting for my less-than-ethical methods of becoming his lawyer to be debated. He didn't shout, or sneer, or even look mildly pissed off. It seemed like a neutral question, like he was just putting it out there on the table, matter-of-factly, like he put the memory stick on the table – *there it is.*

'As soon as I realized you were innocent, I came clean. I didn't have to tell you anything, David. In fact, I still can't quite believe that I told you any of it. It's not like me to be so up front with people.'

Shifting my weight between my feet, I suddenly felt uncomfortable. So I dragged a chair out from the table and sat down. The memory stick lay inches from my reach.

'I've been as honest as I can be with anyone. Don't forget, the only reason you're sitting here and not lying dead in the morgue is because of me and Popo.'

He nodded, shifting his gaze to the memory stick. He touched the cushioned speakers on the earphones that hung around his neck, then rubbed his fingers together. A pack of antibacterial wipes were beside the laptop. Peeling off a couple of sheets, he carefully wiped down his fingers.

'I don't know if I can trust you,' he said.

'Maybe not, but I'm not the one trying to kill you.'

A heavy sigh and a shake of the head.

'But you lied to me,' he said.

'I did, and if I hadn't lied, you wouldn't be alive right now. I want my wife cleared, but she was just attacked, and now I'm more worried about her staying alive. They're targeting her because they don't want me to represent you, so they can control the situation and make sure you don't turn state's witness against them in exchange for a small-time sentence.'

'My God, your wife, is she all right?'

'She's safe. For now.'

A white coffee mug appeared in front of me, steam rising off the jet-black brew.

'Cream or sugar?' asked Holly.

'No thanks,' I said.

She looked at David, and he shook his head. They knew each other well enough that she didn't have to ask him if he wanted anything. Their understanding passed between them, unspoken.

The coffee tasted good, rich, and had enough caffeine to wake up a marine platoon. David refilled his glass from a can of energy soda. The liquid looked almost toxic; it was bright blue and fizzed like a science experiment when it hit the ice at the bottom of the glass. I could smell the sugar from it a mile away. He drained half of the soda, smacked his lips, and leaned forward.

'I'm . . . ah, I'm struggling here,' he said, his voice betraying the facade that he'd put up for my arrival. 'I don't know who I can trust. I need help. What I'm saying here is, I want to trust you, but I can't. How do I know you're not just using me to save your wife?'

I considered this for a moment, sighed. Right then I couldn't think of anything better to tell him than the plain God's honest truth.

'Something happened to me a couple years ago,' I began, and David folded his arms, tilted his head. He was curious but guarded.

'I represented a guy accused of attempting to kidnap a young woman, Hanna Tublowski. I got him off. Before the jury came back with the "not guilty," I realized that my client did try to take that girl. During my cross-examination of the victim, I saw my client's face light up with hate, with excitement, and I knew then that this guy was guilty. Listening to that seventeen-year-old crying as she testified gave my client immense pleasure. It was almost as if watching her fall to pieces made some part of him come alive, a part of him that he kept hidden. He couldn't hide it from me. I did my job and he got off. Later I found the same girl tied to his bed. She'd been beaten and . . . well, you don't want to know what he did to her. By the time the cops arrived, I'd almost killed the guy. I broke my hand on his face.

'I failed that girl. I didn't owe her anything and it wasn't my job to care about her; it was my job to destroy her on the witness stand.'

Child's arms fell by his sides, and he shook his head.

'I promised myself that I wouldn't let that happen again. That I would play the justice game my way, no matter what. I could no more send you to jail for something you didn't do than let that guy walk free again. In my eyes, that's just as bad.'

'But you don't get to decide what happens in a case,' said David.

I took another sip of coffee, replaced the cup on the table, and said, 'The poet Robert Frost once said that a jury is twelve people chosen to decide who has the best lawyer. I believe there's some truth in that. The prosecution evidence is very strong, and I'm not going to promise you that I'll get you off, but I can try, and I'll fight harder than any other lawyer in this city.'

'What are the chances of an acquittal?'

My rhetoric sounded good up to that point. 'Once you walk into court, it's Vegas time. Anything can happen, but I'm not a miracle worker.'

'Are you saying I need a miracle if I'm going to win?'

Pausing, I noted the expectation in his eyes. His open mouth, he'd leaned forward to hear my answer.

'The evidence against you is massive. They have the murder weapon in your car and you're soaked in gunshot residue. You told the detectives you'd never even fired a gun. How do you propose to explain away the fact that when you were arrested, you were covered in GSR? And the security cameras show no one apart from you entering or leaving your apartment at the time of the murder. There's no killer blow here, David. Trying to persuade a judge there isn't enough evidence for your case to even make it to trial is one hell of a long shot. And if we do persuade the judge, the DA gets another chance for an indictment in front of the grand jury.'

His shoulders sagged, and his gaze seemed to disappear into nothing, like he'd become blind.

I'd lied about it being a long shot. From the evidence I'd seen, it looked to be damn near impossible. But I'd been in bad situations before. There was always an angle, I just had to find it.

'Too bad, for both of us,' said David.

'What do you mean?'

He picked up the memory stick and held it in front of his gaze.

'I believe everything you've told me. I really do. But there's too much at stake. People only see me for what I can give them. Clara was the only one who didn't care about the money. I want to see whoever killed her behind bars. I'll pay you to do that. But all I can tell you is that it wasn't me and I need you to defend me.'

He handed me the memory drive.

'This USB drive contains software. The FBI can access Harland and Sinton's mainframe and they can use it to trace the money.'

The little black device was about an inch long. It still amazed me that so much information could be stored on such a small, insignificant-looking thing.

'The stick's yours. If the FBI insert this drive into the Harland and Sinton system, they'll be asked for a password to start the trace. As soon as the charges against me are cleared, I'll give them the password.'

'That's what the feds were offering, a way—'

'No, it's not. They want me to plead guilty to Clara's murder. I can't do that. I won't do that. You get me clear of the charges and I'll give you the firm.'

CHAPTER THIRTY-SEVEN

This was David's play. He'd been running this scenario through his mind for a little while.

'Sell it to the FBI. I want all charges dropped and my name cleared. That's my bottom line. I won't plead guilty even if it means I don't do any time in jail at all. Pleading is not an option. I didn't do it. If I plead, I'll lose Reeler. I spent forty, fifty hours at a time, at my computer in my little dorm room at college, dreaming that someday I would make it. I had a stroke at sixteen. Did you know that? A seventy-three-hour coding marathon for the launch of Reeler. One minute I'm really blasting it on my laptop, and the next – I wake up in the hospital and I can't feel my right leg. When the paramedics brought me in, I had my life savings in my pocket – twenty-three dollars and seventy-eight cents and a forty-thousand-dollar bank loan that I couldn't repay. Three days later I launched Reeler from my hospital bed. A couple weeks after that I'm out of the hospital, fully recovered, Reeler's got nine hundred thousand users, and it's the fastest-growing social network in history. I risked everything, my health, my money, my sanity. And it paid off. I . . . I can't lose that.'

He took off his glasses and set them on the table. From a case in his pocket, he produced a silk cloth and began cleaning the lenses. Quick, almost frantic strokes.

'The problem is that the evidence says you killed Clara. Given time, I can work on it. My wife doesn't have that kind of time, David. Help me, and I'll give you my word I'll help you.'

'If this goes to trial, my reputation is ruined anyway. I need this kicked out now. Make the deal.'

'Believe me, I want this case dead just as much as you do. But what if I can't do it? And making a deal – you know, the city doesn't let murderers walk, even if they are helping the FBI bust the biggest money-laundering operation in US history. They think you're guilty, and they have the evidence to prove it. I can't get a deal that lets you walk.'

'Then prove I'm innocent at the preliminary hearing.'

I let out a long sigh and rubbed my temples.

'The prelim's in two hours. All the prosecution has to do is prove that there's an arguable case against you. We'd have to damn near prove that you're innocent. And there's no jury; a single judge decides.'

Child folded the silk cloth, placed it carefully into his glasses case, and snapped the lid shut.

'Nothing's impossible. I'm innocent; we just have to show that.'

'It's not that simple,' I said. The pain behind my eyes spread over my skull and dived into my neck muscles.

'But it is that simple.'

I got the impression that for David, things were very black and white, clean or dirty, guilty or innocent; gray lines didn't enter into his consciousness. He had a literal thought process that was cast in stone, or green hooded tops, gray sweatpants and red Nikes.

'You don't believe I'm innocent, do you?'

Always the easiest question for a lawyer. The answer is that it doesn't matter what the lawyer believes; it's not our job to believe anyone – all we have to do is represent the client and make the jury believe in the client. David needed more than a stock answer – he needed to trust me – so I told him what he wanted to hear.

'I don't think you're a killer, David,' I said.

My gut told me he was innocent. My mind found it hard to ignore the evidence.

He looked confused.

'If you don't think I'm a killer, then prove it in court. You said we've only got two hours before this thing starts. Shouldn't you be researching case law, or something?' said David. He hadn't listened to a word I'd said. Even so, I admired him. The strength of his belief in his innocence kept me open-minded.

'No, I don't need to do any legal research. I just need to read everything again, watch the DVDs, and find a way in.'

'A way in to what?'

'A way to prove that you were set up,' I said.

CHAPTER THIRTY-EIGHT

Holly slotted the first DVD into the player. I stood, the Lizard took a knee, and David sat on the armchair. Leaning forward, fingers steepled over his mouth, he watched the graphic of a disk spinning as the video loaded.

The screen filled with an image of the lobby of Central Park Eleven – home to more of Manhattan's millionaires than any other. Huge potted plants and small trees lined the peach-colored marble lobby. The camera must have been mounted over the reception desk. In the corner of the screen it read CAMERA 1, but there was no date or time stamp visible on-screen.

A skinny kid in a green hooded sports top, gray baggy pants, and red sneakers came into the lobby. The hood was down. It was David. He was holding hands with a young blond woman wearing blue jeans and a short navy jacket over a white blouse – Clara. I turned away from the TV and glanced at David, leaning so far forward he was barely perching on the armchair. In the flickering light from the plasma screen I saw a tear on his cheek. This was the last footage of Clara before she was murdered.

The couple breezed past reception and the camera view changed. Now we were looking at an elevator camera. The doors opened, and Clara and David entered the elevator. From the pocket of his hoodie, David produced a fob, which he swiped at the elevator panel. He then selected a floor, turned, and embraced Clara. I glanced at Holly – her eyes shifted to the floor and then back to the screen, and when she saw the video, her hand closed over her open mouth.

I looked back at the TV, and Clara Reece was in the corner of the elevator, her eyes on the floor. David moved toward her and she raised her hand. He stopped. She looked awkward, unhappy. Maybe even a little afraid. When the doors opened, she stepped out fast.

I noticed that this footage was date and time stamped MARCH, 14, 19:45.

The view switched again. This time we got the feed from camera fifty-three, which displayed a landing with two doors, fifty feet apart. Clara came out of the elevator first, followed by David, this time with his hood up. He took her in his arms, and they walked toward his apartment. Beside each apartment was a standing mirror, an umbrella stand, and a small table. He used the fob again at the door on the right, then used his keys to open the door.

I paused the video and rewound. One minute they were hugging, and the next she didn't want him near her. I said, 'What was that, David? Clara looked pretty uncomfortable in the elevator. Did you have an argument?'

'God no. She was claustrophobic. Clara struggled being in the elevator with other people, even me. She was forcing herself to do it, trying to overcome that fear.'

David began sobbing uncontrollably into his hands. He turned away, went into the kitchen, and splashed water on his face.

The DA would sell the elevator footage as a fight between David and Clara. It could certainly look like a fight. The prosecution just got their motive.

The screen turned black, fuzzed, and then the same image re-appeared, this time of the empty landing. The figure of David, now with his hood up and a gym bag slung over his shoulder, exited the apartment and closed the door. He hesitated for a second, turned back toward the door. It was almost as if he'd forgotten something. Then he fished in the belly pocket of his sweater, removed an iPod or a phone with a pair of inner earphones dangling from it, placed them in his ears, and called the elevator. Around sixteen to seventeen minutes had elapsed from the time he and Clara had entered the apartment; the clock on the camera read 20:02. He waited for a time, then got into the elevator. There was no footage of the downward journey. The last image was a still-hooded David exiting the elevator at the lobby and leaving the building. The DVD ended with a police serial number and an exhibit catalog reference RM #1 – RM #5.

The cop who'd compiled the footage said he'd watched the camera outside David's apartment. Nobody went in after he left. Nobody came out. The next living soul to enter the apartment was the building security officer, who found Clara Reece dead on the kitchen floor and no one else in the apartment. It was simple – if the cop was right, and nobody went near David's place after he left, then he was the only person who could've killed Clara.

Not a good start.

A buzz as the DVD ejected. I handed Holly the next one, and she fired it up. David was still in the little kitchen, leaning on the worktop.

'David, you need to watch this,' I said.

His face was still wet with tears. He was sniffing and wiping his nose with a wet wipe. He turned toward the TV.

I looked back at the screen and saw a busy intersection in Manhattan. The time stamp from the New York Department of Transport traffic camera read 20:18. Around twelve minutes had elapsed between the footage of David leaving the apartment building and this camera picking him up.

'What are you driving again?' I asked David.

'Bugatti Veyron,' he said.

I saw the distinctive, 1.3-million-dollar car slow at the traffic lights. The Bugatti was facing the camera. Cars pulled out at the cross section for Central Park, moving left to right across the screen. Then they stopped and a few pedestrians crossed the street in front of David's car. Once the last of them had crossed the street, there was a ten-second delay before I saw David's car taking off. He moved quickly, just a touch of the throttle on the thousand-bhp supercar would be enough. The Bugatti took off at speed, and somehow a Ford, going in the opposite direction, veered into the Bugatti's path at the last moment. Such was the force of the impact that I saw the Ford's rear suspension leap off the ground, back tires airborne, chassis buckling with the impact. Steam billowed out from the Ford's radiator almost instantly. Both vehicles remained stationary. The driver of the Ford got out of the car first. The police statement said this guy, John Woodrow, was subsequently charged with DUI and reckless driving. He didn't look too steady on his feet. He wore a white button-down shirt, half tucked into his jeans. As he moved around the car, I could see that he was limping badly.

No, not badly – distinctively.

His right leg flopped out in front of him, his foot swinging. The knee and ankle joints looked as if they were held together with string. Then he sprang forward onto his left before repeating the maneuver.

Two things stuck in my mind.

He could've badly injured his right knee and ankle in the crash. I couldn't ignore that possibility. But in the back of my mind I knew this guy was limping from an old injury, and I thought I'd seen that limp before.

The camera zoomed in as he reached the passenger window of the Bugatti. He leaned in, as if to talk to David, his open, empty hands on the roof of the car. When he brought his head out of the car, the camera was almost framing his face. A row of oversized glistening white teeth shined for his close-up.

I knew right then that David had been framed for murder; the car crash was no accident. The driver of the Ford pickup was a man I'd worked with many years ago. His real name wasn't John Woodrow, and I remembered how he'd come by that limp.

And how he'd gotten his new teeth.

After his close-up, the pickup driver seemed to recoil from the passenger window, took a cell phone from his pocket, and called the cops. Both cars remained in situ until the police arrived two minutes later. A patrolman approached David, got him out of the car, and then he stopped and looked inside the Bugatti, as if he'd noticed something. The cop walked around the vehicle, hands empty, opened the passenger door, then ducked inside. When he came back up, he held the butt of a Ruger with pinched fingers. He spoke to Woodrow, then searched and cuffed my client. A second patrol car arrived and took the pickup driver away. David was placed in the rear of the first patrol car, which left the scene shortly after.

I paused the video, rewound, and watched the pickup driver and the cop approach David's car. The pickup driver's hands never got inside the Bugatti, and the cop wasn't wearing a jacket and I could see his hands were empty when he put his head in the passenger side of the car. A second later his hands reappeared and he held the murder weapon.

David preempted my question.

'I have no idea how that gun got into my car,' he said.

'Is it possible that someone planted it there?'

'I doubt it. The car's security system is state-of-the-art, and besides, I put my bag on the passenger seat. If there had been a gun in the passenger footwell, I'd have noticed it.'

I nodded. If I was right, then the gun had to have been planted in David's car. It didn't look like either the cop or the pickup driver could've planted it. How did they get it from David's apartment to the car in the first place?

'The accident was a setup. The driver is a guy named Perry Lake. He's a hit driver,' I said.

'A what?' said David.

'He sets up accidents,' I said.

I'd worked with Perry Lake for a few months, a lifetime ago. Perry used to race. He was a talented NASCAR driver, until his coke habit got him dropped and a DUI put the final bullet into his career. A man of Perry's skills can always find work, though. With his penchant for narcotics, it was always going to be the illegal, top-paying kind of jobs. He was a getaway driver for a crew that operated out of Atlantic City for a couple of years, then a chauffeur for a high-end pimp that worked girls on the Upper East Side, and then finally he worked for me as a hit driver. Perry set up car accidents to defraud insurance companies with fake personal injury cases. He made a lot of money, too. Then he slept with the wrong kind of woman – the kind that has a possessive, psychotic husband who left him with the limp and a lot of dental work.

'Bottom line, David, somebody paid Perry to swallow enough liquor to put him way over the limit and then slam his car into yours at that intersection, at that precise time on that precise day – so that the cops would find that gun.'

David said nothing. He stared stupidly at the TV, and let his mouth fall open.

'That's what I think, but it doesn't make a lot of sense to me. Why set up a fake accident when the cops were going to come looking for you anyway, as soon as Clara's body was found?' I said.

'You're right. It doesn't make sense,' said David.

I rubbed my chin, twirled my pen around my fingers.

'Holly, can I use your bedroom? I need a little time alone to think this out,' I said.

'Sure,' she said. 'Just don't take too long. We've only got an hour before court.'

I took in David's outfit again, checked the bags.

'David, you're going to need a suit.'

CHAPTER THIRTY-NINE

It takes a lot of care, skill, and planning to set up a car accident. When I was running the con, I took a week to scout the route for the accident. I spent hours timing the traffic lights, measuring the distances between intersections, monitoring the traffic flow at different times. Once I had my preferred location on the target's daily route, I would tail the target for another two weeks. I liked to hit them during the day, usually as they were making their commute to work. That was the most predictable route, the one least likely to change, the one where the accident would cause the most inconvenience. But then there were the professionals, guys like Perry Lake and Arthur Podolske – who could just feel their way into it. Guys like that are few and far between. If you wanted a professional driver to stage an accident and make it look real, there was a very short list of candidates. An even shorter list in New York, and I knew them all. The accident was a setup but I still had no clue why it had happened.

Why go to all that trouble? Why do it then, when the cops don't even know David's girlfriend has been murdered?

The pen my daughter has given to me, the one that had 'Dad' engraved on the side, whispered through my fingers, tumbling in a never-ending sequence that brought it through each finger, around my thumb, and then back again.

It helped me think.

I had the entire prosecution file spread out on the bed: witness statements, crime scene photos, Dr Porter's GSR report, the photos of the car wreck – Perry's busted Ford and David's Bugatti with the front tire all but torn off and the air bags hanging limp from the console, like punctured cartoon ghosts. I even laid out the copies of the security logs, the fingerprint analysis, which had come back negative on the weapon and the arrest report for David. Every piece of evidence, every document, all separated, all laid out neatly on the sheets.

Walking around the bed, pen sliding over my hand, I felt close to something. Some part of this didn't add up. It was right there in front of me, but I couldn't see it.

Without knocking, the Lizard opened the bedroom door and said, 'We gotta split in five if we're gonna make the courthouse.'

As he slipped on a short leather jacket, he noticed the file – separated and spread out in neat columns on the bed.

'Find anything?' he said.

'Not yet, but I'm close. I'd be better if you left me alone to think.'

He chuckled, and from his jacket pocket he removed a pair of leather driving gloves and proceeded to slip them on.

'Well, you're doing the right thing spreading it all out. Helps to order the mind. The Lizard likes to do this with his weapons – take them apart, piece by piece, and lay them out in an exploded view. Clean 'em, make 'em gleam. Then put 'em all back . . . Hey, what're you staring at?'

I must've been wild-eyed. I was looking at the Lizard's gloves. Something about them, something about what he'd just said – it gave me an idea.

I called out, 'David, bring me your laptop right now.'

What I was looking for appeared on the sixth page of my Internet search. A mention in an obscure French forensic science journal. Whatever search engine David used offered me a pretty good translation of the web page. I had to pay for the article. Within a minute I had it downloaded and translated. The article had been presented at a forensics conference run by Interpol last year.

It was there. It was possible.

It was brilliant.

'David, whoever set you up is one smart son of a bitch. I never would've looked for it if the Lizard hadn't given me the idea.'

'The Lizard gave you an idea?' said the Lizard.

My gaze moved from the photo of the totaled Bugatti to the Lizard's gloved hands.

'You can be very motivational, but I need a little favor. I need to borrow your gloves.'

PART TWO

THE PAYOFF

CHAPTER FORTY

27 hours until the shot

Getting back inside the courthouse took a lot of thought and planning from the Lizard. We drove there in two separate cars. I was in the back of an overgrown sedan, driven by Frankie, another of Jimmy the Hat's associates who worked with the Lizard when he needed backup. The leather-clad steering wheel all but disappeared from view, engulfed in Frankie's enormous, calloused hands. Hands that beat dollars out of diamond-tough guys that owed Jimmy.

We drove past the front of the courthouse. From the sidewalk, up the steps, all the way to the entrance, it was like a media convention. You would be forgiven for thinking that the president was due to arrive. Far too many bodies. All it would take would be somebody waiting in the crowd with a .38 and David wouldn't even make it up the first step. In among the crowd, I saw a couple of suits, and in the center of that expensive group was the tall figure of Gerry Sinton, waiting outside to escort his client past the world's media.

'As expected, it's packed,' I said.

We circled around, pulled up a couple of blocks before the courthouse. Waiting for the Lizard's van to appear in the rearview mirror, I thought about the hundred and twenty-five feet of people between the sidewalk and the courthouse entrance. How many shooters could the firm have in that crowd? I'd given the photos of the firm's security team to the Lizard to study. I'd studied their faces, too – and so had David. If we saw any of them, we ran. A blue Ford Transit van appeared in our rearview mirror, slowed. Frankie pulled out into traffic, and the Transit fell in behind us.

The sedan parked alongside the curb, just behind the media trucks with their satellites beaming from the roof. I got out, my files slung over my shoulder in a laptop bag. I wanted my hands free, just in case.

I found Gerry Sinton warding off the handful of reporters who'd recognized him as David's lawyer and were crowding him hungrily. He saw me, made his way down the steps, pushing his way through the TV crews. The reporters in the know sensed they were about to get their shot – they followed Sinton down the steps, toward the sidewalk.

He acknowledged me with a nod.

The Transit pulled up and stopped behind the sedan. Sinton came alongside me, the reporters and cameras on his heels. His voice quivered as he fought to hold down his rage.

'Where's David? He never made it to the hotel,' he said.

'Let's get him inside, and then we can talk. Here he comes now,' I replied.

Frankie got out of the sedan and opened the rear passenger door. Gerry craned over my shoulder to see a pair of red Nikes hit the pavement, and a hunched figure, covered in a white bedsheet, all but fell out of the car and ran toward us.

Gerry grabbed the sheet, guided his hands around his client, and led him toward the now exploding sea of cameras, lights, and voices. Ignoring the reporters, I checked the hangers-on. Didn't see anybody from the firm's security crew. A few members of the public joined the throng of reporters, not really knowing what was going on, but simply overwhelmed with the energy in the air and desperate to catch a glimpse of the accused beneath the sheet. As Gerry plowed through the reporters, his right hand thrust in front of him like a linebacker from the seventies, I let myself drift away just before the media completely enclosed Gerry and his client.

Another scan of the area – no potential shooters. I nodded to Frankie, who stood on the hood of the car, watching.

The rear door of the Lizard's Transit popped open and I saw the small figure of a young man in an ill-fitting suit. He closed the van door and began to walk briskly toward the courthouse entrance. I moved with him and watched Holly coming behind, tossing the keys to the van at Frankie before she broke into her run.

That's when I heard the shot.

CHAPTER FORTY-ONE

'Go!' I yelled, and David turned away from the sound of gunfire. Holly grabbed him by the arm, and together they bolted for the entrance. Their path was clear.

I spun around to see bodies tumbling down the staircase as people scrambled to get clear, to get away, before they were caught in the cross fire. A big guy in a fawn overcoat, still talking into his microphone shouldered me out of his way, and I had to bump past a couple of female anchors to get a view.

Gerry Sinton was lying head down on the concrete. He ran his hands over his stomach, chest, legs, making sure he hadn't caught a stray bullet. The white sheet flew off the head of the Lizard, and with it, he discarded the spent firecracker. Before Gerry could get a good look at him, the Lizard took off. Frankie made a circular motion above his head with his fist. He was going to park and then he'd be coming back. The crowd of reporters caught their breath, cameras steadied, and the screaming became commentary.

As I reached the top steps, I saw David and Holly safely beyond the security check, inside the courthouse.

Holly was holding David's hand.

I made my apologies as I weaved through the group of reporters that had gathered outside the entrance. A hand gripped my arm, and I turned.

The man with *The Scream* tattoo on his throat had taken hold of me. I couldn't move. It wasn't his grip that held me; it was his eyes. His pupils and irises were not dark brown; they were black. Totally black. Each eye looked like a perfect pearl of onyx resting in a saucer of milk. And below that face, the pale man screamed on his throat.

I caught the stink of cigarettes from him when he released his grip and held up his open hands, fingers spread wide. While his skin was dark, his palms were purest white. I noticed more droplets and splashes of white coloring on his fingers and wrists. The skin in these areas was smooth: no wrinkles or lines on his palms or fingers. Everything had been scalded clean, flat, and unmarked. His touch wouldn't even leave a fingerprint.

The man was so unusual, so striking, that for a moment I didn't see that he was hiding something in the pinch between his thumb and index finger.

'Tell your client to keep his mouth shut, *cabron*,' said the man in a thick Spanish accent.

He backed away and spread his right thumb away from his index finger.

I heard the cracking of thin glass. Pushing through the crowd, he trod down the steps. I heard something hissing and looked down. Fragments of glass, no bigger than a spoonful, and surrounding them an amber liquid bubbled as it ate through the concrete.

He'd been holding a small vial of acid. I shivered and scanned the steps. He'd gone.

CHAPTER FORTY-TWO

The courtroom of Judge Knox was filling up rapidly with the still-shaky members of the media. I slowed a little, to make sure David and Holly were right behind me. I'd already decided not to tell David about the warning; he was only just holding it together. I laid out my papers on the defense table and took the seat on the right with David to my left. When he arrived, Gerry would have to take the corner seat.

The rear doors of the court opened, a hundred feet behind us. The prosecution were arriving. Zader hovered at the rear of the pack of assistant district attorneys who hauled evidence boxes and folders into court. District Attorney Zader typed on his iPhone with his thumb.

As he passed me, he leaned down and said, 'I just posted this on Reeler.'

The official reel of the New York District Attorney's Office held a new message:

'THE EVIDENCE WE ARE ABOUT TO PRESENT IN THE PRELIMINARY HEARING IN THE CASE OF DAVID CHILD WILL SHOCK THE NATION. FOLLOW US AS WE LOAD REELS LIVE FROM THE HEARING. #JUSTICEFORCLARA'

'This is going to be public and messy,' said Zader, unable to keep the excitement from his voice.

I saw a box with an 'R' below the DA's Reeler post with a number below it. The number was rolling up every half a second – 257, 583, 1,009. This was the number of times the message had been relayed through Reeler, Facebook, and Twitter.

'Public and messy,' he said again, slowly.

He strode back to his ADAs and waved to a few of the more influential TV anchors who'd taken their prime seats in the front row of the gallery.

'Can he do that?' asked David.

'Pretty much. He's not giving away any details about the case. He's just raising his profile. You're a pretty big fish – he wants to gut you in public. This is the kind of case that could launch his political career. If he wants to be mayor, or governor, he needs the face time on TV. I think he's enjoying the fact that he's using Reeler to destroy you. I guess he finds some irony in that. You're gonna have to face the fact that you're his meal ticket. This isn't about Clara. This is about him, and that sickens me.'

Gerry Sinton took his seat at the end of the defense table without a word. I hadn't heard his approach; for a big man, he walked softly. Sending a warning with a vial of acid wasn't beyond Gerry. He'd worked his way up the chain from the back alleys to the board-room. Dell had told me as much. I thought about reaching across, gripping Gerry's silk tie, and ringing his head off the mahogany a couple of times. I thought better of it when Judge Knox came into the room, took his seat at the bench, and called the case.

No backing out now. This was it. What happened here would save or condemn David. It would save or condemn Christine. It would shape the course of my life. The prosecution had half a dozen witnesses – all of them ready to give evidence that put David Child up for a slam-dunk conviction. It's much easier to tear a witness apart when they're lying. Far as I could tell, with the possible exception of two witness, each of the remaining prosecution witnesses was telling the truth – and that truth added up to David's guilt. I had to swing the truth away from each of them so I could create my own truth and let Knox see the bigger picture.

Trouble was, at that time I didn't know the bigger picture. I couldn't yet see the truth of this whole thing.

I told myself that it would come. Give it time.

Dr Henry Porter was the first big job. The GSR expert. I saw him sitting four rows behind Zader. A man in his fifties, smartly dressed in gray dress pants, white shirt, and blue blazer. All set off with a pale yellow tie. For some reason, like most of his fellow contemporary firearms experts, he sported a graying mustache. I wondered if they handed out the mustache with their forensic expert certification.

He saw me staring and, with forefinger and thumb, adjusted his glasses, then turned his attention to Zader.

The DA stood, ready to give his opening to Judge Knox, who was arranging his own case file in readiness for the evidence.

I wondered then if Zader or Porter had any inclination of what I had in store for them. I hoped not. The DA checked the gallery, making sure his first witness was ready. They exchanged a thumbs-up. I gave myself evens that in an hour Zader would be sitting with his thumb up his ass, wondering where it all went wrong. There was an equal chance that I might be sitting wondering how I'd messed up so bad. It was too close to call.

Judge Knox signaled to Zader that he was ready. The DA took his time. Sipped from a glass of water. A quick scan of the gallery to make sure all was silent, all eyes were on him – that his audience was ready.

The TV cameras started rolling. This case would be on a live feed on damn near every news channel in the country. Zader's last words echoed in my mind.

Public and messy.

Damn, I wished I'd shaved.

CHAPTER FORTY-THREE

'Your Honor, Michael Zader, District Attorney for the people. Second chair is Ms Lopez. Mr Flynn and Mr Sinton appear for the defendant.'

He moved around the prosecution table, taking center stage in the well of the court. I imagined he'd already worked out which spot in the courtroom would give the cameras their best angle.

'I'll keep my opening brief, Your Honor,' said Zader, buttoning his jacket.

He knew Judge Knox didn't care for long-winded opening statements. He liked to get straight to the evidence. The fact that Zader had signposted this meant that Judge Knox would give him a little time for the cameras, without interruption. One of the first things you learn as an attorney is how important it is to find out the preferences of every judge. Some like long speeches, some like strict legal argument with little reference to the facts, and some like it all to be over and done with in the least complicated and quickest way possible – regardless of the fairness of the proceedings. Judge Knox fell into the latter category. The DA had done his homework.

'We shall present a number of witnesses to the court that prove the defendant was the only other person present in his apartment with the victim, Clara Reece, when she was shot and killed. We have camera footage that clearly shows the defendant and the victim entering his apartment. Minutes later, Mr Gershbaum, a neighbor of the defendant, heard the first shots, went to the balcony to investigate, and witnessed a shot coming through the window of the defendant's apartment. A shot that was fired from within the apartment. The security footage then shows the defendant leaving the apartment. Richard Forest, the security guard whom Mr Gershbaum called, will say that he attended with other guards from the building and discovered the body of Clara Reece in the defendant's empty apartment. The evidence will show that in those important and frantic minutes between Mr Gershbaum's call to security and the discovery of the body in the defendant's apartment, security camera footage clearly shows the defendant as the only person who leaves that apartment. It is simple – two people enter an empty apartment and only one leaves alive. We know nobody else was in there, and nobody else came in. David Child leaves his home, and within minutes his girlfriend's dead body is found. In short, he is the only person who could've killed her.'

He paused, nodded to himself as the judge caught up with his notes.

'The medical examiner's report speaks to the manner of the victim's murder. This, Your Honor, is the most shocking part of this case.'

Another pause, building the tension in the courtroom. This guy was very good.

'The victim, Clara Reece, was shot twelve times in the back of the head with a small, highly concealable pistol – a Ruger. Twelve times. She was plainly dead after the first head shot, but her killer, the defendant, emptied almost an entire magazine into the back of her skull, ejected the empty magazine, reloaded, cocked the weapon, and fired another seven shots into her head.

'The overkill involved in this murder clearly marks it out as a crime committed in a blind rage. This is not the work of a hired killer. It is an intensely violent, vengeful murder – one that we say was plainly carried out by a scorned and deeply troubled lover. By the victim's lover – the defendant, David Child.

'Ultimately, the violence with which he perpetrated this heinous crime, combined with a stroke of bad luck, inevitably led to the discovery of the defendant as the murderer. Within minutes of the defendant leaving his apartment building, he was involved in a road traffic collision with another vehicle, not half a mile away from his apartment. The driver of that other vehicle was a Mr John Woodrow. Mr Woodrow was several times over the legal limit for alcohol, and he accepts causing the RTC, a head-on collision with the defendant's sports car.

'When Mr Woodrow approached the defendant's car in the aftermath of the accident, he noticed a gun in the vehicle, in plain sight. He called for police assistance, and Officer Phil Jones attended the scene. It was Officer Jones who found a Ruger pistol in the defendant's vehicle.

'This weapon was independently tested by Dr Porter, our forensic gunshot residue expert. When the defendant was swabbed for gunshot residue, it was discovered and confirmed by Dr Porter's independent scientific analysis that the defendant was literally covered in GSR. In the interview with the investigating officer, Detective Morgan, the defendant denied ever owning a gun, touching a gun, firing a gun, or even being in the same room when a gun was discharged. Given the scientific evidence, it's clear that the defendant was lying.'

To emphasize the obvious disparity with the incontrovertible forensic evidence, Zader raised his hands, closed his eyes, and made a face as if to say, 'I know, this guy's lying his ass off.'

'So, to recap, not only is there probable cause, but the accused is the only man who could've committed this crime. Secondly, given the forensic evidence, the accused lied to the police. That's right, we're saying he lied, because, quite frankly – forensics *can't* lie.

'That is a brief overview of the prosecution evidence,' he said.

He looked at the cameras, something he's not supposed to do. I guessed he couldn't help it.

'Mr Flynn, do you have a short opening?'

My opinion of Judge Knox softened. He knew Zader was playing for the cameras, and he wanted to at least let me have a chance at a quick comeback.

'No, thank you, Your Honor. Let's get this started.'

'Very good. Your first witness, Mr Zader?'

'We're calling Dr Henry Porter to the—'

'Hang on. Isn't he an expert witness? If he is, you don't have to call him in a prelim. I can just read his report.'

'In this case, Your Honor, we feel it would be of benefit to everyone to hear from Dr Porter. He can outline his findings for the court, and I'm sure he'll be able to answer any questions Mr Flynn may have.'

For the cameras, again. The judge knew Zader was calling Porter so that the media could get ahold of this watertight evidence right away. A ten-minute shot of Judge Knox reading the report wouldn't make for good TV.

'If you must, then call him,' said the judge.

The witness was already on his feet and making his way toward the witness stand, his report under his right arm. As he passed me, I detected the smell of gun oil and cheap aftershave. He looked confident, unafraid. At this early stage of the proceedings, there's simply not enough time for the defense to get their own expert to counter the prosecution witnesses' findings. That's what expert witnesses fear most – another expert with better credentials saying that they're wrong. Without that, they have very little to fear. And Porter had a solid record as a witness – he'd never been successfully challenged before in any case.

I told myself there was a first time for everything.

Porter took the oath and sat down.

'Dr Porter, can you briefly outline the nature of your expertise?' said Zader.

'Of course. I'm a trained ballistics and forensic firearm residue retrieval expert. I've previously been employed by the state's own forensic laboratory, and I've been involved in thousands of evidential test situations. I've given evidence in two hundred and three trials.'

He looked relaxed, at home. After all, being a professional witness was his job. And Porter was good, very good. I'd no doubt he'd mentioned the exact number of his court appearances so that he would immediately appear to be clear, precise, and experienced. At the same time, I had little doubt that he'd mentioned the number of cases he'd done to try to intimidate me; in all of those cases, he'd appeared as a prosecution witness, and every single one of them had resulted in a conviction.

'Dr Porter, what is gunshot residue?' said Zader.

'When a shooter pulls the trigger on a loaded firearm, the firing pin is forced against the primer, which ignites the propellant within the cartridge, which then creates a huge amount of gas very quickly. This gas then fires the round from the barrel at roughly a thousand feet per second. The explosion within the primer and propellant releases gasses and fragments of material into the atmosphere, some of which are fused together. These fragments are combinations of minute particles from the pin, the propellant, the primer, and the bullet. All of this material then quickly settles in the environment in which it is created. So the residue of the gunshot will normally settle on the skin and clothing of the shooter.'

'Doctor, did you carry out tests on samples taken from the defendant's skin and clothing?'

'I did. NYPD officers collected samples from the defendant's hands, sweater, and face. I then tested these samples to see if they contained the common material that is found in gunshot residue.'

'And what did you find?'

'I found highly concentrated deposits of barium and antimony on all sample areas. Some of this material was fused together, mostly the barium. This combination of material is scientifically proven and commonly accepted to be gunshot residue.'

'When you say, "highly concentrated deposits," what does that mean?' said Zader.

'Well, if a shooter discharges a weapon once, I will be able to find material on his skin and or clothing that would be gunshot residue. If more than one shot is fired, there will be more than one explosion, so the volume and density of material found increases.'

'In this instance, Dr Porter, what was your conclusion in relation to the high concentration of gunshot residue found on the defendant?'

'Given the wide distribution and concentrated amounts of gunshot residue, I can conclude, with a considerable degree of certainty, that Mr Child was in very close proximity to a firearm that was discharged multiple times and he'd been exposed to this material within the last few hours before samples were taken.'

'Your Honor, if you could just give me a moment to check my notes?' said Zader.

'Of course,' said Knox.

He returned to his legal pad, flicked through a couple of pages. Really he was just pausing for effect, letting that last answer seep into the mind of the judge – and the viewers at home.

He straightened up, returned his attention to the witness.

'Thank you, Your Honor. Now, Dr Porter, I have a note that the defendant, Child, told police that he had never fired a gun and he'd never even been in a room when a gun was fired. Given your findings, would you say that's possible?'

'No.'

'It's just that we've all heard of cases where trace evidence, like gunshot residue, can transfer from place to place, person to person. Is that possible in this case?'

'It's possible that GSR can be transferred. Particles of GSR can be transferred from a person's clothes or skin to other areas. That is not what happened in this case. The sheer quantity of residue I found, in all samples, from the defendant's hands, clothes, and face, rule out transference.'

'And why is that?'

'Because the defendant would've had to take a shower in gunshot residue. In my experience, it's not possible for the sheer quantity and high concentration of GSR found on the defendant to have gotten there through secondary transfer. It couldn't happen. The hard evidence in this case proves that he was in close proximity to a firearm that discharged multiple times.'

Again, Zader paused, letting the answers soak into the cameras. He wouldn't ask any further questions. Zader had slammed home his points and cut off the most likely avenue of attack. I whispered to David, 'Switch on your cell phone; keep it on silent.' As he did this, under the table so the judge wouldn't see, I scribbled a note and handed it to David.

He looked at me expectantly.

'Don't do it yet. Wait for my signal,' I said.

'Your witness,' said Zader, almost as a challenge: *Do your worst. I can take it.*

Porter didn't look in the least bit concerned. As far as he knew, this was a routine test, a routine case, with routine results. He had enough experience to know all the usual defense attorney angles – all the old arguments. Normally the standard line of attack on this type of evidence was to attack the chain. Porter worked in a lab. He didn't collect the evidence and he didn't know which samples were genuine and which were not, which samples had been contaminated and which were accurately preserved. When the defense couldn't argue with science, they argued that science was irrelevant as the expert was testing contaminated material.

Porter folded his arms. He'd heard it all before, many times over. He was ready for anything.

But not for this.

CHAPTER FORTY-FOUR

'Don't go fishing with this guy,' said Sinton. 'He's dangerous – wait until we get our expert. Save it for the trial.'

For the first time, I saw Sinton nervous. Sweat on his upper lip, his pen trembling in his hand. All he wanted was to get the hell out of there and take David with him. The firm couldn't kill him in the courthouse. If they wanted to take him out, they needed him away from the secure building and on the street, vulnerable.

I ignored Gerry, stood, empty-handed, and took in Judge Knox. He looked pissed off. He was waiting for a long, boring argument between me and the witness that would lead nowhere.

But I had a firm destination in mind.

'Dr Porter, you began your evidence by stating that you've testified in just over two hundred cases, yes?'

'Two hundred and four, counting this one.'

'I'm grateful for the reminder. Out of those two hundred and four appearances, how many appearances were as an expert witness for the defense?'

Any other so-called independent expert would've probably squirmed a little. Porter didn't. He just casually let it drop.

'None,' he said.

'None?'

'Correct.'

'Sorry, maybe I don't understand. It's just that you stated, in your testimony, that you are an *independent* expert,' I said.

'I am. I can be retained by defense counsel or the prosecution. My duty is to provide my honest opinion to the court; it doesn't matter which side signs the check for my fees.'

He'd opened the door just a crack. Just enough to let me in.

'So, in arriving at your honest, expert opinion, you have to ignore the name on the check and to base your opinion entirely on the evidence that you've found, correct?'

'Correct.'

'So, just by way of example, if you were asked by the prosecution to state an opinion that wasn't based on fact, or your own evidential findings, what would you do?'

'I doubt any prosecutor would ask a professional witness to do that, but just for the record, I would not make any formal statement of opinion without evidence to back it up.'

'So your opinion flows from the facts and the evidence only?'

'Of course.'

'So you can't base an opinion on speculation when the known facts tell you otherwise, right?'

'Right,' he said, sighing.

I could hear Zader whispering to his DAs, telling them I was getting nowhere fast.

I picked up Porter's report, flicked to the back, which provided a breakdown of the particles and materials found in the samples taken from David's face, hands, and clothes. This was the raw scientific data upon which Porter based his evidence.

'Doctor, in your test results, you found a lot of different particles?'

'Yes. As the explosion happens, the minute material released into the atmosphere by the gunshot will mix with other particles before it settles on the skin, so it sometimes picks up other debris, like dust particles.'

'And the three main indicators of gunshot residue are particles of lead, barium, and antimony?'

'Correct.'

'The barium and antimony particles tend to emanate from the ignition of the primer and propellant?'

'Generally, yes.'

'Lead particles tend to come from the bullet or full metal jacket itself?'

'Yes.'

'You found no traces of lead in your results?'

'That's not unheard of. Some manufacturers' rounds are simply tougher and more resistant than others. The high concentrations of barium and antimony are scientifically well-recognized signatures of GSR.'

'Apart from the high concentrations of barium and antimony, your results show a dense collection of nylon?'

'Yes. It's possible that the shooter was wearing gloves made from this material. The hot GSR material settling on gloves could be enough to burn through the nylon onto the skin,' said Porter, his voice quieting as he reached the end of that statement. He didn't feel solid on this, and I'd already guessed that when compiling his report, he'd been pushed by the prosecutor to explain why he'd found so much nylon and rubber in his samples. It gives the DA an easy argument when the defense points out that no fingerprints were found on the gun; Zader could simply fall back on Porter's thoughts that the shooter may have worn gloves.

I paused, feigned confusion, and looked at the judge. David handed me the Lizard's gloves, which I'd stowed under the defense table. I put down Porter's report and held them up.

'I'm a little confused. These aren't nylon gloves, but surely if the shooter had been wearing gloves, like these, which cover the whole hand, you wouldn't have found so much GSR material on the sample taken from the hands?' I said.

'I take your point, but the material could've been released back into the air and then settled on the hands when the gloves were removed.'

'Are you a liar, Dr Porter?'

Judge Knox's head lifted from his notes in order to make his concerned look register with the defense counsel. The look told me I was on thin ice and I had better be able to back this up.

'I'm under oath, Mr Flynn,' was Porter's reply.

'I know you are; it's just that in your direct testimony you specifically ruled out the possibility of the material traveling onto the defendant's clothes and hands by secondary transfer, correct?'

He nodded at the judge, letting him know that everything was fine.

'Well, I suppose strictly speaking, material falling onto the defendant's hands when he takes off his gloves would be secondary transfer, but some might say it's still primary, as the material is simply being moved around the original source.'

'The lead detective in this investigation is Detective Morgan; are you calling him a liar, Dr Porter?'

'Of course not.'

'It's just that Detective Morgan has viewed a series of private security cameras and street cameras that follow David Child, from the moment he leaves his apartment to the moment he is involved in the RTC. Detective Morgan does not mention in his statement anything about David Child dumping a pair of gloves. No gloves are found in his car, in his apartment, or on his person, and it's obvious he didn't dump them because it would've been seen on camera. So, if you're saying that the shooter may have worn gloves, where did they go?'

'I can't answer that.'

I held up Porter's report.

'In your test results, along with barium, antimony, and nylon, you also found fused rubber, leather, and plastic, correct?'

'Yes.'

'In fact, there was a high concentration of nylon, rubber, leather, and plastic in all samples from the defendant's skin and clothes, correct?'

'That is fair. Yes.'

'Have you ever encountered similar results?'

'No, I can't say that I have, but each environment in which a weapon is discharged is different. One cannot always predict the material one will find.'

'Given that you base your findings on the evidence, and considering that no gloves were found by police, where do you suppose all those nylon, rubber, leather, and plastic deposits came from?'

'I'm afraid I can't speculate.'

'That's because you have no evidence of where the defendant might have come into contact with this material?'

He paused, considering this. His thin fingers ran over his chin. He was suspicious of the question.

'That's correct. I don't have any evidence that could lead me to discern exactly where this material came from.'

Porter had every right to be suspicious. Right then, his entire testimony rested on a knife edge.

CHAPTER FORTY-FIVE

'Dr Porter, please take a look at these photographs.' I handed him stills from the traffic camera that shot the collision between David's Bugatti and the Ford pickup.

'Can you confirm if you've ever seen these photographs before?'

He looked at the judge and said, 'Your Honor, I have never seen these photographs before.'

'It is agreed between the prosecution and the defense that this is Mr Child's car, the Bugatti. You see it, in these photographs?' I asked.

'Yes.'

'You'll see there is extensive damage to the front of this vehicle, from a heavy head-on collision, correct?'

'I'm not a motor vehicle expert, but I agree.'

'So, having seen these photographs, do you wish to withdraw your earlier testimony?'

'I'm sorry, what? I don't understand,' said Porter. The DA knew I was winding up for a sucker punch, but he didn't know where it was going to land. I could hear Zader whispering to Lopez – she didn't know where I was going with this either. It wouldn't have mattered if they'd figured it out. The main thing was that right then, Porter didn't see it coming.

'You are aware, Doctor, that an expert witness has a duty to offer unbiased, expert opinion.'

'I'm aware of my obligations, but I don't understand what part of my testimony you are asking me to withdraw.'

'Your testimony that David Child tested positive for gunshot residue and therefore either shot a gun multiple times or was likely to be in the immediate vicinity of a gun that was discharged multiple times. I will allow you one last opportunity to withdraw that testimony, Doctor.'

'No, I see no reason to withdraw that statement.'

I paused, nodded. Looked at the judge.

'Look at photograph three, Dr Porter.'

He flicked through the set of photographs until he found it. A close-up of the wrecked Bugatti. He'd examined it only moments before, but gave it a further glance and then waited for the question.

'A moment ago you could not explain the nylon, plastic, leather, and rubber particle deposits found on Mr Child's hands, arms, clothes, and face. Can you now?'

Another look at the photograph.

'No.'

I sighed, as if I was having to drag this admission from Porter, when in fact, I wasn't giving him enough to answer the question.

'Dr Porter, we've already established the heavy impact to the vehicle – photograph three is a close-up of that vehicle. As you can see from the interior, no less than three . . .'

He slid down in his chair a little. Closed his eyes. I'd backed him into a corner. Chiseled his testimony on a stone tablet. If he wavered from it, one inch, his tower of evidence crashed, and he knew it. Yet he had no choice.

He'd seen it.

The revelation had come to me when the Lizard talked about laying out the parts of his disassembled weapon in an exploded view. It occurred to me that GSR is the material left behind from an explosion, and I knew for sure that David had been in an explosion that day. A small one, but larger than an explosion from a bullet being fired.

'The air bags,' said Porter.

Behind me, I heard Zader whispering excitedly. I turned and saw an ADA leave the courtroom, powering up his cell phone as he walked. He was young, in his twenties, wearing a gray suit, brown leather shoes, a dark beard set below brown hair. I turned my attention back to Porter.

'Yes, the air bags. When the air bags are triggered in a crash, they explode from the dash and inflate in microseconds, do they not?' I asked.

'Yes,' said Porter.

'That explosive force is caused via a small primer, which would leave traces of barium and antimony. Isn't that right?'

'I'm not sure of the exact composition . . .'

I was already walking toward him. In my hand I held a copy of the French forensic paper on similarities between GSR and trace material found in a vehicle following air bag deployment.

'Doctor, this is a scientific paper published last year that details the forensic analysis of air bag deployment residue and its similarities to GSR. Please turn to page four and you can read the results for yourself.'

The clerk took a copy of the paper for the judge. I left one copy on Zader's table. He didn't pick it up, just stared at me.

As he read, Porter chewed his lip. I gave him a full three minutes to read the entire article. My stomach did a small leap when I saw Judge Knox reading along, too. He was interested. I had to keep it that way.

'Yes, I see that the forensic results detail the standard characteristics of the particle residue from air bag deployment. But it doesn't mean my results don't reveal the presence of GSR.'

Porter was clinging to his opinion, fighting back. Exactly what I'd expected an expert who'd been successful in his previous two hundred and three appearances in court to do.

'Are you sure?' I said.

'I'm confident in my results.'

'In the explosion that punches through the steering wheel cover and the dash to release the air bags, it's entirely probable that small particles of the nylon airbag itself, together with the rubber, leather, and plastic from the dash, would also be fused in the heat, released, and would deposit on the skin, just as the study found?'

'Perhaps?'

'Perhaps? It's very likely to happen. Isn't that correct?'

'Yes,' he said softly.

'This forensic paper on air bag deployment residue states that a very similar material was found in nearly every analysis done. Do you accept that?'

'I have to.'

'You accept that the characteristic air bag deposit material, identified in this paper, is almost identical to the material found in your analysis of the samples taken from the defendant?'

Before I'd finished the question, Porter had already begun to shake his head; he wasn't going down without a fight.

'It's almost identical, and some of the deposits such as the nylon and rubber may have come from the air bag explosion, but that doesn't change a thing. The barium and antimony found on the defendant are characteristic materials of gunshot residue. My opinion remains that I found GSR in those samples.'

He looked around the courtroom, almost relieved. Taking a sip of water and swirling it around his mouth before he swallowed, he had the appearance of a prize fighter who'd just taken his opponent's best shot and come back swinging. He didn't know it yet, but he was already on his way down for a ten count.

'Dr Porter, we had earlier established that the holy trinity of GSR material are lead, barium, and antimony, do you remember?'

'I do.'

'You said that some manufacturers' rounds are tougher than others, so they may not leave traces of lead in GSR. Is that still your opinion?'

'It is.'

'You tested samples taken from the defendant, but you also tested samples taken from the gun?'

His eyes closed slowly. He was way ahead of me. He nodded blindly.

'That's a yes?' I asked.

'Yes,' he said softly, keeping his eyes shut so that he wouldn't see the freight train when it hit him.

'Doctor, your analysis of the weapon recovered from the defendant's car found traces of barium, antimony, *and* lead.'

His eyes opened and he said, 'Yes.'

'No nylon?'

'No.'

'No rubber?'

'No.'

'No leather?'

'No.'

'The results from your tests of the gun material, and the material found on the defendant, are very different?'

'Yes, there are differences.'

'To be fair to you, Dr Porter, the district attorney's office didn't inform you that immediately prior to his arrest the defendant had been in an automobile accident in which the air bags deployed, is that right?'

He knew I was throwing him a bone and he grabbed it with both hands.

'That's right, Mr Flynn. I cannot conduct accurate comparison tests if I do not have the vital environmental facts to feed into my analysis.'

'So, had the prosecutor given you this vital information, would your opinion have been different?'

Even before Porter threw Zader under the bus, I could feel the DA's eyes on the back of my skull; the contempt was palpable.

'My opinion would've been very different,' said Porter.

'It's not possible for a gun discharging lead residue to leave that residue only on the gun and not even a trace of it on the hands or clothes of the shooter, correct?'

I couldn't help but look at the DA, watched as he willed Dr Porter to come up with something, some great scientific trump card, a Hail Mary to rescue his testimony. The expert said nothing for a time. He looked at Zader almost apologetically. I swear I saw Porter shrug.

'Given what I know now, I would say it's highly unlikely.'

'From your results, and what you know now about air bags and the common significant differences between your sample results, it's likely that the material found on the gun is GSR and the material found on the defendant is from the air bag?'

He was drowning, and I was tying cement bags to his legs. Scratching his head, he remained silent for a time.

I spoke slowly, softly even. 'Doctor, may I remind you of your earlier answer? You told this court that your opinion flows from the facts and the evidence before you. Please bear that in mind. Now, I'll ask you again, from the facts and the evidence you are now aware of, the material you found on the defendant was likely to be residue from the air bag explosion and not gunshot residue?'

'Yes, now that I have the full facts, I would agree with that statement,' said Porter.

'Doctor, earlier your sworn testimony was that the defendant had fired a gun on multiple occasions. Now you cannot be certain that he even fired a single shot. Isn't that right?'

Silence. Not even the faintest sliver of breath in the air. All waited for that answer.

Through gritted teeth Porter said, 'No. I cannot now be certain.'

I spun one-eighty and said to Child, 'Send it.'

Under the defense table, David's hands worked at his smartphone. The only sound came from my heels on the floor. Then Zader's chair screeched on the tiles as he stood and said, 'No redirect.'

'Any further witnesses today, Mr Zader?' said Judge Knox.

'Allow me one minute, Your Honor,' said Zader, taking his seat and flipping pages on his file. He was stalling.

David held out his phone to let me see the screen. For a kid on a first-degree murder charge, he looked mightily pleased with himself. I took the cell phone from him and approached the prosecution. The judge had his head down, looking over his notes. I said nothing. Just held out the phone so Zader could see.

It was from David's Reeler account. A new post had been Reeled through all other social media channels. The number of views at the bottom of the screen moved in real time – and accelerated in its thousands. By the time Zader read the post, it had twenty-one thousand views. The post was simple and personal from David to his followers:

I'M INNOCENT. THE DA'S EXPERT WITNESS JUST GOT
DESTROYED. THE PROSECUTION'S CASE IS COLLAPSING.
IT'S EMBARRASSING FOR THE DA.
IT'S PUBLIC AND MESSY.

CHAPTER FORTY-SIX

The ADA that Zader sent out on an errand returned to the court-room. He gave his boss the thumbs-up on his way down the central aisle.

Some steel returned to Zader's face. His jaw set, his eyes lit from behind, no doubt by some kind of move he was planning with the returning ADA.

He couldn't resist the urge to gloat.

'Twenty years on a plea?' he said.

'Drop the charges; let him walk.'

'I hoped you might say that. You did a good job on Porter. Pity it was all for nothing,' said Zader. In his next breath, he addressed the court.

'Your Honor, a matter has arisen, and we would like to see you in private, in your office.'

'Mr Zader, I've already missed my golf day and I'm running late for a dinner tonight, so you'd better make this fast,' said Knox, relaxing into his chair.

Zader and the ADA who'd returned to court with the document stood behind the right-hand chair at Knox's desk. Sinton and I stood on the left. No prospect of Zader making an ass of himself by sitting down. He knew his judges.

Zader took the page from his ADA and handed it to the judge. His tone was solemn and respectful as he addressed Judge Knox. 'Your Honor, I have to make you aware of our intention to file a motion requesting your recusal from this case. We have evidence of judicial bias, and you cannot continue with this hearing.'

A flash of anger rippled over Knox's lips, drawing them into a snarl before fixing his mouth shut, biting down the urge to tear a piece off of Zader. As he read, his eyes broke wide and blood flooded his cheeks, the skin shading into a color that could only be described as sunset pissed.

'How did you come by this information?' said Judge Knox, turning the page over and setting it facedown on his desk.

After looking at his ADA, Zader held out his hands innocently.

'It's for your own good, Your Honor. You should step aside and let another judge hear this prelim. No one is saying that you were aware of this information before the case started. In fact, we just discovered this ourselves. It may be that we've saved you some embarrassment if you withdraw now, voluntarily.'

The judge shook his head, his mouth wide now in amazement. Eventually he turned to me and said, 'What's your take on this, Mr Flynn?'

'I have no idea what's going on. I'm just as surprised as you are, Judge. May I see the docu—'

'No,' said Knox, and his hand thumped down on top of the page. 'You don't need to see it, but I will tell you the contents. It's a statement from my investment agent. I have stocks and shares invested in various portfolios, and my wife deals with the agent and manages these affairs. That's her domain. I just write the checks. It seems as though I have a small investment in the parent company of Reeler, your client's business. I knew nothing about this investment before the case started, I can assure you of that.'

Son of a bitch.

The DA knew Porter's destruction tainted the prosecution case. In fact, it sent it flying into a brick wall, and Zader wanted to kill the evidence. If Judge Knox recused himself, the case would have to start all over again. And this time either Porter would be fully prepared for my line of questioning or, more likely, Zader wouldn't even call him as a witness and would build his case around the rest of the evidence. A fresh start for Zader with no mistakes this time.

'Well, Your Honor, if you didn't know about this, then I can't see how you could be biased . . .' I said.

'Oh, I can,' said Judge Knox, giving a look to Zader that conveyed every inch of the judge's contempt for the DA. If the evidence had gone in the prosecution's favor, there was no way they would ask the judge to recuse himself. I had a suspicion that Zader knew all about the judge's investment before the case even started, so that if there was a disaster he had a recusal motion in his back pocket so that he could wipe the slate clean and start again. Sending out the ADA to retrieve Knox's list of investments was just for show. He'd had this information before the prelim started.

'With respect, Your Honor, the defense has no objection to you continuing with this hearing.'

'Well, of course not,' said Zader. 'The defense isn't going to object because the stock price of Reeler is plummeting every second of this prosecution, and if the defendant has a judge hearing the case who has a financial interest in dismissing the charges and saving the stock price and return on his own investment, well, who wouldn't want a judge like that? The fact is, Your Honor, if you continue and if the press get ahold of this, the prelim will turn into a farce and your career would be seriously compromised.'

'How dare you lecture me on my career and my professional judgment, and don't threaten me with the press, Mr Zader. You're about the width of a page from seeing the inside of a cell. The fact is, despite Mr Flynn's gracious response, I have no choice but to recuse myself. I'm sorry, gentlemen. I will contact the superior judge and have this case transferred to a new judge in the morning. I'm afraid the prelim will have to start over.'

It was the right decision, for all the right reasons, but it still left a bad taste in my mouth. I thought that the points against Porter would give David a sympathetic hearing; it was the first in a series of hammer blows to knock out the prosecution's case. Porter and the air bag was the only hammer blow that I'd found, so far. Now it was gone. Didn't matter that the press knew about it. The new judge wouldn't consider it at all unless Zader called Porter as a witness again – and there was no way he'd do that.

No one spoke. We filed out of Knox's office, and I saw Zader waiting for me in the corridor.

'You see, Flynn, there is no way to beat me. You *can't* beat me. I'm going to blow you away tomorrow, and there isn't a single thing you can do about it. If necessary, I'll continue to kick every goddamned judge off this case until I get one who gives me the right result. I've also got me some backup. We're convening a grand jury tomorrow afternoon. So even if you win the prelim tomorrow, I can still go before the grand jury, who *will* indict Child. You've got nothing. Come to me when you want to make a deal.'

I let Zader walk away, Gerry Sinton following him. Sinton didn't want to be anywhere near me. That huge hand of Sinton's fell on Zader's shoulder. He gave the DA his card, and they talked and walked ever further from earshot. Gerry was building insurance, making plans so that he'd be the first to know if I approached the DA to make a deal. He was probably explaining to Zader that he was really the attorney of record and that any deal would have to go through him. Sinton didn't want a deal. He wanted a tip-off from the DA so that he could make sure to kill young David before he signed up to bury the firm in exchange for an easy ride for Clara's murder. I took the opportunity to lose Gerry in the crowd, grabbed David, and made for the side exit of the courtroom, leading to the cells.

One thing continued to scratch at the back of my head. How did Zader get the goods on Judge Knox? Even if he already had this information before the hearing began, it wouldn't have been easily obtained. Somebody was helping Zader. Somebody with serious connections.

CHAPTER FORTY-SEVEN

Exiting the courthouse without being seen proved a lot easier than getting inside. A courthouse security officer called Tommy Biggs led us down to the ground floor from the secure elevator used to move detainees from the cells to the courtroom. I made it my business to know as many security guards, clerks, secretaries, back-office staff, cops, and detention officers as possible. There were several reasons for this – the first was that they were usually pretty good people to get to know when you're kicking your heels waiting for your client's case to be called. The added bonus of getting to know these good people is that you realize, in reality, they run the justice system. They do the work. All it takes for the administration of justice is a handful of decent judges out of a bag full of assholes and a bank of good support staff.

We waited in the dim corridor while Tommy checked that the service bay was clear. He half turned and peeked through the steel door. I wondered if he had to go through a lot of doors sideways. Tommy was a former Mr Universe contestant, a single dad, and one of the finest detention officers I'd ever met. Barry, an ex-cop and friend of mine who'd spent his last years ferrying prisoners from a van to a cell in the old Chambers Street courthouse, had introduced me to Tommy.

Tommy waved us into the loading area, the secure parking lot where deliveries were made – food, office supplies, and citizens who'd managed to get on the wrong side of the NYPD for whatever reason and got a ride into this area in the back of a prisoner truck. He made his way to the single pedestrian door, which was cut into a block of steel shutters. Tommy made sure there were no reporters waiting by checking the security camera on a bank of monitors beside the door.

'Go. It's clear,' said Tommy.

'Thanks, T. I owe you one,' I said.

He patted me on the shoulder as I passed him, and we made our way onto the street and straight into another dark sedan, this one a heavy shade of midnight blue; the last car was too hot to use again. Frankie took off before I could even get my door closed.

We were out. Thankfully, with David and everyone else in one piece. Now I had a little time to think. But instead of running Zader's moves through my head and thinking about the evidence against David, my mind strayed to Christine. Every piece of ground I'd lost to Zader made the hit on Christine and David more attractive to the firm. They would be desperate now. They would take bigger risks to make sure David didn't talk.

I wanted to hold her so bad I could feel the aching in my arms. Amy didn't need this. She'd been through too much already. I needed to get them somewhere far away and safe.

'What can we do about this prosecution move?' asked David. 'Surely we could get the judge back.'

'I don't think we will. I think the DA has got his chance at a fresh hearing with a clean slate. And he's gathering the grand jury as backup. This guy is a serious player.'

'Can you beat him?' asked David.

'Let's hope we don't have to find out,' I said.

CHAPTER FORTY-EIGHT

Holly must've left the heater on in her apartment while we were out. When she opened the door, it was like being hit by a blast from an industrial paint dryer. I checked the window and watched the Lizard and Frankie separate and take off on foot, covering loops of our route, making sure we hadn't been followed. The quivering voice of my wife echoed in my memory – the fear in her throat as I talked her through her cab drive earlier that day. And the sound of Amy crying. I knew her cry – it was my own. And there was nothing I could do about it.

Holly locked the front door behind us, found another key for a dead bolt, and then slid two security chains across the door. David then approached the door, tried the handle three times, making sure the door was locked. He tapped the security chains and, satisfied, he took off his backpack, unzipped it, and spread out his laptop on the little dining table.

'Sit down, David. I need to know more about this flash drive. You want me to pull off a miracle at the prelim tomorrow – I'm not as confident as you are. There has to be another way to get you and Christine out of this. It's possible I can swing a deal, if I have more to bargain with.'

'I already told you, the software taps into the firm's accounts system. It tracks down and monitors the money trail. The feds just need to insert it into the firm's digital network.'

His unlined, peachy face didn't give an inch. His eyes moved naturally, not deliberately fixed, able to shift, but their intensity never wavered. He was telling the truth. Holly gave him another cold can of his favorite energy drink. He popped the tab and poured himself a fresh glass. Holly poured me a cup from the coffeepot, which had now turned the liquid into a bitter, hot mess. The way I like it. I thanked her. She gave me a tight-lipped smile in return and, as she did so, her eyes lingered on David.

'Did you write this software this afternoon?'

'No. I had it already. Before the firm's security system went live, we had to test the algo and make sure it worked. This software traces the movement of the cash so that we knew the algo was really working. It was a top-level security job, because of the amounts of money involved, so I was the only one allowed to access the algo once it had been coded.'

'And did Gerry Sinton ask you to design this?'

'Yeah. He wanted a backup security system that takes over the firm's client accounts if their database ever got hacked. Once a credible threat is detected, the system my company installed starts running a series of checks. Thousands of calculations per second. If the system decides there's a risk, the security algo kicks in and the money travels for seventy-two hours before returning to one secure account. There are hundreds of dormant accounts in the name of Ben Harland – scattered across five different Manhattan banks. The algo selects one of these accounts at random to be the final destination for all of the money.'

'And by the time the money finds its way home, it's also been washed,' I said.

'To be honest, at the time I created this algo, that had never occurred to me,' said Child dispassionately.

'Structuring' was the term. Albie, an accountant who worked for my pal Jimmy the Hat, used to employ a similar method in what he called the dirty-thirty runs. Splitting down a cash deposit into sums below $10,000 – so the bank doesn't have to write a report under the Bank Secrecy Act and doesn't need to file a suspicious activity call with the Financial Security Task Force.

'And only you have access to this algo, outside the firm, I mean?'

'Yeah, the firm insisted on it. I did, too. I added my own little touches so no one can access the nuts and bolts of the program but me. An algo like this is beyond any standard security tech on the market, and it has to be secure, and that means only one pass. The system is designed to run by itself. It doesn't need updates or maintenance. The firm can use it, but I'm the only one who can pop the hood and access the code that runs the program. But I can only do that from their office, with their knowledge.'

'The firm knows this; that's why you're a target. How would the FBI come by that information?'

'I don't know,' he said, shrugging.

'What does it take to set off this algorithm?'

'A threat or a command.'

'So, somebody in the firm could push a button to set this off?'

'Sure. It has to have that ability; otherwise there's nothing to stop a physical robbery. You see, in a threat situation, it's perfectly legal to move or freeze assets to avoid them being stolen. If the firm is using this as a new method of washing their cash, they're using my system. So it doesn't matter what your wife did. As long as she's not the one operating the system, she hasn't done anything wrong.'

'But she witnessed documents that authorized the share transfers. That effectively covers up the laundering.'

My coffee had reached that perfect temperature, and I took a mouthful and leaned back in my chair. David suddenly noticed that perspiration from his glass had dripped onto the table. He pulled a napkin from his pocket, dried the desk, and placed his drink on top of the napkin.

'So you can access the algorithm and find out where the money's headed?'

'No. Can't be done from here. It has to be done on their system.'

There was no way we could get in and out of Harland and Sinton alive. Too damn risky.

I swept my hair back and locked my fingers behind my neck. The pain in my head had been getting worse every minute, the pressure building again ever since I'd left the courthouse.

'You got any painkillers?'

'Sure,' said Holly, and began searching cupboards.

'I need this, David. My wife's at risk. The firm tried to kill her today, just to take me off your case. I don't want her harmed, and I sure as hell don't want her to end up in prison just because she got conned by her boss into signing something that she shouldn't have signed.'

191

'I feel for your wife. I don't want anyone to hurt her. But if I'm cleared of these charges, the firm will stop wondering if I'm going to cut a deal with the FBI. That takes the threat away from your wife.'

His eyes moved rapidly, and I could almost see his pulse hammering a techno beat through the vein in his neck.

He sniffed, produced another napkin, and blew his nose.

He didn't deserve to be sacrificed for Christine. Of course, I would do the time for her, if I could. She'd trusted her boss and had gotten herself into something big and nasty. Zader would never blow the charges on David given the choice, but I wondered if I dangled a full trace history of the money in front of Dell's face, might he be able to swing something with Zader? And buy Christine immunity? I had to believe that. Right then I couldn't see any other way out.

'Get me the data, David. I'll make sure the charges get blown away. Either the FBI drops the charge, or I do it in court. Either way I'll guarantee you walk away from the murder.'

Right then I wondered how I would be able to deliver on the promise. I couldn't even see a plan of attack on the prosecution evidence at this stage. David flopped into the back of his chair, looked at Holly, looked at the screen, and then looked at me.

'That would be a deal, but I already told you, I can't access the system from here. It has to be done on the Harland and Sinton server, and I can only access that if I'm in their building and I have their Wi-Fi access code. Their mainframe access point is in their conference room. All of their computers, including that one, run on secure Wi-Fi. If I can hack that computer remotely through their Wi-Fi, I can get the data. But we can't go to their office. We'd never make it out.'

Harland and Sinton occupied eight floors in one of the premier skyscrapers in Manhattan. Once we went in there, chances were we'd never been seen again. Unless there was some way to make sure the firm's security team wouldn't make a move.

'I think I know someone who can help us,' I said.

I dialed a number from memory and waited. My call was answered by a female voice that sounded like silk being dragged over smooth pebbles.

'Hello?'

'It's me. I've got a job.'

'Well, hi to you too, honey. It's great to hear from you, but I thought you'd gone straight. Big-shot lawyer and all. You still in the game?'

'Always, Boo. Always.' Boo was a former hooker, and very active con artist, who'd been a friend for many years. I'd had an idea about how to get in and out of Harland and Sinton.

'Say, you still friendly with the guy who used to park his van outside your apartment?'

'I always stay friendly with those kinds of people.'

'Great. I need him, his equipment, and his van. You, too.'

'Sounds exciting. What's the cut?'

'Call it a favor, but I'll make sure you're compensated. I should tell you, it's dangerous.'

She paused, her breath quick and expectant.

'I wouldn't have it any other way,' she said.

CHAPTER FORTY-NINE

25 hours until the shot

Holly drove a car that was smaller than my briefcase. A little Honda that smelled of makeup and bubble gum. The Lizard followed behind us, David sitting low in the passenger seat of the Lizard's new, black Transit. We pulled in at the pier and waited for Boo. Clouds spoiled the full moon. It was past eight, and I'd called Gerry Sinton from a pay phone on Ninety-Eighth Street and told him I was bringing the file and the client to their offices at seven thirty for a strategy meeting.

While we waited, I thought over the evidence against David and wondered how the hell I was going to challenge it the next morning. I put it out of my mind by calling Christine. She said she and Amy were fine. They'd ordered pizza and hadn't left the hotel. I could tell it was bullshit. Amy was crying softly in the background, even with the TV turned up to drown out the noise. My jaw worked at the anger building inside me. Eventually, Christine relented.

'Of course she's terrified, Eddie. I am, too,' she said, the timbre in her voice wet with tears, her throat hoarse.

'I'm going to make this okay. I'll make sure the police don't come looking for you.'

'And what about the firm?' she said.

'The FBI are going to take them down. I can help with that, but I have to make sure you're out of it first. There's something I need from you. It'll help. What's the Harland and Sinton Wi-Fi password for today?'

'Why?'

'I need it. I told you I'm going to fix things, so I need the password.'

'You won't do anything illegal, will you, Eddie?'

'Don't ask questions you don't want to know the answers to. Password.'

'It's chimera87. But they've probably changed it by now.'

I swore under my breath.

'Child says he can probably break in, as long as he's in range. How do you get the password? E-mail?'

'They send a text. Look, you don't have to do this, Eddie. I got myself into this. I should just go talk to the FBI and hold my hands up.'

'No, do not do that. I can fix it . . .'

'Sometimes there are things you can't fix . . .'

'Like our marriage? That's what you were going to say, wasn't it?' Silence.

'No, I'm sorry. I didn't mean that. Amy misses you. I . . . I miss you.'

Neither of us could speak for a time. We just listened to each other's breath.

'Don't get yourself killed. If I go down . . . Amy needs at least one parent,' she said.

'I'll be all right, but if something does happen, don't go to the FBI. Run and take Amy with you.'

Headlights came up behind us. I could tell they were from a van, so I got out and waited for Boo. Boo Johnson was the toughest woman I'd ever met, and one of the smartest. A born con artist. I couldn't make out the livery on the van from my position, not in the dark. So I moved toward them, meeting them halfway up the lane to Pier 39.

The van came to a slow, gradual stop, the passenger door opened, and out stepped a freakishly long pair of pale, muscular legs. She closed the door to the van and, careful to avoid injuring her ankles in her tall stilettos, she strode toward me.

When I'd first met Boo I was a con man. She'd worked a couple of jobs with me, mostly light work, setting up fake car accidents. Boo had that look about her, like she was a movie star; it was a glow, almost. She wore a bright fire-engine-red blouse, cut to her stomach, and a tight black skirt. Her bleached-blond hair had been cut short and was held at an impossible angle by a half bottle of hairspray. The sun had gone down long ago, but Boo always wore her shades. Behind those wide oval glasses were a set of eyes that could throw a priest off the top of a tall building.

She cocked her hip and said, 'Good enough?'

For a second I couldn't connect the question. Then I saw the laminated pass in her hand. I took it from her and examined it. There was no doubt that it looked authentic.

'Not bad for an hour's work. Who's the artist?'

'Little guy in Queens, goes by the name of Georgie,' said Boo.

'Tell him I like his work. I might have need of his services one day.'

The Lizard shook hands with the van driver, a big guy in a blue sweater, leather jacket, ripped jeans, and a baseball cap. He looked handsome. She introduced him as Roger. We shook hands and then he went back to his van.

'Roger and I are just friends, for now,' said Boo, with a smile.

'Will he hold up?' I asked.

'Definitely. As far as he's concerned, it's like any other work night. I'm more concerned about Hansel and Gretel,' said Boo, as she peered at Holly and David.

'Leave them to me,' I said.

Both of them looked nervous as hell. David was staring out at the water, lost. Holly tapped her feet, her hands stuffed into her pockets. They both snapped to attention as I approached.

'Holly, you don't need to do this,' I said.

'He's right,' said David.

'No, I'm his PA. They'll be wondering why I'm not there if I don't show.'

In spite of her obvious anxiety, there was a determination in Holly, and it was something more than loyalty. David was at home in front of a computer or in a business meeting, but I got the impression that when it came to the real world he needed a guide, and that was Holly. He was damn lucky to have her.

'Okay, you know the setup. Gerry Sinton needs you in the ground, David. In fact, they'll kill all of us given half a chance. This is a con.

196

It will ensure that they can't make a move on us tonight without implicating the firm. As much as they want us dead, they're only doing it to protect themselves, so they won't take a chance if they think taking us out can be traced back to them. The con protects us, but it will only work if we all absolutely believe it. You have to live it. If you look nervous, if you look like someone walking into a building full of people that want to kill you – guess what? It's over. We're going to your lawyer's office to discuss your defense, David, nothing more.'

They nodded.

They understood, but I wasn't convinced they'd hold up.

'Just follow Boo's lead. Don't talk to security. Leave it to me and Boo. David, when you've got what you need, I want you to say that you're tired – that you need to sleep before the prelim. That's the signal. We'll wrap up and get the hell out of there.'

'What happens if they see through this? What happens if they try to kill me?' said David.

'They won't,' I said.

David, Holly, and I piled into her car. Boo, Roger, and the Lizard got into Roger's van.

We set off, and I rehearsed with David some code words so he could let me know his progress and the word to let me know he'd been made.

CHAPTER FIFTY

The notorious Manhattan traffic had eased as we made our way to the Lightner Building, home to Harland and Sinton. David sat scrunched up in the back of Holly's car, and I tried not to think about the con. Boo was probably the finest con artist I'd ever met, with the exception of my dad. When our paths had first crossed, Boo was plying her trade as a high-class hooker. She'd been looking for a way out that paid as much as the five hundred an hour she earned turning tricks, and I soon showed her how she could use her acting talent to devastating effect.

In any con, you needed a persuader. Most of the insurance cons I'd run needed a person to deal with the insurance investigators, who, for some bizarre reason, were all men. So for a car accident that I'd set up, with a fake plaintiff, fake injury, fake medical center, Boo usually manned the reception desk of the med center and flattered the investigators until they were convinced she was on the level. She was the ultimate persuader.

My thoughts drifted to the next morning's preliminary hearing. I prayed that if tonight went well I wouldn't have to go to court tomorrow, but part of me knew that I wouldn't get a deal for David and that I had to plan for the worst. I'd never won a preliminary hearing, and I didn't know anyone else who'd won one in the last ten years. They're basically rubber stamps; if the prosecution can show even a shred of tangible evidence against the defendant, they win.

If I was going to win the prelim, I would have to show that David was innocent.

'I'm thinking about tomorrow's hearing,' I said. 'We need another suspect.'

198

'I don't know anyone who could even think about harming Clara. She was . . .' I checked the mirror in my sun visor and saw tears streaking David's face.

'I'm sorry. I shouldn't have brought it up. Forget about it for now. Let me worry about that. Just stay focused on what we're doing here.'

He produced a pack of antibacterial handkerchiefs, wiped his face and blew his nose noisily. How did a beautiful woman like Clara end up with little David? Then I stopped being stupid – *So, Clara, what first attracted you to billionaire David Child?*

'She was older than you, right?'

'Yeah, but that didn't matter. She was amazing-looking and smart, too. She had a good heart, Mr Flynn. She, ah, she was the best thing that ever happened to me. Those six months we had together were the happiest of my life.'

In my peripheral vision, I saw Holly tighten her hands on the steering wheel.

'How did you and Clara meet?' I said.

'Reeler. She was one of my followers and we met up on a Reeler hook.'

'I didn't get any of that,' I said.

'Are you on Reeler?' said David.

'No, can't say that I am, and my daughter is a little too young for social media. I know the basics, nothing more.'

'It's like this – you set up an account and you post your photos, your blog, and all your updates to your Reel. Your Reel is like your own page – and the Reeler algos send your updates to people who it thinks would be interested in your post and hooks into your other social media platforms, like Twitter and Facebook, so you can post everything from your Reeler account. Then there's the big selling point; Reeler is the only social media platform that encourages face-to-face interaction – we call them hooks. So if you're in a bar and you post a pic, as long as you're up for a Reeler hook, Reeler will tell all other Reeler users in the area where you are and what you're doing and invite them to go talk to you. That's why Reeler took off so quickly with college kids – you know how many spontaneous Reeler partiers there were in the first month it was online? Try eight thousand. Reeler is the only true social media.'

'Okay, I get it. So how did you meet Clara?'

He rubbed his hands together and dipped his head for a moment before coming up with the answer.

'I don't go out much. Normally I sit at home or I go to parties at friends' houses. Well, this one night there was a huge Reeler party kicking off in the Loft. You know the Loft – it's a big cabaret bar in the city. Nearly everyone in the bar was posting on Reeler, and there was so much activity the network almost crashed. TV news cameras were headed there to cover the story, so me and a couple guys from the board went down to the party. Get our faces on prime-time news.'

He smiled fondly at the memory; then the new reality of her death spread over his features, strangling his smile.

'Her friend had stood her up for dinner, so she went to the party and she got interviewed by one of the news channels. She was so pretty, seemed the obvious choice for them, and she spoke so passionately about Reeler that I wanted to meet her in person and thank her. So we met, we talked, we left and got coffee. I don't like crowds much. That was it.'

The car went over a drain cover, and it felt like we'd just gone through a crash barrier.

'So tell me about her,' I said.

'She was from Virginia, she studied languages, and she'd worked abroad for a while as a freelance translator. I can't remember how many languages she spoke, maybe seven or eight. She worked all over the world, got tired of it and came back to the States. Her parents had moved out to Florida. There wasn't much sense in going home, so she came to New York looking for work with the UN as a translator. She'd been back only a few weeks when I met her. It was like fate or something. Because she'd been away, she didn't know anybody in New York, and I suppose, really, neither did I. We kind of found each other.'

'Did she get a job at the UN?'

'No, she'd applied. She'd been waiting tables.'

'And there were no ex-boyfriends on the scene, nobody with a grudge?'

'No. I can't think of a single person who even disliked her. She didn't know that many people.'

Holly chimed in. 'I've known David since the eighth grade. He won't mind me saying this, but he didn't date a lot in school or college. When Reeler went massive, David had a good time, but there was nobody serious. Am I right?'

David nodded and smiled.

'I've always looked out for him. We're friends and he took care of me when I got laid off. He also got me through a few breakups. I've gotta say that Clara was different from most girls that David met after the Reeler thing. Most of them wanted David for his status and his money and he didn't get serious with any of those girls. Clara was different. She was, I don't know . . . genuine. In both her affection for David and her lack of interest in his money. You remember you bought her that necklace from Tiffany?'

I could see from David's expression, a smile and then a narrowing of eyes, that the memory was at first warm and then painful. A reminder of the person that had been – and the robbery of the life unfulfilled. I thought of Dell, and for a moment I understood him more. He was convinced by the evidence that David was the killer, and he wanted him to pay. The loss of life, so violent, so sudden, had to be rebalanced.

David couldn't speak, and Holly picked up the story, but she spoke softly, as if her words could wound.

'They'd been dating for a month, and David surprised Clara with a Tiffany necklace that came in at a hundred thou. She told him not to be ridiculous. That Saturday they returned the necklace and went shopping in secondhand stores in Brooklyn. She picked out a little necklace that she liked and David bought it. It cost forty dollars.'

We zipped over another manhole cover and my spine was beginning to protest at Holly's choice of car. I thought about Langhiemer again.

'You think Langhiemer could have set you up on his own? He may be ruthless when he's safely behind a keyboard, but could he pull the trigger?'

'I don't know,' said David.

I thought of the hall footage. No one had left the apartment after David, and the cops had found it empty. Everything pointed to him. If Langhiemer had killed Clara, or even if he'd paid someone else to do the shooting, did they just jump out of the window afterward? I thought about this as we approached the Lightner Building and I was reminded about something my pal Judge Ford once told me – sometimes you reach so far for an explanation that you ignore the solution sitting in your pocket. Even with the GSR testimony I'd wrung out of Porter, David could've shot Clara wearing a pair of gloves and then tossed the gloves out of the broken window, leaving only the GSR from the air bag explosion on his hands. Porter hadn't thought of that, but I bet that Zader eventually would.

I was tempted to call my mentor, but Judge Harry would've told me I was crazy – and that no matter what I thought, or what I believed, the evidence only pointed one way.

I didn't want that conversation. Maybe I was afraid Harry would convince me he was right.

Holly pulled up outside the Lightner Building and my phone began to ring. An anonymous number.

'Eddie Flynn,' I said.

'Why is it you want to meet me, Mr Flynn?' It was Bernard Langhiemer. I recognized his voice, traces of a rural accent being fought down by that Harvard graduate tone. I got out and stepped to the sidewalk.

'I want to talk. Funny, I was just thinking about you. I was beginning to wonder if you were going to call me back.'

'That's strange. I would've thought you've got enough on your mind, what with David's legal difficulties. But you seem to be handling them quite well. I saw David's Reels on the news. That was your idea?'

'Why don't we meet, and we can talk about Reeler all you want.'

'But we are talking. Why do you want to meet me?'

I wanted to look the son of a bitch in the eyes when I asked him if he'd framed David. It's much too hard to discern the truth on the phone.

'It won't take long,' I said.

'Will it help David?'

Only if I figure you're lying, I thought.

'I doubt it, but you never know.'

'In that case, I'll meet you. Tonight?'

'Great. Ted's Diner on Chambers Street. Ten o'clock.'

'I'll be there. Just be careful tonight. There are a lot of sharks swimming in the Lightner Building.'

The call went dead. I stared at my phone. Langhiemer was tracking my cell. He clearly liked to intimidate, play little power games. I still had the cell phone Dell had given me. It would have to do for now. I turned off my own cell phone, dropped it on the sidewalk, and raised my heel, ready to turn it into parts. I stopped. Picked it up and put it in my pocket. If the cell was switched off, he couldn't track the signal. There were better uses for it.

CHAPTER FIFTY-ONE

The automatic revolving doors of the Lightner Building allowed all of us to fit into one of its three segments, and we slowly turned around as it ushered us toward the lobby. A tasteful mixture of steel, granite, and marble made up the grand entrance, and a single reception desk sat twenty feet away, on the right, between us and the elevators.

Four men occupied reception. At this time of night, in most buildings, you were lucky if you could get one receptionist; you certainly didn't need four.

The first man was tall, wide, and wore a sharp black suit with a badge on his lapel that read SERGEI. He had a shock of white-blond hair, and I recognized him from the photos of the security team. Behind him, a formidable middle-aged woman with strawberry-blond hair in a bowl cut sucked on an iced coffee through a straw. Off to the left of the desk, two men, black jackets, in their early thirties, short hair, probably armed – part of the security detail for Harland and Sinton. I also recognized them from Dell's file. The firm was in lockdown, and I'd no doubt these guys were ready to kill us as soon as we stepped into the elevator.

I led the way to the reception desk, followed by David and Holly, Boo and Roger bringing up the rear. The Lizard stayed with the van. He was backup, and he would listen in on everything that happened via my cell phone. I'd called him and left the phone locked and on speaker in the breast pocket of my suit jacket.

'Eddie Flynn and David Child for Gerry Sinton,' I said to Sergei.

'These gentlemen are from Harland and Sinton's security. They will escort you,' he said.

The security team eyeballed me, their jaws clenched, hands clasped in front of them. One of them looked Samoan, his dark hair swept back from his face in a tight braid. The other man was white and smaller than the Samoan, but he looked the meaner of the two.

'Just a second,' I said.

Turning to Boo, I said, 'Ms Feldstein, you wanted an establishing piece?'

'Thank you, Mr Flynn,' said Boo, who walked past David and me. Roger followed behind her. I didn't need to turn around to see the cogs working in the security team's tiny little heads as Roger pulled a large TV camera from his bag, handed Boo a microphone, and hit a button on the camera lighting up the reception.

Boo straightened her blouse, mumbled something to Roger, then began her piece to camera.

'Tonight, the billionaire David Child begins consulting with his legal team in preparation for tomorrow's hearing. At the weekend, Child's lover, Clara Reece, was brutally shot and killed in his apartment. The NYPD believe they have a strong case against Child. Here at *60 Minutes* we will be taking you deep into the heart of this fascinating case. We've been granted exclusive access to the private, attorney-client consultations between David Child and his expert legal team as they desperately try to build a defense for what many believe to be an open-and-shut case.'

She paused. Roger made sure he got the security team in the shot, then flicked the beam off.

'Great, that's uploaded. They'll start cutting it right away – no retakes; you're gonna be big, Lana,' said Roger. Boo smiled.

'What the hell is this?' said the Samoan.

'It's TV,' I said. 'CBS. You watch *60 Minutes*?'

'No,' he said. 'No cameras allowed in here, Mr Flynn.'

'Really? Well, then, we'll just have to go to my office. Make sure and tell Gerry I said hi.'

I turned and began slowly heading toward the exit, Holly, Child, Boo, and Roger came with me.

'Hold on,' said the Samoan, dialing from his cell phone.

We stopped. I kept my eyes on the ground. David stood next to me, and I could almost feel his body shaking through the vibrations passing up from the floor into my feet. I put an arm on his to steady him. Holly's eyes were wide, and she kept rattling her fingers along her bag. Clearing my throat to get her attention, I then made a passive gesture with my hands and she stopped fidgeting.

I knew the Samoan wouldn't take his eyes off of me. He worked a piece of gum in his massive jaws, and I could hear his breathing from ten feet away. He'd more than likely worked himself up into a state where he could pop a couple of people, and now he had to rethink because they'd brought a TV crew with them. His call was connected, and I heard him mumbling, probably to Gerry Sinton himself.

I heard the Samoan say, '*60 Minutes.*' He listened, then said, 'Because it's on the side of the goddamned van.'

It was true. Roger was a veteran cameraman for CBS, and he could take out the van whenever he wanted. The benefits of a long-term business relationship with Boo meant Roger occasionally got first sight of a fresh, hot story. Whatever else Boo had her hand into, she dabbled a little in blackmail and trading the kind of photographs that politicians like to keep secret. Boo was a powerful asset for a cameraman with dreams of stepping in front of the camera one day. The producers had learned to give Roger the van and a little leeway – it always paid off.

The liveried CBS van had proved to be the ultimate persuader. My dad once told me that the heart of the con lies in the eyes.

People believe what they can see. As long as you control their view, you control their mind.

'You can go on up,' said the Samoan.

David nodded frantically, clutched his laptop bag, and followed me. A discreet smile from me seemed to calm him a little.

As we walked past the security team, the Samoan said, 'Take all the time you need. We'll be waiting here.'

CHAPTER FIFTY-TWO

If the lobby of the Lightner Building had been impressive, the offices of Harland and Sinton made the entrance look like the back door of a greasy rib house.

Gold.

Practically everything was covered in some form of gold leaf. Gold lamps, gold lettering on the glass walls, and free gold pens sat in a bowl on a coffee table that looked so delicate I was almost afraid to breathe on it. Ornate antique furniture lined the firm's reception area, and the coffee table looked as though it belonged in a Viennese opera house. From the reception area you could see all the way into the conference room. The glass partition walls were clear and gave the impression of a large open office. The place was still in full swing, with lawyers milling around the offices, looking busy for the dollars turning over on the meter.

I gave Boo a slight nod, and she dipped into her purse, found her cell, and set the timer on her phone to count down from thirty seconds. This was also Roger's signal; he fired up the camera and made sweeping shots of the offices.

'David, Mr Flynn,' said a deep, authoritative voice. It was Gerry Sinton. He came out of a side office and strode toward us with his hand extended, ready to greet. Three younger men in suits, who I took to be associates, came behind him and hung back while he took David's hand.

'You should've called ahead and told us to expect the camera crew,' he said, with a smile that barely masked his disgust. 'I'm sure Mr Flynn has your interests at heart, but letting TV crews into your confidential attorney meetings is a little misguided.'

'Actually, it was my idea,' said David, and even though I could hear the tension in his voice, he'd managed to crane his neck in order to face Gerry as he'd said it.

'I think it's a great idea, but there's a time and a place . . .' began Gerry.

'We need to get out in front of this with the media,' I said. 'It's already out there. Far better that we make the story ourselves. Then we can control it.'

'We're getting the exclusive, so we're amenable to a little editorial input,' said Boo, extending her hand to Sinton.

'Lana Feldstein,' she said.

'Gerry Sinton. Call me Gerry. I don't believe I've seen you on *60 Minutes* before, Lana.'

'It's Ms Feldstein,' said Boo, taking off her glasses and hitting Sinton with all the power from those incredible eyes. Some kind of electricity, or light, shined out of Boo's green secret weapons. She seemed to attract men to those eyes like moths to a lightbulb. They needed it but knew it was too hot to touch.

'Of course, Ms Feldstein,' he said.

He held on to Boo's hand for a second or two longer than was necessary, but he was unable to hold her gaze for the same period; no one could.

Boo's phone rang; the timer had run out, and she canceled the chime and pretended to take a call. 'Scott, did you get the shots?' she said.

'Scott Pelley – the producer,' I said. 'Roger here is able to upload video wirelessly to their editing suite. They're just going over the shots from the lobby with the editor in the studio.'

Sinton nodded, and his lips worked over his teeth, as if he were trying to get rid of a bad taste. He looked over his shoulder at another man who stood in the hallway leading to the inner offices. Whatever was conveyed in that look made this man take off, back into the warren of offices beyond the conference room. There was no way they could make a move now, not with video footage of Child's and my location existing outside of their control.

'You've got the full file?' he said.

I handed him the prosecution file so he could make copies.

He handed the file to one of the associates, who quickly left to copy it. We followed Sinton down a glass-paneled hallway.

For the moment, we were safe. Until we had to leave. Although I didn't want to ride our luck too much. I'd told David we would be no longer than an hour in the office. If he couldn't hack the algo in that time, then we bailed, no matter what.

CHAPTER FIFTY-THREE

Gerry Sinton led us into a conference room with a long table of dark river slate, sparsely flecked with dashes of luminous green. We pulled up chairs and sat down at one corner of the table, the one closest to a wide-screen TV set on the wall. I'd made sure to coach David on seating arrangements. He was to wait until Sinton sat down, and then he was to sit opposite him, and if possible David was to keep his back to a wall or a window.

Roger panned the room, and Boo did a little introduction of everyone present. She explained that although David Child wanted to grant their viewers complete access, CNN didn't want to take any steps that might compromise the trial; therefore, none of the sound in the confidential meeting would be recorded.

'Thank you,' said Sinton.

From his leather bag, David produced a sleek silver laptop, powered it up, opened another can of energy drink, and leaned across the table to Boo. She came over, and they began whispering as Boo read what was on David's screen.

'Ms Feldstein is helping me out with a personal statement that we'll release to the press tomorrow,' said David, in answer to Sinton's searching look.

'I thought I would work on it while you read the prosecution files and got up to speed.'

'Of course,' said Sinton.

As David tapped away on the laptop, his back was to a large window overlooking Manhattan. Sinton and his buddies sat across the table. David could work without any of the lawyers seeing his laptop screen. I swiveled around in my seat to admire the view. Behind David was the Corbin Building, one of the old office buildings in the city that had struggled to find tenants since Harland and Sinton bought the Lightner. 'For rent' signs were pasted on at least one window of every floor of the Corbin Building. Times were tough, even for landlords.

The associate returned with my original prosecution file and five copies. He gave one to Gerry, one to David, and spread the remaining copies out among his other colleagues who sat beside Sinton.

'I'll just take a few minutes to read this,' said Sinton.

I did likewise. Roger continued to pan the room, and Boo and David continued to whisper together, with Holly chiming in occasionally.

'It's difficult to know what to say when somebody accuses you of a crime you didn't commit.'

That was the signal; the network password Christine had given to us no longer worked. David would have to try to hack into the system.

Gerry took his time, scanning each page. His thick fingers worked delicately at the paper, almost reverently. The associates flicked through at a much faster rate, made quick notes on HARLAND AND SINTON headed, yellow legal pads.

I didn't need to reread what was in the file. I'd taken it in the first time, in the cab.

Ten minutes later, turning over the final page, Sinton said, 'Shall we watch the DVDs?'

'Sure,' I said, handing him the first disk. He slotted it into the side of the TV and picked up a slim remote. As the TV came on, the lights automatically dimmed.

'I should've had a PR firm draft this thing,' said David in frustration – the second signal. He was finding it difficult to hack into their system; he would likely need the full hour.

The screen filled with the lobby of Central Park Eleven. I watched David and Clara go hand in hand into the elevator, the swipe from David's key fob and then he selected the floor, Clara's fearful reaction in the elevator, which David said was claustrophobia. Camera change to the landing leading to David and Gershbaum's luxury apartments. Time stamp on the camera read 19:46 as the front door to the apartment closed behind David and Clara. The footage played to 20:02 and David leaving the apartment with his gym bag.

Sinton had made notes while the footage played, the time stamps and camera ID numbers.

I flipped through the file and found the security logs for David's building. The emergency call from Gershbaum went through at 20:02 to security, who must've just missed David as he descended in the elevator. The security team checked in with control when they reached Gershbaum's front door at 20:06.

Sixteen minutes was plenty of time to murder his girlfriend.

While he checked his notes, Sinton wound the footage back so that he could watch David coming out of his apartment. He rewound and watched it again, this time ignoring his notes.

I saw Gerry give David a fleeting glance, then return to the image of his client waiting nonchalantly on the elevator. Of course, I knew what Gerry was thinking – most lawyers have the same thought when they're representing someone on trial for murder; did he do it?

Perhaps Sinton thought David looked just too calm as he exited his apartment. He wasn't fumbling in his pockets, bouncing on his heels to get away. There was no nervous anxiety on display. Sinton was asking himself if David was capable of killing his girlfriend and hiding it so well. I didn't think so. I thought David was the kind of guy to get anxious ordering a latte. If the kid had just killed someone in cold blood, he'd damn near tear the door down to get out of there, and if the elevator wasn't waiting on him, he'd leap down the stairs or throw himself out the goddamn window. Instead, the footage showed David, his hoodie up, close the door behind him, stop, turn around, and take a step toward the door, as if he'd forgotten something, then back away from the door, slip his earphones on, turn casually, and hit the button for the elevator. This was my second time watching this, and I wanted to know what had caused David to hesitate, to turn back toward the apartment, then change his mind and go for the elevator.

David wasn't watching the screen. His attention was concentrated on the laptop.

I had to ask him.

'David, when you left the apartment, did you hear anything in the hallway while you were waiting for the elevator, maybe a shot?'

'No. I would've remembered,' he said.

A fountain pen tapped on Gerry's lips – he put down his pen, made sure it sat straight beside his legal pad, then steepled his fingers. He was evaluating David – weighing it up. Could he have killed her?

But the fact that Sinton was curious about David's guilt or innocence sparked a thought – the firm had nothing to do with the murder of Clara Reece, or if they did, Sinton knew nothing about it. The murder and arrest of David Child threw the firm into a pressure cooker – no, they wouldn't bring that kind of heat down on themselves knowingly.

'I thought we could go over the paper file,' said Sinton finally.

'Okay,' I said. 'That all right with you, David?'

'You guys go ahead and talk it over. Let me finish this and then we can discuss everything.'

Another message: He still couldn't access the system.

CHAPTER FIFTY-FOUR

'It strikes me that the major problem here, apart from the security camera footage placing David as the last person inside the apartment, is the gun in David's car,' said Sinton.

'I agree,' I said.

'So what are we hoping to achieve tomorrow? With this evidence, the preliminary hearing is dead in the water. I say we waive the hearing and get ready for trial.'

'No.'

It took a second for Sinton to register that I'd contradicted him. He leaned back in his chair, folded his arms, and snorted.

'There's nothing to be gained tomorrow, Flynn, we can't say there's not enough evidence to hold David, when in fact, there's easily enough evidence to convict him.'

'David wants the charges thrown out tomorrow,' I said.

'I'm sure he does, but you and I know that's not going to happen.'

David lifted his head momentarily, clocked me. I nodded.

'I've already told David that it's a long shot, but these are his instructions. We fight this the whole way.'

Sinton laughed, shook his head. 'Come on. Even if by some miracle you win the prelim, the DA can go straight to the grand jury anyway. We're wasting time with this when we could be preparing for trial.'

'I want to win tomorrow,' said David.

That cut out the argument. Waving his hands, Sinton nodded, and said, 'Of course you do, and if you want to fight, we'll fight, but there's not a lot to work with.'

Checking my watch, I saw we had less than twenty minutes of the hour left.

Gerry played the accident footage, but I didn't need to see it a second time. Instead I paid close attention to Sinton and his associates, so I was pretty certain they didn't recognize Perry Lake, the professional driver who I was sure had been paid to hit David and had given a false name to the cops. According to NYPD – Perry was John Woodrow. It made sense. Perry Lake had a list of priors for dangerous driving. I suspected that John Woodrow had a clear record.

'Just give me a second and I'll be done,' said David.

With my right index finger, I tapped the back of my left hand. He wanted more time, and I'd signaled that he had five minutes.

We sat in silence for what seemed like ten minutes. In reality it was more like thirty seconds. Sinton couldn't just sit there. He wanted to stamp his authority on the case.

'David, I know that you're innocent. I know that Mr Flynn, here, has passion and skill. But he's also – you'll forgive me for saying so – a small-time criminal lawyer who would jump at the chance of a huge trial like this. No offense,' he said, giving me a look that said he meant every word to be as offensive as possible.

'None taken,' I said.

'The gun, which I think is likely to be the murder weapon, was found in your car.'

'Like I said, I never saw it before . . .'

'David, come on, it was found next to you,' said Sinton.

'You don't believe me,' said David.

'It's not a question of what I believe, David. This is about the evidence. We have to—'

Sinton broke off. It took me a few seconds to realize he wasn't pausing to come up with the right words to appease his client. He was staring straight at David, transfixed. I got up and moved around the table, picking up the remote as I moved. I hit eject and waited for the disk, but really I was trying to see what Sinton was looking at.

His line of sight focused on David, who was ignoring everyone, head down, typing furiously on his laptop.

Then I saw it.

Gerry Sinton wasn't looking at David. He was looking behind David. He was staring at the reflection on the window from David's computer screen.

I was farther away than Sinton and at a worse angle, and even I could see in the mirrored reflection what was happening on David's computer.

The laptop showed two pages on a split screen. On one side was the Harland and Sinton log-in screen, with a large white box below their logo that asked for a password.

On the other screen was what looked like code. Bright green symbols and numbers that David was able to create at blistering speed before highlighting the sequence and then cutting and pasting the code into the password box on the other screen. I saw LOG-IN FAIL come up on the Harland and Sinton page, and David retyped another sequence.

An electric current shot up my spine.

The DVD ejected onto the rich burgundy carpet. I was already moving toward David. I slammed the laptop closed, almost trapping his fingers.

'Enough PR work. Gerry's right. If we don't get you off, then all of this,' I said, gesturing to Boo and Roger, 'doesn't matter a damn.'

The suddenness of my outburst and slam from the laptop closure spread a silence over the room as if all had stopped breathing to let the echoes find a home.

Sinton tapped on the slate tabletop, his pinkie ring making a repeated chipping sound. His gaze seemed far away, across the street to the Corbin Building, over the rooftops and beyond the trees of Central Park. His head swiveled around and snapped those cold eyes on me.

His voice had changed. The deep aggressive drawl had been replaced by a cold, detached tone.

'Your wife went down to the courthouse to speak to you this afternoon. She didn't come back to work afterward.'

He slipped a cell phone from his jacket, typed something, hit send, and returned his stare to me.

'If she's ill, she should've reported sick. A phone call at least. You mind telling me where she is?'

CHAPTER FIFTY-FIVE

'I saw her briefly this afternoon. She said she had someplace to be. We're not together anymore, so I don't know where she went. Where's your partner, by the way? I would've thought Ben Harland would be here, too,' I said.

'Ben is on vacation. I'm more worried about your wife. Maybe she's ill. Maybe you said something to upset her,' he said.

'I don't think so. We had coffee together. It was fine. In fact, David, let's you and I go get a coffee. You can drop me off afterward,' I said. The escape signal.

Roger fired up the camera, and Boo reached into her bag. I didn't know what she had in there, maybe a gun, maybe a knife. Boo could handle herself; she could be lethal with pretty much anything larger than a lipstick.

Holly stood, a little too quickly, but it didn't matter. We'd already been made.

Footsteps in the hall. Fast. Heavy. Two men at least.

The conference room door opened and Gill stood in the doorway. He was still wearing the checkered shirt, but he'd gotten rid of the green jacket. He was on his cell phone. The blond Sergei stood beside him.

'Tell Brond and Fiso to get up here. They're not answering my calls,' said Gill.

I presumed Gill was calling reception, unable to raise the Samoan and his friend in the lobby.

The associates looked confused. They didn't have a clue what was going down.

'That's all of our video uploaded to the studio,' said Roger.

Gill and Sergei exchanged a glance. They hesitated.

'This is Mr Gill,' said Sinton, sweat glowing from his forehead from the glare of the TV screen. 'Mr Gill and his men look after firm security. I'm sure you won't mind them accompanying you to your hotel, David. We can't be too careful.'

I felt my fingers digging into my palms. My legs had spread into a stance, and I was ready to separate Mr Gill's head from his shoulders if he made a move. If they thought David had hacked their system, none of us would leave the building alive. Gerry Sinton looked desperate – the rules had changed.

A low electric hum from the air-conditioning.

David held the laptop across his chest like a shield, but it only drew attention to his panic. It looked like David was using his chest as a pump to inflate the damn thing. He was on the brink of another panic attack.

I didn't move. I was waiting for Gill to reach behind his back for a pistol.

'Mr Gill, would you be so kind as to get that camera for me? I'd like to check it,' said Sinton.

Nodding to the man beside him, Gill stood his ground. He had a good view of the entire room, and his back was to the wall, all of his potential targets and threats in front of him. He wouldn't want to compromise that position. The blond guy from the lobby, Sergei, moved forward, walked behind Sinton and made his way toward Roger and the camera. Before he got to Roger, he had to get past Boo.

Sergei, at around six five and pushing the limits of his XXXL suit jacket at two hundred and fifty pounds, fixed his gaze on Roger. As he approached, he held out his right hand, palm open, to push aside Boo if she tried to intervene. She was half his size. He wasn't even looking at her.

I almost felt sorry for the guy.

Casually, Boo raised her right knee high and then brought her pencil heel down like a hydraulic press on the top of Sergei's left foot. At least two inches of stiletto heel disappeared into the soft flesh where his foot met his ankle. He didn't scream. He didn't have time. His mouth opened, his eyes rolled and by the time he'd hit the floor he'd already passed out.

Gill didn't move forward.

His right arm flexed. His hand rose, and as it drew level with his waist, I saw his elbow extend behind him. He was going for a piece.

The conference doors burst open. Gill arrested his movement, and all heads swung to the back of the room to see the tall, dark figure cradling a Glock.

CHAPTER FIFTY-SIX

'The Lizard's gotta make a small apology,' said the Lizard.

'Who is this?' said Sinton, rising to his full height.

'This is the Lizard. He's a friend of mine. He handles *my* personal security,' I said.

'The two guys in the lobby didn't want to let me up here. We talked. They didn't listen. Cops are on the way. Your receptionist called them, then called the paramedics. The big Samoan guy don't look too good. He might wake up tomorrow to find he's a little shorter than he used to be.'

Sinton stumbled backward, knocked his chair over. Gill put a hand on his shoulder, never taking his eyes from the Lizard. I saw that the Lizard also locked his gaze on Gill. I'd seen this before. Somehow the two most lethal men in any room always seem to find each other; they know instinctively who poses the biggest threat, and neither of them will back down until one of them gets his ticket punched.

I didn't need to check my watch to know that we'd been in the building for seventy minutes. I'd told the Lizard that if we hadn't come out after an hour, he should come get us.

Nobody moved.

I heard the unmistakable sound of a police siren. It was soft and distant, but urgent.

'We should go, Eddie. You got that thing,' said the Lizard.

'He's right. I've got a thing. I think I can speak for David in saying you're fired.'

When Sinton spoke, all of his practiced refinery washed away in his rage. 'That's just fine. We don't represent snitches, anyway. No point. They usually get themselves killed.'

'Why don't we take the stairs; it was a long wait in the car,' said the Lizard.

Quickly, we filed out, Boo and Roger in front, Holly and David, then me. The Lizard's eyes lingered on Gill for a second longer, and then he blew him a kiss.

Gill winked.

We took the stairs two at a time down three flights.

'Here,' said the Lizard.

We followed him through the swinging doors to a dark office reception lit with the interior light from the elevator – a knife jamming the elevator doors open.

As the elevator ran to the ground floor, no one could manage a single word – we were all trying to catch our breath, slow the adrenaline – except Boo and the Lizard, who weren't breathing heavy; they were watching the digital display count down the floors. In the lobby, the female receptionist saw us, screamed when she clocked the Lizard, and hid behind her desk.

On the way out I saw the two security men lying in a heap by the door, their automatic weapons stripped and useless in front of them. One guard was facedown and unmoving. The Samoan sat on the floor, leaning his back against the wall. He gingerly touched his calf. His breath came in short, spasmodic gasps, increasing in intensity as his hands got closer to his ankle. His foot looked as if it was turned in the wrong direction. As the revolving doors swung to let us out into the street, the screams from the Samoan drowned out the still distant police sirens.

I got into the driver's seat of Holly's car and started the engine.

'Don't move; wait,' said David.

I craned my neck to look at him and saw his laptop held up in front of his face.

The code screen had disappeared; only the firm's page remained. Below the Harland and Sinton logo, it read—

YOU ARE NOW LOGGED IN

CHAPTER FIFTY-SEVEN

'Wait, wait . . . If you take off, I'll lose the signal.'

The NYPD response vehicles were maybe five blocks away, the two-tone sirens increasing their pitch and ferocity with every passing second.

I started the car, waited to let the revs die down, and then gently pressed the accelerator. If I revved the car too much, I would flood the engine – I just needed it warm, loose, ready to take off.

'Oh Jesus, they're coming,' said Holly.

She buried her head in the seat and slid down until her eyes met the bottom of the passenger window. Gill and two other men were in the lobby, kneeling over the Samoan.

The Lizard hadn't taken off either. He was waiting to follow me. He leaned out of the van window and hocked his thumb at me. Roger was behind the wheel of that van and he was also pumping the gas.

'David,' I said.

The hollow plastic tinkle of fingers on keys grew in intensity.

'I'm downloading. Thirty percent. . . . forty-one percent . . . Hold on.'

'David, we've got to get out of here.'

Nothing.

The sirens were close now.

Gill was in the revolving door, his right hand behind his back.

I nodded to the Lizard, floored the Honda, and pulled into the street. The dull, throaty noise from the van's V8 sounded behind me. I signaled, turned the corner, and headed deeper into the city as fast as I could.

'No, I'm almost done. Wait!'

'You get it?' I said, looking in the rearview mirror.

'I got it,' he said, removing the USB drive from his laptop.

We drove into Jersey, looped around the suburbs in crazy patterns. After thirty minutes I stopped the car, waited for the Lizard, Boo, and Roger.

'You think the DA will let me walk in exchange for this?' said David, holding up the flash drive.

'I'll push it as hard as I can. You risked your life tonight. I won't forget that. The feds will lean on Zader to get this data. It's all we've got. I just hope they want it bad enough.'

We listened to the wheeze from the engine while the idea floated around.

'You think they can persuade him?' said David.

'I don't know, but I sure hope so.'

I lied. I did know. Dell, no matter what kind of connections he had in New York, wouldn't be able to sell the DA on a withdrawal for David. No way. They would want a full confession and jail time. Nothing else would satisfy Zader. Either I didn't want to tell David, or I couldn't. Whichever, I said nothing more. We'd made our play. The con had burned away the pretense with the firm. It was now open war. I'd already warned the Lizard to be on the lookout for the man with *The Scream* tattoo on his neck. When Roger, at the wheel of the CNN van, appeared in my rearview, I let him overtake and followed.

Weaving through the streets, keeping the van in my headlights, I thought of Christine. I was close to getting her out of this now. She and Amy just had to hang on for a little longer.

The sky had darkened and it was a full moon, bright and tinged with red. I imagined that when the cops arrived at the firm, Gerry would play it down, maybe tell them the Samoan fell down the stairs. I knew Gerry Sinton wouldn't want the cops looking into him or his security team. He would make no complaint about the Lizard beating the hell out of his guys.

Sinton would deal with it his own way. Now that he knew we were on to the money-laundering scheme, he would go all out on having us killed. He had to be careful. Nothing to link it back to him or the firm. But the pressure was on.

'Where's the money gonna land?' I asked.

'Chase Manhattan at 4:05 p.m. tomorrow. I've got the account number.'

I wondered what Gerry would do when the money hit the account. I knew what I would do if I were him. If Gerry was smart, he'd leave the money where it was, take whatever cash he had stashed already, and hitch a private plane to a nonextradition country.

Dell needed the account details and all the evidence to sink the firm before the money became available. His biggest hope was to secure the illegal funds. The amount of money recovered was where the real glory lay for Dell.

'How much money is there?'

'Enough to give Donald Trump heart palpitations. Close to eight,' said David.

'Eight million?' said Holly.

'No, eight billion,' said David.

CHAPTER FIFTY-EIGHT

Our destination following the visit to Harland and Sinton had already been agreed. The Lizard would collect his van from Roger's house and leave Boo and Roger to put the CNN van in the garage. The Lizard was to collect his own van and meet Holly, David, and me at his place. The Lizard said his house would be safest. Turns out, it wasn't so safe after all. But that had more to do with the wildlife in the house than the firm.

I pulled into a space outside a suburban residence in Queens, and the Lizard's van parked behind me. Soon as we stopped I called the Lizard's associate Frankie, whose people were watching the hotel Christine and Amy were holed up in. So far they were safe and there was no suspicious activity. And no men with neck tattoos.

The Lizard's home looked more like a reptile house than a family home in the sleepy corner of Queens.

'Don't go into the yard. Don't even open the door,' said the Lizard, slowly, to everyone as they filed in through the front door. I remembered that out back the Lizard kept his most prized and highly illegal possessions – a pair of Komodo dragons that he called Bert and Ernie. Aside from personal protection, hits, and the occasional hot drop-off, the Lizard's main role for the Italian Mafia was that of interrogator. If they needed somebody to talk, they brought him here. Usually a single look at Bert and Ernie was enough. Most of those guys didn't catch on that the most lethal animal in that house was the Lizard himself.

Holly ate little and went to bed in the Lizard's spare room. The Lizard stood in his kitchen, chopping a twenty-pound rack of pork belly and ribs into foot-long strips. When he was done, he went out back and locked the door from the outside.

Feeding time.

David left the plate in front of him untouched. Although he'd placed his laptop on the kitchen table, he had yet to open it. He sipped at yet another power drink and stared at a tank of tarantulas that the Lizard kept beside his toaster. I suddenly felt both sick and hungry. The Lizard had left a hero sandwich for me, which I unwrapped, cut in half, and then I placed each half on a separate plate.

'You saved my life again tonight,' David said.

I shook my head.

'Boo and the Lizard saved all of us. I just hope it pays off.'

He drummed his fingers three times on the tabletop, adjusted the plate of sandwiches and pickles the Lizard had prepared, turning the plate through forty-five degrees. He took his time with the plate, making sure it was equidistant between his laptop and the edge of the table. When he was satisfied, he examined a pickle, before quickly replacing it and diving for the antibacterial wipes again.

'I'm going to trust you,' said David, handing me the USB drive. 'Here,' he said. 'Try for the deal. I know it's a long shot. But there's no reason your wife should be in danger. You can't change what's happened. I can. You can't win this thing tomorrow. I know you'll try; I understand that now. But quite frankly, there's no reason your wife should suffer. Go on, take it.'

He wrote out a password code on the napkin. I folded the pen drive in the napkin, stood, and put my hand on David's shoulder. He seemed to recoil a little and I gave him his space. I didn't take it as a slight.

'Thank you, but I'm not going to give this to them unless you and Christine walk,' I said.

He nodded. 'Eddie, I know you'll do your best. I almost died twice today. I'm still here thanks to you. I won't forget that.'

I dialed Dell's number on the cell he'd given me.

'I've got what you need.'

'A guilty plea?'

'No, but I have the next best thing. I have the algorithm trace to access the money trail and the account number for the final deposit. Money lands just after four p.m. tomorrow, and I know exactly where it's headed. That's what you wanted, right?'

'Meet me at the St Regis Hotel in half an hour.'

'No.'

Silence.

'What is this, Eddie? A shakedown?'

'Call it whatever you want. I have something you desperately need. I want something in exchange.'

'You want money?'

'I want four things. A private jet, fueled and ready at Teterboro Airport. One pilot. Bring a hundred grand in nonsequential, untampered bills and I'll give you the pen drive. You'll get the DA to withdraw all charges against David Child and an immunity agreement for my wife. My wife and daughter are going to fly the hell out of here, and when I get a call to tell me the plane has landed, I'll give you the password for the algo trace.'

Even though he muffled the microphone I could tell he was talking to somebody else in the room, relaying the information.

'I'll need two hours. You got a deal,' he said.

I hung up, turned to David, and said, 'We're on. I've got just enough time to meet Langhiemer before I have to hit the airport.'

'I'm surprised he's agreed to meet you.'

'It's certainly interesting. Either he had nothing to do with Clara's death and just wants to gloat – or he's involved and wants to find out how much of the setup we've been able to figure out. Either way, once I meet him I'll know.'

CHAPTER FIFTY-NINE

At three minutes past ten I drove by Ted's Diner. It was a pretty small place, and my favorite spot for breakfast. The glass front meant that it was great for people watching. There were a couple of guys in high-vis coats, road workers probably getting a late meal; an old lady in a mock fur coat who was a regular, and a young man in a black hoodie with a MacBook open on the table in front of him. He was the youngest person in the place, fit the description David had given me, and he sat close to the door. It was Langhiemer. I'd bet on it.

I looped around the block and parked down the street from the diner. There were still plenty of people milling around at this time of night. I switched on my cell, locked Holly's car, and tried to hail a cab. While I waited on the sidewalk, I selected the call forwarding service on my cell and entered the number for the cellular phone Dell had given to me. The diner was maybe a hundred yards away. I could see the light spill onto the sidewalk, but no one inside the place could see me. A cab pulled up and I got in the back.

'Where to, pal?'

'Sorry, I forgot my wallet. I'll have to go back to my apartment,' I said, climbing back out onto the street.

The driver shook his head. I closed the door and watched the yellow cab head away from the diner, toward the river, my cell phone tucked behind the seat.

I got back into the Honda and waited.

So far all of my limited dealings with Langhiemer had been on his terms; he had control and intel on me. I needed to switch that up.

My initial estimate was five minutes. I didn't doubt that as soon as I turned on my cell, some kind of program alerted Langhiemer.

He was probably sitting in Ted's staring at the screen and wondering why I was headed in the opposite direction to the diner.

After four minutes the cell phone rang. Call forwarding. My own cell in the cab was on silent, and it shot the call to the phone in my hand. I answered it.

'I'm waiting . . .' said Langhiemer.

'Sorry. Something came up. I can't make it. Can we reschedule?' I said.

'I don't think so,' said Langhiemer, and disconnected.

I started the car. Langhiemer came out of the diner, a laptop bag slung over his shoulder. He made it over the crosswalk onto my side of the street and held out a thumb for a cab. A minute later, a yellow taxi picked him up. I gave it a few seconds before I pulled into a lane of traffic and followed him.

It didn't take long for the yellow cab to drop him on Fifth Avenue. I parked, got out fast, and was maybe twenty feet away by the time he'd paid the driver and made for an apartment block overlooking the park. I watched him enter the building and hung back. I let a few minutes pass, then followed him. A doorman in full regalia, who probably preferred to be called a 'living space concierge' stood at the entrance, eyeing me.

'Hi. I'm from Manhattan Cars. I just dropped off Mr Langhiemer. Thing is, I just found a cell phone in the back of my car. I cleaned the car before I started my shift and didn't find any phones. I think this is his. Would you mind letting me up so I could show it to him?'

I didn't expect to get a pass even though I thought I sounded convincing. I held the cell phone in my hand and looked tired and bored.

'I'll call him and ask him. Wait here,' said the doorman.

A couple of brown leather couches beside the security desk looked real comfortable and I took the one facing the elevators. From where I sat, I couldn't hear the conversation with Langhiemer.

If he was half as smart as I thought he was, he'd figure it out.

'Mr Langhiemer will be down to see you directly,' said the doorman.

Sure enough, before I could get too comfortable, the elevator doors opened and I saw the same man who'd left Ted's Diner. A light beard, dark spots around his eyes. Slim, dressed all in black.

The slight tremble around the lips and the broad-eyed stare gave away his jittery anger.

He launched himself out of the elevator with his hand extended. I took the handshake as I rose and felt him pull me toward the door. I let him. I'd been thrown out of plenty of bars, and this felt eerily similar.

'Let's talk outside,' he said.

'Everything all right, Mr Langhiemer?' said the doorman.

'Just fine,' he said.

Out of the building, on the sidewalk, he let go of my hand.

'You shouldn't have come here. I waited in the diner, like you asked. Nice touch with the doorman. I've got my phone and you knew that. I guess it was your phone taking a ride around Manhattan in the back of a cab. Clever.'

'I thought the message I left the doorman might give you a hint. You're not very hospitable. I was looking forward to taking a look at the view from your apartment.'

'What do you want?'

This was why I'd come. I wanted to unsettle the guy before I popped the question. And I remembered that when he'd first called me, there was a female voice in the background telling him to hang up. The phrase that she'd used was strange: 'Hang up. No calls.'

'You sure you don't need your girlfriend's permission before you talk to me?' I said.

'What?'

'When you called me in the diner today, out of the blue, I heard a female voice telling you to hang up. No calls. It's good to know who wears the pants in your house,' I said.

It was a cheap way to antagonize him: playing on his anger. I'd expected him to explode, to loosen his tongue and maybe, just maybe, he might give something away that he wouldn't have done if he'd been calm.

Langhiemer didn't explode. He didn't let his temper go wild. The opposite.

He stumbled backward, shaking his head. I could tell by the look on his face that he was scared. Not the reaction I'd hoped for, but I decided to take advantage.

'Where were you on Saturday night around eight?'

No words passed his lips. He simply studied me for a moment, giving himself time for the venom to flow back into his system. 'I was murdering David's girlfriend. Is that what you want me to say?'

A flicker from his right eyebrow, and his hands dove into his pockets.

'Where were you?'

'I was at home. Alone. Now get your crummy ass away from me or I'll call my lawyer.'

He didn't move. Neither did I. Then he backed away, holding my stare.

'I value my privacy highly, Mr Flynn. Now leave.'

'Pity you don't think much of other people's privacy,' I said, and I took out my cell phone and snapped a pic of Langhiemer. He thought about making a grab for my phone, thought better of it and went back inside. The doorman got yelled at and fingers pointed at him.

He was holding something back. I knew it. Whether that had something to do with Clara's death, or David, I couldn't tell. Whatever it was, it had something to do with the woman's voice I'd heard on the phone. The fact that I'd heard her scared him. And I had no clue why.

I turned swiftly, conscious that I had to get to the airport for midnight. Just as I turned, something registered in my peripheral vision. Somebody standing still across the street at the park. The man with *The Scream* tattoo. I froze in his stare and began making calculations. Holly's car was parked around fifty feet away. The man was probably seventy-five feet away from me and fifty feet from the car, but on the opposite side of the street. A steady flow of cars on the avenue meant he would have to bob and weave through the moving traffic to get to me.

I thought I could make it to the car, start it up, and get away. But it would be tight. If he was too close by the time I got to the car, I'd have to open the trunk and hope Holly kept a tire iron handy.

The car keys jingled in my hand, the surge of fear in my chest strangled my breath, and I felt my legs itching to take off.

Just before I broke into a sprint, the man across the street smiled, lit up a cigarette, turned his back on me, and wandered away, into the park.

Before he could change his mind, I took off as fast as I could, got into the car and spun the tires into the asphalt.

CHAPTER SIXTY

The wind licking off the runway of Teterboro Airport rocked the little Honda as I drove north along Industrial Avenue, headed for the Homeland Security hangar that served the FBI and a handful of federal agencies whenever they needed a ride. Teterboro sat around ten miles northeast of Manhattan, in Bergen County, New Jersey. It was home to a bunch of private air charter companies which hauled goods and people. I'd once dated a girl in nearby Moonachie, and we'd drive down Industrial Avenue and then sit on the hood of my beat-up Chevy Tahoe and split a six-pack while the planes roared overhead.

As I drove I tried to keep Christine out of my thoughts. In my mind I replayed my conversation with Langhiemer. He had no love for David. Probably hated him. But was that enough to kill Clara to set up David for murder? At my core, I knew David didn't kill Clara. But I wondered if I was either being conned by David, or if I was conning myself into believing he was innocent.

One way or another, I needed to stop this before the firm's tattooed man dropped a bowl of acid on Christine, David, or me.

The Honda slammed over a speed hump that I hadn't seen. My head hit the ceiling and I swore.

As soon as I relaxed my mind and stopped thinking about David and Langhiemer, my mind went straight to Christine. Replaying our phone call not a half hour ago.

Christine told me she didn't want to leave New York. She wanted to stay and tough it out. She was plenty tough, but in the way that lawyers are often tough: crusading against the odds and playing the risks. This was a different situation. I told her she wasn't safe and that if she didn't get on the damn plane with Amy that I would throw her on board and tie her to the seat.

Guilt.

I blamed Ben Harland and Gerry Sinton for their greed, for their cowardice in using the junior associates at their firm as patsies for their fraud.

And I blamed myself.

When Amy was born Christine said she didn't want to work until Amy was well into her teens. I figured it was to do with Christine's upbringing. Her mom had worked long hours and Christine had spent most of her early years with nannies and babysitters, rarely getting much time with her parents, even on weekends.

Guilt.

The only reason Christine took the job with Harland and Sinton was because I couldn't make ends meet for my family. Christine had worked in prestigious firms after she passed the bar exam and so her résumé opened a lot of doors. Just before Christmas, Christine took the job at Harland and Sinton, part time at first, then more hours. By the end of this January she was doing sixty-hour weeks. She didn't want the job. She wanted time with Amy. Time that I denied them both by not bringing home the dollars.

A light rain had begun to fall, and I struggled to see much ahead of me in the tiny headlight beams. After ten minutes with my nose close to the windshield, watchful for speed humps, I saw the taillights of a small aircraft up ahead on the right and the beacon light from an airfield hangar just beyond the plane. I turned in to the lot and made for the hangar.

As I got closer I saw Dell's car parked outside the open hangar doors.

Christine, her sister, and Amy would be arriving soon.

I parked the Honda, folded the collar of my suit jacket around my neck, and jogged to the hangar door. By the time I'd stepped inside, I was wet through. A yellow-orange glow from the overhead lights gave a false impression of heat. The hangar was like a meat locker. Standing by the small plane I saw Dell, Kennedy, and two or three other agents in suits, Ferrar and Weinstein among them. Weinstein still cradled his strapped-up fingers.

A hand in the air from Dell silenced Kennedy as I approached them. Both men wore long overcoats and gloves.

'I knew I could rely on you, Eddie,' said Dell. He nodded and smiled.

'Kennedy knows I always deliver,' I said.

'Thank God,' said Kennedy, in a way that somehow made me understand that he was against the whole setup from the start. While Kennedy and I would never be buddies, I suspected he didn't appreciate Dell's methods. Kennedy had a family, too.

A tech opened up a laptop on the hood of a black truck, and Dell held out his hand for the pen drive. Farther back in the hangar I saw another black SUV, but I didn't pay it any further thought.

'We want to make sure you're not conning us, Eddie. If you don't mind, we want to look at the kind of data that's on the drive,' said Dell.

'You won't be able to read it, not without the password,' I said, handing it over.

The tech inserted the drive into the laptop and I heard the machine purr as it came to life, running its checkups and alert systems as it began to access the memory.

A thumbs-up.

'There's a lot of data here,' said Dell.

'It's there. Let me see the money,' I said.

An agent produced a large sports bag and opened it. One hundred dollar bills – twenty-five of them in each bundle. I emptied the money onto the poured concrete floor and tossed the bag away. Stack by stack, I flicked through the bills, making sure there were no devices like a tracer or an ink bomb and that each bill carried a portrait of Benjamin Franklin. As I assessed each bundle I piled them up neatly beside me and began to build a small tower of cash. They all looked the same, felt the same, and weighed about the same.

'If I find any tracer spray on these bills . . .'

'They're good,' said Dell.

Satisfied, I stood. The rain grew louder on the aluminum roof of the hangar. Even over the pounding noise, I heard a car approach and saw the headlights reflected in the sheets of fat, heavy rain. The car stopped outside the hangar. It was Carmel's Lexus with Christine and Amy inside.

'Your passengers?' asked Dell.

'That's them.'

'Then we're all here. The password, please, Eddie.'

'The agreements first.'

Stepping forward, Kennedy drew out two envelopes, placed one of them on the hood of the truck and gave the other to Dell.

The first envelope contained an immunity agreement for Christine – signed by both Kennedy and District Attorney Zader, confirming that no state or federal criminal charges of any kind would be filed against Christine Flynn arising out of her employment at Harland and Sinton.

But there was a condition.

There's always a condition.

Her immunity hinged on her testifying against Benjamin K. Harland and Gerald Sinton at their subsequent trials.

I folded the document back into the envelope and slipped it into my jacket. Dell mirrored my move and placed the second envelope into his coat.

'I need to see David's agreement,' I said, extending my hand.

'We don't know what you've really got on that drive. If it's good, he'll get what he deserves,' said Dell, who began walking toward the open doors. He gestured for me to follow him. Ferrar grabbed an umbrella, stepped in beside Dell, and winced as he tried to open it. He switched the umbrella to his left hand. His right arm must've still been ringing from the brass knuckles.

I joined them at the threshold of the hangar, where the wind whipped the rain into our faces. The rain seemed to chill the hot, leaden pain in my neck. I let it wash over my face – breathed it in.

'We had a deal. The agreements first,' I said.

'Where are you taking my plane?' said Dell.

'You don't need to know.'

'She'll need to tell the pilot, at least. He'll have to radio in the destination, so you might was well tell me now.'

'When the plane is in the air, I'll let you know,' I said.

'I don't suppose it matters much,' he replied, sniffing the air and letting his gaze fall into the dark sky. 'There's a storm coming,' he said.

CHAPTER SIXTY-ONE

The jet doors hung open. A small staircase built into the frame of the aircraft door beckoned to me. I wasn't going anywhere. I had to stay behind to complete the deal and make sure the charge against David got dismissed in the morning.

I hated saying goodbye.

Christine's hair smelled of cigarettes. She'd quit before Amy was born, but I'd always known that she'd sneakily enjoyed the occasional Lucky with a glass of wine. I held her close. Both of us wrapped ourselves around Amy and hugged in the rain. Letting go, I gently cupped her face in my hands and kissed her. Her lips were cold and sweet, and I tasted the smoke on her tongue. It was the first time we'd kissed in months. Somehow, it almost felt like our first kiss – there was excitement and fear, but this time there was also love and regret. She broke away, looked at the ground, and knelt beside Amy.

'We have to go, sweetie,' she said.

The pins on Amy's denim jacket that bore the logos from a multitude of rock bands I'd never heard of glistened in the light from the hangar. I hunkered down and took my little girl in my arms. I could feel her trembling. I looked at Carmel, a taller, slightly older version of Christine. She had never liked me.

'I love you, kiddo. You look after your mom. You're going somewhere far away – somewhere really safe. I'll be with you soon.'

Amy kissed me on the forehead, gave me another tight squeeze with all her ten-year-old might, took her mom's hand, and they set off toward the plane. I gave Carmel the money. '*I'll* make sure they stay safe,' she said.

Before she ducked into the plane, Christine turned and looked at me again. Her eyes were streaming with tears. She wiped them away.

Her lips moved soundlessly. 'I love you.' I couldn't hear her over the sound of the plane's engines. Maybe knowing that I wouldn't hear her speak those words somehow made it easier for her to say them.

I said it back. She waved and got on board.

The aircraft door closed and I heard the jet engine start up, and then the change of pitch as the plane turned and taxied toward the runway.

'The password?' said Dell.

I said nothing – willing the plane to take off, to take Christine and Amy far away. Away from the firm, away from Dell and Kennedy.

Away from me.

Ferrar switched the umbrella into his left hand with some difficulty and handed his boss a radio.

'Hold here,' said Dell. 'The pilot won't take off without my command. The password, Eddie. Or that plane never leaves the ground.'

'We have a deal?' I said.

Dell nodded.

Bile rising in my throat, I gave Dell the napkin with the password written in blue ink. Dell handed it to Ferrar, who folded away his umbrella and took the password to the waiting tech.

Without looking at Dell, I raised a hand, halting any further talk, and strolled out after the plane. I heard him mumble something to the pilot on the radio. The rain had eased to a light shower, and I saw the clouds clear a little as the jet accelerated down the runway and rose into the tumultuous sky.

I stayed there for a few moments. They were safe. No one could touch them, at least for now. As the plane got higher, the sharp ache in my shoulder blades melted into a dull echo of pain.

'Destination?' said Dell to the pilot on the other end of the line.

'Let me save you the trouble,' I said. 'They're heading in the wrong direction at the moment. Christine won't give the pilot the landing location for a while yet. When she does, you won't have time to set anything up. As soon as the plane lands, there'll be someone to take my family to a safe place, a secret place. All you've done is given them a head start on the firm. They won't truly be out of this until you take down Harland and Sinton.'

He nodded and we strolled back to the hangar. The tech worked quickly, and within a few seconds I saw a smile brush across his features. His teeth shined brightly in his reflection from the polished hood of the Taurus. He popped a bubble of strawberry gum over his lips and whispered to Dell.

'Thank you,' said Dell.

'David's agreement, I need it,' I said.

He handed me the envelope. As soon as took it I knew. The weight, the feel of it. Kennedy saw my expression change. The anger and the boiling fear in my stomach must've leached the color from my face.

'What's wrong, Eddie?' said Kennedy.

I handed him the envelope. He opened it. It was empty. Kennedy tore it up and was about to lay into Dell when the treasury man spoke.

'If you want to avoid a life sentence for David Child, you'll have to talk to him,' said Dell.

The rear passenger door of the black Taurus opened, and District Attorney Zader stepped out. He buttoned his gray, pin-striped jacket and adjusted his tie. He held a larger brown envelope marked EVIDENCE – DAVID CHILD. He handed it to me.

As he spoke he struggled to keep the triumphant tone from his voice.

'You know, Eddie, I'm disappointed. I didn't think I could hustle a hustler.'

I tore open the envelope and found five closely typed pages.

It wasn't a plea agreement. I skim read the document, and a sickening feeling in my stomach grew into a cramp that spread up my abdomen, holding my throat in a tight, bitter grip.

Right then I knew two things.

I'd let my concerns for Christine compromise David; I never should've handed over the password without seeing the agreement. The last kick in the teeth was the knowledge that it didn't matter what I did tomorrow – or months from now in the eventual trial. The document Zader had given me would ensure that David Child would be convicted of murder.

CHAPTER SIXTY-TWO

20 hours until the shot

The document Zader had handed me was a ballistics report. It confirmed, beyond any doubt, that the rounds found in the victim were fired from the same gun found in David's car. I'd expected to see this report but not then, not so soon. And I could not challenge a word of this evidence. The DA was putting the murder weapon in David's car, to match the body of his girlfriend in his apartment. There was no coming back from that scenario.

Game over.

'You used me,' I said, my fingers curling into fists. My legs parted in a fighting stance and my heart kicked into rhythm with the adrenaline soaking through my blood – into my muscles.

'And your wife,' said Dell. 'We don't care about her now that we've got the partners. She can go. She won't face any charges. She is no longer of use.'

'He didn't do it, Zader. We had a deal – the pen drive for the immunity agreements.'

'You didn't have a deal with me,' said Zader. 'You tried making a deal with Agent Dell, but he has no authority in relation to the Child case. I told you, we don't make deals that set murderers free. Not in my office. Best I could do would be twenty years if he pleads guilty. Otherwise, see you in court.'

As he swung away, toward the SUV, I started after him and then stopped myself. If I caught up with him I'd almost certainly lay him out. A night in the cage for assault wouldn't help me defend David.

'This is a joke, right?' said Kennedy.

'You're a big boy, Bill. It's time you started acting like one,' said Dell.

Kennedy tilted his jaw and strode up to Dell, who welcomed him with a burning glare.

'You want to take a pop at me, kid? Go right ahead. I'll kick your ass and take your badge,' said Dell.

Kennedy shook his head, turned to me, and said, 'Eddie, I knew nothing about this, I promise you.' He meant it. He looked even more haggard and disheveled than the day before. His hair was wet with rain, his shirt, too, and I got the impression that the only thing holding him upright was rage. Kennedy was a straight shooter – no way he knew I was gonna be played. And that ate at him.

Dell stepped forward, inviting the attack. Kennedy backed off, got into his own dark sedan, and sped away.

The ballistics report became a ball of paper in my hand as Dell and his men poured into their vehicles and drove out of the hangar.

I'd done the very thing I'd promised myself I would not do. I'd given up an innocent man for my wife. A man who had risked his own neck to help Christine, who had paid for a helicopter to meet her coming off the plane in Virginia – a man I'd let down, badly.

I called Christine's cell, but it must've been powered down for takeoff. The rain beat a tinny drum on the roof. With only me in the hangar, it became an echo chamber for my breath and the tap of my shoe on concrete.

Think.

Dell didn't need me anymore. He'd gotten the code, the evidence that led to the partners and the money. He would take down the firm tomorrow – as soon as the money landed. He would wait with a team outside their offices and swoop in at precisely the same second that the first cent hit the firm's account. He could be no help to me now.

Zader wanted his high-profile murder. He was making a name for himself. A name that he hoped would carry the weight of his political ambitions far beyond district attorney – and on to mayor or governor.

There was only one thing to do. Fight it out in court.

Seemingly from a distance, I heard a ringing, as if it were under-water. When I took the cell phone from my pocket, the noise from the ringtone, ricocheting off the hangar, almost deafened me. It certainly shook me out of my own head.

241

'Eddie, it's Bill,' said Agent Kennedy. He'd never used his first name in conversation with me before.

'What Dell did was wrong and I'll have no part in it. If we can't be straight, what hope is there? I'm sorry, Eddie. I wanted you to know that. And I wanted you to know where I'm headed.'

'I'm listening.'

'Federal Plaza. I'm going to check every police and prosecution file to make sure you've got everything for tomorrow. It probably won't do your client any good anyway, but I want to help.'

'He's been set up.'

'I know that's what you think. Hell, you might be right. But look, what I can get for you – save it for trial. There's no chance of a judge throwing this out for lack of evidence. And even if you did pull off some kind of Houdini stunt at the prelim, I hear Zader's got a grand jury empaneled for tomorrow afternoon and they will definitely find a case against your client because you can't even address them.'

'Let me worry about the grand jury – there might be a way of swinging something, but I'm not sure yet. The main thing is that I get working on this now, and I need you to do something else for me, if you're serious about helping me, that is.'

'Sure, shoot.'

'I need to know everything about the victim. Whatever you can find, I want it. Other than what may or may not be a fight in the elevator, the prosecution don't have a clear motive for this murder yet, and I don't want to be hit with one tomorrow. If I'm right, Child was set up.'

'Sure. I can get background. I'll have that to you ASAP. Anything else you need?'

'I was going to ask you about something. I'm being followed. Hispanic guy with a tattoo on his throat – *The Scream*, by Edvard Munch. He warned me with a vial of acid that David should keep his mouth shut. I'm guessing he's muscle, working for Harland and Sinton off the books. You know him?'

'I only know the firm's security team. Dell told me he already filled you in on Gill and his men. I haven't seen anyone matching that description around the firm. I'll look into it. If you see him again, call me.'

'Thanks. If I see him, I'll call.'

Kennedy's voice became heavy, slow.

'I'm sorry, Eddie. I got you into this. I'd only joined the task force last month. They'd gotten nowhere and I was brought in to look over the evidence, see if there was something they missed. Despite what Dell told you just now, we were going to indict the associates if we couldn't nail Harland and Sinton. We were all set to do it, too. Then Child fell into our lap over the weekend. Dell wanted Child to cut a deal, but we had to separate him from the firm and get him a new attorney. He asked me if I knew anyone who could handle it for a nice payoff. I suggested you. He said he'd heard the name before, and he pulled Christine's file. He had deep background on all of the associates. You were the perfect fit for the job. Eddie, I'm sorry.'

'I know you didn't set me up. You can help me now. Get whatever files you can grab and meet me in my office in an hour. I need to start planning what the hell I'm going to say at the hearing tomorrow.'

My thoughts became lost. Silence filled the line.

'You know, you might be wrong about this. I know you think Child doesn't have it in him, but the security camera footage from the apartment building puts him as the last person to leave that apartment and minutes later his girlfriend's body is found. She's dead from multiple gunshot wounds and the gun is in your client's car. The facts make him good for the murder. Are you sure you're on the right side of this?'

'I'm a defense attorney, Kennedy. I don't have a right side – I just have a client.'

That was what Kennedy expected to hear. All law enforcement think the same thing about attorneys. How do they sleep knowing they set the guilty free? It's even harder to sleep when you've got an innocent man in jail. Well, I was done with nightmares.

'Don't worry. I know I'm right on this one. I can feel it. I'll see you in my office in an hour.'

'Okay, but let me check it out first, make sure it's safe. What are you gonna do for an hour?' asked Kennedy.

I thought it over. There was nothing to be gained from heading back to the Lizard's house. Besides, I'd had an idea.

'I'm going to fry Zader's backup,' I said.

'What? The grand jury? What are you gonna do?'

'I'm going to get my secret weapon, which'll give us a chance at destroying the case if it ever gets as far as the grand jury.'

'How are you going to do that?'

'I'm going to hire Child another lawyer.'

CHAPTER SIXTY-THREE

Finnegan's Pub on Fifty-Sixth Street looked more like a flophouse for the blind than a public bar. A sign on the door read, WE NEVER CLOSE.

I sat outside the bar in the driver's seat of Holly's Honda, the interior light shining on the new ballistics report from CSI Noble. From the unique markings and striations on the bullets found in the victim, he was able to confirm that those rounds could only have been fired from the gun found in David's car. A slam dunk for the prosecution. Only one thing bothered me about the report; from Noble's examination of the weapon, he'd found traces of soil on the grip and some of that soil had made its way into the tiny gap around the magazine, which slotted into the butt of the gun. I told myself I would think about it later, that it probably meant nothing, but all the same, little details like that tugged at my mind. I got out of the car and approached Finnegan's.

The windows of the pub were taped up from the inside, and a second door, just beyond the entrance, was always closed and shrouded in thick green curtains that smelled of rotten beer and cigarettes. It was almost as if the patrons were vampires and if any natural light penetrated the bar at any moment, the entire clientele would burst into flames. It had a reputation as a rough joint and the owner, Paddy Joe, tolerated all kinds of customers. Ten years ago it would not have been unusual to find a gang of bikers in one corner, the 58s in the other corner, the Bloods playing pool, and half of the 16th Precinct's homicide squad hitting tequila slammers at the bar.

'Is Cooch in tonight?' I asked.

Paddy Joe looked up from the bar and for a moment I couldn't take in his face because his head seemed to be as big as a silverback's.

A steel-wool beard hung over his T-shirt and the end of that beard met my eye line at his stomach. Taking a step away from the bar, I was able to focus more clearly on his handsome blue eyes and row of capped teeth that looked like a stack of gold bars lying in the mouth of a dark cave.

'He's in his spot. Good to see you, Eddie. You want a Coke or somethin'?'

When I was hitting the bottle, Paddy had made sure I got home from the bar in one piece – so he knew I'd kicked the booze, or was trying to.

'No, thanks. I'm good. Nice to see you, too, man.'

He held up his massive fist for a bump. I obliged him. It was like a marshmallow briefly touching a wrecking ball.

I turned away from the bar, past the broken jukebox and up a small flight of steps to a large booth in the far left-hand corner of the pub. There, surrounded by three drunk lawyers, Cooch was holding court.

'It's like I always say, you never put your client on the stand. It's suicide,' said Cooch. 'Take Gerry Spence, yeah, best damn trial lawyer I ever saw. Spence practiced for fifty damn years, never lost a case and only once or twice put his client on the stand.'

Two of the male lawyers at Cooch's table were around his age, the third was a younger lawyer, blond, hanging on Cooch's every word. I hung back to let Cooch finish. He was a little deaf and had problems with his volume. You could almost hear him in the street, he was so loud. Cooch also wore a hearing aid, which he tapped occasionally if he didn't hear what you were saying. Like if you reminded him that it was his round at the bar.

'Spence used to say you told your client's story through your cross-examination. Attack the prosecution case. Attack, attack, attack. But pick your battles . . .'

The two middle-aged lawyers had heard it all before – this was Cooch's favorite topic – and they began their own conversation. Undeterred, Cooch switched his attention to the young lawyer.

'Criminal law is war, kid. But don't fight the system; fight the evidence. It's like . . . what's his name . . . Irving Kanarek. He'd fight over a coin toss. You ever hear of him, kid?'

The young man shook his head.

'He was a defense attorney out of LA. He represented Charles Manson. Almost got him off, too. But Irving took it too far. He objected to everything. He made objection after objection after objection. He objected during direct, during opening speeches – everything. He sure pissed off the judge plenty. In the Manson trial Irving got himself sent to jail for contempt, twice. He was just a belligerent guy. Once, the prosecutor called a witness and asked him to state his name for the record. Old Irving was on his feet in the blink of an eye. "'Objection, Your Honor. This answer is hearsay. The witness only knows his name because his mother told him!"'

The young lawyer laughed out of politeness, then stared into his beer.

Moving into the light, I nodded at Cooch.

'Now, here's a real talent, kid. This here is Eddie Flynn. You see him in court, you watch him. Learn from him. He's the next Gerry Spence,' said Cooch.

I exchanged greetings with the other lawyers, who shook hands with Cooch, made their excuses and left. The young lawyer finished his Miller, thanked Cooch for the advice, and made his exit. I took a seat.

'Nice kid, highest score in the bar exam and top of his class at law school. A real prospect. Pity he doesn't have the first freakin' idea of how to be a lawyer, but he'll learn. Like you did, Eddie.'

'You gave me my fair share of advice when I was his age. I was grateful; it helped.'

He waved a dismissive hand.

'What do I know?' he said.

'Look, I need a favor, Cooch.'

'Wha'? Didn't catch that,' he said, and leaned toward me, tapping his hearing aid.

I whispered, 'I'll pay you ten grand for a day's work in court tomorrow.'

'Ten large? Tomorrow? What's the case?' He had little difficulty hearing that.

'Murder. It's the prelim tomorrow. You're second chair.'

Raising his hands, he looked at the patterns of nicotine staining on the ceiling, muttered something, and then returned his attention to me, waiting for the details.

Despite his advanced years, the seventy-year-old lawyer was still as sharp and as dedicated as any I'd ever met. Cooch took a real interest in his clients, getting to know them, getting to know their families, their bail bondsmen, their kids and pets. He survived on repeat business from a large group of clients, most of whom were related and who specialized in low-level organized crime and warehouse robbery. It had been close to a year since I'd last seen Cooch, and in that time he'd aged considerably. The skin around his throat now drooped and his shirt looked too big for him, his hair was now almost completely white. The last strands of Just for Men were a fading memory, quickly evaporating with the spread from his powder-white roots.

'So? Come on, you gotta give me details. How am I gonna prepare when you don't tell me anything about the case? You want me to take half the witnesses? What? Come on, what do you want me to do?'

One of the lawyers who'd sat with Cooch had left a finger of scotch in his glass and the melting ice cube had diluted it. I stared at the dark, amber liquid in the glass for a long second. I shouldn't, I told myself, as I picked it up and swallowed the damn thing.

'Look, don't worry about it,' I said.

'Come on, Eddie, that's not fair. You must want me for a reason. So what do you want me to do tomorrow?'

'At the prelim? Absolutely nothing.'

'Wha'?'

'I don't want you to do anything at the prelim. I need you for the grand jury,' I said, unable to fully restrain a smile.

'Hang on. I can't do anything at a grand jury; I can't cross-examine . . . You know this. It's pointless even being there. You remember what Judge Sol Wachtler said when he was in the court of appeal?'

This was one of Cooch's favorite lines. I knew it by heart, but I let him talk.

'He said, "A prosecutor could persuade a grand jury to indict a ham sandwich." Your client's wasting his money; there's nothing I can do there.'

'I didn't ask you to say anything at the grand jury; you just have to show up.'

Cooch leaned back into the fake leather seats and let his mouth fall open as he thought this through.

After a few moments, he sat up and pointed a clubbed finger at me.

'You don't want me to do anything at the prelim, but you need me to be there, right? And then you want me to go along to the grand jury with a surprise?'

'You got it.'

He shook his head and laughed. 'Eddie, you're one twisted genius, you know that?'

CHAPTER SIXTY-FOUR

I felt like I was taking refuge from the storm in a toy car. The rain bounced off the hood and flooded the windshield. I told myself that I couldn't call Child because I wouldn't be able to hear him over the deafening beat of the rain. He'd called me and I hadn't answered the phone. I couldn't face that conversation just yet, not until I had an answer for him – not until I'd found a way out.

I tried Christine's cell again. Voice mail. Trailing through my dialed call list, I hit the number for the hospital. This time I got through to the nurse on Popo's ward pretty quickly. He was conscious, cooperative, and filled full of morphine so they wouldn't let me talk to him. They weren't letting the cops talk to him either. I asked the nurse to tell Popo I'd called and that I was grateful for what he'd done for David. The nurse said she'd pass it on. I disconnected the call and returned my attention to West Forty-Sixth Street.

There were no people on the street; the rain kept pedestrians inside. I'd been parked for almost twenty minutes and I hadn't seen a single person pass my office. A few cars drove by at speed that didn't appear, to me at least, as if they were casing the place. I'd driven up and down a few times myself, just to look out for anyone who might be sitting in a car, waiting for me to go back to my office. As far as I could tell, the street was clear. I was no surveillance expert, and I'd resigned myself to wait for Kennedy. For all I knew, Gerry Sinton could have half of his security team in my office already with eager guns waiting in the dark for my return.

I was late and Kennedy hadn't shown. I was about to call him when I saw a dark sedan pass me and park fifty yards ahead, just outside my building.

I waited and saw the tall, lean figure of Bill Kennedy exiting the car, a blue plastic folder tucked underneath his right arm. The horn on the Honda sounded like a sick donkey. It was enough to turn Kennedy around. I flashed the lights, got out of the car, and locked it with the ignition key. By the time I'd joined him, I was wet through and the files I carried in my jacket weren't faring much better. The rain was too hard for us to stop and talk and we ran to the entrance to my building.

I hadn't been in my office since early that morning, and with the normal traffic through the front door, there was no point in putting my usual precautions in place. There was no dime and no toothpick to tell me if I had any unplanned guests waiting for me upstairs. We entered noisily and I closed the door too quickly, much too eager to get out of the storm. If anyone was upstairs, they probably heard us come in.

We shook out our clothes, and I wiped the rain from my face and swept back my hair, which had begun to cling to my forehead. Our breath was misty in the cold lobby, and pools of rain water already formed around our feet. I gestured toward my office with a flick of my eyes. Kennedy nodded, handed me the plastic folder, drew his service weapon, and ascended the stairs cautiously. I followed him at a distance.

A reading light shined in my office.

Kennedy put his palm out flat, telling me to remain at the top of the stairs. He moved with a graceful, silent skip toward the door, his gun ready in a two-handed grip. I followed him, and we took our positions on either side of the door. Kennedy shook his head and mouthed that I should stay put. In one smooth, fluid movement, he flicked the doorknob with one hand, then kneed it all the way open as he pushed inside, his gun raised in front of him.

CHAPTER SIXTY-FIVE

Rain trickled down my back, and I pressed myself harder into the wall.

I heard nothing.

Not a sound.

'Kennedy?' I said.

'Clear,' he said.

I breathed out, went inside, and turned on the lights. I must've left my desk lamp burning this morning. That's not like me. I was being careful. If Dell hadn't offered me the cash to represent Child, I had planned to put this month's electric bill on my credit card. We shook off more rain from our clothes. Then I took off my jacket and sat down to read the contents of the folder Kennedy had given to me.

The documents Kennedy brought didn't contain much more than I'd seen already. Only a few other pages of exhibit lists and a clearer, larger version of the map of David's apartment.

'You still think your client is innocent?' asked Kennedy.

I nodded.

'I don't like the way it played out with Dell, so I'll do what I can, but I've got to know why you're so certain about Child,' he said.

'I know how it looks. But I've looked him in the eyes. He doesn't have it in him. It looks bad for David because that's the way it's supposed to look. Whoever set him up wanted him nailed for Clara's murder. By the way, you haven't shown me what you got on the victim.'

The FBI man put both hands in his pockets, drew them out, and held open his empty hands.

'Nothing?' I asked.

'No tax records, no social security number, no medical records in this state. Same with dental. No birth records, no cell phone registered in her name. The only thing I got was a driver's license, library card, and an ATM card all issued around six months ago to Clara Reece.'

'That ever happen to you before?'

'Nope. Come to think of it, I've always been able to get at least one hit, even if it's only birth registration. Her cell phone was an expensive burner. She had cash in her purse – no credit cards, just the checking account. Apparently PD sent a car to the address David gave for Clara. I know that she'd just moved in with David, but the apartment was cleared out. No furniture, no letters, and no TV, even. There wasn't a scrap of paper in that place. Oh, and the smell; apparently the whole place had been steam cleaned and chemically treated a few days before the murder. She'd told her super that she was moving in with David, but he says he didn't clean the apartment. Somebody did, and they were thorough. The cops weren't even able to grab a hair from that apartment.'

'It's almost like she's been erased,' I said.

Nodding his head, Kennedy said, 'I got to admit, that threw me. The DA has got this set up as a wild crime of passion. Somehow, it doesn't feel that way to me. Sounds to me like Clara Reece was running from something, or somebody, and hit the jackpot when she met your client. It doesn't prove anything, Eddie. But it's something to throw into the mix. I just don't know how far any of this will get you.'

'If I'm right, it was a setup,' I said.

He suppressed a laugh. 'Well, if he has been framed, then it's the best setup I've ever seen. Your client says he left his apartment at 20:02, having just kissed Clara goodbye. She was alive and well when he left, according to him. Yet Gershbaum hears the shots, goes to his balcony and sees the window blowing out from the stray bullet and calls security – his call is logged at 20:02. The security camera doesn't show anybody else going near the apartment until the security guards arrive four minutes later. The only person in that apartment is our dead victim. If there's another killer, well, they must have flown away. Child shot her, Eddie. Why can't you

253

see that? So, what's your client's defense? Either he's lying or Clara Reece shot herself in the back of the head twelve times. I don't think she could've managed that, and there's no one else who could've done it, because no one else was there. Gershbaum didn't see anyone escaping onto his balcony, and nobody left his apartment in that time either – you can see his front door from the security footage, too. And if that weren't enough, the murder weapon is in his car. Face it, this man killed her. You have to stop seeing what you want to see and look at the bare facts.'

Something Kennedy said pulled at me, but I wasn't sure what it was. It was like I'd just been flashed a deck of cards and the dealer had held on to one card a microsecond longer than any other as he ripped through the deck. The dealer would show me the card he wanted me to remember – in fact, it would be the only card I could see. The others would go by in a blur. In my mind, I repeated what Kennedy had said, looking for my card.

I found it.

'You said I'm seeing what I *want* to see. And I want him to be innocent,' I said.

'I didn't mean it to sound so blunt, but you needed to hear it,' he replied.

'But that's it. That's the key.'

It was simple. It was the cornerstone of any hustle, people believe what they can see.

Kennedy stretched his back and, as he did so, the file on his knee slipped off onto the floor. I stood and cracked my neck, then walked around my desk to bring the blood back into my feet.

'I need another favor. And I need a ride,' I said.

'Where to?' asked Kennedy, checking his watch.

It was coming up on one a.m.

'Central Park West. I need to take a look at the crime scene.'

'That may be difficult.'

'That building runs twenty-four hours a day. We can get in. We'll figure something out. If this plays out the way I think it will, then I'm going to need you to look into an alternative suspect for Clara's murder. Guy called Bernard Langhiemer.'

'Never heard of him.'

'He's hiding something. David and Langhiemer have history. I talked to him today, and he—' The words caught in my throat. I stood at the window, gazing through the blinds at the street below. A blue Ford had parked thirty feet from my office. The driver's window must've been open. I could see the wisps of smoke gently trailing above the roof of the car.

'We've got company,' I said.

'Who?' said Kennedy.

'I can't see from here,' I said. The light from my desk lamp reflected onto the window, masking the view of the driver.

I heard Kennedy get up from his seat to come take a look. I turned and saw that he'd spotted the lamp's reflection on the glass. He took two steps toward the desk. He was going to shut off the lamp so we could get a better view.

Something in the back of my mind began to grow. It wasn't a theory, or a thought; it was deeper. A feeling of unease that was now exploding into panic.

'Don't move. Wait!' I said.

Kennedy stopped in his tracks, his hand on my desk.

'Before Dell offered me the money yesterday, I was getting worried about how I was going to pay the electric bill.'

He looked puzzled.

'Don't you get it? I'm pretty positive I didn't leave that lamp on. Somebody's been here.'

CHAPTER SIXTY-SIX

Slowly, Kennedy brushed aside the loose pages on my desk to get a better view of the cable switch for the lamp. He picked up the cable from the desk. Carefully, he laid it back down. It was enough for me to see that somebody had tampered with the switch. A red wire led from directly underneath the switch to a freshly drilled hole in my desk.

Kennedy and I exchanged glances. Neither of us could breathe. Sweat broke out on our faces.

With the cable resting on the desk, the switch pointing upward, the wire was invisible. The hole in my desk was only a couple of millimeters wide. Just the right size for the wire. Pushing aside my desk chair with one hand, Kennedy got on his knees and took a small torch from his pocket. Twisting onto his back, he pushed himself under my desk like a mechanic sliding underneath a car.

'Eddie, come take a look. For God's sake, move slowly and don't touch anything.'

Gingerly, I lay down beside him and looked underneath. There were six two-liter plastic cola bottles taped to the reverse side of my desk. They sat way back, so my knees wouldn't touch them if I sat down in my office chair. The red wire ran through the hole and was taped along the base of each bottle. Each bottle was filled with a cloudy liquid and what looked like foil lining the base.

'Whatever you do, don't touch the lamp. We're going to get up very slowly, grab your files, and get out.'

And we did. As Kennedy closed the door to my office, he breathed out and wiped the sheen of sweat from his forehead into his hair.

'It's an acid bomb. The bottles are filled with hydrochloric acid. He added a trip to the cable switch on the lamp. If we'd turned off the lamp, the power would've fed into the red wire and heated the aluminum base of each bottle. Five, maybe ten seconds later, that desk would've been on the ceiling and your entire office would've become an acid shower. Ever see somebody drop baking soda into a bottle of cola? It'll shoot fifty feet in the air. The acid in those bottles would've been superheated and a lot more powerful.'

'It's the guy, the one I told you about.'

'I hear you. I had my suspicions about this guy as soon as you mentioned him. This confirms it. We've got to take him out,' he said as he dialed on his cell phone.

While he waited for somebody to pick up his call, he said, 'Officially, I'm not supposed to be here. I can get Ferrar and Weinstein, maybe. They'll take a risk for me. The man in that car is waiting for you to turn off the lamp. He's waiting to hear you scream.'

We sat in the dark lobby of my building. Kennedy had his Glock in one hand, his cell phone in the other. He was waiting for a call from Ferrar to tell him they were in position.

'The man with the tattoo on this throat, who is he?' I said.

I looked into it. 'Nobody knows his real name. People call him El Grito – the Scream. He's an interrogator, and a hitman for the Rosa Cartel: one of the largest in Mexico. They're at war with the other cartels, but they've managed to hold the White Line – the route from Boca del Rio right through the country, all the way to Tijuana. El Grito is one of the most feared men in South America. In the Mexican drug wars, these guys need a reputation. They build their name on brutality and fear. El Grito likes to use acid and he never gags his victims – he likes to hear them scream. The acid bomb is his MO.'

'I don't like this, Kennedy.'

'The cartel has a lot of money tied up with Harland and Sinton. I guess they're here to help the firm with their little problem.'

'This gets better and better,' I said.

'Eddie, I'd no idea the cartel would become directly involved. The media is all over this thing, and that should be enough to keep them the hell away from it.'

257

'The guy who tried to knife David before Popo got in the way, he was Mexican. And Dell's informant, Farooq, wasn't he burned with acid?'

Kennedy looked at the floor and said, 'It's thin, but it fits. This guy is protecting the firm.'

His cell phone hummed. He listened and told whoever was on the other end of the line to be ready.

'We're good to go. Ferrar and Weinstein drove past. It's him, although he's got somebody hunkered down in the passenger seat. Probably a shooter. My men are in the parking lot a hundred yards up the street. When he runs, they'll block him. Stay here,' said Kennedy.

He drew his Glock, threw open the front door, and bolted to the left, gun in the air, hollering at El Grito to get out of the car.

Instantly I heard an engine fire up, then gunshots. Two different sets of gunfire. The high crack of Kennedy's Glock and the thunderous answer from a shotgun. I peered out my front door. Kennedy was pinned down behind his car, and El Grito was pulling out to pass Kennedy's car. I saw the passenger window of El Grito's vehicle coming down. He was going to stop and take out Kennedy on the way.

I pulled open my mailbox, lifted one set of brass knuckles, and dove into the street. El Grito's dark sedan leveled with Kennedy's car, and I saw a sawed-off shotgun in El Grito's hand, pointed out the passenger window. The shotgun sat over the head of somebody hiding in the passenger seat of the sedan. I hurled the brass as hard as I could. I was only twenty feet away, so it was an easy shot. The knuckles smacked off the windshield, leaving a huge crack.

El Grito hit the gas, his car fired past Kennedy, and I was already pumping my legs up the steps to my front door. I ran inside and slammed the door, but before it shut, it bucked back with a sharp clang and caught me on the forehead, knocking me to the floor. The steel-back plate on the front door was bent and misshapen where it had stopped the shotgun blast. I tore open the door and saw Kennedy standing in the middle of the street, firing into the back of the sedan as it sped away. The back window exploded, but the sedan only sped up, hurtling toward the SUV with Ferrar at the wheel. They'd waited in the parking lot that serviced the restaurants and now they were right across the narrow one-way street. The sedan mounted the curb and was going to slip past.

I took off and caught up with Kennedy as we both bolted up the street.

'He's not going to make it,' said Kennedy.

The sedan must've hit fifty miles an hour as it sheared through the gap between the SUV on the left and the black railings on the right, taking the front bumper off the fed's vehicle. A shower of sparks flew into the air from the sedan's right side and the passenger door fell to the sidewalk.

As the SUV reversed to pursue its quarry, Kennedy and I caught up with it, leaped into the backseat, and Kennedy roared 'Go, go, go!'

Ferrar hit the gas, and Weinstein leaned out the passenger window in front of me with his weapon drawn.

The sedan was almost at the intersection with Eighth Avenue. He didn't slow down. Instead he accelerated, and I saw El Grito lean to his right, toward the passenger side.

Just before he hit the intersection, a body fell out of the passenger side. It hit a parked car and bounced back, tumbling toward the SUV. This block of West Forty-Sixth Street was narrow and with cars parked on either side, the only way to continue the chase was to drive over the person who'd been thrown from El Grito's car.

My head hit the passenger seat in front as Ferrar stood on the brakes. We piled out of the car and watched El Grito drive away. Ferrar got on the radio, but we all knew it was pointless. We'd lost him.

The body on the road had come to a stop. I joined Kennedy as he stood over it. You could tell from the way it had limply rolled across the street that they were dead.

Kennedy stood over the mess. Green padded jacket. Light sandy hair. I joined the fed and stared at the dead man. It was Gill, Harland and Sinton's head of security.

His clothes were ripped, probably from the fall from the moving car. But that wasn't what had killed him. There was no skin on his right hand. I could see white patches of bone and sinew, but there was no flesh. His throat was gone, as well as most of his lower jaw.

Kennedy was still catching his breath as he spoke.

259

'He's been tortured. Then made to drink the acid that dissolved his hand. We can be sure of one thing – whatever El Grito wanted to know, Gill told him.'

He turned to Weinstein and said, 'Call it in. We'll need the bomb squad for the office, too. I'll be back. I need to give Eddie a ride.'

CHAPTER SIXTY-SEVEN

Kennedy parked his car outside David's building. He'd called Dell, told him about El Grito and Gill. He left out the part about helping me. Said he'd come by when I found the bomb under my desk. According to Dell, the Rosa Cartel were by far the biggest client of the firm. Almost six of the eight billion in the accounts belonged to the cartel. They wanted to make sure it was safe, and that meant warning Sinton about what would happen if it went missing. It didn't change Dell's plan; he just told Kennedy to be careful.

We got out of Kennedy's car and entered David's world.

The lobby of Central Park Eleven looked like a lobby from a millionaire's wet dream. Marble floors, antique furniture, oak-paneled private library just to the left of reception, exotic plants that spilled equally unusual scents, piped classical music – Chopin. The receptionist probably made more money in tips in a week than I made in a year. She was tall and blond with a warm face the same color as honeyed milk. Her nails were insanely red, to match lips that sat on her face like twin Ferraris on a Gold Coast beach.

To the left of reception the elevator bank was protected by four security guards. They all looked familiar, as if I'd seen them before on the security footage. Each one weighed two twenty-five to two fifty, with very little fat. They were tanned, with basketballs for shoulders and no necks. Their heads were shaved close, their uniforms a perfectly pressed light blue. Glocks sat on their hips along with radios and cell phones. I guessed they were either ex-cops or ex-army. They certainly all looked as though they could stand around all day with hands on their hips like monoliths of security.

I ignored the looks I got from the guard on the right and turned my attention back to the receptionist.

'Hi. I'm here with Special Agent William Kennedy of the FBI. We need to take a look at the crime scene.'

'It's very late for an inspection. We have instructions from the police not to let anyone near that floor. Do you have ID and a warrant, Agent Kennedy?' said the receptionist.

Before he could answer I stepped in. I didn't want to give the game away that we weren't actually on the same side as the police department.

'We didn't believe that we needed a warrant, ma'am. The apartment is still a crime scene.'

She considered this for all of a second and then slowly shook her head. A Hispanic guy in a gray suit and shirt the same color of light blue as the security guards came out of the elevator and went behind the reception desk. He got the update from the receptionist.

'Could we see some identification, gentlemen?' said the guy in the suit.

Kennedy flashed his ID, and I put my hands in my pockets.

'I'm Alex Medrano. I'm head of security here,' said the man as he read Kennedy's badge and ID.

'Are you Mr Child's lawyer?' he asked me.

Something about the way he asked that question led me to think that if I lied to him, he'd read it in a heartbeat.

'I represent Mr Child,' I said.

'I'll take you gentlemen up myself. Mr Child is very well regarded here. Anything we can do to help, you just ask.'

The wall of muscle and aftershave parted, and Kennedy and I followed Medrano to the elevators. From a key chain on his waist, he selected a polished piece of plastic and waved it over the eye reader on the control panel. Suddenly the controls lit up and Medrano was able to summon the elevator. The doors opened, and we stepped into the lemon-scented elevator car. Mirrors on each wall, tiled floor, polished oak on the ceiling. Again, Medrano swiped the fob at a laser reader and was then able to select a floor.

'If you have your own fob, does that allow you onto any floor?' I said.

'Sure does. We've got a good community here. We like to encourage a neighborly attitude, so there are meetings on various floors, social groups, and, of course, the gym is on the thirty-fifth floor, the spa, just above that, and the wine cellar is in the basement.'

The elevator played the same symphony that had been playing in the lobby, and I guessed it was piped all over the building.

We arrived at David's floor with a pleasant chime, and I checked out the security camera, hidden in the top, northeast corner of the elevator.

The doors opened.

The music continued.

We found ourselves in a rectangular landing a little wider than the elevator bank, maybe fifty feet wide. The door in the northeast corner was Gershbaum's, a door in the northwest corner led to David's apartment, and there was a single door to the right of the elevator that no doubt led to the stairs. Beside the front doors to each apartment was an antique table that held handkerchiefs in a silver box, a bowl of fresh fruit, and a bottle of designer hand cream. An umbrella stand held a few umbrellas bearing branded CENTRAL PARK ELEVEN logos, and a beautiful mahogany-framed standing mirror sat beside each of the tables. I got the impression that before leaving their floor, the residents relished the opportunity to check their appearance one more time before facing their public.

Medrano headed for the door in the northwest corner, which was covered in blue and white PD crime tape and again produced his key chain from his pants pocket.

'This is Mr Child's apartment,' he said, as he looked for the correct key in a bunch of fifty or sixty keys. From his jacket pocket, Kennedy produced a handful of rubber gloves, handed a pair to me and Medrano. Kennedy and Medrano managed to slip their gloves on without a problem. I found it difficult to hold my files and get the damn things on.

Eventually Medrano found the right key, slotted it into the lock, and opened the door. The apartment was everything I expected from the Manhattan elite. Open plan, white and beige furniture to match the thick, neutral carpet. It was probably a Dior design; Christine would've known right away. The living area was a massive open plan space with twenty-foot-long couches that snaked along the center of the room. A musty, metallic, slightly foul smell permeated the room.

The odor lingered almost as a reminder of the violent death that had occurred within those walls. Even with the wind coursing through the apartment from the broken window, that smell remained. At one end of the living area I saw the beginning of white tiles and I headed in that direction. In the kitchen I saw the scene of the murder. One tile had broken up, and a dark, chocolate-red stain covered the broken fragments as they lay in what was now a small depression in the floor. Impact droplets fanned out from the center of the stain. Blood seemed to linger on certain surfaces – a trace that can never fully be removed.

Roughly seventeen inches below the broken tile I clearly saw a stain from a single droplet of blood.

Until the crime scene has been released, no cleaning can be done. The police normally hold a scene for a few days to a few weeks, depending on the progress of their investigation. Where the incident happened in the accused's home, PD will normally hold the crime scene a lot longer so that the accused can't apply for bail at that address, making bail a lot more difficult as it means the accused not only has to pay a bondsman, but also has to find money to stay somewhere else if family won't or can't take them in.

Mostly, this tactic works, and the defendant doesn't even bother applying for bail.

I knelt down to get a closer look at the small bloodstain. The droplet looked to be around two to three millimeters in diameter, dark and perfectly formed. Far as I could tell, it hadn't been trodden on, or smeared, or disturbed in any way since that droplet left Clara's body.

Standing back, I took time to look over the scene, making sure there were no other bloodstains anywhere in the kitchen. There were none. Some six feet ahead of the spot where the body had been found, the wind blew through the panel-sized gap in the glass wall, caused by the windowpane shattering from a gunshot. The safety glass had exploded on impact and tiny fragments spread out from the balcony toward where the body had lain. The fragments had stopped before reaching the broken, stained tile. Most of the glass lay on the balcony. I stepped through the gap left by the broken pane and stood on the balcony. I was glad of my overcoat, and I pulled the lapels around me. The downpour had ceased, but the balcony remained slippery from the rain-slicked broken glass. I looked above and below. There was no way anyone could have scaled up to the apartment or dropped to this balcony from above. The balcony overhead was too high, and the brickwork had been smoothed over with plaster. No foot- or handholds anywhere. Below me, the streetlights dotted around Central Park shined dimly through the trees. We were so close I could smell the grass. The two-lane avenue separated this side of the street from the park, and it felt as though I could lean out and touch the leaves of the oak trees sprouting from the park grounds. The balcony overlooked a quiet stretch of lawn just a bit smaller than a Little League field. It was separated from the park pathway by a row of high hedges. An oak tree sat in the right corner. A collection of empty beer cans scattered around the trunk. You pay thirty million for a park view and you get teenagers and drunks.

Kennedy and I took five minutes each to split up and check every room in the apartment for bloodstains. None were found.

From the files I'd brought with me, I removed the ME's report and flicked through to the drawing of the body. On most ME reports there is a standard, preprinted female form; the ME then adds the location of the bullet wounds and, on the side-profile drawing, they insert the angle of bullet penetration. Aside from the head shots, Clara had been shot twice in the back. The first bullet had lodged in her spine, probably paralyzing her instantly. The second entrance wound was close to the spine, but this bullet had passed through her body and exited through the lower part of the chest wall. An exit wound was marked just to the left side of her chest.

I handed the drawing to Kennedy.

He studied the report again and looked over the scene.

'The angle is a very slight downward trajectory,' he said.

But I wasn't listening to a word Kennedy had said. Instead I was looking at a framed architectural plan on the kitchen wall. It was drawn in white on a blue background, bore a signature in the bottom left-hand corner, but despite this, it looked familiar. I flicked through the prosecution file until I found the sketch that had been drawn of the crime scene denoting the location of the victim's body in the apartment.

Medrano was still waiting at the front door. I beckoned him over.

'Is this what I think it is?' I asked.

'Yes, it's a Claudio. These are in every apartment in the building. The owners were good friends with Claudio, and he designed the refurb in 1981. Residents get a framed print when they take up occupation.'

'No, I'm not interested in the designer. Is this an accurate plan of the apartment?'

'It is. Residents are not permitted to make structural alterations.'

I called Kennedy. He came into the kitchen area and stood beside us, then, realizing how tired he'd become, he reached for a stool and planted himself. It was after two a.m., and he looked completely exhausted.

'Medrano, if I managed to persuade Kennedy to get an agent to come up here in the next few hours with a camera and a bottle of luminol, would you be able to make sure they can get access to this apartment?'

'I'm supposed to finish in an hour. I'm . . . You know we got strict instructions from NYPD not to let anyone up here, right?'

Kennedy was about to speak. I tugged at his jacket to silence him. I wanted to get Medrano talking.

'I think this might be really useful for my client. You said David had a good reputation in the building?'

'Yeah, you could say that. One of my supervisors, Cory, his six-year-old kid got this rare form of leukemia 'bout a year ago. Insurance wouldn't cover the treatment. Building management let Cory put up a fund-raising poster in the lobby and a donation box. He needed to raise four hundred grand for treatment. After a week, he'd raised twenty-five grand; people in this building got a lot of money and they're pretty generous. Anyway, Mr Child had been away on business for a while. When he got back, he saw the poster. He called building management and met with Cory – asked him how much he needed and what kind of treatment the kid would need. Cory said the treatment could prolong his kid's life – maybe five years. But that's all.'

Medrano adjusted his stance, wiped his mouth.

'Well, Mr Child did a little research on the net, found this expert. Next thing you know, he flew Cory's whole family to Geneva, paid more than a million dollars for experimental treatment. Six weeks ago Cory's kid got the all clear.'

Kennedy and I exchanged glances.

'What I'm saying is, will this help him?'

'I think it might,' I said.

'As long as it's between us,' he said.

I smiled and turned to Kennedy. 'Okay, this is what your guy's looking for. We'll just take a peek before we leave,' I said, lifting the framed Claudio from the wall.

CHAPTER SIXTY-EIGHT

Our investigation hadn't yet given me the answers I was looking for, but I was confident that the FBI's forensic officer would give credence to my theory. Right then that's all I had, a theory. But it fit.

'You know what to tell Forensics to look for?' I asked.

'Yeah, I'm good,' said Kennedy.

'Great. I'll need another favor.'

'You're getting pretty loose with the favors,' said Kennedy, but he didn't take it any further. I knew I was pushing it, but I figured he owed me. The bags under his eyes seemed to have grown larger and darker, but there was an alertness to him. He was beginning to doubt Child's guilt, and he wanted to see where this led.

'Anyone in NYPD who could do you a solid and not go running to Zader about it?'

'I know a guy, but why NYPD?' he said.

I handed Kennedy a single page from the file.

'I need the tracker report for this vehicle. FBI wouldn't have access to that system, right?'

'No, we don't. Come to think of it I don't know if my guy in NYPD has access to that system. But I can try,' he said.

'It's important, I'm beginning to piece this together. I'm relying on you. The prelim starts in just over seven hours, and we've got one last thing to check.'

'What's that?'

'Security camera footage of the cops working the crime scene.'

'Let's go to my office. You can watch it there,' said Medrano.

We exited David's apartment. Kennedy punched the button to call the elevator and hung back, waiting for Medrano to lock up. I looked at the CCTV camera, just over the bank of elevators, and moved backward a little, stopped.

'What are you doing?' said Kennedy.

'The camera footage I watched shows David hesitate just after he left the apartment for the last time. He was leaving and then he kind of paused around here and turned back toward the door.'

I examined the door but couldn't see much with Medrano's bulk blocking my view. Kneeling, I checked the carpet; maybe David dropped something and it rolled underneath the table, but I couldn't see anything.

'Looking for something?' said Medrano.

'Not really. David stopped and turned around just after he left the apartment. I saw it today when I watched the footage. Thought he might've dropped something or . . . I don't know.'

'If he dropped something, it's likely the cleaners picked it up. We can always check the camera,' said Medrano.

'You can't see it on the footage. David's blocking the view,' I said, pointing toward the camera.

'Well, we can always look at the other camera,' said Medrano.

'What camera?'

'The hidden camera that covers the stairwell,' said Medrano, pointing to an air vent on the west wall.

CHAPTER SIXTY-NINE

Medrano's office, in the basement of the building, looked more like a TV studio. He had a bank of fifteen flat-screens on one wall, each showing a different live feed from the building's security system. Beyond this room was the locker area for the guards, and behind the monitors there were around half a dozen desks, each with a computer and a phone.

'So, when David's neighbor, Mr Gershbaum, made the emergency call, that call came through to somebody in this room, is that right?'

'Right,' said Medrano.

'And the security system logs the date and time of the call?'

'Yes, and the security officer deals with the police alert,' said Medrano.

'What do you mean?' said Kennedy.

'When a resident makes an emergency call to us, our system sends a text to nine one one telling them we've had a call. Unless our operator contacts nine one one within five minutes to tell them everything is fine, NYPD send a patrol car to check it out. It's like a fail-safe. We've got around twenty of Manhattan's super-rich in this building. If a crew tried to rob us, the first thing they'd do is disable the security control room. So if a resident or a member of staff managed to get to an emergency phone, even though we might be incapacitated, somebody from nine one one will know there's an emergency, and if we don't stand them down, the cops'll come running.'

'I didn't know that. All I have is a record of security calling nine one one when the body was found. Kennedy, you think you can get me a record of the text?'

'I'll do my best.'

'Can I see the whole feed from the camera that NYPD took their footage from? I want to make sure that it hasn't been edited,' I said.

Medrano relieved the security guard at the bank of monitors and started calling up the footage from the hard drive. Within moments, the screen directly in front of us went blank, and then an image appeared of the security guards knocking on Gershbaum's door before letting themselves in.

'Hang on. I'll rewind,' said Medrano.

'No, it's fine. Just let it play,' I said.

A guard came out of Child's apartment and made a call. Nothing happened for a few minutes, so Medrano scrolled through the digital footage until the first pair of cops arrived. Medrano appeared on the screen, and he let the cops into Child's apartment. He fast-forwarded the footage, and we watched Medrano pacing up and down the hallway at high speed until the detectives arrived, followed by a team of CSIs in white overalls to work the evidence. I paid attention to each figure as they moved and asked Medrano to slow it down so I could get a good look at all of the officers. There were periods where there was no one on-screen, and Medrano could fast-forward the footage so that a minute of real time played out on the screen in less than three seconds. After twenty minutes or so of Medrano fast-forwarding the footage, I yelled out, 'Stop.'

Immediately, Medrano paused the video. I knew then that I had a hand to play in court in the morning.

'What am I looking at?' said Kennedy.

'I'm not sure,' I said. 'But I'm going to find out. I'll need to see the footage for the whole day. Can I get a copy of this?'

The head of security rubbed his chin. 'I don't see why not. The cops took the entire day's footage, too. Oh, did you want a copy of the footage from the vent camera?'

'Let me see it first,' I said.

'How come the cops didn't take a copy of this footage from the vent cam?' asked Kennedy.

Medrano cleared his throat, looked at this shoes, and then raised his head to address Kennedy.

'Look, there's a lot of wealthy, famous people who live in this building. We watch everything, and in many ways, we see nothing.

Know what I mean? The paparazzi have been trying to buy some-body, anybody, in this building who'll tip them off when a hooker, a dealer, or another celebrity visits an apartment in this building. We get well paid for our silence and for looking the other way. Up until a year ago there was no camera there. We kind of had an unwritten rule that the stairs were out of bounds for cameras. There was a burglary. We caught the guy and as a compromise we installed hidden cameras on each floor. The cops didn't ask to see this footage, and we never showed it to them. This is the only camera that covers the door to the stairs. It's a balancing act. Lot of potential residents don't want to live under a security camera, not with their lifestyles. So we have to try to make them feel both secure and anonymous.'

After scrolling through menus and entering a date and time search, the footage appeared on the screen above the control panel. It was a side view. We watched David and Clara enter the apart-ment. Medrano sped up the footage until we saw David again, backpack in tow, hooded. He slowed the footage, rewound and played it. David didn't drop anything on the floor. I could see his hands clearly. He turned his back on the door and walked out of view toward the elevator.

'Stop,' said Kennedy. 'Did you see that?' he said.

'No,' I said.

Medrano backed up, played the footage again.

'Right there,' said Kennedy.

'What?' I said.

'Can you zoom in?' said Kennedy.

'Sure. Where?' said Medrano.

The FBI man pointed to the mirror in the hallway. In response, Medrano used two large dials on either side of the keyboard to focus on the mirror. The close-up picture was grainy now, but much larger.

'Play it again,' said Kennedy.

As the footage played, I couldn't help but let out a gasp when I saw it.

'Holy shit,' said Medrano.

The three of us remained silent for a time, our eyes transfixed on the image Medrano had frozen on the screen.

'Are you sure the cops didn't watch this footage?' I asked.

'Yes. They had all they needed from the main camera,' said Medrano.

'So are you going to give this to the DA?' said Kennedy.

I thought for a second. Shook my head. I didn't want Zader to get a heads-up on this evidence. It didn't prove David was innocent, but if handled in the right way, it might just give him a shot.

'No. Better that this comes out in open court. Public and messy,' I said.

CHAPTER SEVENTY

David Child must've heard me trying to park the Honda in the driveway of the Lizard's home. He stood at the open front door, hands in his pockets, his right leg shaking.

'Am I clear?' he said, as I folded myself out of the cramped driver's seat.

'Not yet.'

I told him everything that had happened at the airport over two energy drinks and half a pot of coffee. No wonder David didn't sleep. Those drinks tasted like gasoline and OJ. I didn't tell him about El Grito. He didn't need any more pressure.

'It stands at twenty years – or fight the case and risk a life sentence. The DA has his ballistics now, identifying the gun found in your car as the same weapon that fired the rounds that killed Clara. I read the report from a Dr Peebles, the ballistics expert. It's a pretty straight report. Only thing that stood out was that Peebles couldn't find a serial number on the murder weapon. But that won't cut us any slack.'

He tried to speak. I could see the panic building in his gut, tightening every sinew, stretching every vein, strangling his breath. His head sank to the table.

Then he surprised me again.

'At least your wife is off the hook, from the law, I mean. At least that's one good thing that's come out of this. I could tell by the way the district attorney behaved in court earlier. I just knew. He would never give me a deal. I knew it,' he said, his fists thumping the table.

A long sigh, his fingers extended. Then his body appeared to relax. It was almost like watching someone take the tension out of a coiled spring.

'I'm just thankful your family is safe,' he said. And he meant it.

'Christine has the threat from the firm hanging over her. That won't stop until this charge goes away. You've got the means to hurt the firm, and they won't rest until that threat is removed permanently. Your only chance is to beat this charge tomorrow and pray that the task force takes down the firm before they get to you.'

'But your wife is out of this now. She's safe. You could just walk away. Go be with your family, I'd . . . I'd understand.'

Even staring at the prospect of a life sentence, David was thinking of others.

'No.'

'Why?' he asked.

'Because you need help, because I've let you down enough. I think you should tell the DA to go to hell. That's bad legal advice, but in truth, I'm not much of a lawyer.'

'Really, so what are you good at?' said David.

'Hustling. Grifting. Con artistry. And because of that I've almost worked out how you were framed. But proving it is something else. We do have one new piece of evidence that has potential, but I have to play it right.'

I told him about the footage I'd seen on the hidden vent cam.

'I . . . I . . . don't remember that.'

'From the angle, I don't think you saw it. You must have been aware of it somehow, because you turned around and then stopped.'

'I didn't know what it was at the time. Clara was trying to help me with that aspect of my personality. The compulsiveness. I suppose it worked, some of the time.'

'What we need now is the rest of the story. This won't work unless we can explain the setup.'

From my visit to David's building I had the beginnings of a theory – how he could've been framed. But there were still too many uncertainties and unanswered questions. I didn't have it all. Not yet. And I didn't see any point in telling him how I thought it had gone down. For a start, it was so elaborate, so risky – it was a miracle that it had worked out. So far we'd found one mistake. I was sure there would be others.

'Did you meet Langhiemer?' he said.

I showed David the picture I'd taken on my phone.

'He looks pissed at you,' said David.

'Yeah, there's something going on there. Does he have a girlfriend?'

'I don't know, probably.'

'I can't rule him out, but I can't see how he figures in this at the moment.'

A sudden pain shot through my skull, blinding me. I'd had no sleep in more than twenty-four hours and it didn't look like I was going to get any meaningful shut-eye that night. I closed one eye to the pain, sat up, and drained the last of the coffee from one of the Lizard's mugs that bore the slogan LIZARDS DO IT NAKED. It was almost three a.m., and the sky was just about to change from smoke black to a burgeoning promise of the morning.

'He's the only one with the money and the power to do it,' said David.

'But why? Corporate war is one thing, but murder is a whole different bag. Do you really think he's that ruthless? He'd kill an innocent girl to frame you?'

David rubbed his chin, then thought better of it and plucked three wet wipes from the pack and began to clean his fingers.

I tried Christine's cell for about the twentieth time. Still nothing. I told myself they were okay, they were headed for the open country, in the middle of nowhere, so there may not be a phone signal.

'So what happens tomorrow?' said David.

Folding away the files, I got to my feet, ready to find the Lizard's couch and at least try to get some sleep.

'We fight. At the moment we don't have enough to win. Hopefully Kennedy will come through. In fact, I'm sure he will. I left him at your building – he's searching through the camera footage, trying to clear up a few things. He's also trying to find some information that will help us. It won't be easy to get, but he'll make it happen.'

'So, he's the determined type.'

'I wouldn't say that. He's more like a stubborn son of a bitch.'

Child looked me up and down, shook his head.

'I know you'll do your best, but I can't see this hearing going my way. Whoever set me up saw to that.'

Placing the files on the coffee table, I sat back down and rubbed my temples.

'David, there's always a chance,' I said.

'Because I'm telling the truth?'

'No, because I'm representing you, and I don't believe you killed anyone. I'm sure that's true, but the truth isn't enough. This isn't about the truth. No trial is ever about the truth. It's about what can or can't be proven. It's a game. And tomorrow we're playing to win.'

David got up and held out his hand, a brave gesture for him. I shook it.

I settled on the Lizard's couch, but couldn't sleep. I thought over everything that had happened that day – went over the various ways that the setup for Clara's murder might have worked out. I called Kennedy.

'You still awake?' I said.

'I'm awake. I'm waiting for people to get back to me. I think I'll be able to get you everything you need.'

'That's great. Mind if I run something past you?'

'Shoot.'

'The car accident. David's car was hit on purpose. Whoever orchestrated the accident knew that the air bag residue could easily be mistaken for gunshot residue.'

'Fair enough,' said Kennedy.

'So, you'll look into it?'

'Look into what?'

I sighed. 'I had to buy that article online directly from the university. Maybe whoever framed David got their information from the same source.'

'Okay, I'll look into it. You also asked me to look into somebody else for the murder. What was the guy's name again?'

I told Kennedy all I knew about Bernard Langhiemer.

'I never heard of him, but . . .' He paused.

'What?'

'You said Langhiemer took out some unfriendly bloggers by loading their computers with child exploitation images?'

'Yeah, that's one sick individual,' I said.

'It may be nothing, or it may be something. I saw the video of the interviews between Dell and the informant, Farooq, from last year. Mostly they talk about the firm, its history, Ben Harland being corrupted by Gerry Sinton – that kind of thing. But at one point Dell offers Farooq a deal for testifying. Farooq said that unless he got immunity, he would fight the charges against him.'

'So . . .'

'So Farooq claimed he never saw any of those images before. He said he'd been framed.'

'Take a look at Langhiemer for me, see what else you can dig up,' I said.

Kennedy stifled a yawn and said, 'Anything else?'

'Don't suppose you'd give me an alarm call at seven a.m.?'

PART THREE

THE COVER STORY

CHAPTER SEVENTY-ONE

16 hours until the shot

At 4:05 a.m. the call woke me.

I'd been asleep for less than an hour. Heaving the upper half of my body off the couch, I swung my legs to the floor, knocked over a glass of water and just managed to grab my phone before it fell into the pool of liquid on the floor.

'Yeah? Eddie Flynn here.'

The caller had already hung up. It was Christine. I dialed again – voice mail.

For the next half hour I hit redial – no connection. I knew she'd be in Virginia, in a sparsely populated area fifty miles from the nearest town. Cursing myself for not going with her, I thought of them huddled together. Christine and Carmel would put on a brave face for Amy – that would sharpen Christine and keep her focused.

I couldn't get back to sleep, my mind racing with possibilities. The house was quiet, still. A cold coffee and David's file sat in front of me. I put down my cell, opened the papers, and read them all again.

Within a few short hours, we were on the road.

'Holly, if we all make it out of this thing alive, I want you to do one thing for me.' I said.

'What's that?'

'I want you to take this car to a scrap metal yard and crush it.'

My legs were so cramped in the front passenger seat of the Honda that I thought I might need to get my feet amputated.

In the rearview mirror I saw the Lizard's van hugging our path. We'd driven around for an hour before venturing toward the courthouse, to make sure we weren't followed. Holly found a parking garage and drove to the top level. The Lizard joined us.

We left the vehicle and descended in the elevator to the street. With his hood up, David was pretty anonymous; the baggy hood hid his face well. He wore his suit underneath the loose-fitting clothes.

'So how are we going to get into court?' asked Holly.

'I told you, a friend is giving us a lift,' I said.

The hard rain that had soaked the city overnight was finally letting up. The sun threatened the metallic sky, like a match bleeding through touch paper.

We were six blocks from the courthouse when I stepped into a convenience store. Only when the Lizard told David and Holly to follow me did they enter the small, cramped space. A deli occupied one half of the store. The owner, Lenny Zigler, piled stacks of newspapers, candy bars, foil-wrapped breakfast sandwiches, and magazines at the door. For thirty years Lenny delivered the papers to the local courthouse. A budget cut five years ago led to Lenny's run being dumped, until a new superior court judge was appointed – Harry Ford. Harry had a penchant for hot New York strip sandwiches with lots of jalapeños, especially after a heavy night on the Jack. The morning paper delivery recommenced soon after Harry took up the post – at double the price and with a free sandwich thrown in.

'It's a shit morning, ain't it, Eddie? How's Judge Harry. He hasn't sent you here about that thing last week? I already told him, he wants his sandwich hotter, he's gotta use the microwave,' he said.

'It's nothing like that. Tell you the truth, I need a ride to the courthouse.'

'Somebody break your legs? It's only . . .'

Lenny's words fell away as my mouth opened. He looked at the picture of David on the cover of every paper at his feet, then looked at the young man behind me as he threw back his hood.

The Lizard and I helped load Lenny's van, which was parked at the rear entrance to his business. When we were done, David and Holly hopped in and sat on the stacks of newspapers. I took a seat on the wheel arch, and the Lizard sat up front with Lenny. The smell of ink from the newspapers and the hot meat in the sandwiches mingled with a residual odor of gasoline and oil.

There was no conversation; David rubbed his hands and picked at his fingernails.

'It'll be okay, David,' said Holly.

David returned the sentiment with a half smile. The case was running around inside my head as I tried to make sense out of it. Lenny wasn't getting much small talk from the Lizard; he was too busy scanning the traffic and the sidewalks – alert to any potential threat. To break the awkward silence, Lenny turned on the radio. It was just past eight a.m., and the hourly news bulletin led with David's story. He didn't want to hear it, but he didn't want to be rude to Lenny, so he covered his ears in his hood and plugged his headphones into his iPod.

'In other news, Harbor Police have identified the body of the male pulled from the East River yesterday. Benjamin Harland, a sixty-eight-year-old . . .'

'Hey, Lenny, turn that up fast,' I said, as a cold feeling spread over my spine.

'. . . partner in the successful Manhattan law firm Harland and Sinton. It's believed that the deceased may have suffered an accident while sailing in the bay over the weekend. The boat has not been recovered, and the deceased's twenty-three-year-old daughter, Samantha Harland, is still missing.'

Turning in his seat, the Lizard looked at me, waiting for my take on this.

Holly told David what we'd all just heard on the radio.

'What does this mean? What's going on?' he asked.

I shook my head, trying to make sense of it all.

'Well, with Harland and Sinton about to go down for the biggest money-laundering scheme in US history, I don't think Ben Harland had any kind of an accident. Either El Grito got to him, or Gerry Sinton. Harland was the partner that gave the firm its legitimacy; sure he took the money that Gerry washed, but this was Gerry's scheme and he was using Harland. Now it's all about to unravel and Gerry is scared. He's offing witnesses. Clearing the decks and getting ready to run with the money as soon as it hits the account.

This is an endgame. You can only run an operation like that for so long. Soon everybody gets caught. Gerry is desperate now. The firm is going down, and they want to hide. They'll be even more determined to take you out before they run. We've got to get you clear of these charges so you can take off. The longer you stay in the city, the more dangerous it becomes.'

CHAPTER SEVENTY-TWO

The basement elevator took us to the eighth floor of the municipal court building. I checked the listings and found David's case scheduled in court twelve.

It wasn't a big courtroom, with seating for no more than a hundred spectators. When we got there, every seat was taken either by a TV reporter, a journalist, or a blogger. They'd all been chatting among themselves until we walked in. It was as if I'd stepped on some kind of mute button, because the noise from the crowd instantly stopped, then blew into a frenzy of questions as I led David toward the defense table. We'd discussed this; he was to say nothing.

Holly and the Lizard followed and sat behind us, in the seats reserved for defense lawyers. I let my case files fall on the desk and surveyed the courtroom while David got comfortable. The prosecution table was empty; Zader wanted to make a dramatic entrance. The clerk, Pattie, sat in front of the judge's raised bench. Apart from Pattie, the court guards, and half the media in New York, the courtroom was empty.

At least I thought it was.

Emerging from beneath Pattie's desk, Cooch stood up, adjusted his pants, and then pointed back beneath the desk at Pattie's computer as he whispered his instructions. Pattie nodded.

Cooch lifted a slip of paper from his jacket, removed his reading glasses from his case and put them on, then proceeded to read whatever was on the slip of paper while Pattie typed on the computer.

Pattie smiled and nodded at Cooch. He winked back at her, put a hand on her shoulder, then whispered something in her ear. She laughed. He saw me at the defense table and worked his way around the long clerk's bench, past the prosecution table, then sat down on my right.

'All set?' I asked.

He raised his thumb.

'David, I'd like to introduce you to Cooch. He's the latest member of your defense team.'

David got up from his seat and shook hands warmly with Cooch. As he did so, David couldn't help but look over his new lawyer. The tie that Cooch wore was too wide to have been made this side of 1974, his shirt was yellowing slightly at the collar, but the suit fit Cooch well and was at least bought in the last ten years.

'Thank you for helping me,' said David.

'Pleasure,' said Cooch.

'Eddie, can we have a moment?' said Cooch.

'Sure,' I said.

We took a stroll to the witness box, out of earshot.

'You're not going to win the prelim today,' said Cooch.

'I'm not banking on it. I've got some ammo, but it could go either way . . .' I stopped talking. Cooch was shaking his head. He wasn't referring to the evidence.

'You know who our new judge is, don't you?' I said.

He nodded.

'Tell me it's not Rollins,' I said.

His face creased and he nodded again, apologetically. The one thing I'd focused on in my first year in practice was learning the character of the judges. Some judges are heavier on sentencing for certain crimes. Some won't entertain a self-defense case. Some are high on damages and some are low. Some won't listen to a single word from a defense attorney's mouth.

The worst of them all was Judge Rollins, a man who had just been appointed to the bench and was yet to let a defendant go out on bail for less than a five-figure bond. In the two months he'd been in office, he hadn't dismissed a single prosecution case and gave ninety percent of the maximum sentence to every soul who was unfortunate enough to mount a defense before him.

He was building a fearsome reputation, and the word had spread fast among the defense attorneys. The result, in recent weeks, had been as the new judge had intended. Plea bargains were the order of the day. No contested charges. Every defendant pleaded guilty and the judge's list of cases was already looking light. He'd been home early every afternoon last week, his quota for the day complete.

I needed to figure out a way to handle Rollins. If I couldn't, the case was over before we even started.

'I'll be back in a second. Cooch, come get me if the judge appears,' I said.

Unbuttoning my jacket, I slipped my phone from the inside pocket and began dialing before I left the courtroom.

They should've landed hours ago. David had tried to get ahold of the helicopter charter company that was supposed to meet Christine, Amy, and Carmel as they got off the plane, but he couldn't get anyone in the office to answer the phone. I looked up, scanning the corridor. There was no one looking my way. Slamming my fist into the wall, I swore over and over again under my breath. I had a sensation of falling, my guts slamming into my throat, an overwhelming desire to grab on to something to stop the world from turning. Steadying myself with a palm on the door, I breathed in and out. David needed me with a cool head.

I told myself they were fine. The only thing I could do was pray that there had been some pitfall along the way – no phone signal, or maybe they lost their phones? My throat narrowed at the thought of it, and I squeezed my eyes closed in an effort to banish those thoughts.

Someone tapped me on the shoulder.

I turned, a little startled.

Lester Dell held out a cell phone. With a passive look on his face, he said, 'There's a call for you. You have a major problem.'

CHAPTER SEVENTY-THREE

At the corner of Dell's eyes I detected the ghost of a smile.

I took the phone.

'Eddie,' said Christine. It felt as though I'd been hooked up to the grid power all night, and hearing her voice just pulled the plug, cut the power, and let every muscle in my body relax.

The relief lasted all of two seconds.

'Jesus Christ, what's going on? I've been arrested,' said Christine.

'What?'

'They followed us from the airstrip at Remo. Two federal agents picked us up a few hours ago. The chopper took us to Grey's Point. They must have monitored it. They were waiting for us on the road, almost ran us off the highway. This is bullshit. I thought there was a deal.'

'Hold on. Are you okay? Is Amy all right?'

'She's pretty shook up, and so am I. They left her with Carmel when they grabbed me. I'm in a custody van, headed somewhere. I don't know where. Can't see out of the windows, but I think we're headed—'

The call went dead. I turned my back to Dell, transferred the phone to my left hand, and said, 'Give me a second. Stay on the line, Chrissie. Tell me if . . .'

Spinning on my heel, I slammed an elbow into Dell's face, let my momentum take me full circle, and followed it up with a right cross that took him clean off his feet. Before he could react, I was on top of him, pinning his shoulders to the ground with my knees. I leaned over him and dug my fingers into his face. He bucked and kicked, but I held firm.

'You piece of shit. You had my wife picked up. My daughter was in that car. She could've been killed. We had a—'

Dell's knee slammed into my back. He trapped my wrist, threw a leg over my shoulder, and pushed. As I twisted, I tried to get a hold on Dell's ankle, my hands moving fast, scrabbling around.

But I had a better idea than simply trapping his ankle.

I let him sweep me off of him. For a guy almost twice my age, Dell's speed surprised me, and he was up and on me in a second.

Two quick shots to my kidneys before I heard a guard hollering and Dell's weight lifted from my chest.

'Lester Dell, Federal Task Force Commander,' he said, reaching for his badge. He held out his ID to the guard. I lifted my head and saw Big Tommy.

'That man assaulted a federal officer in the execution of his duty. You saw him. Arrest him right now,' said Dell, struggling to catch his breath.

I stretched my back, got slowly to my feet, and looked Big Tommy in the gut. His head was several feet above me. My head swam, and I half lowered myself, half fell back to the floor. I sat there, my legs stretched out in front of me, breathing hard. Craning my neck, I felt a sharp, burning pain and saw Tommy give me a nod.

'I didn't see shit,' said Tommy, walking away.

Dell watched him go, swore, and sat down on the bench outside of court twelve.

'What do you want?' I said.

He laughed, touched his lip, and spat a little blood onto the floor. The door to the courtroom opened and a reporter stuck his head out. I waved him away with a menacing look. He closed the door.

'Your wife's immunity agreement is in exchange for her giving evidence against Gerry Sinton and Ben Harland at their trial. In case you haven't heard, Ben Harland is dead. Found in the East River this morning. He's bought his ticket to immunity. Sinton is cleaning house. NYPD spoke to him this morning, and he has an alibi for the same time we know that Harland left port. Unfortunately, Sinton is only half the prize. The money is due to hit an account in Manhattan at four this afternoon in the name of Ben Harland. I've no idea how Sinton will access the money, but unless we catch him lifting it or transferring it to his name, we've got nothing on him. Could be that he's not going after the money at all. Maybe he has enough squared away somewhere. I think this is why the final account was always in Ben Harland's name; it's a fail-safe position. If something goes wrong, Sinton can off Harland and lay all of the blame for the money laundering on a dead man. We have literally nothing linking the money to Gerry Sinton. So we have no choice but to go after the associates Ben Harland set up. Your wife is one of those associates.'

He coughed, spat a little more, composed himself, and leaned forward.

'The immunity agreement died with Ben Harland. But I'm going to give Christine one last shot. It's all up to you, Eddie. David Child has lied to you. He's a lot more involved than you think. He didn't design that algorithm to prevent cyberattacks – he designed it to hide the money from the FBI and the Treasury Department. It's not perfect, but it might be enough to get us a conviction. Get me my plea. He gets ten years for murder, gives evidence that Gerry Sinton ordered him to design the program to launder the money, and who knows? Maybe David will get out in five. This is your only option now. This is Christine's only option. You're supposed to get this boy to plead guilty, not get him off. You screw me, I screw you.'

'What about the phone I gave you? Can't you get something from Gill's phone that links the attempted hit on Christine to Gerry Sinton?'

'The phone was wiped remotely about an hour after you gave it to me. We're not even sure how it was done. The FBI's techs are scratching their heads.'

I thought of Langhiemer. If he could trace my phone in less than a minute, he could wipe a cell phone's memory.

'Someone is framing David and helping the firm. The more I think about it, the more I see this guy being involved. I don't know what his connection is to the firm, but he's at the heart of this. His name is Bernard Langhiemer.'

'Who the hell is Bernard Langhiemer? Look, Eddie, this is bullshit. David killed his girlfriend. Gerry Sinton runs the firm's wash house – that's it. Don't get sidetracked. This is your last chance.'

And so it came right down to it. The whole way.

David or Christine?

I couldn't save them both. If I didn't take this deal, the most likely outcome would be that David and Christine spent the rest of their lives in prison. The deal made sense. All I had to do was make my client plead guilty.

Slowly, I got to my feet, smoothed down my suit, and adjusted my tie.

'No deal. I told myself when I got back into practice I would do what's right. David Child didn't kill that girl, and I'm going to prove it.'

'Since when did you care about what's right? You're a defense attorney. I don't care about charging your wife, or the other associates – I want the partners. I can't have Ben Harland now, so I need Gerry Sinton for the whole operation.'

Dell's phone rang.

He took the call, then hung up.

'Gerry Sinton just got into the elevator. He can't see us together. Think about what you're doing. Think about your wife.'

My eyes misted. I wiped them and cleared my throat.

'That's all I ever do, Dell.'

'Be sure to tell her that. My men left Carmel and Amy where we found them. They're out of it now. Christine's on her way here. An hour, tops, until the custody van drops her in holding. If we don't have a plea agreement by then, she'll be charged with money laundering, conspiracy, fraud, everything Ben Harland avoided when he took a dip in the river. Stop friggin' around and get me the plea. Do your goddamned job, and look after your wife,' he said. Then he got up and went back into the courtroom.

Big Tommy stood around twenty feet from me. He made sure Dell had gone, then turned away. There was nobody else in the corridor.

I took Dell's ankle weapon from my jacket pocket, checked that the first round was chambered, tucked the Ruger LCP into the back of my pants, and followed him into court.

CHAPTER SEVENTY-FOUR

The tall, broad figure of Gerry Sinton framed the entrance. With my back to the still empty judge's bench, I stood in the central aisle, my hands in my pockets, waiting for him.

Flanked by the same squad of paralegals, Gerry strode toward me. A bright sheen of sweat covered his face. He looked like a gladiator in a thousand-dollar suit.

Before he took his seat in the gallery, he said, 'I hope to see Christine again soon. I'm sure we'll have a lot to discuss.'

He sat down and folded his arms. I turned and walked back to the defense table, blood roaring in my ears. I wanted to break Sinton's neck.

Instead I sat down and opened the case files.

'David, Dell made me an offer. He says you were hired by Harland and Sinton to design the algorithm for a specific purpose: to launder their money under the guise of a security protocol. I know that's not how it went down.'

'I didn't know the firm's money was dirty. The entire design is based on the premise that they are legit. If the money they brought in was dirty, then, yeah, the algo protecting the money would also clean it. But I didn't know. I swear to you. I won't testify that I created a program to launder money – that's not what I did.'

'Dell's offering ten years if you plead to this murder and testify that the firm asked you to design a digital laundry. I have to tell you, we've got some moves to make today, but the prosecution have a great case and we've pulled a really bad judge.'

I left out the part about Christine. I didn't want to cloud the kid's judgment. All in all, it was a great offer.

'I didn't kill anybody. I've never designed anything with a criminal purpose. I won't do it.'

If there was any doubt left, it disappeared. The guilty don't toss away the deal of a lifetime. They grab it with both hands. Sometimes, even though it's wrong, the innocent take the deal, too; going to trial and risking fifteen years, or pleading guilty and walking out in three, the justice game is a cold house for the innocent. I found myself admiring David; no matter what way you cut it, the kid was brave.

Dell wanted justice for Sophie's killer. I had no doubt about that. People who go through that kind of trauma are never the same. Either they lash out at others, or like Dell, they don't want anyone else to suffer their pain. He couldn't let another victim lie in the dirt with their killer unpunished. Also, Dell knew that Child would never admit to a criminal intent in designing the algorithm – probably because it was the truth. Dell didn't care – as far as he was concerned, Child was a killer and he'd given the firm the means to operate their laundry. He wanted to use David, and for that he needed to take control of his life. A guilty plea and a deal gave Dell all the control he needed to use David as a weapon against the firm. To get his weapon he was putting my wife's life on the line.

I had to play this straight, one case at a time. Get David clear and figure out a way to bury the firm and save Christine.

'I believe you, David,' I said.

The rear doors of the courtroom opened, some hundred feet behind us. I heard another entourage entering.

'I sense a disturbance in the force,' said Cooch.

Zader hovered at the rear of the pack of assistant district attorneys, who hauled evidence boxes and folders into court. Zader looked determined. He didn't have a phone in his hand this time. He was through playing the media for now. He needed a decision that went his way. Then he'd paste that victory over every channel, paper, blog, and magazine.

'I don't think he's got a sense of humor about the whole *Star Wars* thing,' I said.

'Good,' said Cooch.

Cooch stood and held out a hand to the DA.

'I don't believe we've met. I'm Max Coucheron; call me Cooch.'

'Michael Zader,' he said, shaking Cooch's hand.

'Oh, I *know* who you are. I just didn't recognize you without the helmet.'

CHAPTER SEVENTY-FIVE

A hush descended on the courtroom as Judge Rollins came out of his chambers and adjusted his robes before taking his seat at the bench. There was no announcement that court was in session. Rollins had told the clerk that he didn't want a call for silence as he came in because 'the presence of my authority creates the silence.' The story spread fast, and a lot of the more senior defense attorneys made a point of loudly continuing their conversations when Rollins entered court, just to piss him off.

Not that he needed to be any more pissed off than usual.

'Now, the matter of *State v. Child*,' he said, surveying the court-room and drinking in the massive media attention.

He looked at the prosecution table and nodded. 'District Attorney Zader, a pleasure to have you in my courtroom.'

'Always delighted to appear on the side of justice,' said Zader.

I heard fake retching noises from some of the reporters, and a nervous, muffled round of laughter made its way around the room. Rollins ignored it completely and turned his attention to me.

He was a man close to fifty, but on the losing side. He looked to me like he was also losing the battle with his waistline. For all that extra weight, it hadn't softened his face – he wore an angry expression below his light brown hair. He had skin the color of weak tea and dry, fat lips. Rollins had been a tax attorney before he'd applied for a judicial post. Before he became a judge, the closest he'd gotten to a criminal court was driving past the building on the way to his office.

'Mr . . . er . . .' he said, holding out the listing notice in front of him like it was toxic.

'Flynn,' I said, making sure to stand before I addressed him.

'Flynn? I thought that Harland and Sinton were attorneys of record.'

'I am the attorney of record, and there's been a change in second chair. Mr Coucheron now appears,' I said.

Cooch stood and bowed with a smile.

From the distasteful look on Rollins's face, I could tell he'd come across Cooch in his court before.

'Well, before we begin, I wanted to ask if the defendant would be willing to waive the hearing. Surely this is all just a formality, Mr Flynn. Your client must appreciate that he wouldn't have been arrested and charged by the police if they didn't have enough evidence to do so.'

'We disagree. That's why we're here, Your Honor. That's why we have preliminary hearings, so that the defendant can challenge weak and insubstantial evidence . . .'

'I know the basis of criminal procedure, Mr Flynn. I don't need a lecture from you,' he said. Already his palette had changed to a sun-ripened red.

'The prosecution will call their first witness.'

With a thin bundle of papers in his hand, Zader got up from the prosecution table and handed the papers to the clerk.

'Your Honor, might I be permitted to make a short opening statement, to frame the evidence and assist the court?'

'By all means, Mr Zader.'

'Thank you, Your Honor. This will be a short but thorough presentation of the evidence preserved to date in respect to this murder. The state firmly believes that the evidence establishes a strong, circumstantial and forensically sound case against the defendant, Mr David Child.'

Zader spoke slowly, never taking his eyes from the judge's pen as it scattered across the pages of his notebook. Rollins wrote down every word as best he could. Zader knew this and moderated the speed of his delivery to make sure the judge got it all down in his notes. It also meant the reporters, and whichever paralegal from his department, could get a word-for-word note of his speech. He stood with his feet wide apart, his hands lightly pressed together so that he could gesture naturally as he spoke. Zader was a seasoned litigator, and he knew exactly how to portray his own confidence and authority in court.

'Your Honor, we shall call witnesses to prove that probable cause exists here in abundance. This case will show that David Child was alone with the victim when she was murdered. No one else was present, and it is impossible for anyone other than the defendant to have perpetrated this crime. Two witnesses will establish this evidence. Mr Gershbaum, who heard the shots, and the building's security officer, Mr Richard Forest, who discovered the body of the victim.

'The crime scene investigator, Rudy Noble, will speak to the cause of death and reveal the violence inflicted upon the victim as one that can only be described as a crime of passion. A lover's murder.

'Then, in relation to the defendant's capture, Mr Woodrow will testify that he had a car accident, which was his fault, where his vehicle hit the defendant's million-dollar Bugatti Veyron. Mr Woodrow saw a weapon in that supercar. He called the police, and Officer Phil Jones retrieved that same weapon, a small pistol, from the footwell of the defendant's car.

'Your Honor, we have recently received ballistics evidence that proves the weapon found in the defendant's car is indeed the murder weapon. Mr Peebles, our ballistics expert, will testify that the markings on the rounds that were retrieved from the victim match the weapon found in the defendant's possession minutes after the crime was committed. We are reserving our right to submit this expert report without calling Mr Peebles.'

The DA had learned his lesson from the Porter fiasco. This evidence would go before the judge without giving me a shot at cross-examining Peebles. Rollins would accept this evidence verbatim; the gun in David's car was the murder weapon, and I couldn't challenge a word of that. There was one thing that nagged at me about Peebles's report – he couldn't find a serial number on the murder weapon, even using their metallurgic retrieval technology. Basically, every gun in America has a manufacturer's serial number – if that number is filed away, experts can still bathe the weapon in a form of acid that allows them to trace, on a microscopic level, the imprints made when the gun was stamped with the number. Peebles said that even after attempting this method, no serial number had been retrieved.

'Finally,' continued Zader, 'Detective Morgan will testify regarding the CCTV images from the defendant's apartment, which confirm beyond any doubt that he is the killer.

'Unless there is anything else, the people call their first—'

Rollins turned his attention to me with a puzzled expression on his face.

'Mr Flynn, I would ask you to consider, once again, in light of the prosecution's opening statement, whether your client wishes to waive this hearing. This court's time is precious. My time is precious.'

David's leg bounced up and down under the table, the anxiety pumping through his system like caffeine. I looked at Cooch. He was reading the morning paper; he hadn't listened to a word the DA had said. Zader looked like a winner. I became conscious that I was wearing the same suit, shirt, and tie I'd worn yesterday, I still hadn't shaved, my nerves were shot all to hell, my wife was about to be charged with federal offenses, and I'd slept in my suit.

All of these things ran through my mind as I said, 'Your Honor, we are proceeding with this hearing.'

Judge Rollins sighed, shook his head. A sea of mumbling erupted from the gallery, and Rollins let the noise pass without comment. He appeared to be too pissed at me to notice.

'I'm not impressed, Mr Flynn. Surely this case has to go before a jury,' said Rollins.

I had two choices: ignore the asshole and press on with the hearing, or send Rollins a message and risk alienating David further. The safe option was to ignore the remark and get the first witness on the stand.

But I was all about risk. If it paid off, it gave me a way to handle Rollins.

'Your Honor, may I approach the bench?'

'No, you may not. I don't see any need for a sidebar. This is a public hearing. If you have something to say, then say it.'

I'd known he wouldn't grant me a sidebar. He wasn't interested in anything I had to say. Fair enough, I thought.

'Very well, Your Honor. The defense would like to submit a motion for your recusal.'

It was Zader's turn to chuckle with surprise.

Rollins placed his pen on his desk, folded his arms, and seemed to rise up a little in his seat.

'On what grounds do you seek my recusal, Counsel?'

'For bias, Your Honor. My client can't get a fair hearing from you. You've listened to Mr Zader, and it's clear from your remarks that you've already made up your mind in this case. You're biased in favor of the prosecution.'

'In my office, right now,' said Rollins.

As I got up, I felt my phone vibrate. I let Rollins turn his back before I checked my phone. It was a text message from Kennedy.

I've got some interesting reading. I'll be there soon.

CHAPTER SEVENTY-SIX

'I have never been so insulted in my life,' said Rollins as he paced up and down behind his desk. 'I should hold you for contempt,' he said.

Zader shook his head. 'I can understand how upset you must be, Your Honor, but wouldn't that be a little extreme? It might also throw fuel on Mr Flynn's argument.'

I took my hands from my pockets and studied Zader. He was on to me. I had to be a lot more careful. This was a dangerous opponent.

Tapping his index finger on the desk, Rollins fought to hold on to his temper, his collar straining at the bloated veins in his neck.

'How dare you make such an accusation in my courtroom. This is about respect, Flynn . . .' said Rollins. He'd dropped the formal address.

'You will withdraw this scurrilous accusation right now, in open court, and you will apologize to me personally. If you do that, I will consider whether I need to send a letter of complaint to the Bar Association. Do you understand me?'

'I understand, perfectly. Which judge do you propose to replace you?'

'Excuse me?'

'Well, obviously, if you're going to complain about me to the Bar Association, you can't continue to hear my client's case until that complaint is adjudicated. You'll have to recuse yourself. So who is your replacement?'

He caught his tongue just in time. I could tell Rollins was thinking he'd underestimated me. He wasn't the first to do that, not by a long shot.

'I cannot believe you have the audacity to stand there—'

'Your Honor, with all due respect, you asked me twice, in open court, to lean on my client to waive the prelim. You even said that this case should go to a jury, and you haven't heard a word of evidence yet. All you've got is the DA's opening statement. In my mind, you've already decided this case in the prosecution's favor.'

'Of course I haven't decided yet.'

'But you can see where I got that impression.'

He moved to his chair and sat down, cautiously, behind his desk. His extra chin flopped over his collar, his fingers folded across his stomach, and he considered his position. The anger faded – replaced by doubt.

'My comments were strictly obiter, Mr Flynn. Nothing more. I was merely considering the possibility of moving this trial forward. Your client has the right to a speedy trial.'

I didn't reply. Instead I inclined my head and kept my eyes on the judge, who couldn't match my gaze for more than a second.

'You have no cause for bias, really,' said Rollins, opening his hands, splaying his fingers. He was asking me, not telling me. Since he'd cooled, he was replaying his request to waive the prelim over and over in his mind – wondering if he really had overstepped the mark.

I said nothing and let him worry.

Rollins looked at Zader, inviting his cooperation. Zader didn't want to get involved in case it looked like he was backing up his pal, the judge. He avoided the judge's look by leafing through the evidence file.

'I'm not biased against your client, Mr Flynn. Can you accept that?'

Hands on my hips, I nodded and said, 'Your Honor, your word is good enough for me, but I'm mindful of my duty to my client. I will not pursue a recusal at this time, Your Honor, but I will reserve the right to raise it again, should the need arise. I'm sure it won't.'

The judge rose from his seat, nodded, and waved us back into court. With his back to the judge, Zader gritted his teeth and shook his head as we left the chambers. He knew he'd lost the edge with Rollins.

Now I had leverage. As a new judge, Rollins didn't want to make a ruling on recusal, because he was afraid I'd appeal his decision not to recuse himself. The last thing a baby judge needs is a senior member of the judiciary examining his conduct when he'd been in the job only five minutes. Instead Rollins would now make sure that I didn't have the opportunity to raise bias again – by giving me some leeway, being a little friendlier to the defense. And Zader had guessed the exact same thing. I couldn't resist the urge to antagonize Zader.

'Two can play at the bias game,' I said.

A fake smile was all he managed in reply.

Sounds from the crowd dissipated as Zader and I returned to the courtroom, Rollins following. I took up my position at the defense table. Zader returned to the lectern.

'Your Honor, we call the prosecution's first witness to the stand, Mr Gershbaum.'

Cooch gave me the thumbs-up.

We were on.

CHAPTER SEVENTY-SEVEN

9 hours until the shot

After he took the oath, Mr Leopold Maximillian Gershbaum stated his full name for the record in an accent that was pure Borough Park. His voice rattled in his chest, like too much grease on an old, wheezing engine. He unbuttoned his tweed jacket and sat down. I guessed he was pushing sixty. His salt-and-pepper-colored hairpiece looked to be in its early twenties. The reddish brown mustache made the ill-fitting wig look even more ridiculous. It didn't look like he cared. With thirty million in the bank, four divorces behind him, and the future ex-Mrs Gershbaum, a platinum-blond former Playmate of the Month, sitting in the audience for moral support, Leo Gershbaum could afford to slacken on appearances.

I could hear the sound of pages being turned in Zader's file, the muted tapping of Gershbaum's anxious feet, the hum of the air-conditioning, and the swish of my pen moving through my fingers; this was the moment of calm before Zader filled the blank page of the hearing with the prosecution's story.

'Mr Gershbaum, what is your profession?' said Zader.

He'd been prepped for this: Gershbaum turned and gave the judge his full attention as he replied.

'I'm a major motion picture director.'

The judge's eyes widened as a smile invaded his usually sour face.

'Would I have seen any of your movies?' asked Judge Rollins.

'Possibly, Your Honor,' said Gershbaum, rising slightly in his seat. 'A few years ago I directed a picture called *Little Creek Scout*.'

Putting his pen down, Rollins leaned back in his chair.

'Well, Mr Gershbaum, may I say that's one of my favorites. A great American story. Well, well. You may continue, Mr Zader.'

And with that sickening display, Zader had made Gershbaum more or less bulletproof. If I went in hard against the judge's favorite director, I would be pancaked.

Cooch leaned over and whispered some words of advice. 'Go easy on Gershbaum. Rollins is a big movie buff and he loves this guy.'

'Don't worry. I'm going to flip him,' I said.

A pair of unruly but distinguished eyebrows shot up close to the top of Cooch's head. When you have a prosecution witness that the judge or the jury loves, you can't attack them without damaging your case. There's only one option – flip them; the testimony that the judge liked, that he believed, well, you just make that testimony favor your case instead of the prosecution's. The trick was to flip the witness without the prosecutor or the judge even realizing.

'Thank you, Your Honor,' said Zader. 'Now I want to discuss the events of the evening of March fourteenth. Where were you on that night, Mr Gershbaum?'

'I was in my apartment in Central Park West, watching dailies.'

'Your apartment is on which floor?'

'The twenty-fifth. The tower, Central Park Eleven. Only two apartments are on each floor of the tower. The lower floors share three apartments per floor.'

'And what are dailies?'

'Oh, forgive me. Dailies are the collated footage from the previous day's shooting. We'd been filming a gun battle in an alleyway. I was looking over the footage and making notes for the editor.'

'Was anyone else with you in your apartment?'

'No. I was alone.'

'And what time did you begin watching the dailies?'

'Around seven thirty. Right after dinner.'

'And did anything unusual happen that evening?'

'Yes. Just before eight o'clock, I heard a series of loud bangs. Sounded like gunfire. At first I wasn't sure what I'd heard. There was a small amount of noise from the weapons used in the take. But then I turned down the volume on the TV and I heard a series of cracks. They were loud and very fast.'

'How many did you hear?'

'I'm not sure. The shots were rapid. Maybe five? Maybe more.'

'What did you do after you heard these shots?'

'Well, I still wasn't sure what it was. The apartment is pretty well insulated against noise, so I didn't think it came from the street, but I thought to myself that it could only have come from below. So I opened my balcony doors and went out to take a look.'

'And what did you see?'

'I leaned over the balcony, maybe expecting to see smoke from a car backfiring. Or maybe somebody in the park with fireworks. It's close to Saint Patrick's Day, so it's not unusual for some people to start their celebrations a little early. You know what the Irish are like . . .'

'Did you see any of those things?'

'No, sir. I took a good look, and then the explosion happened. Glass just went everywhere. It came from the apartment windows next door. I glanced at them as I ran back inside.'

'Go on, please.'

'Well, I was pretty shaken up. I didn't know what happened. I thought it could be somebody shooting at the building with a rifle, or maybe somebody shooting in the apartment next door. I grabbed my cell and ran for the panic room.'

'I tried calling nine one one, but I couldn't get a signal from in there. I didn't want to step outside the room in case I needed to close the door real quick. So I used the phone in the room, called straight down to security and told them what happened.'

'Did you lock yourself in your panic room?'

'No. I'm a little claustrophobic. I was only gonna close that door if I really had no other choice.'

'This next question is very important, Mr Gershbaum. How much time passed between you seeing the window explode and you making the call to security?'

Like all good, honest witnesses, he took a little time to think about it.

'I called security right away. I mean, I was scared. So, probably within, say, ten seconds I was on the phone.'

Producing a document with a flourish from his file, Zader approached the judge with a copy.

'Your Honor, at this time we'd like to refer to prosecution exhibit TM1. Detective Morgan will formally prove this exhibit in due course. With the defendant's permission it might be appropriate to refer to it now?'

'No objection,' I said.

Nodding his consent, Rollins accepted a copy of the document and asked the clerk to log it.

'Mr Gershbaum, this is a security log from your building. It records, electronically, the timing of emergency calls from residents. As you can see, the log records an emergency call from your apartment at twenty oh two on the night of March fourteenth. Is that correct?'

'Yes.'

'You will see toward the bottom of the page that security officer Richard Forest radioed the security station when he reached the door to your apartment. That time is recorded on the log as twenty oh six. Again, would that fit with your recollection?'

'I believe so.'

'How did the security team gain entry to your apartment?'

'I can buzz them in via the control panel in the panic room. That's what I did as soon as I saw them on the security camera outside my front door.'

'What happened next?'

'I told them what happened. One of the guards went out on the balcony. Then I guess they found her.'

'Apart from the front door of your apartment, is there any other way out?'

'No.'

'Do you know if it's a similar situation in Mr Child's apartment?'

'I believe so. When I leased the apartment, it was on the understanding that no structural alterations were to be made. I assume Mr Child would've had the same lease as I did. I think all residents were told the same. So no, the only exit is the front door.'

'Would it be possible to exit Mr Child's apartment via your balcony?'

Zader was tying off all loose ends – nailing Child to the crime scene and the time of the murder without any possible doubt.

'Not unless you climbed down the outside of the building, like Spider-Man, or something.'

'When you entered your panic room, you said that you kept the door open because you are a little claustrophobic. Would you still have had a view of your balcony?'

'Yes.'

'So, in the time between hearing the shots and the security team arriving, did you see anyone leave Mr Child's apartment and step onto your balcony?'

'No. I kept an eye on the balcony in case anyone leaped over the divide and tried to get into my apartment. Then I would have to close the panic room door. I didn't want to do that unless it was absolutely necessary. I don't do well in confined spaces, not since I spent a six-week night shoot in a tunnel in Pinewood Studios.'

'Nothing further,' said Zader, taking his seat.

I stood, buttoned my jacket, and gave Gershbaum a smile.

I really had only one question. A simple one. I was throwing a snowball up a hill with the hope that this one question would start rolling back down the incline, getting bigger and bigger until it reached the bottom and crushed Zader's case like a wrecking ball through a log cabin.

Clearing my throat, I was about to speak when the rear doors of the courtroom banged open. Two men, federal agents, each of them flanking my wife.

Even from this distance I could see her tears, her trembling hands, and the bright silver cuffs encasing her slender wrists.

CHAPTER SEVENTY-EIGHT

Seats bolted to the rear wall of the courtroom were reserved for court security, law enforcement, and bail bondsmen. One of the agents threw his overcoat across Christine's wrists and guided her to those seats. They'd wanted me to see the cuffs. Now they were being discreet.

From the crowd I picked out Dell's bearded, smiling face. He winked.

Pressure. Dell was all about pressure. And he would use every last piece of leverage to force a deal. I saw Sinton get up from the gallery and leave the court. He nodded at Christine as he walked past.

I felt a cold spike in my back that spread up toward my neck. It was almost as if the gun in my waistband called to me. My eyes grew hot, and I thought about whipping out the piece, grabbing Christine, and running. If we got out of the courthouse, we could hide. But that would be no kind of life for Christine, or Amy.

'Mr Flynn?'

Rollins, calling me. That icy tingle in my spine melted as I turned to face the witness – turning my back on my wife, turning away from her red, pleading eyes.

There was only one way to save her. Her fate and the fate of David Child were linked, bound together as sure as I was bound to her. I didn't trust Dell, but I'd learned the hard way to trust my own instincts. It didn't make sense to me at the time. I just knew. Get this kid off – that's all I had to do, and things would play out for Christine.

'My apologies, Your Honor.'

Just as I knew he would, Rollins rolled his eyes. I was sure that he still thought this hearing was a waste of time.

'Mr Gershbaum, you had heard gunfire and you went out onto your balcony to investigate. Then you saw the glass in the apartment next door exploding. So, you didn't hear any gunfire after the bullet went through Mr Child's balcony window?'

He lowered his gaze, blinked, began shaking his head.

'No. I would've heard it. There was no more gunfire after the window exploded.'

'No further questions,' I said, glancing at Zader. His pen paused on the page. Then he looked to his assistants, hands spread, as if to say, *Is that it?*

I was glad. Zader didn't see it, but if the rest of the case played out the way I hoped it would, then Leo Gershbaum would become the main witness for the defense.

'Redirect?' asked Rollins. Zader shook his head.

'Call your next witness. Let's keep this moving, Counselors,' said Rollins.

'The people call Richard Forest.'

Even as he spoke, Zader eyed me suspiciously. He was beginning to wonder if he'd missed something.

Footsteps in the aisle. I hadn't even heard the doors opening. It was Kennedy, with a bunch of documents in his hands. He almost bumped into the next witness, so eager was he to let me see what he'd found.

Four pieces of paper. Five copies of each of the four documents. A copy for me, one for the judge, the prosecutor, the witness, and the original, which was to be logged into evidence.

I read the documents as security officer Forest took the oath.

'What are those?' asked David.

'Snowballs,' I said. 'Big freakin' snowballs.'

CHAPTER SEVENTY-NINE

Kennedy told me he got a call about Christine, from one of his FBI buddies on the task force.

'I'm sorry, Eddie. This isn't right. My guy told me Carmel and Amy are fine. They're still in Grey's Point. At least Amy is safe,' he said.

'She too young to see all of this. To watch her mother being taken away after what she's been through . . .' I clamped my teeth and said no more. Whatever else happened, Dell would pay for putting my family through this.

It took Zader around five minutes to lead the security officer through most of his evidence. They covered the initial emergency call from Gershbaum, the response time, gaining access to Gershbaum's apartment and climbing over the small gap between the balconies. He was a good witness; he gave clear answers, and I could tell, from the initial questions, Forest had once been a cop. Medrano told me that Forest had left the force because of a ball-busting sergeant. He didn't take too well to that kind of authority but found a home, and better pay, at Central Park Eleven Security. A tall, lean officer with a starched collar and a red handkerchief in his blazer, Forest came across as an accurate, conscientious witness.

'Once you'd made it onto Mr Child's balcony, what did you see?' asked Zader.

'I saw the glass on the floor of the balcony first. I drew my weapon, hunkered down, and peered into the room. That's when I saw the body of a young, blond female, lying facedown on the kitchen floor. I could tell that she'd sustained massive head injuries and in all likelihood she was already dead.'

'What did you do next?'

'I climbed over the balcony and moved into the room, trying not to tread on the glass too much, and I radioed my supervisor that he should enter Mr Child's apartment, that we had a body on our hands and the perp could still be in there.'

'Your supervisor had not entered the apartment prior to your call?'

'No. We can't enter a resident's dwelling without permission, ordinarily. Not unless we have evidence that their safety or the safety of others is at risk. We're not the police. There are a lot of powerful people who live there, and they cherish their privacy more than most folks.'

'Please continue,' said Zader.

'My supervisor called nine one one and informed them that we were entering the apartment to do an emergency search. He got clearance for that from the operator, and he entered through the front door with the response team. We swept the apartment, found no one else. Not long after we finished our search, NYPD finally showed up. Then we cleared the scene and I gave a statement to Detective Morgan.'

'Thank you,' said Zader, taking his papers from the lectern.

'Mr Flynn, do you have any questions for Mr Forest?' said Rollins.

'Yes, Your Honor. Mr Forest, you entered the apartment and discovered the body. You then say you radioed for backup and your team performed a sweep of the apartment. Is that right?'

'That's right.'

'Describe this search of the apartment.'

'We searched the kitchen, the lounge, TV room, first-floor bathroom, ah – then we searched the bedrooms, bathroom, study.'

'Anywhere else?'

'No, well – there was nowhere else to search. Apart from the victim, the apartment was empty.'

My dad's warm breath in my ear: *People believe what they can see.*

The next question was risky. I didn't know the answer for sure. My mouth felt dry as I spoke.

'You didn't search the panic room?'

Warning signs appeared in front of him, big as traffic signs and flashing red for danger. He searched for an answer.

'By the time the security team arrived, they'd already been informed that Mr Child had left the apartment – so there was no point in searching the panic room. He's the only one with access, and he'd already left.'

It was good enough. Time to move on.

'Mr Forest, you were a former police officer, so you would have some training and experience in firearms?'

'Correct.'

'Considering your training and experience, how long would it take to aim and fire a whole magazine from a pistol, reload, and then spend the new cartridge?'

He blew out his cheeks and said, 'I don't know, maybe half a minute?'

'Half a minute. Could you do it faster? Would it be possible to do it in say fifteen or twenty seconds?'

'Fifteen would be very fast, maybe twenty seconds.'

'Twenty seconds, okay. I see that you wear a watch, Mr Forest.'

He was a little taken aback. He screwed up his eyes, let his lips fold down. 'Yes, my wife gave it to me for our anniversary.'

'Do you have your cell phone with you?'

'Yes, it's powered down.'

'With His Honor's permission, I'd like you to turn on your cell phone, just for a moment.'

'Your Honor, objection, relevance?' said Zader.

'I'll be quick, Your Honor. This is relevant and I'm coming to the point shortly.'

'Go faster, Mr Flynn,' said Rollins.

We waited while Forest switched on his phone. That delay gave me enough time to doubt the next set of questions. I decided it was worth the risk.

'While we're waiting for it to power up, can you tell me what time it is, Mr Forest?'

Zader threw his hands up at the judge. Rollins nodded, looked at me. I stared at him hard, my jaw set and tense. I shook my head slightly as my eyes flitted between Rollins and Zader. Like I was waiting for the judge to back Zader, and then I'd be ready to jump in and claim bias.

'Let's give Mr Flynn the benefit of the doubt for now, Mr Zader.'

'Thank you, Your Honor. Mr Forest, the time by your watch is?'

'Eleven oh two.'

'Can you read the time for me from the wall clock just behind you?'

He swiveled around, stared, and said, 'Eleven oh five.'

'And what is the time by your cell phone?'

Pressing a button, he sighed and said, 'Ten fifty-nine.'

'So that's three different times, on three different devices just in this room. Mr Forest, the security log at Central Park Eleven operates on a different system from the security camera system, isn't that right?'

'Yes. They run on two different pieces of software, on different systems.'

'Mr Forest, you did not, at any time subsequent to this murder, check whether the time code on the security footage camera system was synchronized with the time code on your security log, did you?'

He pursed his lips, straightened in his chair.

'No, I did not.'

I lifted the first document from the pile Kennedy had given to me, passed out copies to Judge Rollins, Zader, and the witness.

'Mr Forest, this is a copy of the nine one one emergency log for that night. I take it you are aware that when a resident makes an emergency call, a text registering that call is simultaneously sent to nine one one?'

'I knew that,' he said.

'And from this document, can you read the time that the text was received?'

His eyes flared, and he read, 'Twenty oh four.'

'Thank you,' I said.

I sat down, and Zader was on his feet right away.

Suddenly I was aware of the sheer weight of the evidence against David. And the defense was no thicker than a sheet of ice. I had to tread carefully, slowly, or David, Christine, and I would fall into the cold, dark depths.

Zader was about to send a huge crack across the ice.

'Mr Forest, if there was a difference in the time signatures, would it be possible for the defendant to have left his apartment before the murder occurred?'

Judge Rollins nodded enthusiastically – he'd been thinking the same thing.

The witness shook his head.

'No. It's not possible for the murder to have occurred after the defendant left the apartment. There is only one way in and one way out – the front door. The footage from the security camera showed Mr Child and the victim enter the apartment, and then Mr Child leaves. I spoke to Mr Gershbaum personally. No one entered his apartment via the balcony, and it's twenty-five stories high. When I swept the apartment, it was empty. It's not possible because the victim had injuries that could not have been self-inflicted, and nobody but the defendant left the apartment. The only person who could've killed Clara Reece was David Child.'

CHAPTER EIGHTY

Every nerve ending, every muscle, every ounce of blood in my body wanted me to turn around and look at Christine, but I knew if I did that I risked losing it completely. The battle was in this trial.

I told myself to stay focused.

I whispered to David, 'Don't worry. We're okay.' We were pretty far from okay.

Swallowing down his fear, David patted my arm. He still believed in me.

At least somebody did.

'Officer Noble,' said Zader.

A thin man wearing glasses, blue jeans, a red and blue checkered shirt, and a hopelessly mismatched white tie strode forward and took the witness stand. He wore cowboy boots, which, inexplicably, made the whole ensemble come together.

After Officer Rudy Noble was sworn in, he began polishing his glasses with the end of his tie. The DA's first questions established Noble as the experienced CSI who'd examined both the victim and the crime scene and had documented his investigation with the photographs.

'Officer Noble, given your extensive examination of the crime scene, and given the ME's findings, what were your conclusions as to how the murder occurred?' said Zader.

'Given the wounds on the victim and the rounds found embedded in the victim's skull and in the concrete beneath the tiled floor, the head shots were inflicted when the victim was lying facedown on the floor. That leads me to believe that she was initially shot from behind. There are two bullet entry wounds in the victim's lumbar area. One round became lodged in the victim's spine. The other was a through and through. It is—'

'Sorry, can I just stop you there for a moment? What is a through and through?' said Rollins; tax attorneys didn't deal with too many gunshot victims.

'It's a term used to describe a bullet that enters the victim and passes through the body completely.'

'I understand. Please continue,' said Rollins.

'It's my belief, based on the evidence, that this second bullet went through the victim's back, leaving a large exit wound in the chest, and it was this round that went on to travel through the window.'

'How did you arrive at the conclusion that it was this bullet that shattered the window?'

'We found an empty clip at the crime scene and another empty clip in the murder weapon, which was found in the defendant's vehicle. This weapon holds seven rounds per magazine. Fourteen shell casings were found on the kitchen floor. Altogether thirteen rounds were found either in the victim or in the floor beneath the victim's head. One fired round is unaccounted for. It's a reasonable conclusion that this round passed through the victim, broke the glass, and was subsequently lost to us.'

'What is beyond the balcony window?'

'The window overlooks Central Park. We have searched an area of the park but have been unable to locate the spent round.'

'In the ME's report, it is her view that the bullet that became lodged in the victim's spine may have killed the victim instantly, or certainly paralyzed her. Given your expertise, what view can reasonably be taken of the head shots after the victim has already sustained a near fatal wound?'

'Passion. To my mind, the head shots were overkill. They were not the work of any kind of professional killer – this was a rage killing.'

'What makes you certain of that?'

'The killer reloaded. And then spent the entire magazine.'

'Are there any official statistics in relation to homicides involving this level of violence?'

'Yes. Where a homicide has taken place in the home, and a high level of damage has occurred to the victim postmortem, statistics tell us that in 94.89 percent of those cases, the victim was killed by a spouse or a partner.'

And with that, Zader sat down. My witness.

I stood silently, waiting for Rollins to raise his head from his notes and listen to my question. A whole ten seconds passed before the judge had the courtesy to pay attention. It felt like ten minutes. Noble had time to take a sip of water, then readjust his tie and check his glasses. I had time to think, to worry. Just before Judge Rollins fixed me with a disdainful look, Cooch got up, put a hand on my shoulder, and whispered, 'Shake it off, Eddie.'

My mind cleared and I started slowly.

'Officer, presumably you tested the murder weapon for fingerprints, yes?'

'Correct. None were found.'

'Yes, I read your report. You say that the only fingerprints found were those of Officer Philip Jones, who recovered the weapon from the defendant's car, correct?'

'That's correct.'

'But you also made another observation in your report. You say that when you expended the empty clip, you found a small amount of dirt?'

'Yes, a little soil. It was just an observation. I have to record all of my findings when I examine a weapon.'

Time to move on. Time to start flipping Gershbaum.

'Officer Noble, you were in court just now to hear the evidence of Mr Gershbaum, is that right?'

'Yes. I listened to Mr Gershbaum's evidence.'

'Then why is it that you say Mr Gershbaum is lying?'

Judge Rollins pulled a face, flicked back over his notes.

'Is the witness calling Mr Gershbaum a liar, Mr Flynn? That's not what I have in my notes,' said Rollins.

'That is the effect of his testimony, Your Honor. Please allow me to explore the point.'

'Very well, but I am taking a careful note, Mr Flynn. And please, be more specific.'

I nodded, breathed in and out and tried again.

'Officer Noble, Mr Gershbaum says he heard gunfire, he went to his balcony to check the street below, and then he saw the window of the defendant's apartment explode. He said that after the window exploded, he didn't hear any further gunshots. Do you accept that was Mr Gershbaum's evidence?'

'I accept that he said all of those things. And I'm not calling him a liar,' said Noble, hands open, a smirk on his face.

'But you are, Officer Noble. You say the first two bullet wounds on the victim are in the lumbar area – one shot exiting the body and one paralyzing her and possibly killing her, and then she suffers the shots to the head. Correct?'

'Yes.'

'But on your testimony, the shot that you describe passing through the victim and shattering the window is likely to be the first or second shot while the victim is standing in front of the window – followed by the point-blank firing to the back of the head when the victim was on the ground. Mr Gershbaum did not hear any shots after the window exploded.'

'I can't speak for Mr Gershbaum. I can only evaluate the evidence.'

'The evidence, yes. It's possible that the weapon may have had a full magazine of seven rounds and an additional round already chambered. Isn't that right?'

'It's possible. But we didn't find a fifteenth shell casing in the apartment.'

'You never found the bullet that passed through the glass either?'

'No, we haven't yet.'

'So it's possible the killer could've picked up this shell casing and tossed it out of the window?' I asked.

'I can't say that's impossible.'

'You mean, "Yes, Mr Flynn, it is possible,"' I said.

I heard a wet, unpleasant sound as Judge Rollins sucked his teeth. He shook his head as he took a note of the answer. Noble reacted like a third grader who'd just been put in detention.

'Yes. Mr Flynn. It . . . is . . . possible.'

'I have just a few more questions. I want you to explain why you believe the bullet that passed through the victim shattered the window. Couldn't the victim have been lying facedown when this shot was fired into her lumbar area?'

I'd taken too long. Zader was on his feet. He'd caught the whiff of blood in the air and was desperately trying to limit the damage.

'Your Honor, this is a preliminary hearing, not the Nuremberg Trials. Mr Flynn is dragging this out unnecessarily.'

'I'm coming to the end of my cross shortly, Your Honor. Surely it's in the interests of justice and my client's right to a fair hearing that I am allowed just a little more time.'

'Make it fast,' said Rollins.

'Thank you, Your Honor,' I said, then switched my attention back to Noble. He was smiling. He'd had time to think of an answer, and I prayed it was the right one, the one I'd been waiting for.

'It's impossible for the victim to have been lying facedown when this shot was fired through her body for two reasons. First, we would've found a great deal of blood and tissue on the floor beneath the victim. Second, we would've either found the bullet in the floor or ricochet marks where the bullet struck the tile.'

Blood flushed my cheeks. Zader saw it, and his face dropped. He knew, before I even opened my mouth, that I'd set a trap for his witness, who'd just walked straight in.

'Your Honor,' I said, 'I have rebuttal evidence, which I'd like to submit.'

CHAPTER EIGHTY-ONE

The judge read the document I'd just handed to him, and the crowd murmured and whispered like a soft ripple of water on a midnight lake. The sound of the crowd was broken by the rhythmic slap of David's heel on the floor as his knee bounced with anxiety. Holly put a hand on his shoulder and cut off the noise.

Gripping the pages between his forefinger and thumb, as if they were toxic, he handed me back the report with a sigh. 'Very well. Make sure Mr Zader has a copy of this.'

Cooch flung a copy at Zader, which sailed through the air and landed expertly on the prosecution table.

'Next time, hand it to him, Mr Coucheron,' said Judge Rollins.

I waited around fifteen seconds to allow Zader to skim read the report. When his grip spasmed and tore the corners of the pages, I knew he'd finished reading it. I gave my copy to the witness.

'This is a report written by an FBI field agent named Theo Ferenze. It details an examination of the floor of the panic room, located in David Child's apartment. At the back you will see two photographs that have been printed on plain paper and appended to the report.'

'I see them,' said Noble, through tight lips.

'The annotation for photograph one reads, "Panic room floor, treated with luminol." Now, what is luminol?'

Judge Rollins raised an eyebrow – I got the feeling crime scene analysis didn't feature heavily in his limited experience.

'Luminol is a chemical agent that, when applied to surfaces, highlights blood stains when a black light is shined upon the area,' said Noble.

'Thank you. You didn't search the panic room?'

'I wasn't aware that there was a panic room.'

I held up the Claudio, the architectural drawing clearly showing the panic room, which I'd taken from the wall of David's apartment.

'This was hanging on the wall. Didn't you notice it?'

'No. We don't pay attention to the wall hangings. Anyway, panic rooms are for the occupiers. We understood from building security that the occupier, Mr Child, had left the building.'

'Turning back to the FBI report, it states that a large volume of recent blood staining was found on the floor of the panic room in Mr Child's apartment, as we can see from the purple patch on the floor, correct?'

'Correct.'

'And in addition, photograph two is a close-up of a notch in the concrete floor, in or around the center of the bloodstain, which, according to the FBI expert, is consistent with a bullet having ricocheted off the floor?'

'Correct.'

'According to Agent Ferenze, the bloodstained fibers found in the damaged part of the floor are similar to the T-shirt the victim was wearing that day?'

'According to this report, that's correct. I have not had an opportunity to—'

'Just a second,' said Judge Rollins. 'What does this all mean, Mr Flynn?'

'It means that the victim was shot in the back in the panic room. She likely died there. It means that sometime after this, her body was dragged to the kitchen, where she was shot twelve times in the back of the head. Isn't that right, Mr Noble?'

His mouth clammed up, lips drawn up under his nose.

'That appears likely,' said Noble.

'If that is the case, then considering the accuracy of the other shots, the killer deliberately fired into the window?' I asked.

'That's possible.'

'Perhaps to attract Mr Gershbaum's attention and have him call security?' I said.

'Objection, Your Honor. This is speculation,' said Zader.

After a beat Judge Rollins said, 'Sustained.'

I ignored the hit. The idea had been planted in Rollins's head. One last question.

'You offered the conclusion that the victim had suffered the multiple head shots because of the sheer rage of her attacker, but there is another explanation. Could it be that the damage was deliberately inflicted to wipe out the victim's face, making her impossible to identify from her facial features or dental records?'

'I can't rule that out,' said Noble, shifting in his seat.

I took a moment. Evaluated. I wondered if I'd done enough. The judge looked confused more than anything else. I decided to quit while I was ahead. I thought I'd save my best shots for the last witness, Detective Andy Morgan.

'No further questions,' I said. Zader didn't want any more of this witness.

Noble almost fell over getting out of the stand. He didn't want to stay there a moment longer.

'I suggest we take a short break, gentlemen. Who is your next witness, Mr Zader? You can prep them during the recess.'

'Your Honor, we'll be calling the driver of the car that was involved in the RTC with the defendant, a Mr John Woodrow.'

No, you won't, I thought.

I got up, looking for Christine, and as I passed the Lizard, I palmed his cell phone.

CHAPTER EIGHTY-TWO

My guts boiled.

Scanning the room, walking toward the doors, my pace quickened, I broke into a run, my head swiveling, eyes searching out my wife.

No.

She was gone, and the agents with her. Christine had been taken. I slammed open the doors. The corridor was empty save for two people. On my right, Perry Lake, or John Woodrow, according to the DA. On my left, Dell. I reminded myself that I had a job to do.

Perry Lake leaned against the wall and flicked his thumb across his cell phone. His mouth fell open when he saw me approach.

'Eddie . . . I . . . didn't know you were in this. I'm sorry, man.'

'Take this, Mr Woodrow. There are photographs on this phone. Make sure to answer it when it rings,' I said, handing him the cell phone that the Lizard had passed to me for this very purpose. Without another word, I turned and made my way toward Dell.

Sitting cross-legged on a bench set against the wall, Dell lifted his gaze from his cell phone and said, 'It's your own fault, Eddie. I told you what you had to do. Why can't you listen?'

'Where is she? If she's under arrest, she's entitled to a phone call and an attorney.'

'That's only if she's booked in at a precinct or in federal lockup. You're a lawyer – you should know that.'

'You have to process her as soon as possible. You're holding her illegally.'

'Thinking of suing me? Think again,' he said, and stood. He motioned for me to follow him as he walked toward one of the large windows that overlooked the square. He remained a few feet from the window and gestured that I should take a look.

I felt the vibration from my cell phone. I checked it and found a text message from Christine's number.

Third window, next to the stairwell. Take a look at the street.

I ran to the window and felt my heart plummet ten stories.

Ten floors below, on the sidewalk, Christine stared up at me. It was a fleeting moment, a terrible second of realization that hit like a hammer blow. One of the firm's security men bundled her into a black town car. I hammered the glass, ignored the looks and cries of people in the corridor, and gritted my teeth as I saw Gerry Sinton with a cell phone in his hand, probably Christine's. He slid into the car after her. They sped into traffic and were lost from my view.

'Don't even think about taking a swing at me. I'm through playin' around with you. You try anything and I'll put you down. This is your fault. All you had to do was get me my plea. But you couldn't do that, could you?' said Dell.

'What have you done?' I said, shaking my head.

'I haven't done anything. We let her go. Somebody else picked her up. Nothing to do with me.'

My ears were ringing with blood and my hands trembled. I thought about my hands – slipping around Dell's throat, squeezing his neck, feeling his windpipe collapse, watching the capillaries in his eyes burst.

He checked his watch.

'If Child's algo is right, the money lands in an account in central Manhattan in four hours. If I don't have my plea by then, I can't guarantee her safety. Right now the firm wants to know exactly what Christine has heard about all of this and whom she's told. They'll take her back to their offices. They want to know what the FBI has on them. They already know there's some kind of deal, because an FBI agent is handing you documents in court. That was stupid.'

He was right. I hadn't thought about how that would look if the firm was watching. Stupid move. I turned and heard Perry answer the phone I'd handed to him. Within a few seconds he'd sunk to his knees. I knew how he felt.

'How long can she hold out, do you think? An hour? Five minutes? Five seconds? My guess is they won't make their final play until the money hits Harland's account. We'll keep an eye on things, make sure she isn't hurt too bad.

'I'm gonna give you one last chance, Eddie. I don't want to subpoena David Child. I want him under an agreement, under my control. Doesn't matter what kinda deal the DA is offering. Just take it. I can always get a few years shaved off if he testifies the way I want him to.'

'You mean you want him to lie. You want him to lie about murdering his girlfriend and testify that his system was designed and built for the firm so that they could launder money.'

'You only getting it now? I thought you were smart.'

'He'll never admit to a murder he didn't commit, and as for the system, he built it in good faith. If the firm used it illegally, that's their bad. It's a lie, and it ruins him.'

'He's already ruined. Even if he's acquitted, people will never be convinced that he's innocent. This kind of shit sticks forever. But it doesn't have to go bad for Christine. As soon as he's pleaded, we'll get her safe. It's your call. Don't worry about David Child; it's like I said – shit sticks, and he's in far too deep for you to help him.'

Dell shouldered past me, back into the courtroom. I swung back and saw Perry moving toward me as quick as his limp would allow. He handed me back the cell, mouthed the word 'sorry,' then shuffled into the elevator, almost falling in his haste.

The corridor shrank. I swallowed, trying to hold down the vomit. I fought for control.

The Lizard stepped out of the court and joined me. I had to lean on his shoulder, take deep breaths. We took a corner, so we could talk without being overheard.

'Turns out your old buddy Perry didn't want to meet Bert and Ernie. He said he had to go away for a while, visit his aunt in Topeka.'

'Dell let Christine slip out of court. The firm was waiting for her. This is all pressure to make me bust David's case and force him to plea. Did Perry tell you who paid him to crash into David's car?'

'He recognized the guy from the photos on the phone. Said it was the man in photograph three.'

'Was he sure?'

'One hundred percent. You gonna make David take the plea?' he said.

'I don't trust Dell. He's happy to risk Christine's life. I'm not so sure he's willing to save it.'

The Lizard brought up the third photograph on the camera phone. It was the photo I'd taken of Langhiemer.

'Goddamn it, David was right,' I said.

'You said you needed the Lizard,' said the Lizard.

'The firm has Christine. I think they've taken her to the Lightner Building. You remember the first day I met you, you had a steel box in the back of your van with some toys in it?'

'It's still there,' he said.

'This is what I need you to do . . .'

The Lizard bolted down the steps, headed out with a Hail Mary. He was probably the one man I completely trusted in this whole damn situation. Heavy footsteps behind me. Kennedy tapped me on the shoulder.

'It's Langhiemer. He paid the driver to crash into David's car. I just had it confirmed. He's the one who's set up this whole damn thing. And I can't use it in court. You need to pick him up,' I said.

'We will, but we don't have it all yet. This changes things,' he said, and held out his cell phone. It had an image on the screen.

'You asked me to check out who had access to that French ballistics paper on GSR and air bags. I called the university, and the only person who has ordered it online was you, yesterday. They keep a record. Other than that, the report has never been published in any periodical. The only other occasion in which sections of the report have been made available was at an Interpol conference last year. I got the names of those who attended. Nothing stood out. So I called Interpol and asked for the security IDs for all the delegates who attended that lecture. Fourteen attended. This is the one we're looking for. Sarah Callan.'

I looked again at the image on Kennedy's cell. This time I made the connection.

'You've got to be kidding me,' I said.

He shook his head.

'What the hell does it mean, Eddie?'

Right then I didn't know.

'You got background on this Sarah Callan?'

'My director is e-mailing me. I told him what's happening on the task force, and he's just as pissed as I am. He doesn't want this to blow up in our faces.'

I told him about Christine – he flinched.

'I heard the task force is on their way to the Lightner Building now. The team is gonna clear out the associates and arrest Sinton and the firm's security personnel. She'll be okay. I'll get Ferrar and Weinstein to make sure she's looked after,' he said.

CHAPTER EIGHTY-THREE

'Your Honor, we seem to have had a little difficulty in locating our next witness, Mr Woodrow,' said Zader. 'His evidence was in relation to the automobile accident and spotting the murder weapon in the defendant's vehicle. We can't proceed with that evidence, but we do have the officer who found the weapon in the car and made the arrest. The people call Patrolman Philip Jones.'

A uniformed cop came forward, well built, early forties, dark hair, the shadow of a beard on his cheeks even though he'd evidently shaved that morning.

'Officer, I understand you've recently left the force?' said Zader.

'Not quite. The day I arrested the defendant was supposed to be my last day as a police officer, but since this case has become so important, I've agreed to stay on for another month, to assist with this prosecution.'

Zader thanked him for his dedication, then ripped through the preliminary questions: time on the job, experience, attending at the scene of the accident. Fast questions followed by fast answers; Zader couldn't wait to get to the meat.

'Officer, at the scene of the car accident, what did you see when you were standing at the passenger door of the defendant's vehicle?'

'A handgun, just sitting there in the footwell.'

'Are you sure it was a gun?'

'I could see it clearly. I opened the door, removed the weapon, then questioned the suspect. He said he didn't own a gun and had never seen this gun before.'

'Thank you, Officer. Please remain in the witness stand. Mr Flynn might have a question or two. Although I can't imagine what they might be,' said Zader.

'Are you sure this is going to work?' said David.

'I've got to try,' I told him, patting his shoulder as I stood. He was getting better at handling physical contact – it may well have been the case that he needed it now more than he'd ever realized.

'Officer, you got to the scene of the accident very quickly indeed. How did you accomplish this?' I asked.

'It wasn't all that fast. I got the call from dispatch and I was maybe two blocks from there, so I took the call.'

'And where were you when you received the call?'

He took a breath before he answered, shook his head a little.

'I'm not exactly sure. I was in that area.'

'You said you were around two blocks from the scene of the accident. You must have some idea?'

'I think I was in or around Sixty-Third Street.'

'Are you certain?'

'Yeah, yeah, I'm sure,' he said.

I handed the witness the dispatch record, which Kennedy had gotten for me. I gave a copy to the judge and one to Zader.

'You got any more rabbits in that hat?' said Zader.

'Just a few,' I said.

'This is the transcript from dispatch for the night of the murder. Mr Woodrow, the pickup driver who collided with the defendant's car, gives his location at the intersection of Sixty-Sixth Street and Park. Can you read out your response to the dispatcher?'

He cleared his throat, and confidently, even nonchalantly read, '"Show Twenty Charlie handling. I'm on Sixty-Third coming onto Central Park West." I'm in the Twentieth Precinct and I'm car Charlie. That's my call sign. See, I was right. I remembered. I was on Sixty-Third,' he said with a smile.

'So, you were on Sixty-Third when the call came in. I take it you were on patrol at that time?'

'Correct. I was mobile.'

The judge shook his head. I needed to spell it out for him.

'When you say you were mobile, that means prior to receiving the call, you were driving around the area on patrol, correct?'

A slight hesitation from Jones before he said, 'Correct. I'd been patrolling since that afternoon.'

'And after you picked up the call, you went immediately to the accident scene?' I asked.

'Yes. When I reached the bottom of Sixty-Third I made a left onto Central Park West, and the accident was three blocks ahead.'

Nodding, Judge Rollins looked over his notes. So far Officer Jones had been completely straightforward.

'Officer, you were the single patrolman in Twenty Charlie that day?'

'Yes, I've got a lot of years under my belt. I'm not a sergeant, but I've got enough time on the job that I get to go out on my own.'

'How many times have you failed the sergeant's exam?'

'Relevance?' said Zader.

'A little latitude, Your Honor,' I said.

'I'll allow it,' said Rollins.

He coughed, 'Eight times.'

'I understand you've got a new position; you're leaving the force?'

'That's correct. I'll be working for a private security contractor in Iraq. Security detail. It's a little more dangerous than Manhattan, but the pay is triple my salary as a cop.'

'Very nice. When did you get this new position?'

'I got confirmation a few months ago.'

'And how much was your signing bonus?'

'Do I have to answer that?'

'This is my last question on this topic, Your Honor.'

A nod from Judge Rollins and Jones shook his head. He steepled his fingers, pressing them together hard, whitening the tips.

'Two hundred thousand dollars,' said Jones.

I didn't react. But I watched Judge Rollins blow out his cheeks.

'You'd never met the defendant before that day?'

'No. I'd heard of him, obviously, but no, I'd never met him.'

'So you don't hold any grudges against him?'

'No. I'm a law enforcement officer. We don't hold grudges. And like I said, I'd never met him.'

'And you have no reason to lie about any of this, do you?'

'No reason at all,' he said, shaking his head, pursing his lips.

'It's not like you're looking for promotion. You're moving into a much better paid job, isn't that right?'

'Right,' he said, folding his arms.

'So why are you lying?'

Judge Rollins's head snapped to me, then back to the witness.

'I'm not lying about anything, Counselor.'

I picked up the last of the documents that Kennedy had procured and handed copies to the judge and Zader, then gave a copy to Officer Jones. He took it reluctantly, then scanned it and hung his head.

'Officer, this is a record of GPS locations for your vehicle on the night of the murder. All NYPD vehicles are fitted with a tracker, correct?'

'Yes, we have a tracker, but . . .'

'This is the NYPD record of your vehicle's movements for that evening. Please take a moment to look over it and tell me when the tracker reports your location as Sixty-Third Street.'

He didn't read the report. He shook his head and just looked at the page. He already knew. Zader and Rollins scanned quickly, looking for the relevant entry.

'Perhaps I can assist you, Officer. The report confirms that your vehicle never entered Sixty-Third Street that day.'

'Maybe the satellite was out,' said Jones.

'No, it wasn't. Working backward, the record shows your vehicle stopping at Sixty-Sixth and Park for twenty-three minutes, while you dealt with the accident, found the gun, and arrested Mr Child. Before that the record shows your vehicle having traveled to the accident scene from Central Park West. You actually passed the intersection for Sixty-Third Street on your way to the accident.'

Nodding, but not answering, Jones looked around for help. None was offered.

'So your testimony just now, that you made a left at the bottom of Sixty-Third onto Central Park West, that was a lie?'

'No. It was an honest mistake.'

'Before you drove to the accident scene, the record shows your vehicle parked outside Central Park Eleven for thirty-three minutes. You lied to the dispatcher?'

'So I made a mistake. I . . .'

'You've got a lot of time under your belt as an officer. You said so yourself. Are you telling this court you don't know the difference between Central Park West and Sixty-Third Street?'

'No. I just made a mistake,' he said.

'A mistake, not a lie?'

'No, I made a mistake.'

'So it's just a coincidence that at the precise time that Clara Reece was murdered you were parked across the street from her building?'

'Yes.'

'And it's just another coincidence that you picked up the dispatch call for the accident that resulted in the defendant's arrest with the murder weapon?'

'Yes.'

'You were in court this morning when Officer Noble gave his evidence?'

'Yes, I was.'

'You heard his testimony that he found dirt or soil in the magazine from the murder weapon when he ejected the clip.'

'That's what he said.'

'And you heard him testify that it's possible that the killer deliberately fired into the window of Mr Child's apartment, maybe to alert the neighbor, Mr Gershbaum?'

'I heard that.'

'There may have been another reason for the window to have broken. Mr Child's apartment is on the twenty-fifth floor of that building. At that height, it wouldn't take a strong man to throw the murder weapon across the street and into Central Park, would it?'

Silence. The witness didn't move, not even an attempt to answer the question. His stare moved past me. From the front door of David's building, a fifth grader could pitch a ball into the park. From the balcony of David's apartment on the twenty-fifth floor, you could damn near spit into the park.

'Your vehicle was sitting beside the park for a long time. You were waiting in the park, opposite the building, watching the defendant's balcony. That's a pretty secluded area of the park. You're behind hedges. This was very carefully planned, and you knew, to the minute, when the gun would be thrown into the park from the balcony. You waited until you saw the weapon being thrown from the apartment, retrieved it from the grass, wiped off the dirt, then stashed it in your coat . . .'

'This is bull—'

'Watch your tongue in this courtroom,' said Judge Rollins, staring at Jones. I thought I saw a trickle of light in Rollins, the spark of something in his eyes – the beginning of doubt. I had to make it flourish.

'When you got to your car, you removed your backup piece from your ankle holster, locked it in the glove compartment, and put the murder weapon into your ankle holster, correct?'

'This is . . . lies.'

'Officer, you searched the defendant, his bag, and his entire vehicle, isn't that right?'

'That's accurate. I did.'

'And you did not find any gloves?'

'I did not find gloves.'

'And despite not having gloves, or the means to properly clean the murder weapon, the defendant's fingerprints were not found on that gun?'

'I don't believe they were.'

'The only fingerprints on that gun were yours, Officer Jones?'

'I should've worn gloves when I picked up the gun.'

'You mean when you picked it up out of the dirt in Central Park?'

A moment's hesitation before he said, 'No.'

'You didn't manage to clean all of the dirt from the weapon, did you? I suppose you didn't have much time. No one on the street would see a gun passing overhead, but you had to be quick to pick it up from the lawn.'

He didn't answer.

'Mr Woodrow is not here to testify as to what he saw. There's just you. And when you bent down to look into the passenger footwell of David's car, you retrieved the murder weapon from your ankle holster and held it in the air for the traffic camera?'

'No way.'

'There's only a couple of blocks between Sixty-Third Street and Central Park Eleven. You never expected the dispatcher to notice it, and no one had any reason to doubt your location, or so you thought. You lied about your location because you didn't want to be connected to the murder scene, so no one would piece it together. Right?'

'So I lied to the dispatcher about where I was. I was taking a break. I had nothing to do with that gun until I took it out of your client's car. I'm telling the truth.'

'So you just lied under oath a moment ago, perjuring yourself. But now you're telling the truth, is that it?'

'Yeah.'

'So you're an honest liar?'

Standing now, he pointed at me and bellowed, 'You're full of shit.'

The judge didn't admonish, him – he'd heard enough.

'Just one last question,' I said. 'Is two hundred grand the going rate for planting a gun?'

Jones wiped his mouth with the back of his hand. He wanted to say more, much more. He was all riled up, but he seemed to be trying to put the brakes on, to stop himself from doing any more damage. All eyes were upon him. He leaned back in his chair, looked at the judge, and said, 'I refuse to answer on the grounds that I may incriminate myself.'

I sat down. Without looking at Jones, Zader pointed toward the door. He wanted Jones out of there, but he couldn't bring himself to look at him.

CHAPTER EIGHTY-FOUR

2 hours until the shot

'Eddie, I think the judge is starting to think about this case,' said David.

'Thinking about it isn't enough. He has to believe it.'

'The people call Detective Andy Morgan.'

A blond cop, in a washed-out brown suit, spat his chewing gum into his hand, hung up his cell phone, and put the gum and the phone in the same pocket. Whatever was going on in that phone call caused him some concern. From his flushed aspect, I guessed he was worried about what I was going to ask him. He'd watched two cops get nailed, and now he was next. He took the oath, ran his fingers through his hair, which I noticed had faded to white in a patch at the front, almost as much as his suit had paled. I felt the vibration from my cell, checked the messages; one new message from the Lizard.

Feds just showed up. You want me to make a play?

Under the table, I tapped out a reply.

No. They're gonna take Christine out of there. Watch. Tell me when she's clear.

The DA took Morgan through the story of his involvement: the relay from dispatch that had confirmed that uniformed patrol identified the body in David's apartment as a probable homicide, his arrival at the building and search of Childs's apartment, taking notes of the fatal injuries, calling CSI, everything up until the search for evidence from the security camera footage.

'I then visited the building's security office and spoke to Mr Medrano, their chief of security. He was able to locate the relevant CCTV footage, and I obtained a copy.'

'Is this the disk you're referring to? Exhibit TM2?' said Zader.

'Correct,' said Morgan.

'If it pleases the court, now would be an appropriate time to view the footage.'

'Very well,' said Rollins.

Handing the disk to Morgan, he got up and inserted it into the DVD player that sat below a seventy-inch TV screen to the left of the judge.

Morgan handed the remote control to the DA and resumed his seat.

Start and stop with the footage, while Zader asked Morgan to identify David and Clara. We played through to them entering the room together, then, some seventeen minutes later, David leaving on his own. Four minutes later the security team, led by Forest, is at Gershbaum's door.

'What conclusions can be drawn from this footage?' said Zader.

'There appears to be incontrovertible evidence that the defendant and the deceased entered the apartment together. Only one of them leaves alive. When the apartment is searched, no one else is present. Those are the facts. The defendant is the only person who could've shot and killed the victim.'

'Thank you,' said Zader.

I saw from the digital indicator that popped up on the bottom of the screen that the footage on this DVD, from the hallway camera outside David's apartment, ran on for another eight hours. Medrano probably just copied the entire twenty-four-hour feed onto a disk. I could use Zader's own exhibit against him.

'Any cross-examination?' said Judge Rollins.

I stood and began a series of banal questions, designed to get Morgan talking, to open him up and ease him in. In preliminary hearings, cops are used to being cross-examined at length without it really going anywhere. Just a fishing exercise.

I threw out my line.

'Detective, what time did you get the call from dispatch about a possible homicide at Central Park Eleven?'

He referred to his notes, with permission, before answering. 'I noted twenty twenty-seven.'

'And what time did you arrive at the crime scene?'

'Twenty thirty-eight,' he said with a sigh, wondering how long he'd be in the chair, answering inane questions.

'When you arrived at the scene, what was your first action?'

'I secured the scene. Made sure all personnel had vacated the apartment and opened the homicide log.'

'The what?' asked the judge.

'The log, Your Honor. We log personnel in and out of the scene, significant developments, schedule interviews, record decision making. It's the backbone of our homicide procedure; it's the bible that records our investigation, and it's the starting point for the evidence chain.'

Rollins made a note.

I took the TV remote from Zader, forwarded the footage to Morgan's arrival.

'So at twenty fifty-one, going by the time on the security camera, you and your partner, Detective Algin, were the only personnel in the apartment?'

He checked the log, looked at the camera still.

'Correct.'

'After you entered the apartment, what did you do?'

'I took a look around the apartment, made sure it was clear. After that I examined the body. At first I looked at the wounds, established that there were multiple gunshots to the back of the victim's head and two shots to the lumbar area.'

'What did you do next?'

'I observed a slight bulge in the victim's hip pocket. Thought it could be a purse or a wallet, so I removed it from the victim's person and examined it.'

'And what was it?'

'A pink leather wallet. It contained a library card, a driver's license, an ATM card for a checking account, and around eighty-five dollars in cash.'

'The name on the cards?'

'Clara Reece.'

'What was the date the victim's driver's license was issued by the DMV?'

His head rocked back on his shoulders and his eyes flared open in surprise at the inanity of the question.

'I've got the license here, Your Honor. May I refer to it?'

Zader held his hands out to the judge, pleading, 'Your Honor, this is now a total fishing exercise. This should be stopped right now.'

'I'm inclined to agree with the district attorney, Mr Flynn. I've given you some latitude, but I fail to see the relevance here,' said Rollins.

'This is highly relevant, and I only need three questions to establish that relevance. If you don't see the relevance after three questions, I'll move on.'

He considered this, sighed. Letting his hands fall and slap his thighs, Zader did his best to look pissed off.

'Very well. Three strikes and you're out, Mr Flynn,' said Judge Rollins.

I waited while Morgan fetched the exhibits from another officer and produced the license, sealed in a clear evidence bag. Turning the license around and still keeping it in the bag, he squinted as he examined the plastic.

'Date of issue, is August thirtieth last year.'

'Thank you,' I said, catching Rollins make a strike against his page. He was counting down my questions – I had two left.

'What is the date the victim's checking account was opened?'

From a bag beside him, he flicked open a notebook and turned through the pages, licking his thumb before flipping each page, killing time, stretching out my cross-examination. After maybe half a minute, he found the page in his notebook.

'August thirtieth?' he said. This time he wasn't declaring a date. He was questioning the note.

'And the date the library card was issued?'

Again, he had to search for the library card and found it in an evidence bag. He read the date, looked at me.

His eyebrows crunched in the middle of his forehead as he said, 'August thirtieth, last year.'

'Your Honor, I'd like a little more time,' I said.

Judge Rollins was intrigued.

'A little leeway, Mr Flynn, not much,' he said.

'Detective Morgan, this is not a case of the victim having lost her wallet – or something similar?'

'I can't say that for certain,' said Morgan.

'Her bank account, her driver's license, her library card were all created on the same day last year. It's not as if these accounts or licenses already existed and these were simply replacement cards, is it?'

'No.'

'Clara Reece's ID's were all created eight months ago, just a few weeks before she met David Child, correct?'

'I believe so,' he said.

'So, from this evidence, you were able to identify the victim?'

'Not only that. After the ME had examined the victim, she was turned over, and I found a cell phone on her person. The phone had a social media app for Twitter and Reeler, and each was logged on to an account for Clara Reece. Subsequently we found a digital picture on the phone, which had been posted to the accounts. The image was of Clara Reece sporting a new tattoo of a purple daisy on her right wrist. The body found at the scene also bore a fresh tattoo in an identical spot. From this we were pretty solid on her ID, and combined with the driver's license and ATM card, we had ID'd our victim. Also from the surveillance footage of her entering the building, the security guard identified Clara Reece.'

He cleared his throat, sat up. He was going on the attack.

'We couldn't have a formal identification of the body because, thanks to your client, Clara Reece didn't have a face anymore.'

I heard a sharp intake of breath from Zader. He'd shrouded his eyes and blown a large 'O' through his lips – as if he'd just watched Sugar Ray Leonard sucker-punch a ballet dancer into the hospital.

Rollins seemed to wince, but at least had the knowledge to say, 'Detective Morgan, I can see that you are clearly a passionate and dedicated police officer, but kindly leave matters of guilt to one side. You're a factual witness. You're not here to make arguments.'

'My apologies, Your Honor.'

I moved on, let Zader think I'd taken a hit. For the next ten minutes I took Morgan through the arrival of the ME, Noble and his three CSIs, the two paramedics who'd taken the body to the morgue. At the arrival of each person, I had him check the homicide log, to check the times of arrival for each person as we rolled through the camera footage.

'And you completed the log at the scene?'

'Yes.'

'Where exactly?'

'I believe I stood in the lounge area and completed the log.'

'And according to the homicide log, when did Officer Noble and his team leave the scene?'

'Um, eleven fifteen.'

I found the relevant footage and played the video of Officer Noble and three other individuals in white coveralls, leaving the apartment, only the footage had it timed at eleven sixteen. However, the time difference between the log and the camera wasn't the interesting part.

'And the paramedics?'

He flicked over a page of the log and said, 'Eleven oh nine.'

We watched the paramedics leaving with the body, zipped into a black bag and placed on a stretcher at around the same time on the hall camera.

'And the medical examiner?'

'Ten forty-five.'

Again, I played the footage of the tall ME leaving.

'Apart from you and your partner, were Officer Noble and his team the last to leave at eleven fifteen?'

He took his time, checking the notes.

'That's correct.'

'And what time did you and your partner leave?'

'We left together at eleven twenty-seven. Before we left, I spoke to the building's chief of security, making sure that he understood the apartment was sealed.'

We watched Morgan, and his smaller, younger partner in conversation with Medrano. Blue crime scene tape was spread across the door. The camera logged them leaving at eleven twenty-eight.

'So, by eleven thirty, every member of your personnel has left and the apartment is empty?'

'That's correct,' said Morgan, stifling a yawn.

I fast-forwarded to eleven fifty-one. The view from the camera outside the apartment.

'In that case, do you mind telling me who this is exiting the apartment at eleven fifty-one.'

It was somebody slim, wearing a white hazmat suit and carrying a bag. They exited the apartment, ducking under the crime scene tape. They closed the door behind them and made for the stairs.

He checked the log.

'I'm not sure. I'd closed the scene for the night. It may be one of the CSIs,' he said, still disinterested, believing I was going nowhere.

'But we just watched Officer Noble arrive with three other CSIs, and we watched them leave before you and your partner closed the scene. You logged their exit time yourself.'

He shook his head, stared at the screen.

'Let's put this another way. When you left the scene at eleven twenty-seven, had you logged everyone else out?'

Flicking through his notes, he said, 'I believe I had.'

'Looks like you did log everyone out, from footage we've just seen.'

He nodded.

'Is that a "yes?"' I said.

'Yes.'

'None of the CSIs we saw enter the apartment are as short or as slim as the person who leaves in the hazmat suit. Wouldn't you say?'

Morgan checked his log, looked back at the screen again, where I'd frozen the image.

'I'm not sure I can identify that officer.'

'You agree we don't appear to see this officer enter the apartment after the murder?'

A marble of sweat trickled down Morgan's cheek.

'They may have been missed in the crowd,' he said.

'We don't see this person enter the apartment in the footage we just played, do we?'

'No.'

Judge Rollins threw down his pen.

'Is this leading anywhere, Mr Flynn? Are you alleging there is some breach of your client's constitutional rights by this officer not being logged?'

'No, Your Honor.'

'Then what is the point of highlighting this officer's movements?'

David sat very still, his hands folded in front of him, his eyes on me, and Cooch gave him a whisper of encouragement.

'Your Honor, the person you can see on the surveillance footage is not a real police officer. They are not a paramedic. They are not a crime scene tech. They are not with the medical examiner's office. They are not on the CCTV footage entering the apartment after the murder.'

'So who is it?' said Rollins.

I planted my feet before I spoke, straightened my back, and let the words float softly and confidently up to the judge.

'Your Honor, the defense believes that this person is the real killer. This person murdered Clara Reece.'

CHAPTER EIGHTY-FIVE

I took another DVD from my bag and placed it into the player. I explained that the defense had obtained footage from Central Park Eleven and that, if need be, Chief of Security Medrano would testify as to its authenticity. I forwarded the footage to just after two o'clock on the day before the murder. A shot of the elevator. It was full of people. Clara Reece among them, perfectly calm and definitely not exhibiting any signs of claustrophobia.

I couldn't help glancing at David. He saw Clara, calm and collected in the busy elevator. He knew she'd lied to him about being claustrophobic. I watched Clara exit the elevator with her box of possessions, and another female, same hair color, same style and length of hair as Clara, same body type, same skin color, helped her carry a box into David's apartment.

'This is Clara Reece moving into the defendant's apartment. Another female is helping her.'

I paused as the other woman entered the apartment with the last of the boxes. I skipped forward twenty minutes to see only Clara Reece leaving the apartment.

'The other female is still in the apartment?'

'Yes, from this footage, that's correct,' said Morgan.

'Have you seen this footage?'

'Not as far back as this, no. We understood that the apartment was empty prior to the defendant and the victim arriving that evening. The building's security team searched the apartment. NYPD uniformed officers searched the apartment. I searched the apartment myself. It was empty apart from the victim's body. We didn't need to look at footage that far back. Minutes before the murder, the victim and the defendant enter the apartment together.

The defendant leaves. He was the last person to see her alive. He left her body in his empty apartment – there was no one else there, so we didn't need to go looking at footage from the previous day.'

People believe what they can see.

I hit fast-forward, skipping ten minutes of camera time for every second. If no one was on the floor for an hour, the lights dimmed. An energy-saving system. So it was easy to see when someone stepped out of the elevator, as the lights went up. I stopped the footage at seven thirty p.m., when David and Clara came to the apartment together. Again at nine fifteen p.m., when Gershbaum came to his apartment. No movement after that until the morning, when Clara and David left around nine a.m. and Gershbaum a little before. Nothing until that evening. As Gershbaum got out of the elevator, I paused, rewound, and then let the footage play until he entered his apartment, then hit fast-forward again until David and Clara got out of the elevator for their final visit to the apartment.

'Detective Morgan, from this footage, the female we saw enter the apartment the day before is still in there.'

A huge intake of breath let out in a slow, angry sigh.

'Yes.'

Judge Rollins leaned forward, staring at the footage intently, like I'd just shown him a magic trick and he was trying to figure it out. I ejected the DVD and replaced it with another.

'Your Honor, this is footage that the FBI obtained last night from Central Park Eleven. The camera view you can see is from a small camera hidden in the vent on the east wall. This camera covers the stairs.'

The footage played of David and Clara entering the apartment, and I wound it forward until 20:00, when the front door opened.

'First thing you'll notice is the clock. The time signature on this camera has the defendant leaving the apartment a full two minutes before the call from Mr Gershbaum to security. And in case you were wondering, this clock *is* in sync with the security log clock. I'm going to play this footage, Detective Morgan, and I want you to watch carefully.'

I hit play. The entire room was perfectly silent. I could hear the disk churning in the player, the creak from Rollins's chair as he strained forward, the tap of Zader's pen on his lips, the faint electric burr of the cameras. Maybe two hundred people watched in silence.

All except one.

At the back of the court, Dell watched me.

On the screen, David hesitated, turned toward the door, then stopped, swung around with his earphones on, and made his way out of shot toward the elevator.

'Did you see it?' I asked.

'Did I see what? I'm not sure what you're referring to,' said Morgan.

'Let's watch again. This time I can slow it down.'

I played it again. On this occasion I heard the news cameraman gasp, and one of the ADAs put his hands up, then remembered where he was and folded his arms. He couldn't keep the surprise from his face though.

'I'm still not sure what you're referring to,' said Morgan.

'Nor am I,' said Judge Rollins, but with no indignation in his voice – only curiosity. I gave them both a heads-up.

'Detective, Your Honor, don't watch the defendant. Look beyond him. Look in the mirror.'

The DVD played again, still on slow motion. They couldn't miss it this time.

David closed the door behind him, took a few steps, then stopped, and I wondered if he was resisting the temptation to turn around and make sure the door was locked. But no – he stopped because he'd sensed something. Before he turned, the standing mirror in the hallway, beside the little table, held a reflection of the door. It was there, just for a second. The door handle moved. Down, then up. Somebody on the other side of the door making sure it was locked.

With all eyes on the screen, I took a moment to look over at Zader. He met my gaze – he knew that was game over.

'Detective, door handles don't move on their own. Someone is alive and kicking in that apartment.'

Morgan couldn't answer. Instead he looked at Zader apologetically, raising his hands palms up. *Sorry, we missed that one.*

'Detective Morgan, we know from this camera footage that David Child left that apartment at twenty oh two precisely. A full two minutes before Mr Gershbaum heard the shots and called security?'

'If the time stamp on this footage and the nine one one call time is accurate, then yes.'

'That's more than enough time for the perpetrator to drag the body from the panic room, where, from the residual bloodstains, we now know she was shot in the back, take her into the kitchen, and fire the head shots?'

Teeth gritted, Morgan hissed a 'yes.'

'The perpetrator then had additional time before security entered the apartment – a full four minutes – to shoot through the window, toss the gun into the park, and get into the panic room.'

'That's one theory.'

I had one last roll of the dice. One final piece of evidence to throw into the mix.

'Detective, as investigating officer, you ordered an independent expert to conduct gunshot residue tests on samples taken from the defendant's face, clothes, and hands?'

He looked at Zader, terrified in case he said something that he shouldn't.

'I did.'

'And the result of those tests is contained in this report from Dr Porter?' I said, holding up his paper.

'Yes.'

'The prosecution is not seeking to rely on this report in this hearing, correct?' I said.

His mouth moved like a fish that had suddenly leaped out of the bowl and into the fireplace. Zader stood and addressed the judge.

'Your Honor, that report is not relied upon.'

'I'd like to enter this report into evidence, Your Honor, along with this academic article.'

'Let me get this straight. You want to rely on a prosecution report?' said Rollins.

I handed copies to the clerk, who stamped them and gave them to the judge.

'Detective Morgan, the prosecution had previously sought to rely on this evidential report from Dr Porter, which concludes that the defendant was found to have a large amount of gunshot residue on his person?'

'We did, but we don't seek to rely on that anymore.'

'Why not?' asked the judge.

'Because Dr Porter conceded that the material was probably not GSR, but the remnants of material deposited on the defendant from the explosion that fires the air bags in the defendant's car.'

I almost had him; just a little more.

'At first, Dr Porter believed that the material was GSR, correct?' I asked.

'That's what he said in his report, until you got at him. Then he changed his mind,' said Morgan.

'Detective, if someone wanted it to look like they were covered in GSR, being in a car crash where the air bags deployed might be enough to fool an expert like Dr Porter?'

'It might.'

'In all fairness to Dr Porter, he had not read the scientific study on air bags and GSR comparison, which the defense discovered, had he?'

'No, he had not.'

'If someone had that knowledge and engineered a car accident, they could make it appear that the driver of the vehicle had GSR all over them?'

'I don't know.'

Kennedy gave me the copies of the security pass he'd obtained from the Interpol conference; copies had been e-mailed to him. I distributed the copies and watched Zader turn white. Neither Morgan nor the judge had yet made the connection.

'This security ID was obtained from the Interpol conference where this paper was presented. This ID was presented by a delegate who attended that lecture. Do you recognize the person in that photograph?' I said.

'I can't say that I do,' said Morgan, but he didn't sound at all convincing.

'Let me help you; look at exhibit fourteen.'

Rollins found the relevant exhibit in the bundle of papers. Morgan did likewise.

'The ID is for a Sarah Callan. Compare the photo on the ID to the picture of Clara Reece in exhibit fourteen, the profile picture of Clara Reece taken from her Reeler account. It is clearly the same woman in the footage who accompanies the defendant to his apartment, and it is without doubt the same young woman in the photo ID for Sarah Callan, correct?'

Silence. The judge answered the question meant for Morgan.

'It is the same woman. Clara Reece and Sarah Callan are one and the same,' said Rollins.

No experienced detective handed his ass in the witness stand is going to argue with the judge.

'It would appear so, Your Honor,' said Morgan.

'Detective, the checking account, the library card, the driver's license all issued on the same day last year could be someone creating a history for a false identity?'

'I wouldn't know,' he said.

'Of course. You're NYPD. The police department has never created a false identity for an undercover police officer, have they?'

Even Judge Rollins smiled at that one.

'It's possible,' he said.

'You had no DNA or fingerprint matches for the body in the apartment, did you?'

'No.'

'And the victim's face had been obliterated, so you couldn't ID the body?'

He nodded.

Rollins interrupted me. 'What does this mean, Mr Flynn?' he said.

This was the moment. This was my shot. I took a breath, put down the document and placed a hand on David's shoulder. He was rocking back and forth in his chair, shaking his head, his eyes filled with tears. I steadied him.

'Your Honor, the defense believes that Sarah Callan assumed a false identity in order to frame David Child for murder. Her murder.'

'What?' said Rollins.

I changed DVDs, found the image of the figure in the hazmat suit leaving the apartment just as whoever it was climbed through the crime scene tape.

'Your Honor, the person shown in that video is the person who committed murder in that apartment. It is the same person who

347

attended a lecture in Paris during an Interpol conference on the similarities between air bag deployment residue and GSR under the name Sarah Callan, the same person who would three months later assume the false identity of Clara Reece, the same person who three weeks later met and began dating the billionaire David Child, the same person we saw entering the apartment with a similar-looking young female and then leaving that apartment alone the day before the murder. We do not yet know the identity of the real victim, but I believe that Clara Reece – or Sarah Callan – is still alive, as she was the one with the obscure expert knowledge to know how to produce a convincing false positive for GSR, and I believe she orchestrated the car accident to load the defendant with that false evidence. The real victim was shot in the panic room. That room is soundproof, and a person could easily be hidden there. The real victim had her face obliterated by gunshot wounds so that she could not be identified. The time signature on the vent camera matches the timings on the building's security log, which means the defendant was not in the apartment when the shots were fired. And we know someone was alive and moving around in the apartment after Mr Child had left – the door handle moved. We all saw that. There she is on the screen, leaving the scene of the crime. This was a highly sophisticated but ultimately failed attempt to frame Mr Child for murder.'

'To what end?' said Rollins.

'Your Honor, Mr Child is one of the wealthiest men in this city.' I left it at that, let Rollins fill in the blanks. Let him believe the lie. David had been set up all right, but blackmail had nothing to do with it. The ID for Sarah Callan listed her as a civil servant, which could mean anything, but librarians are unlikely to wind up attending Interpol lectures.

Morgan had been staring at the ceiling, trying to take it all in. He soon snapped out of his contemplative mood when the judge addressed him directly.

'Detective, I don't need to hear anything further. Mr Zader, I take it the detective was your final witness?'

The DA was on his feet, ready to mount a rescue mission. He realized that Rollins was going to rule against him. The footage of the door handle moving had proven to be the final straw.

'Yes. Judge. This is simply ridiculous. The defendant could have arranged this elaborate scheme just as easily as any supposed . . .'

'Do you have evidence of that, Mr Zader?' said Rollins.

'No, Your Honor, not at this time, but . . .'

'Then I suggest you go and investigate. There seems to have been a lot of evidence, which Mr Flynn has presented, that either the police ignored or simply overlooked. And I am not impressed by Officer Jones and his blatant attempt to mislead this court. Given the footage that undoubtedly proves there was someone walking around in that apartment after Mr Child left, and considering the inconsistent time signatures on the nine one one call and the security log, and having regard to the unchallenged testimony of Gershbaum, I am of the view that at present there is insufficient evidence to prove that the defendant was in the apartment when the shooting occurred. There is insufficient evidence to hold the defendant on the current charge, and accordingly, I find in favor of the defense. Mr Zader, if you are sure of these charges, you always have the grand jury. I am not convinced – case dismissed.'

The sound of Judge Rollins pushing back his chair as he rose, closing his notebook, and leaving the court, was lost in the sensational roar of the crowd. What had promised to be a celebrity murder trial and fodder for a few months of news had now turned into a conspiracy-fueled celebrity murder mystery that the journalists knew would haunt the country for years – or more precisely, the media would haunt the public with articles speculating on the identity of the real murderer.

I almost didn't hear David crying. Holly held him close. His shoulders bucked with the ecstasy of release, of freedom, of escape and loss. He'd lost her all over again, because the life he'd had with Clara had been a lie. Clara Reece didn't exist. The life that lay before him was frightening and uncertain, but at least he could make something of it.

'David, don't mourn Clara. The night of the murder, she told you she was freaking out in the elevator because she was claustrophobic. You saw the elevator footage from the day before. She wasn't claustrophobic. She was setting you up: making it look like you scared her, giving you motive.'

He nodded, straightened up.

I heard Zader approach me from behind.

'Get ready for round three,' said Zader.

'I don't think so,' I said.

'Believe it. We've got a grand jury on standby. In twenty minutes' time I'll be leading the same witnesses through their testimony. Pity we don't have time to wait for the transcript from this hearing. None of your cross-examination will get as far as the grand jury. I'll get my indictment. There's no reason for you to even be there – you can't ask questions or make a speech. Just leave it to me. I'll be sure to call you and let you know what happened.'

'The grand jury won't give you an indictment. I know that. But you're right about one thing – I won't be at the hearing. He will,' I said, pointing to Cooch.

'Pity he can't cross-examine any witnesses,' said Zader.

'He won't have to,' I replied, and with that, Cooch approached the bench, retrieved a CD-ROM from the clerk, and joined my conversation with Zader.

'Mr Coucheron here,' I said, laying it out for Zader, 'suffers from poor hearing. He wears a hearing aid. The live feed from that aid is digitally recorded and made available to Mr Coucheron at any time. He can't question your witnesses or make a speech – you're right about that – but he can play this recording. It's court certified.'

I threw the disk at Zader's face. He reacted quickly and caught it.

'I just served the disk on you in open court in front of the cameras. Mr Coucheron will tell me if you don't play it. If I hear you didn't, I'll have *you* indicted for prosecutorial misconduct and misuse of public office. Good luck getting an indictment with that.'

'Goddamn it,' said Zader. He turned to his entourage and said, 'Pull the grand jury for a month.' I walked away, Cooch, Holly, and David behind me. I heard Zader calling after me, 'This isn't over yet.'

I checked my phone; one message from the Lizard:

FBI cleared the building. 2 agents inside with Christine. She's ok.

It was all I could do to hold it together, to keep walking and not collapse in relief. Still, this wasn't over yet.

The solid wall of reporters didn't seem to budge as I approached. The cameras were blinding, the fastball questions lost in a shower of voices, and the pleading hands and thrusting microphones and voice recorders all melted into a single, hungry boiling mass. Something was happening at the rear of the pack; the reporters parted, and two men in suits forced their way through the back of the crowd. One of them held out a pair of handcuffs. I had seen these men before – they both wore dark suits, both in their thirties, fit and with an air of authority in their gait. They were the same men who'd brought Christine to court. One was Latino and the other was an asshole; the asshole wore aviators and looked like he was enjoying himself. I almost held out my hands for the cuffs, but they walked past me and the Latino slapped them on David. With every click and ratchet of the cuffs tightening on David's wrists, the noise and camera flash multiplied in intensity. David was shaking his head, pulling away, his world crumbling before him like a rotten floor-board being sucked into the earth.

'Hey. That's my client and the judge just released him. What the hell are you doing?'

'Dominguez, United States Treasury officer. I'm arresting him.'

'For what?'

'Grand larceny,' he replied, and proceeded to recite David's rights.

'What? This is bullshit,' I said.

The explanation came from behind me. It was Dell, whispering it in my ear.

'I told you not to be taken in by this guy. You messed up. He conned you, Eddie. Your client just stole seven point nine billion dollars.'

CHAPTER EIGHTY-SIX

As we sped through Manhattan in the back of a black SUV, I went through every piece of evidence in my head, every play made by Gerry Sinton, and everything I'd been told in the last forty-eight hours. David was chewing on his lip, at once angry and scared. I found it hard to look away from him. Over and over, a single thought rang loudly in my head.

I've been conned.

As a former confidence man, that thought was a source of some considerable shame. Even though it was evil, even though people had died, I still could not help but marvel at the sheer ingenuity of it. It was possibly the greatest con I'd ever come across.

And it had been played on me.

The SUV slowed and bobbed around the traffic lanes. The Saint Patrick's Day celebrations were gearing up for the evening. Hundreds of people in green and white littered the sidewalk. Irish souvenir stalls, hot dog carts, and coffee stands fought their way along the line of parade-goers, vying for any last-minute trade. The parade had passed a half hour ago. It would take us at least that long to get to the Lightner Building in this traffic. NYPD were reopening the roads, and the SUV sped up. The city was readying itself for Skyfest, the Saint Patrick's Day firework display that started in Dublin, then moved city to city. Paris had it last year, and New York wanted to put its own stamp on the tradition.

I sat beside David in the eight-seater SUV. He looked numb, shaking his head, muttering to himself. I told him to keep quiet. The treasury agents sat in the additional seats behind us. Kennedy had taken a seat in the front, beside Dell, who was driving.

'This is a mess,' said Dell.

'Your operation is way out of control,' said Kennedy. 'I'm here to make sure you don't harm any civilians on this crazy mission of yours.'

Dell shot him a look and said, 'You can bet I'll be talking to your superior officer after what you pulled. You're supposed to be my number two on this task force. You're supposed to be focusing on the firm, not the Child case.'

'Where are we going?' I asked for the third time. I'd insisted on accompanying David to processing, but I knew there was no way he would be brought to a precinct or the FBI premises. I knew where we were headed – I just wanted confirmation.

Dell provided it after the fifth time I asked.

'That algo trace your client gave us enabled our tech to follow the money, just like you said. But fourteen minutes ago it crashed. Just before it died, it reported that all of the funds – almost eight billion – did not make it into Ben Harland's account as planned. Instead it transferred into a Harland and Sinton client account. The name on the client account is "David Child." Forty-three seconds after it hit the account, the money disappeared. We're going to Harland and Sinton now, to meet the rest of the team who have already made the arrests. Your client is going to log on to their accounts system, and he's gonna tell us where he's hidden the money.'

'I didn't take the goddamn money,' screamed David. He was on the brink of another panic attack. I spoke to him softly and gripped his arm hard. The pain brought him down, made him focus.

I whispered to him, 'David, tell me you didn't do this.'

He looked like he was drowning. His eyes glazed over, and he simply shook his head.

Was this the face of a man falsely accused for the second time? Or the face of a man who'd stolen the world? I couldn't tell. I'd allowed myself to get too close.

I trusted my gut. I'd backed David. I was pretty sure he wasn't a killer. Would he steal eight billion dollars? I had no clue. I was with him as his counsel, and we were on our way to the building where Christine was being held. Right then all I cared about was getting my wife out of there.

'Let this play out,' I said.

He put his head in his hands, and I knew I would get nothing more out of David.

I typed out a text to the Lizard.

I'm on my way. Do nothing until I give the Ok.

'You're the only person with access to that algo, Child. You altered the code last night when you logged into Harland and Sinton's database and traced the algo – that means either you stole the money or, at the very least, you know where it is. And we're not leaving that building until you show us exactly what you did and how we trace the cash,' said Dell.

I looked at David and he leaned back, wiped his hands on his pants, and puffed out two whimpering breaths.

It took an hour to get to the offices of Harland and Sinton. In the distance, the final traces of daylight were disappearing behind the Chrysler Building as we stepped out of the car. There was no one waiting for us outside the Lightner Building. Nobody in reception, not a soul standing by the elevator.

'They're supposed to have this place locked down,' said Dell, taking a cell phone from his pocket. As we waited for the elevator, I thought I caught a familiar smell.

Stale cigarettes.

The elevator opened and the treasury agents fanned out of the doors. Through the glass partition I could see Christine sitting in the conference room with two men. Dell led the way into the large conference room, dominated by the center table.

Ferrar and Weinstein sat at the conference table drinking coffee. Beside them, Christine, hands cuffed to the front. I ran to her, but Ferrar stood in my way.

'You can't approach her. She's in federal custody,' said Ferrar.

'If you don't move, you'll be in the state hospital,' I said.

A hand on my shoulder, Kennedy.

'Eddie, calm down. This isn't helping,' said Christine. Dirty tear tracks on her face. She looked tired, beaten, resigned to going to jail because of the firm. I shrugged off Kennedy's hand and made for Christine. Ferrar moved for his weapon but stopped, realized his dominant arm still hurt like hell, and he switched hands to grab for his piece with his left. I pushed past him and embraced Christine.

'Let him go, Ferrar,' said Kennedy.

She placed her hands on my stomach and I took her in my arms. I could feel her trembling. I kissed her head and her mouth and held her close, tight. I whispered, 'When you get out of here, you keep going and do not come back, no matter what happens. Amy's okay. She's with Carmel.'

She said nothing, but I felt her legs shift and give way. I held her tight. Her worry for Amy was all that had kept her going. Now that she knew our daughter was safe, her body was ready to give up.

Dell addressed Ferrar and Weinstein. 'You two, where's Schaffler? He's supposed to be downstairs covering the entrance.'

'Damned if I know,' said Weinstein.

'Associates cleared out?' asked Dell.

'Every single one. Gerry Sinton is in the office next door. Agent Patton led the raid. He made the arrest. Apart from that, the whole building is clear,' said Weinstein.

'Good. We'll need Sinton.'

Weinstein buzzed Agent Patton on the radio, told him to bring Gerry Sinton to the conference room.

Dell dragged David forward by his handcuffs and pushed him into a chair at the end of the slate conference table. An open laptop sat on the table, and Dell snatched it, placed it in front of David, and instructed Dominguez to take off the cuffs.

'Find me the money,' said Dell.

From his jacket pocket, Dell produced a pen drive and slotted it into the laptop.

'This is your program, the trace for the algo. This is your only chance. This can go easy or hard. I'm going to ask one time only – tell me where you sent the money.'

I put my back to the window of the conference room, and for a second Kennedy's eyes met mine. Christine pulled herself closer to me.

'I didn't take the money. It's supposed to land in a new account in Ben Harland's name – that was the trace result. I checked it myself. If somebody altered the final account destination, it wasn't me. Here, let me show you. I'll pull up the trace.'

His fingers worked fast on the soft keys. No one spoke. The only sound I heard was Christine, her chest fluttering like a startled bird as she breathed.

'What the hell is this?' said David. Kennedy leaned over David's shoulder.

'Oh my God, it's a virus,' said David. 'It's eating the data. It's burning everything – here and at the bank. I'm locked out. I can't do a single thing,' he said.

'You put a virus through the system?' said Dell.

David's mouth was open, hands wide. Shivering now, afraid. He swiveled the screen around. It was fuzzy and frozen – the images distorted.

Pulling the drive from the laptop, David held it in front of Dell and said, 'The virus came from this drive. It uploaded as soon as I opened it.'

'Bullshit. You've been playing us the whole way,' said Dell, snatching the pen drive from David. 'This is evidence. That was your last chance. You're done, Child.'

David stood, anger pulling him upright.

'I've done nothing.'

'Goddamn it!' said Dell, slamming closed the lid of the laptop. 'Kennedy, Ferrar, Weinstein, take Ms White and Child into custody. Charge them both. The full spectrum of charges for White – laundering, racketeering, the whole damn cake. Book Child for grand larceny and whatever RICO charges you can think of. Either he's hiding the money for Gerry Sinton or he's stolen it for himself. Either way he'll talk at the federal lockup. Take them. Eddie, you stay here. I need to know what David told you about the algo. I'm not sure you haven't been playing a con the whole damn time. If I find out you knew something about it, you'll be sharing a cell with your client.'

'Go,' I said to Christine. 'I'll find you and I'll get you out.'

'This is all wrong,' said Kennedy. But Dell didn't listen. Reluctantly, Kennedy, Ferrar, and Weinstein led Christine and David to the elevator, David protesting his innocence. I was thankful for Kennedy as he led Christine gently into the elevator. She lowered her head and shook it, wiping away fresh tears, unable to let anyone see her like this. I saw the muscles in Kennedy's jaw working overtime. His gaze fixed on David. The elevator doors opened and swallowed them up.

CHAPTER EIGHTY-SEVEN

Dominguez left by the stairs. He was going to man the reception and secure the building. His partner adjusted his sunglasses and took up the coffeepot. Poured himself a cup, pulled up a seat at the conference table. Dell turned and punched on the glass partition of the conference room. A large man with a bald head and wearing a blue tee, whom I guessed to be Agent Patton, marched Gerry Sinton into the conference room. Cable ties around Gerry's wrists. Agent Patton stood behind him, his hand on the back of Gerry's neck, forcing his head down.

'No one else in the building?' said Dell.

At the sound of Dell's voice, Sinton's head shot up, and his eyes met Dell's.

'Clear and secure, Mr Dell,' said Agent Patton.

'What is he doing here?' said Sinton, looking at me. He'd lost the suit jacket. The cable ties were cutting off the circulation in his wrists. His hands were red – same color as his face.

'Your former co-counsel might help me clear some of this up,' said Dell.

'Why don't we talk in private,' said Sinton. Dell shook his head.

'Not until we work this out. Eddie, Sinton says he doesn't have the money. He was waiting for it to hit his partner's account. He killed his partner because he knew the money would end up in an account in Harland's name. Under their partnership agreement, in the event of a partner going missing, the other partner has power of attorney to manage their financial and partnership affairs. I figure Gerry here was going to lift the entire pot of eight billion and make it look like Ben Harland took it and disappeared in his yacht. But Gerry didn't account for Ben's body washing up yesterday. That gave him a problem. The money had to move again, into a different account that couldn't be traced to him. So either Child took the money or Sinton did. Or maybe they're working together. Either way, we're going to stay here until somebody tells me where it went.'

Sinton sure was smart. He could kill his partner, frame him for the whole enterprise, and walk away with the money. Had he changed his plans when Harland's body was found? The way David had talked about the algo, I'd gotten the impression that it couldn't be altered, but that all depended on whether David was telling me the truth.

Patton delivered a savage kick to the back of Sinton's legs, dropping him to his knees.

The treasury agent wearing the sunglasses suppressed a laugh and said, 'You heard Mr Dell; start talking.'

'Let's talk alone,' said Sinton, his eyes pleading with Dell. Agent Patton kicked Sinton again.

My cell rang. Kennedy.

'Hold on, Dell. Let me take this.' I accepted the call. 'Hey.'

'Eddie, it's Kennedy. Listen to me very carefully. David and Christine are safe. You are not. Whatever you do in the next five seconds, do not react to what I'm about to tell you.'

CHAPTER EIGHTY-EIGHT

'I'm listening, Cooch,' I said.

'Good,' said Kennedy.

My heart was banging. My eyes closed. Deep breath.

Dell shook his head. He couldn't believe I had the audacity to take a call and interrupt him. 'Can you believe this guy?' said Dell, throwing a hand at me.

'I just got a call from the associate director of the FBI. I'd asked for intel on Sarah Callan, the woman who posed as Clara Reece. It just came back at the highest level. Sarah Callan was an alias for Sophie Blanc – a CIA operative. She's listed as KIA last year in Grand Cayman, following an armed assault on her convoy, which was targeting a witness in an ongoing investigation.'

'Cooch, you know what that means?' I said.

'Patton, was Sinton carrying a weapon?' said Dell.

Patton pulled a Glock from his waistband and gave it to Dell. The treasury agent in the aviators slugged back the coffee.

'Dead women don't go to lectures on GSR. Dell lied to us. Sophie and Dell have set this whole thing up together. They're going to steal the money and frame David for murder and the theft of the eight billon.'

All I could do was bite my lip. Dell and his girl framed David for murder. They wanted him to take the plea so he would be sent to jail to die. And he would surely die, because they'd framed him not only for murder, but for the theft of the money itself. It was brilliant.

Dell checked the weapon Patton gave to him. Popped the magazine, slotted it back in.

'What does the DA have on this guy?' I said.

'We don't have much yet. But we've got enough to arrest. We're coming up. Full tactical assault. Hold on for two minutes.'

'Call me when you hear back from the DA,' I said. I put the phone down on the table.

Dell widened his stance, turned, and casually shot Agent Patton in the face. The treasury man dropped his coffee and swung his feet off the desk, and Dell put a bullet through his aviators. Dell lowered the gun, pointed it at Sinton. I was on the opposite side of the table, and as far as he was concerned, I was unarmed and no threat.

I had two choices. I could clap my hands. Or I could make a move myself. The situation was too complex to rely on anyone else.

I ducked, and in half a second Dell's backup piece was in my hand, the barrel pointing over the table at Dell's head. The piece was still warm from sitting at my back all day.

'Don't move,' I said. I had the drop on Dell.

My hands were shaking, my back soaked in sweat. The sight on the Ruger's slide quivered in my grip as I tried to hold it firm, and I saw something on the weapon. Or rather, I didn't see something. There was no serial number on Dell's Ruger. Same as the murder weapon. The only place you can get a gun without a serial number is if you tell the manufacturer that's the way you want it. The United States government could do that, if they didn't want weapons traced back to them. The kind of weapons used in CIA Black Ops.

Dell looked at the gun in my hand.

'That's my piece. I want it back.'

Nobody moved.

'Dell, you double-crossing son of a bitch,' said Sinton.

The CIA man silenced Sinton with a punch to the face.

'Hands in the air, Dell,' I said. He stepped back, kept the piece pointed at Sinton, and turned slowly to face me.

'You ever shot someone before, Eddie? It's not as easy as it looks. You don't have to kill anyone and you can walk out of here, you know. There's always a deal to be made, right? But I need to understand how much you know. And how much it would cost for you to keep quiet. I'm going to put two rounds in Gerry's head. You see, Gerry Sinton just killed two treasury agents. Then I'm going to leave here and meet a special friend. And that friend can send you fifty million dollars. You'll have it by tomorrow. That same friend is gonna spread traces of the money over Gerry's accounts – seventy or eighty million, say. And the same for David Child, you, me, and your wife. We'll be clear and rich. So tell me, how much do you know, and is it worth fifty million?'

'No . . .' said Sinton.

I kept my eyes on Dell's hands as I spoke. I needed time. Kennedy was on his way.

'It's worth a damn sight more than fifty, Dell. You told me Grand Cayman was the Panama Canal of dirty money. My guess is you knew every operation going and you made a lot of money skimming off the top. But that kind of business is risky. You said so yourself. The fewer people involved, the better. I think Sinton got the idea of using technology to move the cash, and he laid you off along with the other money mules. You didn't like that. I think Bernard Langhiemer is in the CIA's pocket – your pocket. I think he's your special friend. You got him to frame Farooq so you could lean on him and get whatever information you needed to pretend to go after the firm. Farooq told you about the algo, the piece of tech that replaced you, so you wanted your revenge on David as much as the firm.'

Dell nodded, smirked.

'Sarah, or Sophie, or whoever she is, created Clara Reece to get close to David. She faked Clara's death, murdering some other poor girl and wiping out her face so the cops couldn't ID the body. Then Clara hid in the panic room until it was clear and walked out of the apartment in a hazmat suit. Langhiemer helped you frame David by setting up the car crash. You used me, you used Christine, and you used David. His arrest put the firm into meltdown and caused them to trigger the algo. They didn't want David talking to the FBI. You needed the firm to panic and hit the wash button so you could be waiting to grab the whole pile when it landed, framing David for the robbery of eight billion dollars.

'If you wanted information from David, you could've picked him up and scared him into giving you whatever you wanted. No, you needed a patsy. You needed David to plead guilty to the murder. That's the only reason you got me involved. Shit sticks, right? You told me that yourself. Nobody would believe David didn't steal the money after he pleaded guilty to killing his girlfriend. You weren't just setting him up for murder. You were setting him up to take the fall for your robbery. This was always about the money. David's setup was elaborate and brilliant – easily worth eight billion. That's how much I know. That costs a lot more than fifty,' I said.

'You son of a bitch!' screamed Sinton.

Dell had turned his attention on Sinton. 'You paid me to wash the money, but you didn't need me anymore after Child came up with his algorithm. I don't like being fired from the criminal organizations that pay me for my services; it sets a bad example for the rest of them. This is the greatest robbery of all time. Don't you see that? I set you running like a hare, and you were very quick to kill your old partner. I got to say, I enjoyed that. It made things easier for us. How do you feel now? I'm taking it all, Gerry.'

The gun shook in my hand, I'd never shot anyone before, but now seemed a good time to start.

'Eddie, I'm going to pull the trigger. It's all over for Gerry. Don't shoot. Before I do that, I need to know, do we have a deal? One hundred million sound fair?'

'If it's dirty money, why the elaborate frame-up, Dell?' I said. I needed to buy time. I wasn't about to give up David or anyone else, and I knew Dell would kill me the second he had a chance. I knew I shouldn't have pulled the gun. I should have clapped my hands. Come on, Kennedy, where are you?

'Oh, I'm not worried about the cops. No, I'm worried about the organizations who own big chunks of that money. The cartel already sent their man up here to check this out. Only way I can survive this is if they go looking for someone else – someone like David Child.'

The elevator chimed and the doors opened. I thanked God that Kennedy had made it. Slowly, Dell turned, shielding the gun as he did so. My gut tightened when I saw that it wasn't Kennedy. Twenty feet away, standing in front of the elevator, were the last two people on earth that I'd expected to see.

A figure in black. The man with the tattoo of the screaming soul – El Grito. In one hand he held a gun. His other hand was wrapped around the throat of Sophie Blanc. Her hair was cut short and dyed black. A livid bruise seemed to almost fold her face in two. But it was her. Sarah, Clara, Sophie, did she even know who she really was anymore? Right then it probably didn't matter. She knew she was dead already.

'We've been watching you,' said El Grito, in a thick Latin-American accent. 'Langhiemer is dead. No one is coming to get you out of this. I found this little whore in Langhiemer's apartment. Drop the gun and take me to the money. And then she will die quickly. This is the best I can offer. You know this, *puto.*'

The cartel's hit man gave me a small window; a single moment of distraction was all I needed. I dropped the Ruger at my feet. I raised my arms above my head and clapped my hands. The window came in around me, covering me in a wave of shards. The thunder of breaking plate glass was answered by gunfire. El Grito threw his hostage on the floor and started shooting. The doors beside the elevator burst open – Kennedy came in low, Weinstein and Ferrar behind him.

I ducked, leaned over the slate table, grabbed the edge with both hands, and heaved the whole thing over onto its side. The table weighed a ton, and as I pulled it, I tore the muscles in my back and let go of the damn thing just as it smacked into the side of my head. I went down behind it. The lights in the whole building went out. Standard FBI tactical assault.

Deaf.

I could feel the vibrations from the weapons. Blood and teeth-shattering cracks roared in my ears.

Blind.

The visceral dance from the coruscating muzzle flash. Fireworks from the parade bloomed phosphorous flowers in the black Manhattan sky. Inside, the deafening ballet was punctuated only by the teeming black of the room, which seemed to fight against the glimmer of muzzle flash. The dark wanted this place, and fought for it. I couldn't tell if it was the darkness or the men that did the killing.

I lay flat on the floor and watched sparks from the exploding TV ignite the carpet.

And then silence.

The quiet came before the smell – that sour odor from hot metal burning and tearing through flesh and bone and life. The shattered window let the Manhattan breeze into the place – almost in a futile attempt to wash the smell away on the air.

My body would not move. It felt as if my limbs were betraying me, paralyzing me, so that I couldn't get up and catch a bullet. I thought of Christine, and Amy, and somehow I moved.

I still couldn't see much. My eyes stung from the smoke coming off the burning carpet. On my hands and knees, I couldn't find the Ruger. Ahead of me, a Glock. I took it and stood up.

CHAPTER EIGHTY-NINE

I thought everyone was dead.

The offices of Harlan and Sinton, attorneys-at-law, looked like a war zone. I could taste blood in my mouth, probably from the table tumbling over on top of me. The metallic taste mixed with the smell of burnt acid rising from the spent cartridges rattling around on the floor. A fat moon illuminated ghostly trails of smoke that seemed to rise from the floor and evaporate just as I caught sight of them. My left ear felt as though it were filled with water, but I knew I'd merely been deafened from the gunfire. In my right hand I held a government-issued Glock 19. I moved around the table, and in the firelight from the smoldering carpet, I saw Sinton crawl across the floor, reaching for a gun. Without another thought, I pointed the Glock at him and fired. The bullet took him in the thigh, and he rolled over. His rasping, blood slicked breath gave out. There was already a mass of bullet wounds in his chest. I took comfort from that. I hadn't killed him – he'd been dead already.

The Glock was now empty. Sinton's legs had fallen across the stomach of the corpse next to him and, in a curious moment of realization, I noticed that the bodies on the floor of the conference room all seemed to reach out to one another. I didn't look at each one; I couldn't bring my eyes to bear on their dead faces. I saw the treasury agents, Patton and the man in the sunglasses. Dell's victims. I looked around for Kennedy, but I didn't see him.

My breath came in short bursts that had to fight their way through the clamp of adrenaline threatening to crush my chest. The chill wind from the broken window behind me began to dry the sweat on the back of my neck. The glass partition that moments before had separated the reception area from the conference room lay in thick, beady chunks on the floor.

The digital clock on the wall hit 20:00 as I saw my killer.

I couldn't see a face or even a body; my killer took shelter in a dark corner of the conference room. Green, white, and gold flashes from the fireworks bursting over Times Square sent patterns of light into the room at odd angles that momentarily illuminated a small pistol held by a seemingly disembodied gloved hand. That hand held a Ruger LCP. Even though I couldn't see my killer, the gun told me a lot. The Ruger held six nine-millimeter rounds. It was small enough to fit into the palm of your hand and weighed less than a good steak. Three possibilities leaped to mind.

Three possible shooters.

This was Dell's piece. Maybe he'd found it.

I hadn't seen El Grito's body. He could've picked up the gun, or brought it with him.

A third possibility: Dell's lover.

No way to persuade any one of them to drop the gun.

Considering the last two days I'd had in court, they all had a good reason to kill me. I had an idea about which one it might be, but right then it didn't seem to matter somehow.

The Ruger's barrel angled toward my chest.

I closed my eyes, feeling strangely calm. This wasn't how it was supposed to go down. Somehow this last breath of air didn't feel right. It felt as if I'd been cheated. Even so, I filled my lungs with the smoke and the metallic tang that dwelt long after a shooting.

I didn't hear the shot, just a dull *thump*, which couldn't have been a gunshot. My eyes were tightly shut, so I didn't see the muzzle flash – I only felt the bullet ripping into my flesh. That fatal shot had become inevitable from the very moment I'd made the deal to persuade David to plead guilty in exchange for Christine's immunity.

My pants felt wet and warm. I guessed it was my blood.

Only then did I hear the shot; it sounded like a bullwhip cracking.

Instantly, I knew that sound was different – it wasn't the deafening *thump* of muzzle blast from the bullet and its gas propellant exiting the bore – this was different. This was the sound of the bullet breaking the sound barrier. I knew I wouldn't hear the shot because the shooter was too far away. He was in the building across the street, behind a 'for rent' sign with an M2 sniper rifle, one of his favorite toys. He'd watched Christine from the Corbin Building, and if anyone had tried to take her out, he'd take their head off with one squeeze of the trigger.

I opened my eyes. The Ruger was no longer there; neither was the gloved hand. A bloodied stump of bone and matter, the hand taken clean off by the Lizard's shot. I heard the scream then. A woman's voice, yet deep and agonized. She stepped forward, into the moonlight, and Sophie Blanc raised a Glock with her other hand.

I'd thought everyone was dead.

I was wrong.

Four quick shots. Her body crumpled to the floor.

I turned and saw Kennedy leaning out from behind a couch.

The pain in my chest grew from something similar to a burning cut, into an ice pick plunged through my rib cage. I forced myself to look down. There was no bullet wound. Instead, the slide from the Ruger protruded from my chest. The handgun had been torn apart by the hollow-point boat tail fired from the Lizard's sniper rifle. I guessed that the gun part was maybe six inches long, and most of it was buried in my chest.

I don't remember falling, but I remembered Kennedy shouting my name. And then Weinstein was in the room beside Kennedy. His head framed in the blare of the fireworks.

'Eddie, stay with us. We got 'em. We got 'em all. We heard it all on your call,' said Kennedy.

I hadn't disconnected Kennedy's call. Instead I'd put the phone on the conference table and let Dell talk.

'Your wife's safe. So is David. It's okay. Paramedics are on their way . . .'

My head wouldn't stay upright. It kept flopping to my left. Each time it did, I saw Dell's body, the top of his head missing. The Lizard would have taken out Dell first. Beside him I saw El Grito's corpse, his dead eyes staring at me.

I heard Kennedy hollering for the paramedics.

And I lost my battle for the light.

EXTRACT FROM THE NEW YORK TIMES
Wednesday, 18 March

The 20th Precinct of the New York Police Department has released some of the names of the individuals who lost their lives in a bloody gun battle that took place yesterday evening in the heart of corporate Manhattan. Lester William Dell (54) and Sophie Blanc (31) were law enforcement officers working with the Treasury Department. Eli Patton (28), Joel Friend (29), and Sonny Ferrar were agents with the Federal Bureau of Investigation. Gerald Sinton (49) was a named partner in Harland and Sinton, one of America's most respected law firms. His partner, Benjamin Harland, lost his life in a boating accident just two days before. Police sources believe the two incidents are not linked. One dead man, believed to have links to the el Rosa Cartel, has not yet been named. And finally, criminal defense attorney Eddie Flynn (37), also lost his life. The district attorney's office has yet to fix a date for a grand jury hearing into the murder of Clara Reece. No official statement has been issued on why this violent episode occurred.

CHAPTER NINETY

Six weeks after the shot

'How's it feel to be a dead man?' said Kennedy.

Even though he'd had time to rest and recover from the ordeal, the fed still looked like hammered shit.

'I feel a damn sight better than you look. You ever sleep?' I asked.

'Not much. Not since Ferrar's funeral. I saw you there, but it wouldn't have gone down well with the rest of the Bureau if we'd spoken. You understand?'

I nodded.

'Look, I know your business took a dive after the *Times* told everyone you were dead, but we had no choice at the time. We had to let this blow over. The State Department, the Treasury Department, and the Justice Department are all up in arms about renegade CIA operatives setting up a joint task force to carry out the largest robbery ever committed on American soil. The CIA have said they're carrying out their own investigation.'

'I'm sure that'll be extremely thorough. They have to know exactly what happened so they can make sure it's buried for good.'

Kennedy smiled and said, 'You could be right. I'd say none of this will go public – too embarrassing. It'll all blow over. In the meantime, I figured it would be good to take the heat off you and your family for a while, if everyone thinks you're six feet under. The cartel won't go looking for a dead man.'

'You find the money yet?'

He shook his head. 'The virus David unwittingly uploaded wiped the whole system. We believe the virus and the money switching into David's client account and then into the wind was Bernard Langhiemer's work . . .'

His face darkened at the mention of Langhiemer.

'You find him yet?' I asked.

'Most of him,' said Kennedy. 'It looks like Dell's partner, Sophie, was hiding out in Langhiemer's apartment. El Grito found them, got Langhiemer and Sophie talking. It wasn't pretty.'

'So you think the cartel knows it was Dell who robbed them?'

'We think so, but we're making sure of it. We don't want a bloodbath while they go looking for the money. At the same time as we're covering this up in the press, we're leaking to our sources in the cartel that Dell went renegade and that we recovered the money. That way no one will come looking for it from David or Christine. The cartel are sore about their man getting plugged, but it turns out El Grito had already fed back to his boss that the firm was tearing itself apart, what with Sinton killing Ben Harland and his daughter.'

'His daughter?'

'We got a positive ID last week on Samantha Harland being the body in David's apartment. DNA profiling from her old man's body. We also got a toxicology report. Turns out she'd been given a powerful sedative. We figure Sophie brought her into David's apartment the day before the murder, drugged her, and stashed her in the soundproof panic room. The next day, after David leaves the apartment, she shoots Samantha in the back, then drags her into the kitchen and unloads into the back of her head. Samantha was twenty-six years old. Assholes like her father never think that what they get into might end up hurting their kids.'

I gazed out at the street.

'Sorry, I didn't mean . . .'

'It's okay,' I said.

'I think it's best if you lie low for a while, and when you want to practice law again, we'll get the *Times* to print a retraction. If the cartel found out you'd made it out of there alive, they'd kill you on principle. But they've got short memories when it comes to straitlaced lawyers. Sometimes killing an ordinary member of Joe Public is much more difficult than taking out a player.'

'I understand,' I said.

'Don't suppose your memory has improved?' he said.

'What do you mean?'

'The sniper hole cut in the glass on the thirty-eighth floor of the Corbin Building, the fact that Dell and Sophie Blanc all had bullet wounds consistent with a round from a high-caliber rifle? Any of this ringing any bells yet?'

'I already told you, I don't know anything about that.'

I finished off my stack of blueberry pancakes, drained the last of my coffee, and left forty bucks on the table for the check and the tip.

'David pay you for the prelim?' said Kennedy.

'Way too much,' I said. My financial worries were over, at least for now.

A horn sounded outside Ted's Diner, and I shook hands with Kennedy.

'That's my ride,' I said.

'Oh, I almost forgot,' said Kennedy, handing me a large manila envelope. I checked its contents, shook hands with Kennedy again, and placed the envelope in my bag, beside two others of similar size.

It was late April, and the blossoms were tumbling through the puddles on the sidewalk. I opened the rear passenger door of the Range Rover and climbed in.

'This is a mighty step up from that Honda,' I said, gritting my teeth at the stretch to get into the high vehicle. The wound in my chest still hurt like hell when I least expected it. It would heal, but I'd been told to expect an ugly scar.

Holly pulled into traffic and looked at me in the rearview mirror. 'I know,' she said. 'You could say our relationship has moved on. David wanted to get me a Ferrari, but I told him it was too ostentatious. This is nice.' David leaned over from the front passenger seat and whispered something to her. She patted his knee and they laughed softly together. When David got released the day after Saint Patrick's, Holly took him in. Through all the shit they went through over those two days, they'd somehow found each other. I was glad.

'So, you ready?' said David.

The question wasn't meant for me. It was directed toward the other passenger, in the seat beside me. He didn't answer. He just stared out the window.

David and I talked a little during the drive, and Holly told me all about their plans for a romantic weekend away – their first. The other passenger never spoke. After an hour, when we were well into upstate New York, we fell into silence as we approached our destination. Holly and David were very much in love. It was nice to see, but it made me ache. Christine and Amy were staying at Christine's parents' house. I'd seen them both, briefly, once I got out of the hospital. We'd agreed to meet in the park.

I'd watched Amy on the swing. Christine and I sat on the grass in the little park close to her parents' house. After a while I purposefully tuned out Christine and watched my daughter. I didn't want to hear what she was saying. She said there was something about me that brought danger to our lives, that somehow, as long as I was in the law, I would attract bad men. And bad things would happen, whether I wanted to do the right thing or not.

Christine and Amy would live with her parents in the Hamptons. Amy would change schools. I could see Amy once a month, at their house. No more. Not for a while. Not until Christine was sure they would be safe. I tuned out again and stared at Amy.

'So what do you think?' said Christine.

'I'm sorry?' I said.

'You haven't really been listening, have you? I said how would you feel if we tried things again in six months?'

'You mean us?'

'Yes, I mean us.'

The creak of the swing drew my eyes to Amy again. She was getting taller. Her feet were dragging on the ground on every low point of the swing. I'd taken her to this same park the year before and her feet couldn't touch the ground then. I thought about finding a bloodied seventeen-year-old girl in my client's house, not a mile from here; I thought about David, fighting for air in the courthouse conference room as he begged me to help him; I thought about Christine, that moment in Harland and Sinton before I got her out.

'I can't. I love you both too much,' I said.

'What do you mean?'

'Bad things happen around me. Maybe I let them happen. I don't know, Christine. I can't take the risk that something might happen to you or Amy. I don't want to put distance between us, and I want to watch my little girl grow up. But it's more important that she gets the chance to grow up and be with you. Whatever has happened to me, whatever's happened to us, I can't change that. All I can do is make sure that I don't do any more harm than I've done already.'

'Eddie, it's not forever. I want to try again when things have calmed down. It's your job; it's not you. I thought you could think about winding down the rough cases, maybe even trying a new career. And hey, I'm not blameless here either. What happened with the firm wasn't your fault.'

'You're wrong. Dell told me I was the target, not you. They wanted to use me to get to David. You were leverage to them, nothing more. I can't expose you or Amy to that risk. As things stand, I'm a dead man. That facade won't last for long. I can spend the weekend here, but I need to go back.'

'Why?'

'Because I have to. I can't really explain it, but I need this. I need to work. I can help people. David reminded me of that.'

'There are other lawyers . . .'

'I know, but most of them are probably like I was before I pulled Hanna Tublowski out of that house. If I'm not there, who'll pull out the next girl?'

She dragged herself close to me, rested her head on my shoulder.

I was going to be on my own. For the good of my family. That made me think about what kind of a man I was, that my family was better off without me – without the hustler, the lawyer, the con man.

Holly made a left and drove along a narrow gravel path that led to a large mansion, set in acres of open green fields.

We pulled up outside the house. Several men were waiting outside, dressed in white hospital uniforms. I got out of the car, walked around, and opened the other passenger door. The low morning sun blazed into the car. This place wasn't advertised on the Internet, or anywhere else for that matter. Maybe a hundred doctors in the whole country knew of its existence. As far as I knew, the house didn't even have a name. Rock stars, movie stars, the überwealthy came here to get clean.

373

Popo wept as he got out of the Range Rover. He was shaking, and his lips were cut and bleeding. I told him to stop biting his lips. David and Holly joined us.

'You'll stay here until you're better. Until you're clean,' said David. 'And when you're clean, you come see me, and I'll make sure you have a job at Reeler.'

'I don't know what I'm supposed to say,' said Popo.

'You don't need to say anything. You saved my life. Whatever I can do to save yours, you got it,' said David.

I knew Popo would make it. He'd been given a chance to turn his life around, to become another version of himself, a better version, a stronger version, a purer version. A chance to get back to who he really was.

I hoped I would get the same chance someday.

We waved goodbye to Popo and got back into the Range Rover.

'Okay, now to business,' I said. 'You can drop me off at Hogan Place.'

CHAPTER NINETY-ONE

'Dead man walking,' said Zader, as I closed the door to his office in 1 Hogan Place.

I took a seat and admired the headlines in the newspapers he'd spread out in front of him. Most of them were speculating on his next move in the David Child case and when the grand jury would hear the evidence. The DA looked tired; his eyes were heavy and his collar was undone.

'So, think your client will be ready to face the grand jury next week?' he said.

I opened my bag, removed the three envelopes, and set them on top of the papers.

'Say, can I get a drink?' I said.

He converted a sneer into a half smile and pressed a button on his desk phone.

'Miriam, two coffees, please. Oh, sorry, cancel that. One coffee for me, and see if you can rustle up a scotch for Mr Flynn. He looks like he could use it.'

'I don't drink anymore,' I said. 'But you knew that.'

'Miriam?' said Zader into the intercom. 'Miriam, are you there?'

'Maybe she's picking up your dry cleaning?' I said.

He leaned back in his leather chair and said, 'We're going with your client as an accomplice to the murder. It's not the full beans, but . . .'

I could see his eyes focus on something behind me, which cut him off in full flow. Miriam entered his office with two coffees on a plastic tray. She placed one coffee in front of me and the other beside it. She pulled up a seat and took the second cup of coffee for herself.

'Cream and sugar?' she asked me.

'Thanks,' I said.

Zader stared at both of us.

'There isn't going to be a grand jury,' I said, picking up the first envelope and tossing it to Zader. He opened it, began to read the two-page document, and was about to say something pithy when I cut him off.

'The Justice Department, the State Department, and the Treasury want the whole David Child case to go away quietly. It's too messy for them. I can't tell you why, but I'm sure you already know this; somebody on high has probably already had the same conversation with you. I'll save you the trouble of reading this for now. It's a press statement that your office is releasing this afternoon. It confirms that as a result of your extensive inquiries, David Child is innocent of all charges in relation to the murder of Clara Reece. It hasn't been released yet, but Clara didn't actually exist. The dead girl in David's apartment is Samantha Harland, matching tattoos and all. There's a full public apology to David Child, which I want you to read out, on camera. You'll notice this statement is drafted by the Justice Department. They're sending you a clear message to make this go away – you mess this up, you're making an enemy of the US government.'

'You've got to be kidding me if you think I'm going to be pressured into—'

'You put pressure on innocent defendants to plead guilty to crimes they didn't commit. You do this every day of the week by dangling plea agreements in front of them. Take five years on a plea, or fight the case and risk a twenty-year stretch. This is what it's like, this pressure. Open this . . .' I said, handing him the second envelope.

This was a bulky package, and he tipped the contents onto his desk. He saw photographs of dry-cleaning receipts, e-mails ordering Miriam to reduce her caseload by handing her most serious cases to junior ADAs. There were video stills of Miriam bringing him coffee, cleaning his office, vacuuming the carpets, washing the coffee cups. In among the photos and e-mails were also several microcassettes with recordings of Zader's juiciest sexist remarks.

'When you ran against Miriam for district attorney, you gave an interview stating how much you admired her skills as a lawyer and how honored you would feel if she agreed to stay on as a senior prosecutor in the event of your victory in the election. Yet there's a mountain of evidence here to show you've treated her like shit. And you've done it because she's a woman. The tapes are particularly good. My favorite is the conversation you had with Miriam three weeks ago, where you tell her female trial attorneys will always be beaten by male attorneys in court because men are more credible. Nice. I'm thinking that statement alone is good for a hundred grand from the jury.'

Miriam smiled at him.

'Miriam, this is outrageous. If I've treated you poorly, it's simply because you were my opposition. I would've done the same thing if you were a man,' said Zader.

'That's a great defense,' I said. 'Your Honor, I didn't harass Ms Sullivan because she's a woman. I demeaned her simply because I'm an asshole, and I would've done the same thing to a man.'

I heard Miriam tutting.

'You'll also find, in that pile, two documents that you will need to read. The first is the copy of my draft sexual harassment suit, for my client, which I'll file this afternoon if you don't sign the agreement right now.'

'What agreement?' said Zader.

I found the agreement on his desk, handed it to him.

'The highlights are that you will resign first thing tomorrow morning. You can say it's for personal reasons and you'll give your full backing to Miriam Sullivan, whom you're appointing as acting district attorney until a new election can be called. If you refuse to call the press conference for David, or if you refuse to sign this agreement, I'll file suit for Miriam, she'll win, and your career will be over. This way you get to walk out of here without a court judgment against you.'

His gaze flickered between the photographs and the agreement. A drop of sweat hit the desk, and he wiped at his forehead, pulled at his tie even though it was already loose.

'I'll fight this the whole way. You think you've won, but you're wrong. I don't scare easy.'

I turned toward Miriam and said, 'You were right. He is stupid.'

'Told you we'd need more,' said Miriam.

'You called it. You do the honors,' I said.

From her inside jacket pocket, Miriam produced two pages and handed them to Zader without another word. The first page was an affidavit sworn by Assistant District Attorney Billy White. He stated that he had been asked by Zader to contact a private investigator in order to obtain confidential, and highly sensitive, personal and financial information on every single judge in New York. The private stock information Zader had used to get rid of Judge Perry was already in his possession when the case began, and he didn't bring it up until it looked like Perry was going to find for the defense. This alone would be enough to launch a state inquiry into prosecutorial misconduct, but the fact that he'd illegally obtained personal information and built dossiers on every judge would end his career in a heartbeat and probably send him to jail. The second page was clearly labeled as a draft e-mail. It was addressed to the FBI and the current governor. The e-mail listed Billy White's affidavit as a single attachment. The draft e-mail was just as good as pulling back the hammer on a pistol and holding it to Zader's temple.

'You can't be a felon and a DA. Mayor maybe?' I said.

'You're a bastard, you know that?' he said. 'I can't possibly call a press conference today. It would take . . .'

'The press are already in the briefing room,' said Miriam. 'I took the liberty of calling them. You want me to hit send on that e-mail?'

He shook his head. I ignored him and waited.

He spotted the last envelope, sitting unopened before me.

'What's in that?'

'That's option B,' I said.

He held out his quivering hand. I gave him the envelope, drained my coffee, and stood. I buttoned my jacket and said to Miriam, 'It's good to have you back.'

She smiled.

Zader ripped open the envelope just as his office door closed behind me. Silence. Then I heard Miriam's stern tones. Before I left the open-plan office, I waited for a spell at the coffee machine. I'd left because this was Miriam's victory. She left Zader's office, caught my eye, smiled, and gave me an excited thumbs-up. The signed agreement and press release were in her hands. In the third envelope, I'd given Zader the same option he'd given David Child – the envelope was empty.

I stepped into the elevator, waved goodbye to Herb Goldman on the reception desk, and hit the button for the ground floor. Zader appeared at Herb's desk, watching me leave with a look of utter contempt on his face. His skin shone under the lights; fear and hate danced in bulbs of sweat. He slapped Herb's desk and swore at me.

I said nothing.

Herb's keen eyes passed over both of us, and he chuckled to himself. Somehow Herb knew that he'd soon be serving under yet another new district attorney.

The elevator doors began to close. Before they shut, I heard Herb offer some final advice to the departing DA.

'You know what they say, Mr Zader,' said Herb. 'You can't hustle a hustler.'

Acknowledgments

There are an enormous number of people to thank. First on the list is my wife, Tracy, who is a constant source of great ideas, insights, support, inspiration and gingerbread lattes. I owe her more than I can ever say.

My agent, Euan Thorneycroft, and all at AM Heath for their support, advice and expert representation.

My editors, Jemima Forrester at Orion Books and Christine Kopprasch at Flatiron Books, for their patience, expertise, and dedication to making this novel the best that it could be. Also huge thanks to Jon Wood, Angela McMahon, Graeme Williams and everyone at Orion Books and Hachette Ireland. Also huge thanks to my US team, Amy Einhorn and Marlena Bittner at Flatiron.

My family, friends, readers, everyone who has reviewed the books and especially the booksellers that have championed me from day one – I owe you all a pint and a hug.